PRAISE FOR
SHANNON K. BUTCHER'S
THRILLERS

NO ESCAPE

"An exciting, suspenseful ride that goes from zero to sixty on the first page . . . A first-class romantic suspense that satisfies from beginning to end and one that shouldn't be missed."
—FallenAngelReviews.com

"Suspenseful . . . palatable danger and plenty of sexual tension . . . Stunning."
—SingleTitles.com

"A nicely paced and involving romantic suspense that will keep readers flipping the pages well into the wee hours."
—BookLoons.com

"Solid, quality romantic suspense that's well worth reading."
—LikesBooks.com

NO CONTROL

"Tense, fast-paced . . . Believable and gut-wrenching . . . Butcher is in control."
—*Publishers Weekly*

"Butcher is one to watch! Characters that tug on your heartstrings and a well-formed plot make this romantic suspense a must-read!"
—ArmchairInterviews.com

NO REGRETS

more . . .

LOVE YOU
TO DEATH

LOVE YOU TO DEATH

SHANNON K. BUTCHER

FOREVER

NEW YORK   BOSTON

Book design by Giorgetta Bell McRee
Cover design by Diane Luger

Forever
Hachette Book Group
237 Park Avenue
New York, NY 10017
Visit our website at www.HachetteBookGroup.com.

Forever is an imprint of Grand Central Publishing. The Forever name and logo is a trademark of Hachette Book Group, Inc.

Printed in the United States of America

First Printing: October 2009

10 9 8 7 6 5 4 3 2 1

ATTENTION CORPORATIONS AND ORGANIZATIONS:
Most HACHETTE BOOK GROUP books are available at quantity discounts with bulk purchase for educational, business, or sales promotional use. For information, please call or write:

Special Markets Department, Hachette Book Group
237 Park Avenue, New York, NY 10017
Telephone: 1-800-222-6747 Fax: 1-800-477-5925

This book is dedicated to all the loving sisters out there, but most especially to mine.

ACKNOWLEDGMENTS

I'd like to thank Robert Schneider for his invaluable insight into the mind of a serial killer. You saved me hours of difficult and creepy research, and I'm sorry if I messed anything up in the process of breathing life into the profile.

My thanks also go out to my faithful critique group: Sara Attebury, Dyann Barr, Julie Fedynich, Sherry Foley, Liz Lafferty, and Claire Ashgrove. I can't tell you how much I appreciate your putting up with my never-ending requests for feedback.

LOVE YOU
TO DEATH

CHAPTER ONE

Breaking into a house was a lot harder than it looked on TV.

Elise McBride held the small flashlight in her mouth, smoothed the warped edge of her credit card with her fingers, and tried to shove it between the door and the jamb again, with no luck. All she managed to do was take off another layer of plastic and shred the magnetic strip.

Fantastic. Getting a replacement card while she was traveling wasn't going to be any fun.

Defeated, Elise dropped her head against the cool wood of her sister's front door and tried not to cry in frustration. After days with no contact from her gabby sister, Elise was sure Ashley was in trouble. The deep kind.

Her gut churned with worry, warning her that something was wrong. Ashley had a tendency to disappear, wandering off on bizarre, artistic tangents with whatever hot guy was at hand, but never for this long, and never without returning a phone call.

Elise had left dozens of messages on her sister's phone over the past few days, and not one of them had been answered.

The police had promised her they'd check Ashley's home, but what if they'd forgotten, or lied to Elise just to get her to stop bugging them? What if she was inside, hurt or unconscious and unable to reach a phone? What if she was lying in a hospital somewhere with amnesia, unable to call for help because she couldn't remember who she was? What if she'd driven her car into a ditch, gotten trapped, and no one had found her yet?

Stop it. Get a grip. All that doom-and-gloom stuff sounded like Mom talking. If Elise had listened to her, she'd believe that everyone died in a ditch wearing dirty underwear after being attacked by boys who wanted only one thing.

Ashley was fine. She had to be. Elise just needed to figure out where she'd gone this time, and the key to that mystery was likely inside her sister's tiny house.

Elise briefly thought about breaking a window, but it was around three in the morning. Haven, Illinois, was as still and quiet as the cool morning air, and she was afraid one of the nearby neighbors would call the police if they heard breaking glass. She wasn't about to get hauled to jail for breaking and entering while her sister was in trouble.

Maybe Ashley had stashed a key somewhere. Heaven knew she was always forgetting or losing things. Including keys. After years of being coddled by family, Ashley was on her own now, developing coping mechanisms to combat all her flighty, brainless habits—like misplacing keys. At least that's what she said. She'd told Elise many times how she was fine living on her own and didn't need a keeper, no matter how much Elise worried.

And she did. Every day. She worried that Ashley would get lost in a particularly engrossing series of paintings and forget to eat. She worried that Ashley would be driving along, see a bird she wanted to paint, try to follow it, and crash her car into a tree. She worried that Ashley would go home with the wrong man one of these days, and rather than spending a fun weekend in bed, she'd become a victim.

Ashley was way too trusting with men, way too easily swayed by a sweet smile and a confident wink. One of these days, it was going to get her in trouble.

Maybe it already had.

Elise had to get in her house and find out.

The front porch was littered with springtime lawn ornaments and pots of flowers—both fake and dead. A dozen wind chimes hung in stillness, though Elise wished for a wind to kick them up and cover any noise she was making. A blown-glass globe sat in a wrought-iron stand right next to the door. The base of it was mosaic tile depicting a stylized peacock—Ashley's design, no doubt.

Elise tipped the stand, shined her flashlight under it and took a look, praying she'd find a key. No luck. She searched under all the flowerpots, sculpted frogs, lawn gnomes, and even the doormat with no success. Her flashlight beam bobbed over the porch, glinting off the wind chimes.

Frustration and a growing sense of panic gripped Elise hard. A cold sweat formed along her spine, making her shiver in the cool May air.

She was going to have to break a window. There was no help for it. She couldn't stand around out here in the dark when the key to her sister's disappearance might be right inside that door.

Elise clamped the slim flashlight in her mouth to hold it while she took off her jacket. She could use the fabric to mute the sound of breaking glass and hope the neighbors were all heavy sleepers.

She tipped her head back a bit when she slid the jacket off, and the silhouette of a key appeared on the porch ceiling. Elise followed the beam of light to the small wind chime dangling near the door. It was made from a variety of household bits, including a tarnished knife, a can opener, chunks of broken colored glass, and wire. Everything was painted in lazy swirls of color that Elise instantly recognized as Ashley's work. Even the key was painted.

Surely, Ashley wouldn't be foolish enough to dangle the key to her front door in plain sight? It had to be an old key.

Then again, this was Ashley. If the key was at hand when she went into that creative zone, she wouldn't have thought twice about using it.

Being careful not to make a racket, Elise gripped the wind chime in her hand to keep everything quiet and eased it from the suspended hook. She separated the key from the rest of the piece, then slid it into the lock. It went in easily and turned without effort.

Ashley's front door swung open and Elise stood there, dreading that first step. If she failed to find her sister now, it was completely her fault. She couldn't blame it on a locked door.

Part of her was terrified she wouldn't be able to find Ashley. The rest of her was terrified that she would, and that it would be too late.

Pretend you're not afraid. That's what she always did whenever the story she was covering got dangerous. She'd straighten her spine, pretend she wasn't queasy and shaking, and move on. As a freelance reporter, she had no choice but to move on or go hungry, so she moved. But the stakes were higher this time. Her sweet, too-trusting sister needed her, and she couldn't fail.

Elise stepped inside.

Trent Brady's flighty neighbor was out of town again, but someone was creeping around her house all the same. At three in the morning.

Cop instincts he'd tried for two years to kill came roaring back to life, making him reach for his gun. Of course, there was no weapon strapped to his hip, nor would there ever be again, but it was a reflex he hadn't been able to stifle.

Trent set the sleeping pill he'd been about to swallow aside. It wouldn't have worked anyway. They never did.

Through his kitchen window, he watched the intruder's flashlight beam dart around clumsily. Whoever he was, this guy was a novice. Judging from what Trent could see of his build, he was young, too—just the right age to learn a lesson.

A slow smile pulled at Trent's mouth. It had been a long time since he'd had the pleasure of educating a youngster. He'd almost forgotten how much he missed it. Almost.

It took him only a few seconds to slide on a pair of

jeans and shove his feet into grass-stained sneakers. He was out the door before he realized he hadn't called the police. In all the excitement, he'd forgotten that it was no longer his duty to deal with this. No longer his right.

Trent turned around, made a quick call to his buddy on the Haven police force, but refused to wait for him to show up. Little Ashley McBride was a sweet kid, even if she couldn't remember what day of the week it was. He wasn't going to let some punk trash her place when he was able to stop it.

The fact that said punk might have a gun, when Trent didn't, didn't even slow him down. Maybe an action like that deserved some careful thought, but he'd do that later. Much, much later. His life was bad enough without adding a bunch of psychobabble crap on top of it.

He hurried across the street and slipped silently onto the porch. The front door was closed again, but a slow turn of the knob told him it wasn't locked.

Amateur.

Trent eased inside, listening for which way the intruder had gone. Ashley's house was an artistic mess, with canvases stacked everywhere. Every horizontal surface was covered with clothes, paints, brushes, or papers. There was more furniture in her living room than there was in his entire house, leaving only a narrow walkway open for him to navigate.

This whole neighborhood had been built in the housing boom after World War II, and Ashley's house was an exact copy of his own, so he had the advantage of knowing the layout, even in the dark.

A low scraping sound came from the back bedroom, like someone was rummaging around in there.

Trent's body flooded with adrenaline and he slid into that comfortable space where each heartbeat stretched out for an eternity. The rush of strength and clarity nearly made him giddy, and he realized it had been way too long since the adrenaline junkie in him had gotten his fix.

The streetlights outside shone through the front window, outlining the entrance to the hallway. His eyes had adjusted to the dark enough that he could see vague shapes, but little else. He crept toward the bedroom where he'd heard the sound.

A thud followed by a muffled hiss of pain came from the back room. Trent eased through the doorway just as the intruder stood up from a crouch.

He was only three feet in front of Trent, and a sudden rush of instinct took over Trent's body as he moved. He grabbed the kid and shoved him hard against the door. He used his body to pin the kid there while he took control of the intruder's hands and any weapon he might hold.

The kid let out a high shriek of fear that was cut off too soon, like he'd run out of air. He struggled, fighting Trent's hold, but wasn't strong enough for it to do any good. Those struggles did, however, press the intruder's breasts against Trent's bare ribs.

Breasts? For a brief second, shock rolled through him, freezing him in place. The intruder was a woman, not a kid. Not that it mattered. She was still breaking the law.

She used his moment of surprise to wrench one hand free of his grip and slammed her fist into the side of his head. The blow rattled his cage, but it didn't slow him down. He recaptured her hand and leaned his weight into her harder, crushing her ribs.

Her knee came up toward his groin, but they were too close for the blow to have any force behind it. She kind of grazed his thigh, but it was enough to make him want to prevent it from happening again, just in case she got a lucky shot.

He spun her around, twisting her arms behind her, and leaned his weight against her. She tried to head-butt him, but the top of her head only came up to his chin, so all she hit was his collarbone. Her pale hair was tucked into a bun, which cushioned the blow. Trent doubted he'd even have a bruise.

He had to give her an A for effort, though. She was completely outclassed, apparently weaponless and alone, and yet she kept fighting.

Her foot slammed down hard on his toes, and pain screamed up his leg.

"Bad move," he told her as he wrenched her arms higher, putting enough force on her shoulders to make a grown man cry.

She let out a willowy gasp of pain that was so feminine it made Trent feel like an ass for hurting her. Not that she would have thought twice about hurting him, given the chance.

He let up, releasing some of the pressure, which only proved how soft he'd gotten over the past two years. Soft and useless.

"Let me go," she ordered. The fact that her words came out as a breathless whisper robbed them of some authority.

"Not gonna happen. Who are you, and why are you here?"

"I should be asking you the same thing. Why are you in my sister's house?"

"Sister?" Oh, crap. Not good.

Trent turned her around, a lot more gently this time, and looked at her face. It was hard to see in the dim light, but the flashlight she'd dropped created enough of an ambient glow that he could make out the basics. Her mouth wasn't quite as full and pouty as Ashley's, but she had the same dainty chin and nose, the same pale eyes and hair.

"What's your name?" he asked her, just to be sure.

"Elise McBride."

Trent knew that name. He'd heard Ashley talk about the revered Elise often enough he remembered it. He let go of her like she'd sprouted quills. "I'm so sorry," he rushed to tell her. "I'm Ashley's neighbor and I thought you were breaking into her house. Did I hurt you?"

She rubbed one shoulder, sagging against the door, breathing too fast. "I'm fine. Heck of a neighborhood watch you have here."

Well, hell. He'd gone and fucked up good this time. And the sirens in the distance told him that in a few minutes his humiliation would be complete.

Elise couldn't stop shaking. For a moment there, she was sure that she was about to witness what had happened to her sister, up close and personal. She'd thought she was going to die, that the man who had complete control over her body was going to kill her.

And there hadn't been a thing she could do to stop him.

Suddenly, Ashley's disappearance became even more sinister. In that one brief moment of helplessness, Elise had gone from hoping to find her sister safe and sound to knowing that she was fooling herself indulging in that kind of fantasy.

Bad things happened. That nagging itch in her gut told her that Ashley had been a victim of one of them.

Her whole body trembled, and it was still a little hard to breathe. Her lungs felt flat, heavy. The surge of adrenaline was wearing off, leaving her sagging and queasy in its wake.

Sirens outside grew louder, but she couldn't bring herself to face the police just yet. She had to get a grip and regain her composure. She didn't want to look like a wilting flower when she demanded that they help her find Ashley.

Elise straightened her shoulders, which ached almost as much as the back of her head. Whatever the hell this guy was made of, it was tough stuff. She'd nearly imploded her skull trying to bash him with it.

Not the smartest thing she'd ever done.

"Sit down a minute," he said, urging her toward Ashley's bed. "You look a little shaky."

Elise sat down, grateful to have the solid surface supporting her trembling legs. "Who are you?" she asked him.

"Trent Brady. I live across the street."

The name was familiar, and it took her only a second to place him. "Ah. So you're Ashley's 'Hot Lawn Guy.'" She'd talked about him so often that Elise was beginning to wonder if Ashley was making him up. No guy was as helpful as the Hot Lawn Guy without wanting something in return.

"Uh. I mow her lawn, yeah."

"And fix her car, and get rid of wasp's nests, and repair broken garbage disposals. She talks about you all the time."

He shifted uncomfortably from one foot to the other, as if she'd embarrassed him. "Ashley likes to talk."

Elise couldn't make out much in the dark, but she'd felt enough of Trent's body pressed against hers to know the guy was in great shape. He was helpful, and apparently modest about it.

It was a wonder Ashley hadn't fallen in love with him at least three times by now, but she'd always said he wasn't her type. Maybe he was gay.

He reached over to flip on the light.

"Don't bother. I already tried. The fuse must be blown."

"I'll take care of it," he said. "As soon as the police get here and I sort things out."

Elise heaved out a weary sigh, dreading the job she had to do now. "They were on my list of people to talk to anyway. I guess now is as good a time as any."

Suspicion tightened his voice. "Talk to about what?"

"About my missing sister and what they're doing to find her."

CHAPTER TWO

Elise met the officer at the door to her sister's home. He was in his fifties, she guessed, with short salt-and-pepper hair and a matching mustache. Although he wasn't wearing his uniform, his car bore the emblem of the Haven Police Department.

He looked her up and down briefly, then his gaze went over her shoulder to the man standing just behind her. "Morning, Trent," he said. "Wanna tell me what's going on here?"

"Sorry, Bob. False alarm. I thought she was a kid out for a little B and E."

Officer Bob's mouth turned down at the corners as he looked at her. "Did you break in?"

"No. This is my sister's place. I used a key." All of which was technically the truth, even if it didn't convey what really happened.

"Good. It's too damn early for paperwork," said the officer. "And trouble. What's your name, ma'am?"

"Elise McBride, Ashley's sister."

"Ah. You're the one who called in the missing person's report."

"Yes, sir. That's why I'm here. To find Ashley. I'm hoping you can help."

In the houses around them, people wakened by the sirens peered out lighted windows.

The officer's thick chest collapsed on a heavy sigh. "Let's take this inside, kids. No sense in making a scene on the front porch."

Elise stepped back to make room for the officer, grazing Trent's bare chest with her arm. The heat from his skin soaked into her, and until now, she hadn't realized she was cold. Stupid nerves.

He moved out of her way, taking all that warmth with him, and the officer shut the door behind them.

"Why's it so dark in here?" he asked.

"A fuse blew," said Trent. "Happens all the time. I'll take care of it." He crossed the room like he lived here, opened a door and went downstairs.

Elise briefly wondered just how close he'd been to Ashley that he knew her fuses blew often, and exactly where to go to fix them. Her sister told her about all her boyfriends—in great detail, much to Elise's dismay. In all those breathless ramblings, Ashley hadn't mentioned Trent as anything more than Hot Lawn Guy.

"So, Ms. McBride. How 'bout you tell me why you showed up here at three in the morning?"

Elise shrugged. "I got off the plane in Chicago, rented a car and drove here. It took as long as it took."

"Where'd you come in from?"

The power came back on, bathing them in light. From the kitchen, an appliance beeped, begging for attention.

The ceiling fan in the living room started spinning in a lazy circle.

Elise blinked as her eyes adjusted. "Hong Kong."

His bushy brows lifted. "That's a long way off. Do you live there?"

She caught a glimpse of herself reflected in one of the windows, and the sight of her frizzing bun made her cringe. She'd been traveling for hours, and every one of them showed in her hair.

Elise worked the hairpins out of the knotted mess of curls and untangled them with her fingers. "Sometimes. I'm a reporter. I was working on a story."

As soon as the word *reporter* came out of her mouth, Officer Bob flinched. "You're not going to be stirring up any trouble here, are you?"

Elise knew exactly what he meant, but she pretended ignorance. "Trouble? What do you mean?"

"I mean you starting stories about women disappearing from Haven."

"A woman has disappeared. I'd say that's newsworthy, wouldn't you?" He didn't have to know that wasn't the kind of story she usually covered—that her work was mostly about the changes in foreign economy with a bit of fun stuff thrown in on the side, just to keep her interested, even if it didn't pay the bills. Let him think that his town's dirty laundry was going to be aired for the world to see. Maybe it would get him to cooperate.

"We don't know she's disappeared," said Trent from the top of the stairway. "Ashley has a tendency to run off for days at a time."

Elise turned her head to give him hell for talking

about her sister in such a flippant way, but the words stuck in her throat.

Hot Lawn Guy was more than just hot. He was scalding.

He wasn't wearing a shirt, but for him, covering up should have been a crime. Golden skin stretched tight over delicious slabs of muscles. His shoulders were wide and heavy, his arms thick and long. The ridges in his stomach stood out every time he breathed. But the beautiful part was that none of that was a show. He hadn't removed his body hair or oiled himself up, or sprayed on a tan. He wasn't coiffed or groomed. In fact, he was in desperate need of a haircut.

He wasn't trying to look good. He just did.

"Oh, for heaven's sake," muttered the cop. "Would you put on a damn shirt? You make the rest of us mere mortals look bad."

"In a minute," said Trent, staring at Elise. His eyes slid over her from top to bottom and back again, making her wish for a hairbrush. "I think the lady here was about to say something."

Yes, she was. Elise couldn't remember what it was, so she ripped her eyes away and tried to concentrate.

"Trent's right, Ms. McBride. We had a couple of officers check things out when you reported her missing. They questioned the neighbors and everyone said the same thing. She goes away for days at a time. It's not unusual."

"Yes, but she never goes this long without phoning me."

"Maybe her phone broke," said Trent. "Maybe she's low on minutes and doesn't want to pay the overages."

Elise refused to let his good looks intimidate her. She did, however, keep her eyes fixed on his face. It didn't help much, since the man's face was a compilation of fascinating masculine angles, and nearly as attractive as the rest of him, but she managed to maintain her focus. "Ashley can't go a day without talking to me. She tells me everything. She would have borrowed a phone, or called collect from a pay phone—something—if she was okay. I'm telling you that this is not like her. It may appear to be normal to her neighbors, but it's not. If it was, I wouldn't have abandoned the job I was on and flown halfway around the world to find out what's wrong."

Trent's blue eyes flickered with interest. "When was the last time you spoke to her?"

"Friday afternoon."

"Trent," said Officer Bob in a warning tone. "If you want to investigate this, you know there's always a job waiting for you, but so long as you're not wearing a badge, I want you to stay out of it."

Trent all but snarled. "We've talked about this. I'm not going back into police work."

"Then go home. Mind your own business."

His mouth tightened until his lips all but disappeared. "Fine. I'm going."

Trent slipped past them, the muscles in his back tight and his hands in fists. Elise tried not to stare, but she had no choice. The man's ass was like a magnet, drawing her gaze. Not that she minded the view.

She had no idea what was going on between these two men, but she really didn't care. All she cared about was finding Ashley. If the officer thought Trent would be in the way, then she'd avoid him.

Even if it meant not getting to see that magnetic ass ever again.

Trent had never squirmed before in his life, but there was no better word for what he was doing now. His whole body was crawling with anxious need. He wanted to hear what Elise was telling Bob so he could throw out his opinion. He wanted to be a part of the investigation, to help find Ashley.

He wanted to be useful again for something more than digging holes and trimming grass.

Too bad what he wanted no longer mattered.

Bob's reminding him of the open job offer on the Haven police force was a cheap trick, and Trent was sure the man knew it.

Most of an hour had passed, and his neighbors had finally gone back to bed. Their houses were dark again, just like Trent's. Though, unlike Trent, he figured they were all back in their beds, snug and warm. Instead, he was standing in the dark, staring out his kitchen window, hoping for a glimpse of something that would tell him what was going on across the street.

Sure, chances were that Ashley had just found another one of her random men and hooked up with him for a long weekend, but what if he was wrong? What if she really was in trouble?

It was none of his business. He wasn't a cop anymore. Protecting and serving was someone else's problem. He needed to get some more sleep so he'd be able to install that sprinkler system tomorrow. Digging ditches. That was his job now.

At least the work had honed his body to the point that

women took notice. That was definitely one of the perks of manual labor. Especially when the woman noticing had the kind of compact curves that fit into a man's hands just right. Ashley was wisp-thin and walked around covered in paint more often than not. She made him think of grade school kids and butterflies. Her sister, on the other hand, was all woman. She wasn't very tall, but everything was in the right proportions—some more right than others.

He could still feel her breasts against his chest. No silicone there.

As if it mattered. He wasn't getting involved. Not with whatever had happened to Ashley, and certainly not with Elise.

Across the street, Bob Tindle got back into his cruiser and left.

Trent gripped the countertop to keep himself from calling Ashley's house to see what Elise and Bob had talked about.

None of his business.

Then why the hell couldn't he walk away from the damn window and try to get a couple hours of sleep before work?

A minute later, Elise walked out, locked the door, and headed for her car.

Trent was halfway across the street before he realized he'd left his house.

Elise saw him coming and halted at the door of her rental car. "What do you want?"

"What did Bob say?"

She looked at his bare chest and lifted an irritated brow. "Ask him yourself."

"He won't tell me. Said it's none of my business."

"Then why should I tell you?" She tucked some of her blond hair behind one ear. The wild nest of curls had been brushed and tamed, leaving behind silky waves that fell past her shoulders.

"Because I might be able to help."

She cast a *yeah, right* look his way. "How? I don't need any gym equipment modeled."

Trent ground his back teeth to keep from spewing out the angry words he wanted to fling her way. He hated feeling useless, but seeing that uselessness reflected in Elise's eyes made his chest burn with frustration. "I used to be a cop."

"Used to be?"

"Yeah."

"But not now?" she asked with more than a hint of suspicion.

"No."

"Why not?"

He was not going to talk to her about that. Not in a million years. "Long story."

"Another time, then," she said, opening her car door, preparing to leave.

Trent had to stop her. He had no clue why he felt so frantic about this whole mess, but he did. Maybe it was the adrenaline rush she'd given him earlier. He wanted more. He didn't want her to walk away and leave him out of all the fun.

"Wait," he said, grabbing her arm. "Where are you going?"

Her shirt had short sleeves, baring the silky-smooth skin of her arm to his touch. His fingers nearly encircled her biceps, but her feminine muscles were firm and strong under his grip. He fought the urge to slide his thumb over her skin so he could get a better feel.

"To look for Ashley's car."

"It's late."

She gave him a look that screamed *duh*. "Not in Hong Kong. I'm still on their clock. Can't sleep."

"Hong Kong?"

"That's where I was when Ashley went missing."

She flew all the way here to check on her sister? She really was worried.

"Let me go with you." The words fell out of his mouth without going through his brain first, which wasn't at all like him.

She stared pointedly at his fingers around her arm. Trent let her go, but he couldn't help but let his fingertips slide along the delicate skin of her inner arm as he did. It was a dirty trick, but it was worth it. It had been a long time since he'd felt anything quite so soft as Elise McBride's skin.

"Haven's fairly small. I can manage on my own."

"It might be small compared to Hong Kong, but the town sprawls all over. You'll never find your way."

Elise shrugged. "Ashley talked about all the places she liked to go. Since I have ovaries, I'm not incapable of asking for directions."

Trent ignored the jab at his gender. "At four in the morning? There aren't a whole lot of all-night gas stations around once you get away from the interstate."

She stared at him for too long. "Why should I let you come?" she asked. "You don't believe my sister's in trouble."

"Maybe she is, maybe she isn't. Either way, I know this town a lot better than you do."

"I'm used to strange towns. I'll manage."

"It'll be faster if you have a tour guide. Faster is better, right?"

One side of her mouth lifted in a grin. "Spoken like a true man."

And just like that, his mind went there, to that lovely place where sex with a woman like Elise was more than a fantasy. It was a short trip that ended with her impatient, humorless snort.

"Get in. I don't want to waste any more time."

Gary Maitland smoothed the blond curls off his wife's forehead. Even though Wendy's eyes were closed, he could still recall the vivid shade of blue, and the way they used to sparkle when she laughed. Or cried.

"I can't stay long, but I wanted to visit you before I went to work. I've been so busy, it's been hard to find time to spend with you the way I should."

He traced the delicate arch of her eyebrow, stroking her as he spoke. He wasn't sure whether or not she could hear him, but these visits were more for him than they were for her anyway.

Since the accident, he missed her so much he ached. Filling the void she'd left behind had been impossible, but he'd managed to find a way to cope and move on with his life.

"You'd like what I've done to your parents' place. The pond is so much bigger now. Deeper, too. I kept the dock, though—the one we used to sit on at night when we were dating all those years ago."

They'd done a lot of things on that dock—none of which her parents would have approved of. Those planks of splintered wood held a lot of memories for him.

That dock was the first place he'd ever made her cry.

She'd been so beautiful under the moonlight, with tears glistening in her eyes. It was one of the memories he held closest to his heart—one of the many memories he used to get through each day.

"I've renovated the basement, too. There's lots of room for guests now, so you won't be lonely when I'm at work."

Speaking of which, Gary checked his watch. He had more than an hour's drive to get to work from here, and it was nearly time to go. Besides, his fingers were getting numb from the cold.

He leaned down and kissed Wendy's forehead. "I'll bring you something special tonight. I've found just the perfect gift for you."

Wendy would never be the same again, but he knew his wife well enough to know what she liked.

She always liked to be around people. His little social butterfly would flit from one person to the next, making everyone she met smile. Now that she was no longer able to go out into the world and make new friends, the least he could do was bring them to her.

She didn't have to know that the presents he brought to her were his leftovers—the women he found lacking. Telling her that would only upset her.

Gary pulled the sheet back over his wife's head and walked out of the giant freezer where he stored her remains. He made sure the door was locked and pocketed the key.

Now that Wendy was dead, his search for the perfect woman was consuming him. The void her death had left inside him had to be filled. The emptiness was eating him alive; he had to make it stop, and the only thing that would fill him up again was the perfect woman.

He hadn't found her yet, but he refused to give up hope. She was out there somewhere, and Gary was going to find her.

"Turn left here," said Trent.

Elise did, maneuvering her rental car down a dirty street. This was the older part of town, well away from the tidy historical downtown section, and the buildings here were sad, run-down piles of brick.

"Slow down a bit so I can scan the alleys."

Elise activated the auto locks on the doors and gripped the wheel tighter. "Surely, Ashley wouldn't be hanging out around here?"

Trent shrugged. "Sally's Bar is a hot spot in town for young singles, especially the college crowd. Ashley went where the men were."

Indignation made Elise's back straighten. "You make it sound like she's some kind of slut."

He held up a hand, and his long fingers cast a shadow over her lap. "Stop right there before you get all defensive. I like Ashley. She's a great kid, but that doesn't change the fact that she dates a lot of men. If you think that makes her a slut, then that's your interpretation. I'm just stating the facts."

"The fact is that if a man dates around, he's a player. If a woman does, she's a slut."

"Life is full of double standards. Deal with it."

Elise stared at him in silence for a moment before pulling her attention back to the road. "You know, it's a shame for such a fine body to grace such a cynical man."

He grunted in amusement. "If you think that's cynical, you've led a sheltered life."

He hit the nail on the head, and it sparked years of frustration and anger. How many years had she wasted under the protective umbrella of her mother? She was nearing thirty and had really spread her wings only three years ago. After Mom died.

It was sad that she'd had to wait for her mom to die in order to live herself.

"Stop the personal commentary or you can walk home from here," she told him.

"Did I hit a nerve?" he asked sweetly.

Elise stopped the car and unlocked the doors. She turned in her seat and glared at him. "In or out?"

Trent had the gall to grin at her. "You're nothing like your sister."

"And you're nothing like a gentleman."

His grin widened. "I think I'm going to like you, Elise McBride."

"It's highly unlikely."

Trent settled back into his seat, making himself look comfortable. "Sally's is two blocks up on the right. After we check the parking lot, I'll take you to the community college where Ashley goes to school."

"Does this mean you're going to be good?"

"Angelic."

Elise snorted in disbelief. "Yeah, right."

"Now who's being cynical?"

Elise drove to the bar, but Ashley's bright lime-green Volvo was nowhere in sight. They cruised the streets around the community college with similar results. It was already light by the time Elise pulled into a grocery store parking lot to figure out where to go next.

"Could she have gone out of town with one of her boyfriends?" asked Trent. "Maybe out of the country where her phone wouldn't work?"

"She didn't mention she had a trip planned, but she has a tendency to be spontaneous."

Trent let out a bark of laughter before Elise's glare cut him off. "I'm sorry," he said. "But spontaneous doesn't even begin to describe Ashley."

"You say that like you know her better than I do."

"She's lived across the street from me for over a year. Did she ever tell you how we met?"

"She mentioned you, but that was all."

"Her grass was so long it was breaking city code, so I went to mow it for her. I figured she was sick or something."

"She calls you Hot Lawn Guy. She mentioned your name once, but after that, I think she forgot it."

Trent rolled his eyes. "She hardly knows what day of the week it is, so I can see how names would be difficult."

"She's not stupid," said Elise, gathering steam to let him have it for insulting her sister.

He held up his hands to ward her off. "Of course not. She strikes me as one of those people who are so smart they do dumb things."

Placated, Elise released her mental tirade.

"So," Trent continued with his story. "I go across the

street with my mower to take care of her yard, and when I get there, her car is running. The car door is wide open, so is her front door. I worried that she was sick or hurt, so I knocked on the open door. She yelled for me to come in without knowing who I was."

Elise's stomach sank. Ashley had always been too trusting for her own good.

"I go in," said Trent, "and she's in her kitchen with her arms sunk up to the elbow in some kind of clay or plaster. All her dirty dishes are on the counter and her sink is full of the stuff."

"She likes to experiment with different mediums."

"Yeah, she said something along those lines, right before she asked if she could smear me with the stuff to make a mold. The woman didn't even know my name."

"Were you shirtless?" asked Elise.

"Yes. I was getting set to mow, and it was hot."

"You did it to yourself, then."

He ignored her opinion and went on. "My point is, I found out that she'd been home for two hours with her door open and her car running. She forgot to turn off the engine or close any of her doors. If she found something that interested her, she might go running off after it without letting you know."

What if he was right? What if Elise didn't know as much about her sister as she thought?

"I hope you're right, Trent. I hope that Ashley is off in Paris with some sexy guy smearing him with clay or something. But I have this feeling, you know? This sickness in my stomach that tells me something's not right."

"Gut instinct. You should listen to it. If you don't, you'll be sorry."

"You say that like you know from experience."

He looked away, staring toward the doors of the grocery store. "When did it start? This feeling?"

"Saturday morning, your time. Ashley always called me to tell me about her Friday night adventures, but this time, she didn't. I left her a message and tried not to think anything about it. I went to bed, slept badly. When I got up and she hadn't returned my call, I tried again. Over and over. Pretty soon, her phone went directly to voice mail, like she'd turned it off."

"Or the battery went dead."

"Yeah. I called the police, and got on the next flight into Chicago."

"You're a good sister to drop everything like that."

She pushed out a long breath, wishing it would ease some of her tension. It didn't. "I guess we'll see how good I am."

"What's that supposed to mean?"

"It means I never should have let her live alone to begin with. I know what she's like—how distracted she can get—but she wanted her freedom. So did I. We agreed to go our separate ways after our mom died, but I never should have left her alone."

"She's a grown woman, not a child. You can't be responsible for her forever."

Elise shook her head, feeling the sway of her curls against her neck. They were probably frizzy again. "I agreed because it's what I wanted, not because it's what was good for Ashley. I see that now."

Trent frowned at her. It was getting bright enough to could see his face more clearly. His eyes were pale blue highlighted in gold at the center. When the sunlight hit them, the golden flecks seemed to glow.

Elise shouldn't have noticed, but when he was looking right at her with that expression of concern tugging at his features, it was hard not to notice. Just like it was hard not to notice the faint shadow of stubble lining his jaw, or the way his hair fell in an artfully mussed disarray over his ears.

Trent Brady was a distraction Elise couldn't afford, but one she welcomed nonetheless. With him sitting beside her, the gnawing fear seemed to ease. With him nearby, she didn't feel quite so alone.

"So, what? You're going to move in with her and live there the rest of your life?" he asked.

"No, just until she gets married. There's got to be some guy out there who will love her enough to take care of her, hopefully better than I have." She shot him a grin. "What about you? Care to fill the position?"

Trent let out a single laugh. "Sorry. She's a sweet kid, but she's not my type."

Elise bit her tongue to keep from asking him what his type was. She didn't want to know. She didn't need to know. She was only going to be here long enough to find Ashley, then get back to work.

Time for a change of subject. "So, what should I do next? I've never done anything like this before. I have plenty of experience investigating stories, but I'm not sure if I have the skills to investigate Ashley's disappearance."

"You need to let the police handle it."

Easier said than done. "It's not enough. I can't sit around and wait for her to show up, wait for someone else to find her. What if they can't? What if it's too late by then?"

"It won't be," he said with such confident authority she couldn't help but believe him. "She'll turn up safe and sound and you'll give her hell for scaring you like that."

She gave him a long look, searching his face for a hint of the lie he'd just told. She saw none. "You said you were a cop. You know better than anyone that things don't always work out like that."

"No one loves her like you do. No one will work as hard for her as you will. Stay on Bob's back and he'll do the rest."

"Is that what you'd do if it was your sister? Sit back and let someone else do the work alone?"

"No."

"What would you do?"

He scrubbed a hand over his face and let out a long sigh. "Are you asking what *you* should do or what *I* would do?"

"I'm asking you to give me the truth. What do I do to find Ashley?"

He was quiet for so long Elise didn't think he was going to answer her question. He stared at her as the sun rose higher, heating the car. "You're not going to stop, are you?"

"No. I'm not."

He let out a weary sigh. "If Bob asks, you didn't hear this from me."

"I don't even remember your name."

He nodded, satisfied. "Call the airport police and ask if her car is in one of the lots, just to be sure she didn't hop a flight out of town. Go through her bank and credit card records. See if she's made any recent charges that might tell you where she is. If there are none, try to re-create what she was doing during the time leading up to her disappearance. Look for changes in her spending habits. See if her cell phone company will give you information about which cell tower her calls went through. That will help map out her movement, too."

"Anything else?"

"Nothing you should do alone."

"Fine. I won't."

"You're lying."

She hated it that he could see through her so easily. "Just tell me, damn it."

Trent shook his head. His shaggy hair slid over his brow, nearly hiding his eyes. "Nope. But I will show you one more place to check for Ashley's car before you take me home. I don't want to be late for work. My little brother's the boss and he'll give me hell."

"Why won't you tell me?"

"Because you'd get yourself into trouble. Do the things I mentioned."

"And if they don't pan out?"

A slow, satisfied smile curved his mouth. "Then you're just going to have to let me help you."

CHAPTER THREE

Trent was late for work. His brother's truck was already at the job site, bristling with PVC pipes.

He pulled up behind Sam's Ford, and braced himself for a scolding as he crossed the client's dead lawn.

"You're late," said Sam over his bare, sweaty shoulder. He dug the shovel into the hard ground, biting into the orange line they'd painted on the grass yesterday.

"Sorry."

"No explanation? No stories of sexy women tying you to the bed against your will?"

Trent grabbed a shovel, picked a spot and started working. "Nope."

"You're not going to kiss and tell, huh? Oh, wait. I forgot. You don't even kiss these days."

Trent shoved his boot against the shovel and dug in deep. "Leave it alone, Sam."

"You show up late, you take your punishment. Besides, Mom is worried about you."

Trent felt his shoulders creep up toward his ears as the

muscles in his neck clenched. "Since when is that new? She's been worrying about us since we were born."

"Can you blame her? You never visit. You never call. You work and go home. What the hell kind of life is that?"

"The one I picked."

"Then you're as stupid as you are ugly."

"Can we just work and stop yammering like old women?"

Sam chuckled that same wicked chuckle he'd had since they were kids—the one that told Trent he was in for a world of hurt. "Mom and Dad are having a cookout this weekend. You've been ordered to attend."

"I'm busy," said Trent.

"That's not going to fly this time. Besides, Mom's invited some girl from church she wants you to meet. Dad says she's busty."

The idea of his dad looking at any woman's breasts was unsettling enough without the commentary. "Not interested."

"Fine. I was going to call dibs, anyway."

"She's a woman, not a slice of pizza," said Trent.

Sam gave him a *whatever* shrug. "So, are you going to tell me why you were late, or should I invite Mom to bring us lunch?"

That was a threat worth paying attention to. Sam was the Golden Boy. He'd taken over the family lawn-care business so Dad could retire. He graduated from college. With honors. He was actively searching for Mrs. Right to provide their parents with grandchildren. Sam wouldn't think twice about having Mom out to watch them work, bring them lunch, stay and chat for a while. He'd bask in the attention.

Of course, Sam wouldn't be stuck avoiding intrusive questions about his love life and whether or not he should "talk" to someone about what happened in Chicago. Nor would he be getting all those wonderful bits of helpful advice about how to find and keep a good woman so his life would be worth living.

If he never had to hear his mother ask him how his sex life was again, it would be too soon.

"You wouldn't do that to me," said Trent.

"The hell I wouldn't. I'd do it just for the entertainment value. I love to see you squirm."

Squirming twice in one day. That had to be a record. "You're a horrible brother."

Sam grinned. "That sounds a lot like defeat to me. So, spill it already. Why are you late? You're never late."

"My neighbor's sister came to town last night."

"Oooh. I like where this is going. 'Dear *Penthouse*,' . . ."

"My neighbor has gone missing, dickhead. Have a little sympathy."

All the humor in Sam's face fell from his expression, leaving it bleak and barren. "You're not talking about Ashley, are you?"

"Yeah. I am."

"How long?"

"How long what?"

"How long has Ashley been missing? Has anyone talked to the police? Filed a report?" Sam slung the questions at him like closed fists.

"Since Friday. Yes, and yes. What the hell, Sam?"

Sam pulled his shovel from the ground. "We should be out there looking for her. That girl doesn't have two brain cells left to rub together. All those paint fumes killed them. Someone's got to look out for her."

"The police know what's going on. It's not our business."

"I don't care. Let's go look for her." Sam turned to leave.

Trent stepped in his path. "The police have it covered. They'll find her."

"Are you sure?"

"Yes," lied Trent. He knew the kinds of things that could happen to a young, beautiful woman, and he didn't want his little brother to witness any of them.

Sam's posture relaxed somewhat. "We should still go look for her."

"I already have. That's why I was late. Her sister and I were cruising around, looking for her car."

"That screaming-green Volvo? Shouldn't be hard to find."

No, it shouldn't have been, which only made Trent worry more that Elise was right and something bad had happened. But, since his brother was already getting riled up, he skipped stating his worry and stuck with the facts. "We didn't see it."

"Maybe she's out of town." Sam sounded hopeful and worried all at the same time.

Trent shrugged. "That's what I told Elise, but she's sure there's a problem or Ashley would have called by now."

"Well, hell," spat Sam. "Like I needed one more thing to worry about."

"Then don't worry. The police are on it. So is Elise."

Sam's body relaxed more, deflating him. "Let's hope she's smarter than her sister."

"She is. Cuter, too."

"Like hell she is. God doesn't make 'em any cuter than Ashley. That's why no one's killed her yet."

"Let's hope."

"What the hell is that supposed to mean?"

"Elise has a bad feeling."

"People have bad feelings all the time." Sam sounded like he was trying to convince himself.

"Last time I had one was two years ago." As soon as the words were out of his mouth, Trent regretted them. He hurriedly added, "But I'm sure you're right. It's nothing."

Sam buried his shovel in the ground and leaned on it. He stared intently at Trent, speaking in a low voice. "You can talk to me about it, you know. About what happened."

No, he couldn't. Not to Sam. Not to anyone. That part of his life was locked up tight, sealed and buried. It was the only way he could keep moving each day, keep living.

Trent gave his head a brief shake. "Won't help. Why bother."

"John called me again last night. He said he tried to get ahold of you several times, but the number he had was disconnected. Apparently, he doesn't have your cell phone number."

A sick sense of panic flooded Trent's stomach. He couldn't talk to his former partner. He couldn't face the mistake he'd made and the lives he'd ruined. "You didn't give it to him, did you?"

Sam sighed. "No. I figured I'd talk to you first, make sure it was okay."

"It's not. I don't want to talk to him."

"You shot the man. I think you owe him the courtesy of a fucking phone call now and then."

No. The best thing he could do for John was leave him in peace. Anything he tried to do now would only make matters worse. "Leave it alone, Sam. I mean it."

"I can't. Your life is a pile of shit. Do you think I like seeing you live like this?"

Rather than see the look of pity on Sam's face, Trent focused on the sun-dried ground, biting into it with his shovel. "If you don't like it, then don't look."

"You're my brother. I can't let you go on punishing yourself for an accident."

Accident. It was funny how such an innocuous word could symbolize the devastation of so many lives. John's, his wife's, his kids'. Tyler Craft's and his mother's. Trent's. "It's none of your business."

"Like hell it's not. How much longer do you think Mom and Dad can stand to see you moping around? They should be enjoying their retirement, not worrying about you."

"Are you telling me I should leave town?" He'd thought about it a lot lately. Maybe it was the right thing to do. Sam had taken over the family business, and it was once again running smoothly under his vigilant care. The transition from father to son was complete, and Sam didn't need Trent's help so much anymore.

"No, dickhead, I'm telling you to get some help. Talk to someone."

"I'm not going to get my head shrinked."

"Fine, then talk to *me*. I'm standing right here."

What good would talking do? It wouldn't change anything. "I just want to get back to work. Can we do that? Please?"

Sam shook his head. "You're losing it, man. You're not like you used to be when you were a cop. You used to care. About everyone around you. About yourself."

"I still care." It was another lie, but an easy one to tell.

"Then you'll tell Mom you'll show up this weekend, make nice with Busty. And get a damn haircut. You look like a junkie."

"If that's what it takes to get all of you to leave me the hell alone, then that's what I'll do."

Sam uttered a low curse. "If that's the way you feel about it, then it's already too late. You're already dead."

Finally, after two years, Sam was catching on.

After spending the day in Ashley's home, Elise was finally starting to figure out her filing system. She found her sister's phone bills under the phone book in the kitchen cupboard. Her credit card bills and bank statements were in her closet with her purses. Her unopened mail was on top of the washing machine, which didn't make any sense to Elise, but probably made some to Ashley.

The bills weren't current enough to cover the past few days, but she was able to use them to create a pattern of Ashley's normal routine. Nearly every weekend night, she went to Sally's. The weeknights she spent mostly near campus at one of three coffee shops.

Ashley had saved all of her account passwords on her computer so she wouldn't have to remember them, which made Elise's job of getting the most current information easy.

What she found left her reeling in shock.

Ashley used her bank card or credit card for everything. There were charges for a couple of dollars here and there, proving Ashley still forgot to carry cash around. Nearly every day, Ashley had purchased something, even if it was just a cup of coffee. Friday night, there was a charge at Sally's, then nothing. Not one of her cards had been used since just before midnight on Friday.

It was as if Ashley had fallen off the face of the planet.

Panic grabbed Elise by the throat, cutting off her air. That sick feeling in her gut welled up until she had to sprint to the bathroom to throw up.

Elise retched into the toilet and sank down, her knees too weak to hold her up. She sat there on the worn vinyl floor, tears streaming down her face, shaking.

Ashley was gone. There was no hint she was still alive. No scrap of hope to which Elise could cling.

Despair hung over her, blocking out the light and air in the room. If Ashley was dead, how could Elise go on?

"You left the door unlocked," said Trent from the bathroom doorway. "You should be more careful."

Elise jumped at the sound of his voice, but couldn't find the strength or the will to get up. She sat with her forehead propped on her arms, which muffled her voice. "You should have knocked."

"I did. Guess you were too busy puking to hear me." He stepped into the bathroom, wet a washcloth, and filled a paper cup with water. He handed her the cup, and Elise was grateful to wash the taste of bile from her mouth.

She flushed the toilet, but her arm felt too weak and heavy for even that small task. Getting up wasn't going to be fun, but sitting here with an audience was too much for her pride to bear.

Elise moved to get up, but Trent pressed his hand to her shoulder. "Stay put, just in case you're not done yet. Neither one of us want to clean that up." He lifted her hair off the back of her neck and draped the cool, wet cloth at her nape. "This will help."

Miraculously, it did. The cloth sucked away some of the nauseating heat coursing through her body and eased her stomach.

He sat down on the edge of the tub, making himself at home. The room was small, and the hair on his legs brushed her bare arm. "Any better?"

"Yeah. Thanks."

He nodded. "Do you have some sort of Asian stomach flu, or was it a case of nerves?"

"Definitely nerves."

"Want to talk about it?"

Elise shook her head. "Not really, but I guess I have to."

He waited in silence, his elbows propped on his knees, his hands dangling down between his shins. A fine layer of dirt clung to his shoes, socks, and shins. The scent of the sunshine and hot male skin swirled in the air around him, somehow calming her nerves.

Pride or not, she was glad she was no longer alone in Ashley's house. Sure, she didn't really know this man, but he was real and solid—something to grasp onto when the rest of the world seemed to be spinning out of control.

Trent sat there, watching her, casual and patient as if he had all the time in the world. It was probably some sort of interrogation skill he'd learned as a cop.

Elise pulled in a deep, steadying breath. "You said to look for changes in her spending habits. Ashley hasn't used her credit or debit cards since Friday night. Before that, she used them every day."

His mouth flattened and she thought she saw his shoulders drop a fraction of an inch. "What about her phone?"

"The phone company wouldn't tell me anything, but Officer Tindle said he'd call and see about getting them to release the information."

"That's good."

"No, it's not. It's not enough."

"Let me call Bob and talk to him for you. Once he finds out that her spending habits changed, it will light a fire under him. It's proof that something has happened and it will get the police to work harder to find her."

"He told me he's already doing everything he can, but he was evasive on the phone, like he didn't want me to know what he was going to do."

"He doesn't want to worry you."

She let out a scathing laugh. "Like I could be any more worried. I'd feel better if I knew what he was doing."

"Would you really?" asked Trent. "Or are you just saying that?"

"I'd rather know than not. I'm tough, but I need some kind of hope to grab onto—something to focus on so my mind will stop eating away at itself with worry."

Trent sat silent for a moment, studying her, like he was trying to decide if she was lying. Whatever he saw must have satisfied him, because he let out a resigned sigh and said, "Bob will contact area hospitals to see if anyone matching her description has come in for treatment. If she was in an accident, she could still be unconscious or unable to tell the doctors who she is."

That sounded smart. In fact, she should have thought about that herself. She was just so tired. She hadn't had time to adjust to this time zone yet, and she'd worked all day during the hours she'd normally be sleeping. "Why wouldn't he want me to know he was doing that?"

"Because it logically leads to the next step."

"What next step?" she asked.

"Checking morgues for any Jane Does that have come in since Friday."

The image of her sister's lifeless body lying on a cold metal slab slammed into her, making her sway. The room spun around and Elise held on tight to the toilet to keep herself from spinning away with it.

"Easy," said Trent. His voice sounded like it came from a long way off, even though she could feel his strong hands on her arms, anchoring her in place.

Her stomach gave a heavy lurch, like she was going to be sick again, but nothing came up. Her eyes watered until all she could see was wavering blobs of color, which made her feel even worse. She closed her eyes to shut out the nauseating sight and felt hot tears stream down her cheeks.

His warm, work-roughened hands slid up and down her arms, holding her steady. His soft, low words of comfort seeped into her, but she didn't understand them. They gave her something to focus on, something to think about other than the horrifically real images of her dead sister.

Ashley wasn't dead. She couldn't be. Elise would have known if her sister had died, wouldn't she?

Elise frantically clung to that notion, gripping it tight in desperation. She needed a shred of hope to help her move on—to keep her strong—so she would use this one. She'd hold it close and let it give her strength.

Ashley was alive, and Elise was going to find her.

Slowly, she regained her composure and wiped the tears from her cheeks. Her skin was cold with sweat and her hands vibrated with tension, but at least she could see again.

Trent was crouched beside her, stroking her spine with a repetitively soothing sweep of his wide palm.

"Better?" he asked.

Elise gave a weak nod. "Yeah. Thanks."

"I'm sorry," said Trent. "I guess I shouldn't have said that."

"No. I needed to know. I don't want to be coddled. If I'm going to find her, I need to know how to do it."

"The first thing you need to do is take care of yourself. It's important that Ashley has a voice to make sure everyone remembers she's still missing."

"Are you saying the police will forget?"

"No, of course not, but this isn't their only case. Every

time a new one comes in, it pushes Ashley down farther on the list of priorities. You need to be there to keep her at the top."

"Believe me, I know how to make myself heard."

"I'm sure you do, so long as you don't get sick. If she *is* in trouble and something happens to you, no one else will be here to champion her."

"I'm the wheel that needs to keep squeaking. I get it. This was just a temporary case of nerves. It's already passed."

She pushed away from the toilet, needing to put some distance between her and the nauseating reminder. Trent's hand fell away, leaving her feeling oddly chilled.

She washed her hands, rinsed her mouth, and felt him standing behind her. When she glanced in the mirror, she saw the gold flecks in his eyes glittering with concern.

"I get that. Believe me. But what starts out as a case of nerves can get worse fast. Why don't you come over to my place for some dinner?"

The idea of food was immediately revolting. "No, thank you."

"You've got to eat. Besides, you can show me what you found today. A fresh pair of eyes never hurts."

Elise shook her head as she dried her hands and walked to the kitchen for a drink. "I appreciate the offer. I really do, but I have plans tonight."

"What kind of plans?"

"I'm going to Sally's Bar to talk to anyone who might have seen her Friday."

"I don't think that's a good idea. Researching her

credit card charges is one thing, going out asking questions is something best left to the police."

"I'm not going to sit around and do nothing. I can't. Someone there might know something."

"Suppose they do," said Trent. "Suppose you find whatever guy she was with Friday. What then?"

She reached into the fridge, pulled out two bottles of water, and handed one to Trent. "Then I start asking questions."

"Like what?"

"Like where she went after she left, who she was with."

Trent ran a hand through his shaggy hair in frustration. "We searched for her car between here and the bar. There was only one stretch of road where her car would be hidden if she'd had an accident. We saw no signs of bent guardrails or tire marks. I checked again on my way to work, just to make sure we didn't miss anything in the dark."

"So? All that means is we know she didn't drive her car off the road *there*." She opened the bottle and sucked down about half of the cold liquid. It did nothing to ease the worried burn in her stomach.

Trent watched her mouth as she drank, like he was dying of thirst, but didn't take a drink. "It also could mean she didn't drive her car off the road at all. Sure, she could have had an accident driving home from some guy's house, but the longer she's missing, the more likely it is that she . . . met with foul play."

Elise was pretty sure he was going to say something different but censored himself for her benefit. "You mean that someone hurt her."

He cracked open the bottle and drank. She watched his throat move, watched his tongue lick away a drop left on his bottom lip. "It's possible. What if you start asking questions of the guy who did it? You're putting yourself in unnecessary danger."

"I may be putting myself in danger, but I don't think I'd call it unnecessary. You know as well as I do that the longer she is missing, the more likely it is she'll be found too late."

Or not at all.

Elise couldn't bring herself to say the words, but she knew it was a possibility. So would Trent. It just wasn't one she could deal with yet. Not if she wanted to stay sane.

"There are other things you can do to help—things that won't put you in danger."

"Like what?" Elise had finished off her water, so she tossed the bottle into the trash. She wanted more, but those were the last two bottles in the house.

Trent must have read it in her expression. He offered her his half-empty bottle, and Elise's throat burned enough she was willing to take it. She thought she could taste some spicy hint of him on the plastic, but it had to be her imagination.

"Talk to the press," he said. "Get her name and photo out there."

"I already did that. I contacted all the Chicago stations and did a live interview earlier today—before the noon news. Guess you didn't see it."

Trent shook his head. "I ate at the job site. No TV."

Good. She'd cried during the interview, despite her promise to herself that she wouldn't. She didn't really want Trent to think she was a basket case. Even if she was.

He seemed to know what he was talking about, and she needed all the allies she could get. She didn't want to scare him away with her tears. The fact that he'd seen her get sick was bad enough.

"I've done all the safe things I can think to do," said Elise. "Now, it's time to move on."

He shot her a hard, level look of disbelief. "To unsafe things? That's stupid."

"Not stupid. Desperate."

His mouth twisted with contempt. "Either one could end up with you just as dead."

Elise ignored his harsh words. She knew he was trying to protect her.

She pulled in a breath, hoping it wasn't a mistake to bring him in on her plans. "I have a plan I think is safe enough. Want to hear?"

He crossed his arms over his wide chest, making his biceps bulge in a mouthwatering display. "Why the hell not. At least this way I might be able to tell the cops where to find your body."

Elise was not going to dignify his cynicism with a response, so she pretended he hadn't spoken. "I'm going to Sally's to talk to people who might have seen her. Show her photo, offer cash for information. If it's like most bars, there are a lot of regulars at Sally's and someone as colorful and flamboyant as Ashley is bound to get noticed."

"You have to be careful who you talk to. There are a lot of dangerous people out there."

"How dangerous could it possibly be to go around asking questions about my sister?"

"Some people protect their privacy more viciously than others. No one likes a nosey reporter."

Elise let his thinly veiled insult slide off her. "Story of my life. I'm used to it—and used to getting around people's need to keep information to themselves."

Trent shook his head. "At least let me come with you."

"No. Ashley would have gone alone, so I need to, too."

"So, what? You're going to dangle yourself out there as bait, hoping that if someone picked her up, they'll do the same to you?"

The thought had crossed her mind, and it must have shown in her face.

"Shit," spat Trent. "What makes you think that you won't end up disappearing the way she did? How can you help her if you're de—missing, too?"

He'd almost said *dead* before he caught himself. Too bad Elise caught it, too.

"You think she's dead?" she asked, barely able to force the words through her dry throat. The empty water bottle dangled uselessly from her fingers.

Something in his hard expression softened, making him look inhuman in his beauty. His voice was low and quiet—the kind of voice reserved for funerals. "I don't know."

But he used to be a cop. He knew the odds.

So did Elise. She'd googled them earlier today when she'd gone through Ashley's e-mail. She knew that the chances of finding her sister alive were dwindling by the second. She had to *do* something, even if that something didn't help. If she stopped doing, she'd start thinking, and that was dangerous.

If she started thinking about Ashley and what could have happened to her, she'd crumple into a soggy heap and never get up again.

She never should have let Ashley live alone, no matter how much she begged. She should have moved in with her. Taken care of her. Protected her from herself.

But Ashley wanted to be free—she craved it the same way Elise did. After years of being overprotected by their mother, they both deserved a little freedom. Or so Elise thought. It was clear now that she'd been wrong. Selfish. She wanted to pursue her own dreams to see the world, and she couldn't do that if she was tied to her scatterbrained sister.

Elise refused to be selfish any longer. She was going to do whatever it took to find Ashley, even if it meant putting herself in danger. She'd do whatever she could to minimize the risk, but she wouldn't back off. And anyone who stood in her way had to go.

She looked up at Trent. "Thank you for all you've done. I appreciate it, but I think it's best if you leave now."

"Why? So you can go and do something stupid?"

"I need to get cleaned up." She moved toward the front door.

Trent didn't take the hint. He stood in her path, unmoving. "You're going to get yourself hurt."

She grabbed his thick arm and pulled him toward the door to help get him moving. "Don't worry about me. I'll be fine."

"I see stupid runs in your family."

Indignation flared hot inside her, making her words sharp. "Ashley isn't stupid."

"So, it's just you, then?"

Elise refused to let his insult pull her in. He was trying to distract her, and she didn't have time for it. "Please leave."

Trent shook his head and opened the front door, giving her a disappointed frown. "Let the police handle this. You're going to get yourself killed."

"I've got pepper spray in my purse. I'll be fine."

"Pepper spray? You really think that's going to help if you get in trouble?"

"Yes." She had to think that. Anything else was too scary to deal with.

He stepped onto the front porch and Elise started to close the door. Trent slapped his hand against it, stopping her. "Did Ashley carry pepper spray?"

"Yes. Mom made sure it was a habit for us to have it with us all the time."

"It didn't help her, did it?"

Somewhere in the back of her mind, Elise already knew that; she just didn't want to admit it.

She shoved the door shut, blocking him and any further disturbing statements he might make. She had enough to deal with without his help, thank you very much.

And just to make sure he didn't come marching in here again, uninvited, Elise locked the door and went to get dressed up.

Tonight, she had a part to play, and she was going to

need all the time she could get to make herself look like she hadn't been crying and sick with worry all day.

And then, once she poured herself into one of her sister's daring dresses, shoved her feet into high heels and heaped on the makeup and hair spray, she'd be the perfect bait.

Tonight, she was going hunting.

Gary had watched the clock all day, counting the minutes until he could leave the bank and get back home.

He was looking forward to seeing Wendy again. And to tonight's project.

Through the glass wall of his cubicle at the bank, Gary saw one of the tellers approach with another woman. They were headed right for him.

He clenched his jaw in frustration at the delay. It was just his luck that he'd get a customer two minutes before the bank closed.

Gary plastered a fake smile on his face as they came through the open doorway. "Mr. Maitland, this is Gloria, and she needs to make a change to her student checking account."

"Thank you, Candice," said Gary.

As the teller left, Gary got a clear view of the customer. She was young and moved with exceptional grace. Though her face wasn't beautiful, she was pretty enough. And she was blond, just like Wendy. He'd always loved blondes.

Gary reached out his hand in greeting. The young woman put her hand in his and time seemed to slow. Her fingers were long and slim, her skin so warm and soft, it reminded him of Wendy's hands before the accident.

She always knew just how to stroke him, just how to touch him.

His erection was swift and startling, and it took him a moment to remember his manners. The slight tug against his palm reminded him to let go of the woman's hand.

Before she could see his arousal, Gary eased himself into his chair. "Have a seat, Gloria," he said. "I'll be happy to help you."

She sat, lowering herself to the chair in a single, fluid movement.

"You're a student?" he asked.

"Yes. I major in dance."

Ah. That explained her gracefulness. No wonder he was drawn to her. He'd always had a thing for creative women. "That must be fun."

"It's hard work, but I love it."

"So, what can I do for you today?"

"I just moved out of my ex-boyfriend's apartment and got a place of my own, so I need to change my address." She slid a piece of paper across the desk. "Here's the new one."

He clamped down on the urge to ask if she lived alone until it made his head throb. He never found his women at work. They'd be too easy to trace back to him. He knew better, but Gloria was so lovely. So perfect.

Maybe just this one time he could break his own rules. He owed it to himself to at least find out more about her. He owed it to Wendy.

"I'll need to see your ID."

Gary watched as she reached into her purse and pulled out a wallet. Those slender, graceful fingers of hers sorted through the cards until she came up with her driver's license. She handed it to him, and he couldn't stop himself from grazing one finger against hers.

He shifted in his seat, trying to ease the discomfort his trapped erection caused.

Rules were meant to be broken, and if ever there was a woman worth taking a risk for, it was the one sitting across his desk. There was just something about Gloria that gave him hope that perfection was real and waiting for him to make the first move.

Gary finished updating her records and watched as she walked away, each stride fluid and graceful. When she was finally out of sight, he took the slip of paper with Gloria's new address on it and slid it into his pocket.

If she hadn't wanted him to come visit her tonight, she wouldn't have left her address behind. She may not have shown it, but he had a feeling that she wanted him as much as he did her. There was probably something in her that had sensed the kind of man he was, the kind of things he liked to do to women.

Wendy had been drawn to that darker side of him. She'd liked the pain he gave her.

Gloria would, too.

CHAPTER FOUR

Stupid, foolhardy, brainless woman.

Trent's feet still burned from stomping all the way home, and that had been twenty minutes ago. It was good she didn't want him around. He didn't want to watch her self-destruct. Hearing about her foolish plan was bad enough.

The cold shower he'd taken hadn't done anything to cool off his frustration with her and her "plan."

He turned on the TV to drown out the instincts that were screaming at him to stop her. It wasn't his business. If she wanted to throw herself on a fire, she could. He didn't care.

Or at least, he wished he didn't.

His hair was still wet when he sat down with his microwaved TV dinner. It was nearly seven, and the last few minutes of the news droned on while he waited for the next show to start. He needed to get his mind off Elise, and TV was easy. He'd been leaning on the thing for years as a means of distraction.

The anchor came on, her voice perfectly modulated

to somber professionalism. "And for those of you who might be tuning in late, please take a look at this photo. Ashley McBride went missing from her Haven, Illinois, home sometime late Friday."

Trent looked up from his food to see a recent photo of Ashley glowing bright on the TV. Her face was frozen in a laugh and there was a smear of blue paint on one cheek.

"If you've seen her, or have any information that might lead to her whereabouts, please call the Crime Stoppers line."

The image cut to Elise, standing in front of Ashley's house. Several microphones were thrust in her face, but she ignored them and looked directly into each camera, one at a time. When her gaze connected with this station's camera, Trent's breath swelled in his chest. He felt like she was pleading with him personally. Sunlight glinted off the streaks of tears sliding down her cheeks. Her voice wavered with emotion, but she held steady, saying what needed to be said. "I'm offering a reward of ten thousand dollars to anyone who can help the police find my sister. Please, if you know anything, call the Crime Stoppers Hotline. I need to—" Her voice broke and she cleared her throat, regaining her composure. "If you want to remain anonymous, that's fine. I just want to know where she is so I can bring her home."

She'd said more, but the story was already aging, and she was cut off before she finished. The reporter repeated the Crime Stoppers Hotline number and moved on to the next bit of news they wanted to shove in before the last few seconds of airtime were gone.

Trent sat there with the image of Elise's grief-stricken

face burned into his retinas. He wanted to help her, to make it all go away. He wanted to find Ashley and bring her home safe and sound.

He missed being a cop, missed helping people so much it felt like part of him had been gouged out and the open wound left bleeding.

If only he'd been more careful. Smarter.

Hell.

Trent dropped his fork and shoved the TV tray away. No way was he going to be able to eat now, not with all that guilt swirling around in his gut.

He went to the kitchen for some antacids and stared across the street. Through Ashley's sheer curtains he could see Elise's shadow moving around in the living room, likely trying to maneuver around all that damn furniture.

The woman was going to get herself killed looking for her sister. She was going to poke her nose into places it shouldn't be and end up getting it lopped off.

None of his business.

Any minute now, she'd walk out that door and get in her car. She'd drive over to Sally's and start asking dangerous questions. Even if no one there knew what had happened to Ashley, he'd bet his house that several people there had secrets to keep. That place wasn't exactly the safest hangout, which was why it was popular among the younger, thrill-seeking crowds.

It was the first place he'd go if he wanted to find drugs, especially party drugs. He didn't know if Ashley was into them or not, but if she was, Elise was going to run into the wrong person fast when she started asking around.

And when she did . . .

None of his business.

Trent was not going to crack. He was not going to go over there and stop her. If she wanted to get herself killed, it was her decision. She was a grown woman and perfectly able to make whatever stupid decisions she wanted.

Not stupid. Desperate.

That's what she'd told him.

What lengths would he go to if Sam went missing? Would he sit around doing nothing, or stick to only safe routes of investigation if it was his brother's life on the line?

Not a fucking chance. He'd be out there, doing whatever he could—whatever it took to find Sam. He'd take on drug dealers and their thugs ten at a time if that's what it took. He'd do just what Elise was doing.

Only he'd know what he was getting himself into; he'd have the muscle and the attitude to keep the low-life scumbags from thinking he was an easy target, which would make it a hell of a lot safer.

Elise didn't have any of that going for her. All she had was a burning need to find Ashley and a mouth that was likely to get her into trouble.

She came out the front door and locked it behind her. The porch light was on, bathing her body in light, making her bare skin glow. And there was a whole bunch of it glowing.

Her dress looked more like a long, clinging shirt, ending only a few scant inches below necessity. Her shoulders were bare but for two minuscule straps holding the dress up—if that's what one could call up. The thing plunged down so far in back he was sure he could see a couple of dimples only her lovers or doctors should have been able to discover.

As she headed for the car, the black dress caught and held splinters of light, shimmering in a way that caught his attention, even from across the street. She was drop-dead gorgeous. Once she got inside the walls of Sally's Bar, every eye would be on her.

Trent was sure she'd done it on purpose. He was equally sure that there was no way he was going to let her go alone. Not dressed like that. If she got into trouble, she couldn't even run away on those tiny, stilt-high heels.

He tossed the antacids in his mouth and chewed them as he headed out the door.

Detective Ed Woodward covered what was left of the woman's body with a sheet.

"How'd you find her?" Ed asked Officer Talley, one of the uniformed officers who had secured the scene.

"Report came in about two hours ago. Homeless guy called it in from a pay phone about a mile away. He was long gone by the time we got here."

"Did he say anything else?"

"Just that she'd been decapitated. That's why we called you."

Ed had been investigating the recent headless, hand-less victims' deaths for two months, and he still had nothing to go on. Whoever had killed these women knew how to keep evidence of themselves off the victims— assuming it was even the same guy. Of course, dumping them in the river helped wash away anything the perp might have left behind.

In the moonlight, the white fabric glowed in stark contrast to the muddy ground. Without the head, the drape of the fabric was oddly distorted. Sickening.

"How many does this make now?" asked Talley.

"Depends on how you count it. This is the third woman we've found like this so far this year." There were a·lot more victims than that, some of them dating back ten years. All young, all with the same general size and build. Most of them had been natural blondes, though some of the other women may have dyed their hair. There was no way to know without the heads.

"Think it's the Outfit? Trying to hide the identity so prints and dental records are no good?"

Ed shrugged, pretending ignorance. His gut told him it was more than a Mafia hit, but he had no proof of it yet, so he kept his mouth shut. "Hell if I know. We'll get forensics out here, see what they can find."

"It's not gonna be much," said Talley. "She's been out here for a couple of days, at least."

That meant the interval between deaths was shorter this time. A lot shorter.

It could be coincidence, but Ed wasn't much of a believer in that, and he sure as hell wasn't going to sit around with his thumb up his ass while he waited for the next victim to show up and test his theory.

Like it or not, he had to face the possibility that they had a serial killer on their hands.

*   *   *

Gloria was sure someone was watching her. She could feel his eyes on the back of her neck, making the fine hairs rise up in protest.

She pulled into the driveway of her new home, thankful that the neighbors on the other side of the duplex had left their porch light on. Her half of the duplex was dark, and her garage was still too full of moving boxes to pull into it, so she had no choice but to walk up to her dark doorway and let herself in with the key.

With two heavy sacks of groceries on her arm and her backpack slung over her shoulder, it took her several long seconds to wiggle the key in the lock just right.

The whole time, she kept looking over her shoulder, scanning the darkness for Ken, her ex. She didn't trust that the restraining order she'd taken out would do anything to keep him away. At least not for long.

Ken was too arrogant and stubborn to let a piece of paper come between them. She knew that. She also knew that the first time he violated the order, she was going to see to it that he went to jail. Metal bars would keep him away, even if nothing else would.

And then, finally, she'd be able to relax. She could stop looking over her shoulder every minute and focus on her studies, and her dancing.

That would certainly make her parents happy.

Gloria slipped inside, locked the door, and flipped on the porch light. The fact that she was safe and sound inside her home should have made her relax, but it didn't. That eerie feeling that someone was watching her was still there.

Maybe it was just nerves. She'd been through a lot

these past few weeks, and the stress was probably getting to her.

As she put her groceries away, the feeling grew heavier until she could no longer ignore it. She grabbed her cell out of her purse and dialed Ken's number. He picked up on the first ring, as if he knew she'd be calling.

"I know what you're trying to do," she spat at him.

"Whoa, honey. What are you talking about?" Loud music and chatter filtered through the phone between his words.

"I'm sick of your games. Why don't you be a real man and stop slinking around in the dark?"

"I don't know what the hell crawled up your ass, Gloria, but I'm not doing any slinking. I'm at the bar with my buddies. Don't even try to call the cops. There are dozens of witnesses here."

More background noise from the bar filled the line. He wasn't lying. He was at the bar.

Which meant he wasn't watching her. Someone else was.

Gloria hung up, trying to control her breathing. This was ridiculous. She was overreacting—making things up because she wasn't used to the new place yet. Her mind was playing tricks on her. That was all this was.

None of her rationalizations helped make that creepy feeling go away. It was like a rabid dog panting on the back of her neck, waiting to attack.

She had to get out of here and go someplace else. Someplace public with lots and lots of light.

Elise saw Trent jogging toward her car, and she briefly considered tearing out of the driveway before he could catch up to her. The man was shirtless again, wearing only a pair of khaki shorts, and she wasn't sure she could stand the distraction right now.

Instead of running away, she waited for him with her car door open, hoping he'd say what he had to say and then leave.

He glared down at her, his gaze sliding over her body. It paused briefly at her thighs, then kept on going all the way down to her too-high heels. "You're not going out dressed like that, are you?"

Anger flashed just below her skin, making it grow hot. She knew how provocatively she was dressed, and she'd done it on purpose. Men's tongues loosened up when they couldn't keep them in their mouths, and Elise wasn't above using her body if that's what it took to get information about Ashley. "If that's what you came to say, then move away from the car. I'm leaving."

He didn't budge. He kept his body in the way of the door, preventing her from closing it. His abdomen was at eye level, giving her an up close view of all those lean ridges. The dome light in her car cast his muscles into stark relief, accentuating how well sculpted he really was.

The urge to reach out and touch him grabbed ahold of her until she was sure her hands were shaking.

Thankfully, Trent crouched down to eye level, keeping her from doing something stupid. His hair was damp, and the scent of some manly soap wafted up from his skin.

He was close. Too close. She could see flecks of gold glinting in his blue eyes, fine lines of paler, sun-starved skin fanning out toward his temples. She doubted they were smile lines, since he didn't seem the smiling type.

"I'm not letting you go out like that." He acted like he had some sort of say in the matter. She wasn't sure if it was because he always poked his nose into other people's business, or if it was because she'd allowed him to see her in a moment of weakness earlier.

Either way, she had to resist the urge to laugh in his face. "You say that as if you have some sort of control over me. My mother's been dead a long time. I'm not looking to fill the position."

He scrubbed a hand over his face in frustration. "You're going to get hurt, snooping around, asking nosey questions, dressed like you're offering more than you are."

"I'll be fine."

"Ah, yes. That's right. You carry pepper spray."

"Want to test it to see if it works?" she asked sweetly.

"Damn it. Do you think I'm standing out here half dressed because it's fun?"

Elise shrugged one bare shoulder and Trent's eyes darted toward the movement, locking onto it. "I assumed you liked showing off. You seem to do it often enough."

"Showing off?" He muttered something low and indecipherable that Elise was likely glad she hadn't understood. "Would you please just go back inside with me so we can talk about this?"

"There's nothing to talk about. I've got a plan. I'm executing it. End of story."

"Executing might have been a poor choice of words."

He had a point, but it was one she was happy to ignore. "Move out of the way, Trent."

"At least let me come with you."

She eyed him up and down. "You're not exactly dressed for the occasion."

"Give me five minutes."

"Why?"

"Because it takes that long to put on some damn clothes and comb my hair."

"No. I mean why bother? Why come with me?"

His lips pressed shut for a long minute as if he didn't want to say it. "Because it's not safe to go alone."

"I'm perfectly capable of—"

"And, because I feel responsible."

"For what?"

"Ashley. I should have done a better job of looking out for her."

Elise knew how that felt, even if it wasn't entirely rational. "You were her neighbor, not her keeper." Not her sister.

"Maybe, but I knew how scatterbrained she could be. I knew she left her door unlocked most of the time. I knew she was easily distracted and never paid attention to her surroundings. I knew she went to places she shouldn't. Just like you're about to do."

She could hear the guilt making his words clipped and harsh—the same kind of guilt she felt for not being here for her sister. It was a horrible feeling, one Trent didn't deserve to suffer through simply because he was trying to look out for a woman he barely knew.

In the end, it was his guilt that won her over. If she

didn't let him come and something happened to her, she didn't want him to feel like it was somehow his fault.

"Fine. You can come. But don't you dare try to stop me from doing what I need to do."

He rose up to his full height, which put his abs back on display at eye level. "I won't let you do anything stupid."

"Have you seen the shoes I'm wearing? I'd say it's a bit too late for that."

CHAPTER FIVE

Sally's Bar was crowded for a Monday night. Or, at least more crowded than Elise had imagined. Maybe it was always like this.

Based on the decaying brick facade, Elise had expected the place to be a little less like a club and more like a dank little hole where people came to get drunk. Instead, Sally's gleamed with chrome and glass, giving it a sophisticated industrial vibe that clashed jarringly with the traditional brick exterior.

Music pulsed from dozens of speakers, and lights flashed in time with the pounding beat. Bizarre, fragmented images glowed along one entire wall of connected TV screens, throbbing along with the music, changing color with the tempo.

Trent had changed into a tight-fitting pair of jeans and a T-shirt that clung to his chest. He wasn't as well-dressed as many of the men here, but he looked a heck of a lot better. Sinful, even.

He carried himself like he owned the place, parting the crowd easily as they made their way to the bar. His hand was warm and solid around hers, giving her something to hold on to as she followed behind him.

There was one empty seat at the end of the gleaming metal bar, and Trent lifted her up onto the high leather perch before she embarrassed herself by trying to shimmy up there without showing off her underwear. He stood beside her with one hand at the small of her back, looming, glaring at anyone who was close enough to see. The feel of his hand on her bare skin, so warm and unexpected, sent a little thrill racing through her, adding to her already frayed nerves.

Elise had conducted plenty of interviews in her lifetime, but she'd never done an investigation like this before. Her insides were quaking with nerves, and she had no idea how Trent could stand there completely calm and unfazed.

He flagged down the bartender and ordered them drinks. He hadn't asked Elise what she wanted, but it wasn't as though she was going to drink anything, anyway. Not with her stomach on edge the way it was.

She opened her purse to pay, but Trent gave her a tiny shake of his head as he reached for his wallet. He gave the bartender a tip big enough to make Elise cringe at the thought of paying him back. She'd already offered her entire retirement fund as a reward for information about Ashley, and that was all the financial padding she had. Freelance reporting made her enough to live on, but just barely. She had to be careful about her spending, and hopping on a last-minute flight from Hong Kong had cost her a fortune.

There were always credit cards. Debt would be worth it if she was able to bring Ashley home.

Trent slid his hand up until his arm draped over her shoulders, his fingers dangling down until they were just a hairbreadth away from grazing her breast. Everything about his pose screamed proprietary possessiveness. In the car, he'd told her he was going to put on a show, and that she should play along, but she hadn't expected anything like this.

"I was hoping you could help us," he said to the bartender.

The man was in his fifties, wearing the clothes and hairstyle of a man half his age. A diamond winked in his left ear, and his shirt was unbuttoned down far enough to show off a thick thatch of chest hair—with gray roots.

He glanced at the tip, smiled, and said, "What can I do for you?"

"My lady and I were in here Friday. We met this hot young thing, but she left before I could get her number. Her name is Ashley."

The bartender glanced at Elise, then back to Trent. "I don't catch many names. What does she look like?"

Trent leaned closer, giving the man a conspiratorial smile. "A lot like my lady. Blond. Light eyes. Great tits. Maybe five and half feet in her fuck-me heels. She's into threesomes."

The bartender's brows lifted with interest and studied Elise more closely. His beady gaze made her squirm, but she held her ground and went along with Trent's story. She even found the strength to plaster a vapid smile on her face.

"I wish I could help you, man. I really do. Sorry."

"Were you here Friday?"

"Yep. I'm always here. You might check with

Gus when he comes in Wednesday. He was here Friday, too."

Trent nodded. "Thanks. I'll do that."

The bartender left to see to another customer and Elise stared at Trent in irritation. "Threesomes?"

"It was all I could think of. We came in together, and I wasn't about to leave you unattended for every hairy-assed loser to hit on."

"The point of being here is to mingle. Ask questions. I don't care how hairy their asses are if they were here Friday night."

"Fine. Mingle. Knock yourself out. Just stay where I can see you, okay? And don't let your drink out of your sight."

"I'm not an idiot, Trent."

"Wearing that outfit here says differently."

That was it. Elise was done trying to reason with him. She was here to hunt for information, so she was damn well going to go hunting.

Gary fed his guests, then bundled himself into his winter coat and pulled a knit hat down over his ears. He would be more comfortable if he put on gloves, but then he wouldn't be able to feel Wendy's skin under his fingertips.

He unlocked the walk-in freezer and sat on the wooden stool beside his wife. He uncovered her head and found her frozen fingertips beneath the sheet.

"I met someone today," he told her. "Her name is Gloria. I think you're going to like her."

Her fingers were stiff in his—not at all like they used to be before the accident. He remembered how supple and warm they were as they twined with his, as they slid over his body. How they turned the prettiest shade of pink when he tied her up.

She had such beautiful hands, just like Gloria.

Gary had always loved women's hands. Some men preferred breasts or asses, but he liked hands. They were the outlet of a woman's creativity, the way she cared for others. They could bring exquisite pleasure, and yet it took so little effort to cause them excruciating pain. So many nerve endings, so many delicate bones.

Without her hands, a woman was helpless. Gary could see it in her eyes—that moment when she realized what she was missing, that she could no longer create, no longer feel, no longer fight. It was the same look Wendy had given him moments before her death. That one, single look of helpless pain had changed his life.

"I drove by Gloria's place on the way home. It's a little duplex tucked back away from the main roads. She just moved in and hasn't put up curtains yet. I saw her moving around inside, putting away groceries. There's a kind of grace about her that you're going to love."

Gary paused, even though he knew Wendy couldn't respond. It was a habit he'd developed over the years they'd spent together. There was a natural cadence of conversation that flowed between them, and even though she'd been silent for a long time, he still felt his silence was a necessary courtesy.

"I'm going to go see her again tomorrow. I'll video-tape her so I can show you. I know how much you like that."

He slid his finger down her cheek, following the ridge

of a cut that had never healed—a cut she never would have had if he'd been more careful.

Guilt made his finger shake, but he didn't tell her he was sorry. He wasn't. She'd given him a precious gift that night—shown him a side of himself he never would have known about.

Her death had been both his deepest sorrow and his greatest joy. One day, he'd find a woman to replace her—maybe Gloria—but until then, he'd have to satisfy himself with the imperfect women he kept in the basement.

Their screams would have to fill that void until his search was over.

From his view on the balcony at Sally's, Trent had no trouble keeping an eye on Elise. That sparkling dress made her easy to spot in the throbbing crowd of dancers. She was currently dancing with her third partner, writhing in time with the music.

Elise McBride was sexy as hell. Each movement was sinuous grace, a blatant invitation to stare. Her compact curves were fluid under that scant bit of fabric, and a couple of times, Trent thought he might have gotten a shadowy glimpse of cleavage—both front and back.

The music morphed to a different song and Elise pulled her partner from the dance floor toward the booth they shared with two more of her dance partners. Her drink had been left behind at a table with the other two men during the dance. Who knew what they could have drugged it with? Trent had meant to keep an eye on them, but the show Elise had put on had been a potent distraction.

She shimmied herself into the booth and toyed with

her glass. She didn't drink, even though he was sure she had to be thirsty after all that dancing.

Maybe she was smarter than he'd thought.

Not stupid. Desperate.

The man sitting next to her put his arm around her and slid his fingers over her bare shoulder. Trent knew for a fact how soft her skin was, and he hated it that this guy knew now, too.

It wasn't as if he wanted to stake a claim or anything. He wasn't even interested in dating. It just bothered him that she had to resort to using her body to get information.

Assuming there was any information to be had.

Whether or not he was interested in dating, Elise still had a way of heating his blood. Trent took a drink of his soda, praying it would help cool him off.

He wanted her, pure and simple. Not that he was going to do anything about it. There was no way he was going to take advantage of any woman when she was frantic and desperate, much less his neighbor's sister.

Maybe after they found Ashley and everything had calmed down . . .

Nope. Not going to happen. Don't even go there.

Trent scanned the crowd, more out of habit than because he thought he'd actually find something useful. There were a lot of sexy women here. A lot of bare skin and glowing female curves.

He wasn't interested.

Maybe he should let Mom set him up with Busty. It wasn't like he had anything better to do. He could make his mom happy and maybe even get laid in the bargain. It wasn't a bad idea.

After they found Ashley, that's what he'd do. If Sam didn't get to Busty first with his juvenile claim of "dibs."

Trent's gaze went back to Elise. She was showing the three men at the table a photo of Ashley. One of them nodded and said something that made Elise hop up from the booth. She leaned down and hugged the man and then hurried off on those too-high heels, scanning the crowd.

On the off chance that she was looking for him, Trent ditched his empty glass and made his way down the metal stairs, keeping her in his sights.

A guy at the edge of the dance floor looped his arms over her neck and pulled her out into the mass of writhing bodies. Trent saw her trying to slip out of the man's hold, but he'd wrangled her deeper into the crowd until she was caged in by dancers with no room to maneuver.

Trent cleared the stairs, but without the advantage of higher ground, he could no longer see her. He pushed his way through the mass of sweating bodies, heading toward the last place he'd seen her. It took forever to move, and the urge to simply shove people away was nearly overwhelming.

The only thing that kept him from doing just that was knowing that it would undoubtedly start a brawl, which would only make things worse for Elise. Not to mention it would get his ass thrown in jail.

Wouldn't Mom love that?

He collected dozens of dirty looks from the dancers—the ones who weren't already so high they didn't even notice he was pushing them around. Finally, he spotted a flash of glowing blond curls against a shimmering dress.

Another pair of dancers glared at him as he pushed past, but he didn't give them a second look.

Over the crowd, he saw the artificially black hair of the man who'd taken her, only five feet away.

"Hey, watch where you're going!" shouted a young man, barely audible over the pounding music.

Trent ignored him and kept on wading through the mass.

Finally, he saw her. The guy with her had one arm locked around her waist and was grinding his dick against her, pretending it was a dance move.

Elise leaned back, trying to put some distance between them. Her hands were on his chest, pushing, but the guy didn't seem to notice, or care. He'd covered her hands with one of his and was leering down at her.

Elise's eyes darted around as if looking for a means of escape. When she saw Trent, her gaze locked on his, begging for help.

With pleasure.

Trent squeezed past the last few dancers in his way and said, "Hey, baby. There you are." He glanced at the asshole. "Find yourself a plaything?"

Elise shook her head, her eyes wide with relief.

Trent gave the asshole an expectant stare. "Sorry, buddy. The lady's with me."

"Not right now she isn't. I'll give her back when I'm done."

Elise straightened her backbone and dug her fingernails into the asshole's chest. "Done? Do I look like I don't have an opinion?"

"We're having fun. Tell your boyfriend to go chill for a while and I'll show you a really good time."

She laughed, and somehow the sound of her mockery rose up through the pounding beat. "I'm sorry, but the only thing you can show me is why I'm with a real man. Now. Let. Go."

"You heard her," added Trent. "I'd rather not have to beat the hell out of you, but I will."

The asshole gave a derisive snort and lifted his hands from Elise's body. "Whatever. She's not worth the trouble." He turned around and muscled his way through the crowd, knocking one drunken woman off her feet.

"Thanks," said Elise. Her voice shook, as did the rest of her.

Trent was still running hot, anger burning low and steady inside him. "I told you this place was dangerous."

"And I believed you. That's why I let you come."

"We're sticking together from here on out."

"Yes, sir," she snapped, but it didn't have the same anger behind it as before. Her voice was still shaking too much to pull that off.

An enthusiastic dancer bumped into Elise and she grabbed Trent's arm to steady herself. The feel of her fingers on his skin swept through him in an unexpected rush of pleasure. It had been so long since he'd felt anything like it, he simply stood there, staring at the spot where her slender fingers met his tanned skin.

"Sorry," she said as she let go.

Trent wanted to grab her hand and put it back, but he resisted. He wasn't thinking clearly. His fear for Elise still pounded through him, bringing out his more primal urges—ones that had no place anywhere near her.

"Let's get out of here."

"No, wait. I got a lead."

Another dancer jostled them, so Trent moved toward an empty spot along the wall. He maneuvered Elise so she had her back to the wall and put his back to the crowd to keep them from bumping into her.

There wasn't a lot of space, and they stood close enough that they could hear each other over the music. So close he could smell the sweet fragrance of her perfume and the underlying scent of warm woman. "What lead?"

"One of the guys I danced with says he remembers seeing Ashley here Friday. He said she was with a man, and she left with him before the party really got started."

That would all fall in line with what they knew—she'd left before midnight.

"Did he know the guy's name?" asked Trent.

"No. And he didn't really remember what he looked like since he was so busy staring at Ashley. But he said that they have cameras all over this place, especially in the parking lot. I thought we might be able to get a look."

"We should tell Bob. Let him get a search warrant."

"What if they retape over old recordings? I don't want to wait that long and take a chance that we might lose the evidence."

"If something happened to her and we find evidence, it might not be admissible in court."

"I don't care about that. I only care about finding Ashley."

Trent knew she'd change her mind about court if Ashley had been hurt, or worse, but the desperation glowing in her pale eyes made it impossible to fight her. Not to mention the fact that finding a lead sooner might actually prevent the worst from happening. "I'll go talk to the bartender."

"Let me do it. I'm less intimidating."

"I'm not going to intimidate him."

She raised her brow. "You may not try to, but you probably will. Besides, you catch more flies with honey. And cleavage."

Against his will, Trent's eyes dropped to the low neckline of her dress. It wasn't as scandalously low as the back, but it was low enough. He could see the swell of her breasts, gleaming with moisture. Whether it was the sweat of fear from being swept away by the asshole, or her body heating from all the dancing she'd done, he wasn't sure. What he was sure about was that it made her glow like a beacon, trapping his gaze.

The bartender had no hope.

"Right. Honey." Sweet and sticky, begging Trent to taste.

His mouth had gone dry and he desperately needed another drink anyway. Time to hit the bar.

Trent cleared a path the best he could. Elise clutched the back of his shirt, pressing herself against his spine to avoid being swept away by another asshole. He could feel the swell of her breasts brush against him every few steps, and remembered just how nice they'd felt against his chest, too. If he ever got the chance to have her pressed up against a wall again, he was going to take the time to enjoy it.

His dick swelled and twitched below his belt, and he quickly moved his thoughts elsewhere before he got carried away and had to face Elise with an embarrassing hard-on. He wasn't sure who it would be more embarrassing for, but he wasn't exactly dying to find out.

Like the rest of the place, the bar was crowded, and there wasn't an empty seat to be had this time, so Trent found them a relatively open spot between two men. Nothing like being surrounded by burly guys to show off just how sweet and sexy Elise was.

Honey. He was dying to watch her go to work on this guy, while simultaneously dreading it. He didn't like the idea of her using her body to get information, but even more, he didn't like the idea of her doing it with a guy who dyed his chest hair and oozed slimy intentions.

Trent felt the change in her demeanor as she shimmied up between the seated men. Her movement went from a form of locomotion to something more silky and fluid. She gave each man flanking her a coy smile, then turned that smile on the bartender.

He sloshed some vodka into a glass and shoved it in the general direction of the customer who'd ordered it. The whole while, he was leering at Elise, licking his lips.

"Well, if it isn't Miss Threesome," he said.

The men beside her both turned and stared at her as soon as they heard that.

Trent was right behind her, close enough to touch, but not doing so, watching her face in the mirrored backsplash. Her grin widened and she leaned on the bar, pressing her breasts upward on display.

"In the flesh," she told him.

"Lots of it, too. What can I get you, sugar?"

"Tickets to your back room."

The bartender looked up at Trent, then back at her. "I only have one left."

Elise pouted, and if it wasn't the sexiest damn thing Trent had ever seen, he didn't know what was.

"Spoilsport."

"Sorry. I'm not into guys."

"Then I'd make him watch. He likes to watch."

Holy shit. She was pushing too far, tempting fate, offering something Trent would never let her give.

He put his hand on her bare back in silent warning. Supple muscles rippled under her skin as she straightened her spine, but she gave no indication that she'd understood his warning.

Was she desperate enough to actually go through with her promise? Would she fuck this guy if it got her a peek at the security tapes?

Desperate.

Over Trent's dead body. Either the guy would let her see them or he wouldn't. Sex wasn't going to change a thing.

"We just want to talk," said Trent, butting in before she got herself in too deep. "That's it."

"Is this about that girl you're looking for? I saw her picture on the news today." He looked down at Elise. "I saw you, too. I know you're just playing me with that whole threesome bit."

Elise moved back from the edge of the bar, taking her breasts off display. Thank God.

The movement pressed her more fully against his palm until he could feel the delicate bones of her spine. Trent should have pulled away, but he couldn't. He left his hand right there, bathing in the softness of her skin, the damp warmth her body was putting off.

"Please, just give me a few minutes. I'll pay you for your time," said Elise.

The bartender's eyes brightened at the promise of cash, but he shook his head. "Sorry. I'm too busy tonight."

"Don't they give you a break?"

"Breaks don't earn tips."

"I want to talk to the owner," said Elise.

"She's out of town. I'm in charge."

It was a lie. Trent could smell the man's deception all the way across the bar.

"Please," begged Elise. "My sister was in here Friday. She left with some guy and we need to see your security tapes."

"No way. Not without a warrant."

"What are you trying to hide?" asked Trent.

"I'm not trying to hide anything. I'm trying to protect business. If I go letting you snoop through my tapes, it'll drive away a lot of customers. Do you have any idea how many of the guys in here are married?"

The man on Elise's left stood up and moved away so fast he nearly knocked a waitress down.

"See?" said the bartender. "You're driving people away. Now leave or I'll have you escorted out."

"If you kick us out, we'll be coming back here with the cops," warned Elise.

"Fine, bring 'em on. Tell 'em to bring a warrant or I'll kick them out, too."

They weren't going to get anywhere like this. Trent took ahold of Elise's arm and gave her a small tug. "Come on. We'll call Bob and do this by the book."

Elise let him lead her back through the throng toward the door. "We need to tell him to hurry. I don't trust that man not to destroy the evidence just to protect his cheating clientele."

"Neither do I."

Trent looked over his shoulder, and sure enough, the slimy bartender had gotten a waitress to take his place, and was headed toward a door marked "EMPLOYEES ONLY."

As soon as they got outside, Trent dialed Bob Tindle. Bob wasn't going to enjoy getting another late call, but that was just too bad.

Steve hated leaving voice mail, but he had no choice. "Just had a couple of people snooping around here, asking questions about the girl your brother was with Friday night. Smells like trouble. If you want to hear more, come to Sally's. And bring plenty of cash."

He hung up the phone and it began to ring almost immediately.

"Sally's," he answered.

"Never leave a message like that for me again," said the man on the line.

Steve recognized his holier-than-thou tone in a heartbeat. Lawrence Maitland, the owner of one of the most well-respected funeral homes in the area. Word was he dabbled in more than just bodies, but Steve wasn't stupid enough to repeat any of the gossip. He liked breathing too much.

"Pick up your goddamn phone, then," griped Steve. "You're the one who asked me to keep an eye on your brother. Don't go getting all pissy with me when I do what you asked."

"I offered to pay you. I expect you to behave in a professional manner."

"I called and told you within seconds of them leaving. That's about as professional as you can get."

"Who was there?" asked Lawrence.

"The girl's sister and some guy. I'd bet money he's a cop."

"What did they want?"

"To see the security footage from Friday night."

"Gary was there?"

"Yeah. He left here with a blond chick." Gary liked blondes. Steve had never seen him with anyone else.

There was a long silence on the end of the line before Lawrence came back on, issuing orders like he owned the place. "Destroy those tapes. Destroy any backups. If you have any receipts tying Gary to your establishment, destroy them as well. If this man was a cop, he'll be back, and when he is, I don't want there to be one scrap of evidence left for him to find."

"Whoa," said Steve. "You're not pulling me into this mess. I'm not destroying anything."

"How much?" asked Lawrence, his tone dripping with disdain.

"Five grand. In cash. And I want it here tonight."

"Fine. I'll have the delivery made before you close. But keep in mind that you'll be asked to show proof you've already complied before payment is made."

"Yeah, yeah. I'll kill the video. He paid in cash, so that's not an issue." Gary Maitland always paid in cash, as did all the other people here who didn't want a spouse to track them down.

"Good. At least he wasn't that stupid."

"This is the second time he's walked away from my bar with a girl who never showed up again. I have no idea what he's doing with these broads, but it can't be good."

"That is none of your affair. I expect you to keep your mouth prudently shut."

Steve did not dare let the words "or else what?" leave his lips. He bit down on the smart-ass reply until he thought he'd draw blood. "I will."

"See that you do. I'll be watching."

CHAPTER SIX

Detective Ed Woodward hated visits to the morgue. The chilly, sterile stench of the place never failed to turn his stomach.

"Couldn't this wait until morning?" he asked Dr. Foster.

"Why? You got someplace better to be?"

Dr. Foster looked younger than she was. She had to. There was no way they'd let a twenty-year-old perform autopsies. She didn't even look old enough to have graduated college, much less med school.

Her dark hair was tied back away from her face in a severe bun, and even though her eyes were devoid of makeup, she still had the longest, darkest eyelashes Ed had ever seen.

"As a matter of fact, I do."

She looked up at him in jaded disbelief. "Hot date?"

"Ball game on TV."

"Ah. TV. Haven't watched it since I was a kid."

Ed bit back his reply that she still *was* a kid. "Just tell me what you've got, so I can get back to my worthless existence."

Dr. Foster pulled open a refrigerated drawer and extracted a tray like the one Ed had eaten lunch on today. She set it down on a stainless-steel table and carefully peeled back the white cloth covering the lumps on the tray.

It was a severed hand. A woman's severed hand. The flesh had barely started to decay, and the manicure was still perfect, glowing bloodred against the pale skin.

Ed's stomach heaved, but he kept his frozen pizza down. No way was he puking up his guts in front of the kid.

"Where did it come from?" he asked, working hard to put an edge of clinical detachment in his tone.

"Some teens found it along the river and brought it to the hospital."

Great. They'd probably destroyed the scene, assuming they could even remember where it was.

"I assume there's a reason you called me instead of whoever had the pleasure of investigating the kids' story."

"I've always loved jigsaw puzzles. How about you?"

"Not really."

"You should give them a try. They're incredibly relaxing and satisfying."

Ed preferred his satisfying relaxation in the form of a cold beer or a hot woman. "Sure. I'll get right on that. Is there a point here?"

"I have an eye for matching pieces, which is why I saw the match right away."

"What match?"

"The body you brought in this morning? This hand goes with it."

"Are you sure?"

"I am. The sawed ends of the bones are a perfect fit. A jury might not be convinced without a DNA test, but I'm confident the results would come back positive for a match on tissue samples."

Ed trusted her judgment. He'd worked with Dr. Foster before and she'd always been completely competent and professional. For a child.

"Who was assigned the case?"

Dr. Foster handed Ed a file folder. He flipped through the pages until he found the report and the cop who'd written it. "Mind if I make copies?"

"Go ahead."

"Thanks." Ed turned to leave, glad to be getting out of there.

"Wait. I didn't tell you the cool part."

Oh, no. Anything she thought was cool was going to end up making him sick. As it was, he was never going to be able to eat off one of those lunch trays ever again.

"What?"

"The hand is less decayed than the body it belongs to."

"So, what? The guy kept it in a freezer or something after he dumped the body?"

"He must have, but there's something odd. See these marks here?"

Ed looked because he was paid to, not because he enjoyed it. She pointed at the severed edge to small dots spaced evenly along the skin.

"It looks like there were sutures here," she said.

"The hand was sewn on?"

"Yeah, only there were no matching marks on the body."

"Then what?"

Dr. Foster shrugged. "I'd only be guessing, but it seems odd to have the stitches here unless the hand was sewn onto someone else. Or some*thing* else, I suppose."

That pizza was not going to stay down much longer. "Did you see any sign of sutures on the wrists of the other handless Jane Does?"

"No."

"Could you have missed it?"

"No," she said with total confidence. "I'm good at what I do, Detective Woodward."

"Of course. I didn't mean to imply you weren't. I'm just trying to figure things out here."

"Besides, the last two bodies were different blood types than this one. If someone had tried to transplant a hand, the tissue would have been rejected immediately."

"So, some guy is lopping off women's hands to sew them onto someone else? Like black-market organ transplants?"

"If the person who did this was connected to that kind of business, then why didn't he take the heart, kidneys, and liver? There's a huge market for those."

"I have no idea. I'll run the prints on the hand and see if our Jane Doe shows up in the system. Maybe that will give me a lead to work."

Ed checked the file, saw that Dr. Foster had already taken fingerprints from the severed hand.

"I'll ask around online and see if any other MEs have seen anything to help make sense of this."

The idea of a bunch of MEs chatting online about dead body parts gave him the creeps. "That would be great. Thanks. Anything else you can tell me about the girl?"

"I haven't opened her up yet, but I can tell you that she was young, thin, with very little muscle mass. She might have been starved for a while before her death. The only thing the body was missing—besides the obvious—was a small patch of skin on her back."

"How big? Could it have been scraped off by rocks in the water?"

"Two inches square, and no, it was definitely removed by someone. The cut was too perfect to be accidental."

A trophy, maybe? One of the other bodies had also been missing a square of skin, but the others had decomposed too badly to tell if they also had the same missing piece. It was something to look into. He'd go back over the ME's reports again to be sure he hadn't missed it.

"Anything else that might help ID her?" he asked.

"She had no scars. In the file, there's a photo of the bird tattoo on her right shoulder. That might get you somewhere."

It wasn't likely, but he'd give it a shot anyway. "Thanks, Doc. Call me if you find anything else."

"I always do."

Ed left, and instead of going back home, he went to the station. Might as well get to work. Sleep wasn't coming anytime soon tonight.

*   *   *

Bob Tindle was waiting for them by the time they got back to Ashley's house. Elise pulled up beside his car, praying he'd managed to get a search warrant for the security footage at Sally's.

"This isn't good," said Trent.

He'd been quiet the whole way back, and Elise hadn't felt much like trying to hold up a one-sided conversation.

"Why not? He must have already gotten the warrant."

"Not this fast, not at this time of night. Something else is up, or he wouldn't be here in person so late—not after my wake-up call early this morning."

"Maybe he's here to tell us we're grounded—that he doesn't want us working on the case anymore."

"Maybe," he said, but he didn't sound convinced.

Elise turned off the engine and unbuckled her seat belt. "I'm not going to stop, Trent. I don't care if he wants me to or not."

Trent gave her a brief look that verged on pity before he got out of the car and shook Bob's hand. Bob didn't smile in greeting.

She scrambled out of the car as fast as her ridiculous shoes would allow. Her feet hurt like crazy, and she was glad to be almost out of her sister's half-size-too-small shoes. She teetered around toward where the men were already speaking in low voices. She couldn't hear what they said, but Officer Bob's face was grim, and Trent's jaw tightened. He swallowed and nodded at what Bob had said, then Trent turned his head and caught her gaze. His blue eyes were bleak from whatever Bob had told him, and shining with sympathy. He reached out toward her.

Elise stopped in her tracks, her body going still with shock.

"No," she said.

Officer Bob's mouth turned down in grim acceptance and he let out a weary sigh. "We should go inside."

So he could tell her that Ashley was dead. That's why he'd come here. That's what he'd just told Trent. "No."

"It's not what you think, Elise. We don't know anything," said Trent.

She couldn't move. She couldn't take another step. Her worst nightmare was coming true, and there was nothing she could do to stop it. The best she could hope for was to stay suspended in time, here at the moment before her world was shattered. She couldn't stand to hear the words.

Trent came to her and tipped her chin up so that she was forced to look at him. "A woman is dead, but we don't know if it's Ashley."

The officer let out a disapproving grunt. "We don't know it's not either. We need to go inside and talk."

Talk? About what? How could they not know if it was Ashley?

Trent wrapped his arm around her and led her toward her sister's house. He took her purse from her numb fingers and dug in it until he found the painted key. He unlocked the door and let them all inside. Elise let him do it. She wasn't really there to stop him. She was hovering above everything, suspended in the agony of impending doom.

When he eased her down on the puffy purple couch, Elise went. When he pushed a cup of water into her hands, she took it.

He sat down beside her, close enough that his thigh brushed hers, but she couldn't feel it. She was numb. Reeling in shock.

A woman was dead. It might be Ashley.

"Tell her," said Trent.

The officer sat on the edge of the chair. His knees bumped the coffee table Ashley had made out of old vinyl record jackets. She'd glued them together in crooked stacks, arranged in a dizzying shift of bright color. A slab of glass etched with peacock feathers sat on top of the twin stacks.

Ashley's sketchbook lay open, a set of pencils close at hand, like she'd come back any minute and pick up where she left off.

"The body of a young woman was recovered early today. They don't have an ID on her yet, but she's about the right height and build. Can you tell me if your sister had any indentifying marks?"

"Marks?" asked Elise, trying to get her mind to work so she could make sense of his words.

"Scars, tattoos," explained Trent.

Elise went blank. "I . . . can't remember."

Trent took the cup from her hands and set it on the table. He took her cold, limp fingers and pressed them between his, warming them. "Did she ever have any surgeries?"

"No. She was always healthy."

"What about tattoos? Did she ever tell you about getting a bird tattoo?"

Elise shook her head. "I don't think so. She likes change too much for something so permanent." But Ashley loved peacocks. Maybe she had gotten one, but

Elise couldn't bring herself to ask them what kind of bird. She didn't want to know.

"Look at her," said Bob. "She doesn't know what she's saying. She's not going to be able to help until she calms down."

Anger at the officer's toss-away attitude helped burn off some of the fog in her brain. "I'll do whatever I have to to help Ashley."

"Then think harder. Did your sister ever get a tattoo?" asked Bob.

"Not that she told me about."

"What about piercings?"

Elise nodded. "Her left ear was pierced twice. The right once. She said she got her nose pierced for her twenty-first birthday, but I haven't seen her since then." Why hadn't she made more time to visit Ashley? Why had she let her career become a higher priority than her sister?

The officer rubbed his eyes as if they stung. "Those piercings aren't going to help us ID her. Sorry."

"Why not?"

"You did great, Elise," said Trent, cutting off whatever Bob had been about to say. "If you remember anything else, make sure you tell us, okay?" His voice was gentle. His tone careful.

He was hiding something.

"Why won't knowing about her piercings help? If this has something to do with Ashley, I have a right to know."

"We don't know if it is Ashley. There's no point in putting yourself through this if you don't have to."

"Putting myself through what? I'm already dying

inside, not knowing if the woman you found dead is my sister. How much worse can it get?"

"Plenty," said Trent.

Bob shook his head. "I don't like it either, but she's going to find out from the news soon anyway. I'd rather her hear it from me."

"Hear what?" Elise nearly screamed it.

"The woman was decapitated. They haven't yet located the head."

Oh, God, no.

The world slipped out from under Elise, leaving her reeling and stunned. Her vision failed, casting her into blackness. She reached out for something to grasp onto and found herself pressed against something warm and hard.

A sob of agony tore through her, ripping her apart.

Sweet, precious Ashley. Headless.

Elise couldn't breathe. The force of her grief was too much, too heavy. It was going to crush her. It was going to drive the life right out of her.

She wished it would hurry the hell up and kill her.

"Just go." She heard the deep male rumble of Trent's voice vibrate against her ear. "You really should get that search warrant before it's too late."

"I will, but first, we should call a doctor. Get her sedated."

"No. Everything will still be there when she wakes up. She's strong. She'll be better in a minute."

Better? Elise was never going to be better again. Her world had come to a screeching halt and nothing else would ever make it spin again.

Ashley was dead. Elise had let it happen.

Another jagged sob ripped through her and there was nothing Elise could do to stop it.

"Leave the file," said Trent.

"It's police property."

Trent's voice lashed out like whip. "Leave the fucking file, Bob. I'll bring it back to you tomorrow."

Tomorrow? Didn't he know there weren't going to be any more of those? How could there be if Ashley wasn't around to see them?

From a world away, Elise heard the sound of a door shut. A car started, drove away.

"We don't know it's Ashley," said Trent.

A sliver of hope speared through her, making her heart start beating again. "We don't?"

"No. It could be, but what if it's not?" He was stroking her hair and over her naked back. She could feel that now, the slow, gentle sweep of his hand.

Elise opened her eyes and tried to find some sense of reason, some shred of calm. Tears blurred her vision, and all she could see was Trent's lap wavering through a sheen of tears.

"How do we know?" she asked.

"You'd have to look at some pictures. Do you think you could do that?"

No. She didn't want to see that lifeless body. She didn't want to have those images burned into her memory.

But Ashley needed her to do it. No one else knew her sister as well as she did. She loved Ashley enough to put her own wants aside. "I'll do whatever it takes."

"When you're ready," he told her. "No rush."

His hand kept moving over her hair and skin, soothing

her with the repetitiveness of it—the lazy stroke of warmth over her chilled skin.

Somewhere in the room, a clock gave off a muted tick, marking the passing seconds.

Elise managed to get control over her emotions enough to stop the sobs that shook her body.

Ashley might still be alive. She had to look at those pictures and see for herself. She couldn't give up hope. What if Ashley was still out there, needing her?

What if identifying her body was the last thing that Ashley ever needed from her?

Elise pushed herself away from Trent. The shoulder of his gray shirt was soggy from her tears. Under other circumstances, she would have been embarrassed, but there was no room for that now. She was already dealing with too much. Embarrassment seemed petty and self-ish, somehow.

"Better?" he asked her.

She couldn't look him in the eye. She didn't want to risk seeing sympathy shining there. If she did, she was afraid she'd crack, break down again into a swampy mess of hysteria.

"Show me."

Trent leaned forward and took a file folder from the coffee table. "Let me look first, okay?"

Elise gave him a shaky nod, willing to put off this horrible task a few seconds longer.

"I'm going to cover up part of the photo—the part you don't need to see."

She knew exactly which part he was talking about— the place where the head should have been.

Her stomach twisted and she sucked in a deep breath

to steady it. Throwing up now would only make her feel weak, and she couldn't face this if she was any weaker than she felt right now.

"Are you ready?"

"No. Show me anyway."

Trent pulled the photo out of the file, using both hands to cover up parts of the image. Elise focused on the part she could see, doggedly ignoring the rest.

The woman's body was the wrong color—too pale. Too blue. Her arms were skinny, her collarbones protruded, but her stomach was distended, stretching her skin. Her legs were long. Her pubic hair was dark blond, trimmed into an unnaturally small patch.

Did Ashley do that? Elise had no idea. It wasn't something they'd ever discussed.

What else hadn't they discussed? Elise thought her sister told her everything. Apparently, she'd been wrong.

"I can't tell," said Elise.

Trent pulled the photo away and tucked it back into the file. "That's okay. It's hard to tell from a photo. I'll check to see if we can get a DNA test done."

"Won't that take awhile?"

"Weeks, likely. You might be able to expedite it if you pay a private lab to do the work yourself. We'd still have to get the okay to take a sample from the body."

Elise couldn't wait that long. She couldn't stand not knowing. "I want to go see her."

"What?"

"I want to go see the body in person. Maybe I could tell better if I was there." Standing close enough to touch her, close enough to feel the chill of her dead body.

"We can do that if that's what you really want, but I'm not sure it's a good idea."

"Why not?"

"I won't be able to hold my fingers over the body. You'll see everything. Do you really want that image in your head?"

"No, but I have to know."

Trent's jaw tightened, making him look harder. "You didn't notice, did you?"

"Notice what?"

"The fact that I was covering up her hands, too?"

Elise had been so consumed with not looking where his fingers covered the picture that she hadn't consciously taken note. "No," she whispered.

"Yeah. Her hands were missing, too. If it is Ashley, I don't want you to see her like that. Do the DNA test. Wait for the results."

"I can't. I have to do this. Now. Tonight."

"Damn it, Elise. You're going to regret this."

"I can't regret anything more than I already do. I should have been living with her, taking care of her. If suffering through some personal trauma is my punishment, then that's what I'll do."

Elise stood, waited for the wave of dizziness to pass, and picked up her purse.

"I'm not letting you go alone."

"It's better that way." Better that he didn't see her break down again. She knew she would. She wasn't sure if she'd ever be unbroken again.

"Like hell. You're in no shape to drive across town, much less up to Chicago. You don't know where you're going. You don't even know who to talk to."

He was right. She'd been ready to jump in her car and drive. She probably wouldn't have even realized she didn't know where she was going until she was miles away.

"Do *you* know?"

"Yes. I used to work for Chicago PD."

"Can you give me directions?"

"No, but I'll drive you."

"I'd rather go alone."

He crossed his arms over his chest and the wet patches her tears had left behind. "Then you can wait until tomorrow, after you've had some sleep."

Sleep? Was he serious? Elise felt like she was never going to sleep again. She couldn't even fathom lying down and closing her eyes. She knew exactly what she'd see.

Headless. Handless.

Ashley.

Trent grabbed her arm, and until then, she hadn't even realized how unsteady she was.

"Go change. I'm going to call my brother and tell him I might not make it in to work tomorrow." And just to make sure she didn't leave without him, he snatched her keys and shoved them deep into his pocket. "We'll leave in five minutes."

Elise was ready and waiting on him in three.

Gary stored the dead woman's lower leg in his refrigerator. He wouldn't need the whole thing, but there wasn't time to finish the job now. He needed the cover of dark to get rid of the body.

He laid what was left of the woman inside the body

bag and zipped it closed. Her head and hands were already in separate bags and stowed in the trunk of his car. As pretty as they were, he no longer had a use for them, and he knew from experience that separating them from the rest of the body made identification much more difficult and time-consuming for the police.

Gary was enjoying himself too much to allow the police to find him.

He'd just lifted the body to carry it up from the basement when his cell phone rang.

Gary pulled off the surgical gloves, dug under the disposable plastic poncho, and retrieved the buzzing annoyance from his pocket.

It was his brother.

"Hello, Lawrence," he answered.

"Care to tell me what you've been up to?"

Gary knew what he meant, but he found it more amusing to pretend ignorance. "Work, mostly. You?"

"Stop playing dumb. I heard about the woman you met at Sally's."

"I meet a lot of women there." Among other places. "You're going to have to be more specific."

"You're doing it again, aren't you?" asked Lawrence in a whisper.

"Doing what?" he asked, just to get a rise out of his stuffy brother.

Lawrence made a strangled sound of frustration. "You're going to ruin everything. I have a business to run. I can't have my brother behaving in such a deviant manner."

"Deviant? Some would say playing with dead people was deviant."

Gary could practically hear his brother's spine straighten, each vertebra clicking into place. "I do not *play* with them. I perform an invaluable public service."

"You burn and bury corpses. It's not curing cancer."

"I have a reputation to maintain, and you're going to destroy it. You're going to destroy everything I've worked for."

"Only if I'm caught," said Gary. "And that's not going to happen, is it?"

"Well, I'm certainly not going to report you, if that's what you mean."

"If you're so worried, then you could always help me. Like you used to." Getting rid of bodies was a lot easier when his brother cremated them. No muss, no fuss, no evidence. Too bad Lawrence had put his foot down a few months ago.

As if that was going to stop Gary from finding all those women and bringing them home. He'd almost found enough pieces to finish stitching together the perfect body for Wendy to replace the one that had been crushed in the accident. The leg in his refrigerator was one of the last bits he was going to need. Just a few more pieces, and he'd be done. Wendy would be whole again.

Then he could start all over. Give Wendy a sister to keep her company. Or a daughter. She'd always wanted a child, and now he could give her one.

The thought made his heart pound as he gripped the phone tighter.

"No," said Lawrence. "I run a legitimate business. I won't risk it for you or anyone else."

"That's not what I hear," said Gary. "I hear you're

working for one of the families, helping them the way you used to help me."

Haughty indignation rang in Lawrence's tone. "I don't know what you're talking about."

"Yes, you do. But I don't mind. The more the merrier, right?"

"Stop it, Gary. I mean *now*. No more."

"Or else what? What do you think you could possibly do to me? Have me offed by your new Mafia friends?"

"Don't tempt me."

"You won't do it. It's too late for that. You're an accomplice now," said Gary, just to goad his brother.

Lawrence was terrified of prison. He was homophobic to the point of paranoia, and convinced that if he went to jail, he'd end up as some con's plaything.

There was a long stretch of silence on the line before Lawrence spoke. "You're getting sloppy. People are asking questions. It's only a matter of time before your depravity is uncovered."

Depravity. Gary had often wondered if there was something wrong with him—if his need to take these perfect, beautiful creatures apart made him sick. It wasn't as if he'd sought out this passion. It had landed in his lap—literally—the night Wendy died.

It was a gift she'd given him as she departed. A way for them to stay connected even beyond death. How could that kind of love be depraved?

"You'd better hope my hobby stays hidden, because if it doesn't, I'm taking you down with me." With that, Gary hung up and pocketed his phone beneath the waterproof poncho.

He pulled on a new pair of gloves, picked up the body

and headed for his car. He still had a lot to do tonight if he was going to keep to his schedule.

Gloria wasn't going to wait forever to be caught.

And Wendy wasn't going to wait forever for a new pair of feet.

CHAPTER SEVEN

It wasn't Ashley. That poor, mutilated woman wasn't Ashley.

Elise knew it as soon as she saw the irregular birthmark on the back of the woman's left shoulder—right above a missing patch of skin. She didn't dare ask why they'd removed that patch. She preferred to believe it had been done for some sort of forensic test.

"It's not her," she managed to choke out.

"You're sure?" asked the young woman who'd met them.

"Yes."

She pulled the sheet back up. "I'm sorry you had to go through that, but thank you for coming."

Elise nodded. "I need to get out of here."

"Thanks, Dr. Foster," said Trent.

His arm at her waist held her steady, guiding her back through the hallways. She never could have found her way without him. She hadn't been paying enough attention.

She still wasn't. She was trapped in that thick, numbing fog that had settled over her during the drive here. Nothing quite seemed to penetrate except the warmth of Trent's hand on her arm.

He stopped and spoke to a man Elise didn't know, signed some paperwork, then guided her out into the darkness and tucked her into the passenger's seat of her rental car.

"I'm going to find us a place to rest for a while, okay? Maybe get something to eat?"

He was probably tired and hungry. It was nearing two in the morning and he'd missed a lot of sleep the night before helping her search for Ashley's car. "Sure. That's fine."

He got them a room at a motel and led her inside.

Elise sat on one of the beds, staring at the black screen of the TV. All she saw was that woman's mutilated body, the dead-fish pallor of her skin, the ragged flesh of her wrists. Her neck.

"I'll be right back," he said.

She wasn't sure how long he'd been gone, but the door opening startled her when he came back inside.

He opened a cold can of soda and handed it to her. "Drink this. You could probably use some sugar right now."

Elise sipped the drink because she simply didn't think to not do as he asked. The ginger ale fizzed in her mouth and slid down her throat, easing the dryness she hadn't noticed before.

"Do you think you could eat?" he asked.

She wasn't hungry, but she hadn't eaten much today. Or yesterday. Ashley was still out there, and she needed her strength to find her. "Maybe."

"I can run and get something, if you think you'll be okay here alone for a while."

"Okay."

He knelt down in front of her and took her hands in his. He was so warm. She had no idea how he could be so warm when that room had been so cold.

"Elise," he whispered, making her look at him instead of the TV. His blue eyes were rimmed with dark lashes that curled at the tips. They were ridiculously beautiful in the midst of such a ruggedly masculine face. Golden shards of determination glowed, radiating out from his pupils. "We'll find her."

"Not like that. I can't find her in one of those drawers, Trent."

"Not like that," he agreed. "We'll find her before it's too late."

"How can you be sure?"

"I'm not, but what I do know is that if we give up now, she has no hope. Wherever she is, whatever she's done, she needs us. If we lose hope now, we're putting her in that drawer."

"Then I won't lose hope," said Elise, wishing she felt the words. "I'll keep looking."

"*We'll* keep looking. You're not alone in this."

No, she wasn't. She hadn't realized how much she needed him until now. "Thank you."

He squeezed her hands. "I won't be long," he promised. "Why don't you get a hot shower while I'm gone? Your hands are like blocks of ice."

That sounded good. Maybe a shower would help wash away the stench of that morgue and help her drive away the image of that poor woman's body.

*   *   *

Trent made sure the door shut and latched behind him. Elise was completely out of it, and probably wouldn't have noticed if he'd left it hanging wide open.

Seeing the corpse hadn't broken her, but it had come damn close.

If that woman had been Ashley . . .

He didn't even want to think about it. Just the possibility that it could have been had nearly killed Elise.

She wasn't strong enough to do this alone. Not that he could blame her. He wouldn't have been strong enough to hold himself together if it had been Sam who'd gone missing.

She needed him, and for the first time in two years, he felt like himself again. He really shouldn't get involved, but what choice did he have? She didn't have anyone else—certainly no one else with the background he had.

It wasn't as if he was doing anything more important with his life. Sam could handle things without him. In fact, Trent was pretty sure Sam didn't really need him at all—he just told Trent he did so Trent wouldn't feel like he was taking a handout from his little brother. It had fooled Trent for a while, but he knew better now. He'd just been playing along because it was the easy thing to do. It made everyone in the family happy, and it paid the bills.

It wasn't enough.

Trent knew himself well enough to realize that if he let go and threw himself into helping Elise find Ashley, the thrill of the hunt would come roaring back to him.

He'd get hooked again and be back where he was two years ago, mourning a friend and a career.

He wasn't sure he could walk away from doing what he loved twice.

He'd told Elise he'd help, and he would, but he had to be careful about how much help he allowed himself to give. He had to be careful to remember that this was only temporary. Not his real life. His real life was back in Haven, not here in Chicago, where memories of his mistakes were everywhere. He could give her advice, but that was all. He couldn't go out looking for Ashley with her. He couldn't go to bars, asking questions and finding leads.

What if he ran into John?

Just the thought was enough to make Trent scan his surroundings, like his old partner was going to jump out and surprise him.

John didn't jump anymore. He couldn't run, couldn't walk. He couldn't even stand. Trent had taken all of that away from him.

He'd taken even more away from Regina Craft. He'd taken her son.

Trent squeezed his eyes shut, trying to drive away the memories of that night.

So much blood. It had spread out over the cracked alley, making the pavement gleam under the yellow streetlight nearby. The smell of garbage mixed with the metallic tang of death had filled his nose, choking him almost as much as his panic.

He'd managed to stem the flow of blood from John's back, but there hadn't been a thing he could do for Tyler Craft. He was already dead.

Trent sucked in a breath, filling his lungs with fresh air. He wasn't in that alley. He couldn't go there now, not while Elise needed him to stay solid and help her get through this. He wasn't going to be any good to anyone if he started taking a trip down memory lane. That road led only to helpless rage and debilitating grief.

Trent shoved his personal hell aside long enough to find something for them to eat. He figured breakfast was going to be easiest on her iffy stomach, so he found a nearby diner that served it all day and night.

When he got back to the room, her hair was wet from a shower. She wore the same clothes she'd had on before, because neither of them had thought about bringing an overnight bag. He'd intended to drive back home tonight until he'd seen how unstable she'd been after viewing the body.

Elise sat on one of the beds. The TV was on, but the sound was so low Trent couldn't hear any of the dialogue.

When she looked at him, she seemed clearer—more like herself.

"Good shower?" he asked, more to engage her in conversation than anything else.

"Uh, yeah. I'm warmer now."

"Good." He set the food down on a small round table in front of the window. "I got pancakes, eggs, and bacon. Want some?"

She didn't answer, but she came and sat down in front of one of the divided Styrofoam containers. Trent handed her a pack of syrup and took the lid off her orange juice.

She looked fragile and uncertain, staring at her food like she didn't remember what to do next.

Trent opened the plastic pack of utensils and fixed her pancakes the way he ate his. He wasn't sure if she was one of those women who never touched butter, but she didn't stop him from spreading it on, or drenching them in syrup.

He handed her the fork, and she looked up at him, blinking. "Do you think Ashley's hungry right now?"

Oh, God. He couldn't let her go down that path. He'd seen how badly that could end. "No. I think she's asleep. Safe." He didn't even care that it was probably a lie. He'd keep on lying to her if that's what it took to keep her grounded. "She'd want you to eat and take care of yourself."

Elise gave him a distracted nod, but she started eating, staring off into space. Thinking.

Trent needed to distract her and keep her mind from heading into dark places. "Tell me about you and Ashley. Where did you grow up?"

She answered automatically, without pausing. "Wisconsin, mostly."

"What about your parents? Are they still there?"

She shook her head, and a damp curl stuck to her cheek. "Dad divorced Mom right after Ashley was born, and found a family he liked better."

"Ouch. That had to suck."

"At first. We got used to it. Mom married again a couple of times. Divorced again a couple of times."

"You make that sound like something everyone does."

Elise shrugged. "Look around. Seems pretty normal to me. How many times have your parents been married?"

"Once. To each other."

"Huh. I didn't think that happened anymore."

And she thought *he* was cynical. Rather than debating a touchy topic, Trent steered her back toward safer ground. "What did your mom do?"

"Office work during the day, waited tables at night."

"Who took care of you kids?"

She gave him a confused frown. "I took care of Ashley."

Which left no one to take care of Elise. Suddenly, her desperate need to do whatever it took to find Ashley started to make more sense. Elise felt responsible for Ashley because she'd grown up being responsible for her.

"Were you two always close?" he asked.

She ate a bite of bacon, grimaced, and went back to her pancakes. "Yeah. Right up until I graduated. Mom wanted me to skip college and stay home with Ashley. She'd just started high school and everything was a drama."

"Sounds pretty standard for that age."

"No. Not like this. She didn't cope well with Mom's last divorce. She went wild. We had to watch her constantly, or she'd run off with some guy—usually a much older guy. It's a wonder she didn't end up pregnant by the time she was fifteen. At least that's what Mom always said. She was a big fan of the Lecture."

Trent remembered getting a few of those himself, though he doubted they were the same as the ones Elise got. "What was the Lecture?"

"It started differently, but always ended the same way. If we went to a movie with a guy, or hung out at the mall or went miniature golfing, we were going to end up raped, pregnant, full of STDs, and dead in a ditch by sunrise."

"Wow. I had no idea miniature golfing was so dangerous."

She smiled a little and it made his heart lift to have been able to make it happen. "Needless to say, I didn't date a lot. Or at all. At least not until college."

"Were you the kid who sat in her room studying all the time because you were too afraid to come out, or were you the one getting wasted at parties because it was the first time you'd been able to spread your wings?"

"Neither. I lived at home, but there were a couple of really hot study groups I belonged to. The fact that there were guys there made it as close to a real date as I'd ever gotten."

"So, how did you get from there to spending the night in a cheap motel room with a man you hardly know?"

"Mom died a few years ago."

"Ouch. Now I feel like an ass for trying to make a joke."

"Don't. I loved Mom, but she'd been sick for a long time and said she was ready for a rest. She said death was the only way she was ever going to be able to stop working so hard."

"I can't imagine life without my parents. Good thing they're still young. They had me when Mom was eighteen. Dad just turned fifty last month."

Elise sipped her juice. "Eighteen? That is young. I was still a virgin at eighteen."

"The last of a dying breed."

"I suppose."

"So you're on your own now, living by your own

rules," he said, to get her to keep talking. She'd finished off half her meal, and as he'd hoped, the distraction was helping her get it down.

She nodded. "I get to see the world now, which I always wanted to do."

"You're a reporter?" he asked, already knowing the answer.

"Freelance. I mostly cover dry economic stuff, but I want to branch out more into other areas. I'd love to shed some light on parts of the world that are bleaker than ours—get people to think about how they can help others, maybe help them be grateful for what they have."

"That's no small feat."

"I'd only be contributing a drop in the bucket, but at least there'd be one more drop."

Trent got that. He knew that as a cop he couldn't stop every crime, or help every person in need, but he could do something. It wasn't much, but it was a lot to the people whose lives he touched.

That was the part about being a cop he missed most— knowing he'd made a difference.

She set her fork down and leaned away from the food.

"Full?" he asked.

"Yeah. But I think I might be able to sleep now."

"Go ahead. I'll take care of cleaning this up."

She stood and put her hand on his shoulder. Her gray-green eyes were shadowed with fatigue and red from crying, but she seemed aware of her surroundings now. It was a big step in the right direction.

"Thank you, Trent. I don't know what I would have done without you tonight."

His throat closed up, clogging with a rush of emotion. He'd helped someone with something important. He'd helped a sweet woman get through one of the most horrific moments of her life. That gratitude shining in her face made him feel like a hero. Made him feel useful again.

Something inside him that had long been dead came rushing back to life. He wasn't useless. He still had something to offer. Maybe it wasn't much, but it was something.

He nodded, unable to speak. Elise didn't seem to notice his awkward emotional state. She crossed the room, got into bed, and slid her bare feet under the covers. She rolled over, putting her back to him, and he was grateful for the privacy.

Trent wasn't sure how he was going to handle going back to that desolate uselessness his life had become, but he knew he had to find a way. Pretty soon, they'd find Ashley. Or they wouldn't. But in the end, it would be the same. Elise would get back to her life of traveling the world and making a difference, and he'd go back to his life of . . . not.

Maybe he should go back to being a cop. It was the only thing he'd ever truly loved doing. It was part of him.

But what if he had to face down another armed kid? Would he hesitate again? He'd barely lived through the guilt the first time, and John had survived. What if next time, his hesitation got his partner killed?

He'd never be able to live with himself if that happened. He'd end up eating a bullet. His family would suffer. His parents would be devastated. His brother would find a way to make himself believe it was some-how his fault. Sam was good at absorbing blame, which was why he'd spent half his childhood grounded.

No, it was too much of a risk. It was best if he left well enough alone. He was getting along fine. Sure, he wasn't bubbling over with happiness, but he didn't deserve that. John sure as hell wasn't doing any bubbling. Neither was Tyler Craft's mother.

He'd do what he could to help Elise and let it end there. This would be his last hoorah, so he was deter-mined to make the most of it.

Gary peered through his binoculars and watched Gloria move. She was graceful. Beautiful.

Alone.

A thrill raced along his limbs, making his hands shake. He pulled in a deep breath to steady his nerves so he could continue to watch his sweet dancer. Getting up this early had its downside, but the fatigue was worth it. He didn't want to miss a minute of his early bird's workout.

Watching her dance only proved how perfect for him she really was. There was something special about ar-tistic women, something that drew him to them. He'd sensed it in Gloria the moment he'd met her.

His instincts were never wrong.

Gloria had finished stretching and began to dance, bouncing and jiggling for his enjoyment. He especially liked the part of her routine where her hands were in the air, waving around where he could see them clearly.

She had such pretty hands.

He unzipped his trousers and gripped his erection.

There was no way for her to know he watched, but he had always thought that women in his life were connected to him from the very beginning. There was a link running between them that tied them together. Pretty soon, she'd feel it. She'd start looking over her shoulder for him, the way the others had.

The last one hadn't been perfect as he'd hoped, but it wasn't her fault. He forgave her, as he always did. Perfection was rare, and Gary had to be patient.

Even though his latest find was beautiful and graceful, she still had a long way to go to prove herself to him, to prove she was worthy to become a part of his beloved Wendy.

Patience. It wasn't time to take her yet. He still had to clean the traces of the last woman from the guest room to make space for her.

Gary had found over the years that there was always room for one more.

CHAPTER EIGHT

Elise woke up from a series of bloody dreams starring her terrified sister. She was sweating and shaking. There was blood under her fingernails from where she'd dug them into her palms while she slept. Her knuckles ached from being clenched into tight fists.

That feeling that something was wrong writhed in her gut, insistent and demanding. Wherever Ashley was, she was in trouble, and it was getting worse by the day.

Elise washed her hands at the sink and splashed water on her face, wishing she knew where to go from here. All she wanted was to find Ashley and get her back home, safe and sound. For the first time in her life, she understood why her mother had been so overprotective.

If Elise had the choice, Ashley would never leave her house again. She'd have armed guards posted at all the doors, and no one would get in her home without a background check and security clearance.

Talk about repeating her parents' mistakes. Even her and Ashley's carefully controlled lives had been less restrictive.

Elise let out a long sigh and had to bite back the sob that threatened to rise up out of her. She needed to get a grip. Seeing that body had rattled her, but she couldn't let it continue to do so. She had to push it from her mind so she could move forward. Keep searching.

Ashley was not going to end up like that woman, not while Elise still drew breath.

Trent was sprawled on the far bed, his long body stretched out on top of the bedspread. His tight shirt clung to his torso, revealing muscles that not even the relaxation of sleep could diminish. His face was softer, though. More intriguing. Light from the bathroom shadowed his jaw and accentuated the angular line of his cheekbones.

Elise stepped closer to his bed and watched him, feeling all the tight, worried places inside her start to loosen up. There was something about him that made her feel stronger, safer. Maybe it was the way he helped her keep going despite her consuming fear for Ashley. Maybe it was simply that he was the only one who'd stepped up to help her, been there for her. Maybe it was the fact that he seemed completely capable of handling whatever came their way.

Even asleep he looked invincible. She had no idea why he'd decided to help her like this, but she was grateful he was here. She didn't think she would have made it through the past few hours without him at her side, supporting her.

Under different circumstances, she could fall for a man like Trent. Hard.

Maybe after they found Ashley.

If they found Ashley.

No. Elise wasn't going to go there. Not yet. There were

still things she needed to do to help the police find her sister. She wasn't sure exactly what those were yet, but she had a long drive back to Haven to figure them out.

Trent would help her, too. She trusted his guidance and judgment.

"Are you going to stand there and stare at me all night?" he asked in a quiet voice.

"Sorry. Did I wake you?"

"I was just dozing." He pushed himself up on the bed, making dozens of muscles bunch. What she wouldn't give to have half his strength right now.

"How are you feeling?" he asked.

"Better. Sorry I freaked out on you like that."

"It was completely understandable."

She sat down on the edge of her bed, giving him some space. "Why are you doing this?"

"Doing what?"

"Running off in the middle of the night with a near stranger to ID a body."

He let out a big yawn. "You needed me," he said, as if that was a complete explanation.

"You don't even know me."

"I know Ashley. Isn't that enough?"

Maybe for him it was, but for other people, she didn't think so. "I want to go back as soon as you're ready."

He glanced at the bedside clock. "You should try to get some more sleep."

"I don't think I can. I need to *do* something. I can't just sit around and wait for another call that a body's been found."

Trent nodded and rubbed his eyes. "I understand, but

I also don't want us to crash the car on the way back because neither of us is awake enough to drive."

"I'm fine."

"You slept for three hours. From the looks of the circles under your eyes, my guess is that you haven't slept since you left Hong Kong."

"I slept on the plane."

"Sunday night. It's Tuesday. Granted, just barely, but still, you'd be foolish to drive, and I'd be an idiot to get in the car with you."

"I need to get back."

"Why? Bob has your cell number, and mine. He can reach us if he hears anything."

"There has to be some clue that I missed—something to tell me where to find her."

"Now you're just grasping at straws. I get that you want to do something proactive, but there isn't a whole lot left you *can* do."

"I'll put up flyers, start a Web site, launch an e-mail campaign. Someone somewhere has to know where she is."

Trent came and sat down beside her. The mattress dipped under his weight. He took her hand in his and laced his fingers through hers. The comfort of human contact radiated out from that touch, helping to calm her frantic nerves. His thumb stroked the back of her hand. "Do those things if it makes you feel better, but you have to be realistic. We already know she left the bar with some guy. The police know it, too. I talked to Bob and he said he'd send one of their artists to get a composite sketch from the man you talked to at Sally's. In the meantime, they're searching all the security footage from the bar.

Let the police work this angle. Give them a few hours to do their job."

"It's not enough."

"It's going to have to be. I know you feel helpless, but you're just going to have to deal with that the best you can. You can't control this situation. These kinds of things happen *to* you, and there's nothing you can do to stop it."

"Are you speaking from experience?"

He looked away from her, turning his head so that it was hard to read his expression. "I was a cop. I saw a lot of people in a lot of bad situations. The ones who came through it best were the ones who accepted that they were not in control. They took things in stride, did what they could, and let go of the rest. That's what you need to do here. Let go. Take care of yourself. If Ashley is hurt when they find her, or even if she's just scared, she's going to need you to be there for her. You need to stay strong."

"I'm fine."

"No. You're not. You need to sleep, just for a few more hours. Let your body recover from the strain you're putting on it."

He was right, but what he was asking—letting go—was a lot harder to do than it was to say.

"I dreamed about her," whispered Elise.

Trent squeezed her hand. "Do you want to tell me about it?"

"No. I just don't want it to happen again."

"I could go get you something to help you sleep," he offered.

Elise shook her head. "I don't want to do that. I want to be alert if Bob calls."

Trent nodded. "Is there anything else I can do? Anything you need?"

She gathered up her courage. She knew what she needed, even though she knew it would bruise her pride to admit it. "I don't want to feel alone. Having you near me helps." His touch helped calm her, but she didn't want to make him uncomfortable by telling him so. "You've already done so much for me, and I hate asking . . ."

"Just ask, Elise. I want to help."

She forced the words out, knowing it was the only way she was going to make it through the night. "Do you think you could hold me, just for a while?"

He hesitated for a long moment, so long she was sure he was going to turn her down. For all she knew, he was in a committed relationship. His girlfriend certainly wouldn't appreciate him holding another woman in a motel room.

"Sure," he finally said. "I'd like that."

Trent had overestimated the width of his heroic streak. He never should have agreed to sleep with her, no matter how vulnerable and fragile she looked. But he had, and now he was stuck in the lovely position of physically comforting an alluring woman in need.

The comforting part he could handle. He understood exactly why she would need to not feel alone right now. It was the part where he remembered why he shouldn't seduce her that was starting to elude him.

Elise had fallen asleep about ten minutes ago. He felt the shift in her breathing, felt her fingers loosen their tight hold on his arm. Her chest expanded, pressing her breast against his side, and all he could think about was how he promised himself that if he ever got to feel that again, he'd take the time to enjoy it.

Too bad his tense muscles and throbbing erection kept him from enjoying much of anything.

The woman turned him on, and if that didn't make him a total ass, he didn't know what would. Just thinking about her in a sexual way was taking advantage of her. She was in a vulnerable mental state, not thinking rationally. She was all relaxed and sleepy, and totally trusting of him. It wouldn't have taken any effort at all to seduce her.

Hell, he could literally do it with his eyes shut.

Trent kept his eyes wide open, staring at the ceiling. He wasn't going to touch her—at least not like he wanted to. He was not going to be the asshole who took advantage of a woman in need.

And then, when the sun came up, and his dick was still safely in his jeans, he'd congratulate himself on a job well done. Maybe he'd even go and buy himself that motorcycle he had his eyes on.

He'd sure as hell deserve it.

Elise shifted, curling into his side more closely. Her cheek was pillowed on his shoulder and her fingers were splayed over his abdomen. Every bit of her fit against him just right, making him grit his teeth against the urge to pull her even closer. Instead, he kept his hands to himself, balled into fists so he wouldn't accidentally forget and start touching her.

He knew for sure that if he started touching her, he wouldn't stop until she'd come, and he was the lowest form of scum on the face of the planet.

The happiest, lowest form of scum on the face of the planet.

CHAPTER NINE

Elise pulled into Ashley's driveway just before nine.
Trent had slept most of the way back, giving her quiet
time to think, which wasn't necessarily a good thing.

At least she now had some idea of what she needed
to do next. After printing up flyers and finding someone
to get a Web site up and running fast, she was going to
go through Ashley's house, looking for address books,
phone numbers, names, and anything else she could find
that might help her locate the mystery man. Then, she
was going to head over to campus to talk to Ashley's
friends and see if any of them knew who he was.

Maybe the cops were already working on that angle,
but she could help.

Having a plan made her feel better, as had the few
hours of sleep she'd been able to find in Trent's arms.
Whatever it was about him that made her feel stronger
had also managed to replace the nightmares with something pleasant. She'd dreamed about Ashley as a little
girl, covered in finger paint and chasing the bubbles

Elise had blown for her. Ashley was smiling and happy, a carefree spirit going whichever way the wind blew.

The memory gave Elise the strength to keep going, to face another day of uncertainty and fear for her sister. She had Trent to thank for that.

She put her hand on his shoulder. "We're back."

He straightened and stretched his long body, filling the space next to her. He blinked a few times to clear his eyes, then looked at the clock. "I have to go to work, but I'll make time for breakfast if you want some."

"Thanks, but I'm going to get to work, too."

"Are you sure? You had a pretty rough night." He reached over to caress her cheek. He wouldn't have done that yesterday. She wouldn't have let him. But today was different. He'd spent hours touching her last night, which, somehow, gave him the right to keep doing so.

Elise leaned into his touch, soaking up the comfort it brought her. "I'm sure. I need to keep looking for her."

"You're not going to do anything dangerous, are you?"

"I'll be careful."

He nodded. "You've got my cell number. Promise you'll call if you need anything."

"I will."

He got out of the car and jogged across the street to his house. Elise watched him go, appreciating the view and the pleasant distraction it gave her. It had been more than a year since she'd taken a lover. She'd chosen, instead, to focus on her work. But Trent was making her think about taking another one. He was kind, caring. Not to mention gorgeous. She could see herself getting swept away by a guy like him, just for a little while.

Elise was sure that after a few days in his bed, she'd be able to go another year without sex.

Maybe after they found Ashley, that's what she'd do.

Once he was inside, she was able to stop staring and unlock the door. After a quick shower and a cup of coffee, she got to work.

It was noon by the time Elise had gone through all of Ashley's recent e-mail, and her e-mail address book. Most of the entries were merely online names and meant nothing—none of them screamed "Abductor of Women." Elise drafted a letter explaining what had happened to Ashley, and e-mailed it to every one of them, asking them to please pass it along to whomever they could. After that, it was time to make the flyer she'd post on campus later today.

She needed a recent photo of Ashley that showed her face clearly, but more than that, she was looking for one that would get noticed. She needed something sweet and full of life that would make women want to help. Something that showed off how sexy Ashley was, which would make men stop long enough to read the text.

She couldn't seem to find the right one in all the photos on Ashley's PC. Most of her pictures were of other people, or objects she'd captured so she could paint or sketch them later. There were hundreds of images of birds, squirrels, and other animals; dozens of snowy landscapes all dated last winter; a handful of children's faces Elise didn't recognize.

Like most of Ashley's house, there was no real method to the madness of her organization, leaving Elise to click through all of the photos, one by one.

She got to the last folder, which Ashley hadn't renamed, so it was identified by the date the photos had been uploaded to the computer.

It was the day Ashley went missing.

Elise almost didn't open it. She wasn't sure she could face seeing what her sister had spent that day doing, how life had been normal right up until that night.

In the end, there was no alternative. Elise had to open it.

The first dozen photos were taken from Ashley's front window. Trent had been outside, mowing his lawn. He was shirtless and glistening under the bright morning sunshine.

Elise's pulse sped up at the sight, and guilt rushed through her that she was actually taking the time to enjoy seeing Trent when she had more important things to do.

She clicked through that series of images quickly, moving on to the next. Ashley had taken four photos of a bird in her backyard, three more of a squirrel, one of a bunny, two of a passing jogger and her dog. There were two more that she'd taken in her bathroom mirror, photographing herself taking a photograph.

Elise smiled at her sister's ridiculousness, even as she felt tears sting her eyes. That uninhibited abandonment was so like Ashley.

The next photo was one of Ashley, too, only this time, she was holding the camera out at arm's length, photographing herself. Her mouth was puckered in a kiss, and her green eyes were lit with a smile. Life and happiness poured out of that photo. She was so beautiful it made Elise's chest hurt to look at it.

That was the picture Elise needed for her flyer. That

was the image that was going to make people stop dead in their tracks to look.

Elise renamed the file so she could find it, then moved on through the rest of the pictures to make sure there were no others that were better. There weren't. Just more of the same. Lots of birds, even a close-up of a housefly. The last few of the pictures were of a blue jay sitting on a tree branch in her backyard. It was sunset, and the lighting was oddly pink, but there was something about this picture that made Elise slow down and take a longer look.

She stared at the bird, seeing nothing at first, but there was a prickling along her spine. Her eyes had seen something her mind had not quite recognized yet.

Elise printed the photo and took it to the window where Ashley had taken the shot. She compared everything she saw with what was actually outside. At first, she couldn't find anything different, other than the missing bird, but then she saw an odd knot on the trunk of the tree in the photo—one that was no longer there.

She looked closer, squinting at the blurred background.

That wasn't a knot. It was a hand, a gloved hand. On the ground beside the tree, outlined in pink light, was the long, distorted shadow of a man standing behind the thick tree trunk.

Someone had been outside Ashley's house.

Fear slid though her, chilling her bones.

She stared at the photo until it began to shake along with her hand. She rushed back to the computer and went through those last few photos, one by one. Slowly, she scanned each one as she printed it.

The last image showed the very edge of a man's face. She could see his cheek, one eye, and part of his jaw.

He was staring right at the camera. He'd been watching Ashley.

Elise sucked in a deep breath, trying to calm herself enough to figure out what to do.

The police needed this photo. So did the press. She needed to get it out there so that someone would come forward and identify this man.

There was no longer a question as to whether or not Ashley had been involved in some kind of auto accident. She hadn't driven off the road. She was not trapped in her car. Elise didn't know where she was, but this man did.

Elise was going to find him.

That feeling of being watched was getting worse.

Gloria glanced in her rearview mirror, certain she'd see the devil himself on her bumper. Instead, all she saw was a weary-looking woman with a pile of kids in the back of her minivan.

Gloria turned left at the next intersection, which was going to make her late for class, but so be it. She needed to see who was behind her—or at least see that someone was there so she had something to report to the police. After all the documentation she'd had to provide to get a restraining order against her ex, she didn't think the police would accept her creepy feeling as proof someone was after her.

Even Gloria's best friend didn't believe there was anything to worry about. She said it was probably just one of Ken's buddies playing a sick joke on her.

Maybe she was right. Ken was still mad at her for leaving him. Maybe it was just a joke, but it sure as hell didn't feel like one.

She made another left, then merged back into heavy rush-hour traffic near a line of fast-food restaurants. The whole time, she kept glancing at the road behind her but saw nothing odd. There were lots of cars, but none seemed to be following her.

Gloria glanced at the clock, wincing at the time. Her class started in ten minutes and she was still five minutes away from campus. Stalker or not, her parents were going to kill her if she let her grades slip. Attendance in her morning dance class was mandatory.

Besides, there would be lots of people on campus. She'd be safer there than anywhere but the police station.

By the time she pulled into a parking spot, she still had three minutes to make it to class. If she ran, she might make it, so she took off at a jog down the sidewalk.

A car horn blasted not ten feet away from her, making her tightly strung nerves vibrate in shock.

An angry young man flipped off a car that had slowed down to a crawl, then sped around it. The offending car had tinted windows, making it impossible for Gloria to see inside. What she did see was that the car was keeping pace with her, slightly behind her so she wouldn't have noticed it if not for the honking horn.

Whoever was in there was watching her, and that car was way too nice to belong to one of Ken's loser buddies.

Gloria stood frozen for a second before anger washed

away some of her fear. She'd spent the last two years walking on eggshells, worrying that she'd set Ken off. It had taken a lot of guts to get rid of him, and there was no way she was going to let some other creep ruin her life.

She charged the car, preparing to face down whoever was inside and give them a piece of her mind, but before she could, whoever was in there gunned the engine and sped away.

The car behind him was right on his tail, making it impossible for her to get the license plate. All she saw was a shadowy silhouette of a man behind the wheel.

The good news was that she wasn't crazy—she hadn't imagined any of this. The bad news was that someone was definitely following her, and she had no idea why.

Elise handed Officer Bob Tindle the printouts of the photos she'd found.

He stared for a long moment at each one, his mustache twitching as he chewed on his lip. "Did you bring the original files with you?"

Elise handed him the camera. She'd checked and the photos were still in the camera's memory. "I also e-mailed the files to the address on your business card."

"I'll have someone look at them and try to clear up the image. In the meantime, I'll get with the composite artist to see if she can make anything out of this."

"Can she combine it with the sketch she got from the guy I talked to at the bar?"

"He didn't remember anything except what your sister had been wearing that night, and how short it had been. I'm sorry, but that was a dead end."

"You could show him this picture. Maybe that would spark his memory."

"Sure," he said, nodding. "We'll do what we can."

That sounded too evasive for Elise's comfort. "What have you found out?" she asked. "Have you managed to find any leads?"

"We put out the description of her car, so there are a lot of officers looking for it. My guess is that the car is either not in the area, or it's been hidden. Otherwise, we would have found it by now, seeing as how it's such a unique paint color."

"Is that all you've done? Drive around? I already did that. You need to be out there looking for *her*, not just her car."

His eyes narrowed in irritation. "We are looking for her. And we interviewed several people that were at the bar that night. We even went through all the video footage from the bar, and there was none there showing her going in or out of Sally's. I'm sorry that we haven't been able to find her yet, but you've got to be patient. Give us time to do our job."

"My sister clearly had a stalker. She's been missing since Friday night. You *do* believe she's in trouble, right?"

His mustache flattened in a grimace. "Yes, ma'am. That's clear now."

"Maybe if you'd believed me when I reported her missing earlier, you would have been able to find her."

"I understand that you're angry, but getting mad at me isn't going to help. We're doing all we can do. I suggest you do the same. You mentioned putting out flyers, and I think that's a great idea."

"You're just trying to get rid of me so you can go back to drinking coffee and eating donuts."

Officer Tindle's face darkened all the way up to his salt-and-pepper hairline. "Stress and grief can make people ugly, so I'm going to ignore that comment. I suggest, ma'am, that you leave now, before you make one I can't ignore."

He was right. She was lashing out at him when none of this was his fault. "I'm sorry. I'll go now." She picked up the photos of Ashley's stalker.

"What are you going to do with those?" he asked.

"Take them to campus. Ask around to see if anyone knows who this guy is. Get them on the news."

"That's not a good idea, nor is it safe. You need to leave the investigation to us." He held out his hand for the photos.

Elise ignored his outstretched hand and tucked the papers in her purse. "If I'd done that, Officer, we wouldn't have this new lead, would we?"

"Fine, then go back to her place and look for more photos; just stay off the streets and out of harm's way. And for God's sake, don't give these to the press."

"Why not?"

"If this guy sees his face on the news, he might panic and do something . . . desperate. If he's still got Ashley, we don't want to do anything to set him off."

Elise hadn't even considered that, but he was right. "Fine, I won't go to the press, but I'm not going to sit back while Ashley is still out there with this psycho. I'm going to find her, with or without your help."

She turned and left his office, got in her car and drove toward campus.

*   *   *

Bob dialed Trent's cell phone. He didn't know if Trent had any pull with the feisty young lady, but he sure as hell hoped so.

Someone needed to rein her in before she got herself hurt. Or worse yet, before she disappeared right along with her sister.

CHAPTER TEN

After a quick trip to a local office-supply store, Elise was armed with several hundred flyers, a loaded staple gun, and a dozen rolls of tape.

She plastered the campus with flyers, handing them out to anyone who would take one. Several of Ashley's friends from the art department pitched in and helped her cover more area, but none of them had any idea who the mystery man was.

Elise was bathed in sweat, dirty and worn out after spending the afternoon under the hot sun. Campus had seemed to clear out from one moment to the next, and every bulletin board she could find now bore a picture of Ashley. It was time to leave.

Tonight, she was going back to Sally's in the hope that the man in the photo would show up, or that someone might at least know who he was.

When she pulled into Ashley's drive, Trent was sitting on the front porch next to a sculpted frog. His hair was damp, and a crisp white shirt glowed against his bronze skin.

The muscles between Elise's shoulder blades started to unknot just looking at him. She felt like she could take a full breath again, that the weight pressing against her chest had been lifted.

As Elise got out of the car, she pulled in a deep breath and let it out slowly.

"Rough day?" he asked, eyeing her up and down.

Her clothes were a mess, and she could only imagine how bad her hair looked, weighed down with sweat that had not yet had time to dry. "I actually made some progress today, so it was worth it."

She pulled the key out of her purse, sliding her fingers over the subtle ridges of paint that Ashley had layered on the surface.

"Bob Tindle called me today," he said, following her into the house. "He's worried about you."

"He needs to worry less about me and more about Ashley."

Elise headed for the fridge and took out a pitcher of water she'd put in this morning. She poured two glasses, handed one to Trent and started in on her own. She hadn't had anything to drink out there today, and she hadn't realized how thirsty she was until just now.

Trent watched her as she drank. "I went over the case with him. He's not missing anything. He's doing everything he can."

The cold water pooled in her belly, making her shiver. "It's not enough. If it was, Ashley would be safe at home right now."

"Don't make him the enemy here, Elise. Don't alienate the men who have the most power to help your sister."

Elise sank down on the purple couch, giving her weary feet a rest. She speared her fingers through her damp hair and rested her head in her hands. Flecks of colored paint stained the hardwood floor under her feet, blending with pencil shavings and plenty of dust.

Ashley wasn't much of a housekeeper, and proof of her life was everywhere, reminding Elise how much was at stake.

Trent was right. She had to be nicer to Officer Tindle. Taking her anger out on him wasn't going to bring Ashley home. "I'll apologize to him again tomorrow, and this time I'll actually sound like I mean it."

"He's a good man. I'm sure he understands how upset you are."

Elise didn't agree—how could he understand unless he'd been through what she was going through right now? But she kept her opinion to herself and sucked down more water.

Trent disappeared into the kitchen. She could hear him shutting cabinet doors. He came back with a bag of potato chips in his hand. He opened them and held them out to her. "You need salt. It looks like you lost quite a bit today."

"Is that your way of saying how sweaty I look?"

One side of his mouth lifted in a teasing grin. "I don't mind a sweaty woman, I just prefer to be the one to get her that way."

Something soft and liquid shifted inside Elise, releasing even more of the tension that had built up inside her today. "Is that an offer?" she teased back.

His grin disappeared and his gaze darkened as he

stared at her. "Under different circumstances, yes. But I won't take advantage of you."

"Because you're a nice guy? Because Ashley is gone and I'm not thinking straight?"

"Exactly."

Elise stood and looked right up at him, making sure he'd pay attention. "If I were to let something happen between us, it wouldn't be because you took advantage. It would be the other way around. I'd be taking advantage of *you*, using you to bleed off some stress."

His dark brows shot up in surprise, and there was more than a spark of interest glowing in his eyes.

"But I don't have time for that now. I've got to get dressed and ready to go."

"Where?"

"I'm going back to Sally's to show off the picture I found today. I'm hoping someone will know who the guy is. So, if you don't mind, please let yourself out so I can shower."

She turned to leave, expecting him to do the same, but instead, he grabbed her arm, stopping her dead in her tracks.

"I'm sorry," he said. "But I can't let you do that."

Was she out of her mind? What the hell was she thinking, deciding to go back to Sally's with the picture of some stalker in hand? Didn't she have any idea how dangerous that was?

"What do you mean you can't let me?" she asked. Her voice was quiet, but the threat of violence running through her words was loud and clear.

"Bob told me about the photo. It's too dangerous for you to go around asking questions."

"Did I ask your opinion? Did I even ask you to come with me?" She jerked her arm away and thrust her chest out at him in defiance.

Trent was too much of a dog not to be distracted by the sight of her breasts on display. Even sweaty and disheveled, there was still something alluring about Elise. All he could think of was that if he ever got her in bed, she'd look just like that when he was done with her. Her skin would be glowing and dewy, pink from exertion. Her hair would be a mess. Her eyes would be shining and sleepy.

All the previous signs of sleepiness were gone now, though. In front of him stood a fiery, enraged woman who looked like she'd just as soon slug him in the mouth as kiss him.

"It's too dangerous. Let Bob and his men do the questioning."

"Like hell I will," she snapped. "And if you can't keep the macho urge to stick your nose into my business in check, then you can just go home and leave me the hell alone."

"Excuse me?" he said, feeling his temper rising fast. She had no idea what she was getting herself into. He did. He'd been a cop long enough to see the myriad scum that walked the face of the planet. He wasn't about to let her saunter into Sally's and piss one off. "It was me sticking my nose into your business that got you into that morgue last night. If not for me and my connections, you'd still be in Chicago, wading through red tape. And even if you had managed to get in to view the body last night, who would have been there to help you get through that trauma? You were barely able to stand."

She was silent, but her mouth was tight in anger.

"Do you think I wanted to see that woman's corpse?" he demanded. "Do you think I enjoyed giving up a decent night's sleep so I could wallow in the devastation some sick fuck caused? I did it because you needed me. I did it because you didn't have anyone else. And I'm going to stop you from getting yourself hurt for the same reasons."

"Leave," was all she said. He knew she'd heard every word. He could see her struggling not to let the tears pooling in her eyes fall.

"No."

"I'll call the police."

He waved toward the phone. "Be my guest. I know Bob will back me up in this. He doesn't want two missing women on his turf."

Her bravado disappeared and her whole body deflated, like the life had been sucked out of it. The tears she'd been trying to hold back fell. Her voice was weak, and the sound of defeat trembling through her words made Trent want to kick himself.

"I can't stop," she whispered. "I can't sit around and wait. I have to keep moving, keep doing. If I don't . . ." She trailed off and a sob shook her body.

Trent couldn't take it anymore. He couldn't stand to see her cry and do nothing, which probably made him a hypocrite for asking her to do just—nothing.

•He pulled her into his arms and hugged her tight. Her breasts felt soft and perfect against his ribs, but he did his best to ignore the feeling. He stroked her limp curls, and she let him. There was no fight left in her.

"It's going to be okay," he told her, praying it wasn't a lie. "They'll find this guy. They'll find Ashley." Hopefully alive. "You've done all you can."

"No. I haven't." She sniffed and looked up at him. Her gray-green eyes were bright and filled with desperation. "I understand that asking questions is dangerous. I don't care. I'm the only person she's got left. I can't sit back and do nothing, even if the only things left to do are the dangerous ones."

"You don't have the training to deal with this kind of thing. What if you make it worse? What if you find this guy, but he gets away? He'll know the police are on his trail and it might make it even harder to find Ashley." He might even skip town, leaving her locked up somewhere to die of starvation, but Trent couldn't bring himself to say that to Elise. It was too horrible for her to think about and would only make her more desperate.

"I'll be careful," she said.

"You don't know how to be careful."

"No, but you do."

Damn it. He'd hoped she wouldn't ask this of him. Helping her duck a bunch of red tape was one thing, but she wanted more than that. She wanted him to hit the streets with her, to work the lead she'd found today.

Trent wasn't equipped to do an investigation anymore. He was rusty, out of practice. He didn't even own a gun. After what he'd done to John and Tyler, he couldn't even stand to have one in his home. If he ran into trouble, he'd be hard-pressed to deal with it.

And if he went after the guy in the photo, he was definitely going to run into trouble. There was no question in his mind that this guy was responsible for Ashley's disappearance. Whoever he was, he had the upper hand. No one knew who he was, where he lived, or what he wanted.

If they were lucky, he was keeping Ashley for sex and would let her go once he was bored with her. She'd be traumatized, but she'd live. If that's not why he took her, then the options swiftly got bleaker after that. He'd had her for four days now. A lot could happen in four days.

Trent didn't want to get involved any more than he already had. He didn't want to step back in that world where people depended on him, trusted him to help keep them safe. He liked it too much. He knew that if he got another taste of that—if he felt that thrill again, that sense of purpose—he might never recover once he went back to his real life. And he had to go back. He couldn't be a cop again. He swore he'd never again pick up a gun—never again risk shooting someone he cared about. Never again kill another kid because he had no choice.

So where did that leave him?

He either had to risk losing all the progress he'd made over the past two years of getting on with his life, or he had to look into Elise's hopeful eyes and tell her he couldn't help. If he did that, he didn't trust for a second that she wouldn't go out on her own and try to do the job herself.

If he didn't keep her in sight, there was no telling what she might do.

In the end, there really wasn't any choice to make. He had to protect Elise from herself.

"Okay. We'll go to Sally's and see what we can dig up, but you have to promise me that if we don't find out who this guy is, you'll accept it. We don't even know that the guy she left the bar with is the same guy as the one in the photo."

"I never even considered that, but you're right. Maybe she came home from the bar, and he was waiting for her here."

"Stop right there," said Trent. "Going down that path is not going to do anything but scare you. Let's take this one step at a time. We'll go back to Sally's, ask around, and then we'll go back to my place."

"Your place?"

"This guy might already know you're living here. It's not safe for you to stay here alone anymore."

Elise nodded. "I can get a hotel room."

He liked the idea of having her in his home too much to let the opportunity slip by. "You'd be safer with me. Besides, I want to make sure you're not doing anything stu—desperate."

She gave him a weak smile. "What? Don't you trust me?"

"Not an inch. Pick out what you need to bring with you, and I'll help you pack. You can get dressed at my place."

Ashley heard Gary coming down the hall, and every muscle in her body tensed. She wasn't sure how long she'd been here, but it had to have been days. Without any clocks or external light source, she couldn't really tell.

At first, she'd thought he was a perfect gentleman, but

it hadn't taken her long to realize how wrong she'd been. She'd woken up with that devastating hangover, wanting nothing more than to go home, but Gary insisted on taking care of her.

It hadn't been until after the grogginess wore off that Ashley realized two things. First, that had not been any normal hangover. She'd been drugged. And second, Gary was not what he seemed.

He told her he wanted to keep her all to himself, just for the weekend, and proceeded to turn on the charm.

Stupidly, Ashley had fallen for it and ignored her instincts that something was off. Right up to the point when he'd told her good night and locked her up again without sleeping with her.

As soon as he'd come back hours later, she'd demanded that he let her go. When that didn't work, she lashed out at him physically, raking the skin of his arm with her fingernails. The change from nice Gary to demonic, frothing-at-the-mouth Gary had been instantaneous and scary as hell. He'd locked her back in this room and hadn't come back for her since.

The room wasn't bad. She had a comfortable bed, a bathroom stocked with all the toiletries she needed to keep herself clean and groomed, fresh clothes in a tiny closet, and a small area where she could sketch with the supplies he'd left for her. The room's colors were a bit drab for her tastes, but everything matched. There was even a print of an English garden on the wall over the bed—the only splash of color that wasn't some form of beige.

If it hadn't been a prison, it would have been a nice place to stay.

But it was a prison. And she wasn't alone. She could hear pitiful moans of pain and desolate weeping coming through the walls. There was another woman here.

Gary's steps paused outside her door.

Ashley stood up and forced herself to appear calm. She didn't want to do anything to set him off again. She'd spent hours going over every inch of her room, looking for a way out, and found nothing. If she was going to get out of here, it was going to be through him.

He unlocked the door and swung it open. The space behind him was dark, giving away nothing of the layout of the building. She'd been so drunk or stoned when he'd led her down here, she couldn't remember a thing other than going down a long flight of wooden stairs.

He stepped inside, and she could see he had a plate of food with him.

Thank God. She was starving.

He stood there as if waiting.

He was a handsome man, well dressed. But it was his confidence that had attracted her to him at Sally's. He moved like the earth was his domain and he was just letting everyone else live here out of the goodness of his heart.

If only Ashley had realized that it was all an act. There was no goodness in him. How could there be when he held women against their will? When he did to her whatever it was that made her cry out in pain?

Ashley prayed he wouldn't do the same to her—that she'd find a way out before he could.

His dark hair was neatly trimmed, neatly combed. Everything about his grooming was fastidious—nothing at all artistic or expressive. Except for his eyes. He had the oddest-colored eyes—golden, yet dirty, like sunlight reflected off an oil spill. They seemed to glow from inside, but they only did it when she was afraid.

Demon eyes.

"Are you ready to apologize?" he asked.

Ashley had never been the smartest person in the crowd—in any crowd—but she was smart enough to know that playing along was her best shot at getting out of this mess.

She looked down at the floor, hoping she seemed apologetic enough. "I'm sorry."

"For what? You won't learn if you don't know what you did wrong."

She was sorry that she'd let him come on to her. She was sorry she'd been stupid enough to drink whatever it was he'd drugged her with. She was sorry that she'd let him bring her home with him.

"I'm sorry I hit you."

"Apology accepted. Now, come and eat. We have plans for tonight."

Hope soared inside her. "We're going out?" She could run away, jump out of the car. She didn't even care if it was moving at the time.

He set the tray down on the small table and motioned for her to sit first. "In a manner of speaking. There's someone here I'd like you to meet."

Ashley sat down, watching him slide gracefully into the chair across from her. It took all her willpower to pretend her skin didn't crawl getting this close.

She took a bite of the sandwich, wondering if it, too, might be drugged. At the moment, she was too hungry to care, and too worried she'd piss him off to lift the bread and check for signs of drugs. "Who?"

"You'll meet her soon enough. Slow down. You're eating too fast, chewing like a cow."

Ashley slowed down.

"How long have I been here?" she asked.

"Why? Don't you like your room?"

She swallowed her sarcastic comeback along with a dry bite of bread. "It's not that. I'm just curious. It's odd not being able to tell time."

"I'm giving you the gift of timelessness. You don't have to worry about anything here. There is no work, no school. No bills or obligations. You're free."

"Free? But I can't go anywhere or do anything."

"You'll be busy soon enough."

She looked up to see him smiling. His eyes were glowing, making a sick sense of dread pool in her stomach.

The food in her mouth turned to putty and threatened to choke her. She took a sip of water, hoping to wash it down. He watched her struggle. She could see his amused enjoyment lifting the sides of his mouth.

He was toying with her, and heaven help her, she didn't know if she would be better off feeding his enjoyment or trying to destroy it. The idea of making him angry again scared the hell out of her.

After another drink of water, she finally won the battle with her food and asked, "What does that mean?"

"It's a surprise."

"I don't like surprises."

His smile fell away. "Are you complaining? Whining? Perhaps you need a few *days* alone this time to think about what you've done, rather than a few hours."

So, that period of confinement hadn't been days? It had only been hours? If so, there was no way she'd survive longer. "No," Ashley shouted. "Please. Don't leave me alone again. I'm sorry. I won't complain anymore."

"See that you don't."

After a moment of silence, Ashley decided she was safer if she got him to do the talking. Her mouth was bound to get her into trouble. "How was your day?" she asked.

He settled back in the chair, pulling the king-of-the-world cloak around him again. "Tedious. I'd hoped to come home early to see you, but I had paperwork to do."

"What do you do?"

"I work at a bank."

"Which one?"

He shook his head slowly as he stared at her. "This is beginning to sound like an interrogation."

"I was just trying to make conversation."

"Idle conversation is for women. Come with me and I'll give you someone to talk to."

"Really?" she asked, putting down the last few bites of her sandwich.

He gave her a magnanimous smile and reached out to stroke her cheek. Ashley managed not to flinch away from his touch, but it left her feeling dirty and used.

"You're beautiful like this. Perfect. I may have to give you gifts more often."

She almost asked him to give her the gift of freedom, but she didn't want to come across as whining again and risk losing her chance to talk to someone else.

He wrapped his fingers around her wrist in a painfully tight grip and led her down a dark hall. There was just enough light to see doors lining either side of a long hallway. Ashley counted five more besides her own.

At the end of the hall was a wider door. He unlocked it and led her inside. He flipped on the lights, and bright whiteness stabbed at her eyes. She blinked fast, hoping to help them adjust. If there was some way of getting out of this place, she didn't want to miss seeing it.

The room was large, tiled completely in white. It had a distinctly medicinal smell, and beneath that was the familiar sharpness of bleach. The walls were lined with stainless-steel cabinets and shelving. Two video cameras were aimed at the center of the room, pointed directly at the woman who was strapped to a complicated chair.

She was in a hospital gown. Her arms and legs were held down by wide straps. At her left was a small rolling table covered by a blue cloth.

The woman's blue eyes were wide with fear, and tears streamed down her temples, wetting her blond hair. A wadded rag hung from her mouth, muffling the sounds of her terror.

"Ashley," said Gary, "I'd like you to meet Constance."

Ashley stood in shocked stillness. She couldn't seem to make sense of what she saw. If she didn't know better, she would have thought she was in a hospital. It certainly looked like one.

Gary tugged her wrist, jerking her forward. "Constance, this is Ashley."

Constance's eyes pleaded with Ashley for something, but she had no idea what it might be. Or what she could possibly do to help.

"What's going on here, Gary?" she asked. "What is this place?"

He ignored her questions and waved to a stainless-steel stool on Constance's right. "Sit there. Comfort her. Your job now is to take care of her."

Ashley still didn't understand. "What's wrong with her?"

"She's afraid." Gary stroked Constance's cheek, his touch a mockery of gentleness.

Constance's eyes closed in defeat. Ashley didn't know what to do, so she covered the woman's chilled fingers with her own, hoping to offer some kind of comfort.

"That's good. You two are going to get along perfectly. I can tell." Gary snapped on a pair of rubber gloves and pulled the cloth off the table, revealing a tray filled with gleaming metal surgical instruments.

Next to them lay an equally sinister handgun.

Gary looked across Constance's body to where Ashley sat. "If you move from that chair, I'll kill her first, then you. Do you understand?"

No. She didn't understand any of this, but his threat was clear, as was the fact that he was deadly serious.

Ashley gave a numb nod and squeezed the woman's hand.

When Gary made the first cut along Constance's wrist, Ashley screamed right along with her.

Elise was dressed to kill in a short blue dress with way too many tiny buttons holding it closed. It had taken her ten minutes to get the thing on, but it went with the shoes she'd picked out for tonight. They were a bit more sensible—still heels, but they laced up her ankles, so if she had to run in them, at least they wouldn't fly off her feet.

And the chances she'd need to run were going up by the day.

Elise knew what they were doing was dangerous; she simply didn't care, not if that's what it took to find Ashley.

Sally's was nearly as crowded as it had been the night before. The music seemed louder tonight, the lights brighter. Maybe it was just her fatigue and constant worry that made everything harsher.

Elise shielded her eyes as she made her way across the dance floor toward the bar.

"Let me ask the questions," said Trent, right by her ear. The feel of his warm breath sweeping over her skin made a shiver run through her limbs.

She was sleeping at his place tonight. She wasn't sure if it had been smart to agree to that, but she hadn't been able to tell him no. She hadn't wanted to even try.

Truth was, she liked the idea a bit too much.

Elise nodded and handed him the photo. She didn't mind letting him take the lead at all, especially since he hadn't tried to make her sit at home while he came and did the dirty work himself.

As if she would have let him. He probably guessed as much and saved himself the breath.

Trent slid the photo across the bar toward the bartender they'd spoken to last night. A twenty-dollar bill peeked out from beneath the edge. "Have you seen this man?"

The bartender ignored Trent and smiled at Elise. "Hello, Miss Threesome. What can I get you?"

Elise couldn't bring herself to flirt with him. "Look at the photo," she ordered in a cold, no-nonsense tone.

The bartender picked up the photo with the bill, pocketed the money and brought the picture to his face to make it out better in the dim light. A frown pulled his brows together. "Nope. Sorry."

"Thanks anyway," said Trent.

The bartender walked away, moving to the end of the bar to wait on another customer.

"Now what?" she asked him, trying to keep the disappointment from her voice.

"Now we go see if the guys you talked to last night are here. I'd like to know if this is the guy Ashley left with."

"And if it's not?"

"Then we start looking for the guy who walked her out of here Friday, and hope he can give us something more to go on. He's likely the last person to have seen her."

Elise hoped that the man who'd watched Ashley leave had been paying enough attention to tell if the man in the photo had been with her Friday. At least then they'd have another piece of the puzzle.

Trent put his hand at the small of her back and they made their way across the crowded dance floor.

Steve slipped into the back room to make a phone call.

"Yes," answered Lawrence on the first ring.

"They're here again, asking questions."

"I already paid you for that information. I'm not paying again."

"This time, they have a photo of Gary."

Steve could practically hear Lawrence giving him his full attention in the stunned silence that followed. "A photo? How?"

"It wasn't from any of my cameras. I swear. I took care of all that just like you asked."

"You'd better have been thorough. For your sake."

"I was. The photo wasn't very good. I could only see part of his face, but I know it was him. He was standing behind a tree, so most of it was hidden. They don't know who he is—that's why they're asking around."

"You mean they're showing that photo to other people?"

"Yeah. Right now. Do you want me to stop them?"

"No, it will only draw unwanted attention. I'll deal with it."

"What about my money?" asked Steve.

"You'll get it."

The line went dead and Steve hurried back out to the floor. He wanted to keep an eye on that couple, just in case. So far, they'd been worth a small fortune. If he played his cards right, he might be able to cash in even more.

Gary finished the surgeon's knot, stripped off his gloves and answered his brother's call. "It's a little late for a social call, isn't it?"

"I knew you'd be up. I assume you've still got company."

"In a manner of speaking." Gary looked down at his creation and smiled. He'd taken the best parts of dozens of women and sewn them together into a beautiful body for Wendy to replace the one crushed in the accident.

The head and the left hand were Wendy's, dug up after her burial, but the rest had been taken from the women he'd met over the years. Each little stitched slice of flesh was a thrilling reminder of time he'd spent with them. A sweet memory of their fear, their perfection. The pieces fit together in a beautiful patchwork—his wife's hand stitched to Jackie's right forearm, stitched to Melinda's elbow, and so on.

He kept her frozen, taking her out only long enough to use a hair dryer to thaw out whatever part of her was necessary to sew the next bit on. Right now, he was sewing Susan's left shin into the puzzle.

She fit perfectly, as he knew she would. Only the very best was good enough for Wendy.

"The woman you met at Sally's. You need to get rid of her."

"When I'm finished with her."

"No. Now. Bring her here and I'll see to her cremation."

"I thought you said you wouldn't help me anymore," said Gary.

"That was when I thought it would make you stop. I understand now that you'll never stop, will you?"

How could he? How could he abandon his quest to give his wife back what he'd taken from her? The accident had been his fault. Her body had been crushed, ruined. They wouldn't have even been in the car that night if he'd been more careful with her. Her death was *his* fault.

Wendy had been the only woman who could make him feel whole and alive. She was meek, submissive, obedient. She never questioned his needs or diluted his pleasure with demands of limits or "safe words." She put herself in his hands wholly, without reservation or condition. No other woman would ever be as perfect for him as Wendy was. When she'd died, a part of him had died with her, leaving a gaping, hollow spot inside. Some days, the screams of his guests filled up that void, but only some days.

Nothing had filled it today, and he was left aching and desperate for solace.

That's why he'd come here, to this walk-in freezer where he kept his beloved. She wasn't finished yet, but adding Susan's piece would make her more whole. Make him more whole.

"I'm busy tonight," he told Lawrence. "I can't come."

"You're going to get caught. You're not being careful enough."

Good thing Lawrence didn't know about Constance. He wouldn't have liked that at all. He probably thought that Ashley was downstairs alone right now. He had no idea there were others waiting for their turn to help complete Wendy's new body. Constance was next, but she wouldn't be the last. Wendy deserved only the best.

And there was still Gloria and the hope that she might be the one.

"I've got to go now," said Gary.

"No, wait. Listen to me. You've got to be more careful. I know you won't stop, but you've at least got to choose runaways and prostitutes. No one will look for them."

Gary had started there, but they'd been unclean, soiled. Imperfect. He needed something more—that spark of creativity that Wendy'd had. It wasn't easy to find, especially among the dregs of society.

"You're not worried about the women at all, are you?" Gary found that interesting and turned it over in his head, studying it. Maybe he and Lawrence were more alike than he thought.

"I'm worried about our family name. My business, my reputation. No one is going to put their loved one in my care if they find out my brother is a psychopath."

"So turn me in. You'll be a hero."

"It's too late for that. It was too late for that the first time I cremated one of your victims."

Lawrence had done it to cover up the murder. Even then, he'd been more worried about his reputation than the law. Lawrence had put her body in with another and no one had ever known.

It was the first time Lawrence had helped him, but she hadn't been Gary's first. Sarah Ann was number seven, and she'd been so sweet—so unlike the foul, used-up hookers he'd found up to that point.

Gary slid his finger over Sarah Ann's frozen neck, remembering how soft her skin had been when she was alive and warm. She'd tried so hard to make him happy, but in the end, the only thing of value she had to offer was her pain and the slender length of her perfect neck.

"I need to go." He needed to finish his work before the skin froze up again and became too stiff to stitch.

"Promise me you'll bring the girl out. I'm cremating another body tonight. Hers can go in at the same time."

"No. I'm not done with Ashley yet. You'll have to wait."

"What do you mean you're not done with her?"

"I need her."

"For what?"

Lawrence would never understand Gary's needs, so he didn't waste his breath trying to explain it. "Good night."

"Wait," said Lawrence, but Gary hung up on him. It was getting late and he needed to finish this and get to bed. He had an early meeting at the bank tomorrow and didn't want to be late.

CHAPTER ELEVEN

Trent drove them home. Elise was too shaken to drive.

The man in the photo was the same guy Ashley had left Sally's with Friday night. And yet there was no footage of him coming or going from the bar. Mr. Dyed Chest Hair had definitely tampered with the tapes.

But why?

Trent turned the question over in his mind. Had it been as simple as the bartender claimed and he was only trying to protect his clientele? The only tapes the police found were of the day they got the warrant. Bob had told him that much. Everything else was blank.

It was likely the bartender knew more than he was letting on, but if so, he had a good poker face. Maybe one of the businesses across the street had a security camera that had caught something that would prove the bartender a liar. He'd mention it to Bob in the morning and make sure they were working that angle.

In the meantime, he was taking Elise home. His

home. And that was it. He was going to tuck her into his bed, then sleep on the couch.

"I don't know what to do next," she said, though it somehow sounded like an admission of guilt.

"You get some rest. Maybe some food. When's the last time you ate?"

"Do potato chips count?"

"Hardly."

He pulled out his phone and ordered them a pizza.

"If this was your case, what would you do next?" she asked.

"We're not going to talk about this tonight. Tomorrow, maybe, but you've got to relax."

"My baby sister has been taken by some guy who was watching her from her backyard. There's no way to spin that so I can relax."

Trent let out a long sigh of frustration. "We should go see Bob tomorrow morning and see if he's learned anything new."

"What about tonight? What do I do right now?"

"How are you at researching things online?"

"Decent, why?"

"You could look up other recent disappearances, I guess. I'm not sure you'd find anything helpful, but it would keep you busy at the very least, keep your mind occupied. You might stumble onto something useful."

She gave him a distracted nod and kept staring out the window. "I hope she's okay."

"Me, too."

"I think I'd know if she was dead—that I'd feel it somehow, like a light had gone off inside me. Is that stupid?"

"No. Not at all. I've seen it happen before with mothers and children. Why not sisters? You should hold on to that." It would keep her strong, maybe even keep her out of trouble.

Trent pulled into his garage just as the pizza delivery car pulled in behind him. Elise went inside while he paid the bill. When he went inside, he found she'd made herself at home, going through his cabinets until she found his plates and glasses.

His house was a lot emptier than Ashley's, making it look bigger, even though it wasn't. He hadn't bothered to paint or change the wallpaper since he'd moved in, and the small dining space off the kitchen was still a hideous riot of faded pink and yellow roses with blue ribbons weaving throughout.

He'd never really cared what was on the walls, or what someone might think of the worn carpet. It had never even occurred to him to care until now, when Elise was standing there, surrounded by all that shabbiness.

"My interior decorator quit on me," he joked as he set the pizza down on the dusty table. At least the chairs matched—a housewarming present from his parents.

She eyed the wallpaper. "Saved you the trouble of having to fire them."

They dished out pizza and Trent dove in, starved after a day of hard labor.

Elise stared at her food as if she wasn't sure what to do with it.

Distracting her with conversation had worked before, so he tried it again. "Where do you live?"

"I have a room at a friend's house in Atlanta. Well, more of a closet, really. I store my stuff there—the things I can't part with, clothes that are out of season or won't fit in my suitcases, that kind of thing."

"What about Hong Kong? Do you have a place there?"

"I had a room I rented by the week, but I gave it up when I came here. I wasn't sure if my assignment would still be there when I got back, and if it is, I figure I can always find another place."

"So no permanent home?"

She shook her head as she took a bite. "No. I prefer to go where the jobs are. Being mobile has helped me cover some really neat stories. Besides, there are too many places left for me to see."

"Where will you go next?"

"Russia, I think. Or maybe Africa. There are a lot of stories to be told there. All I have to do is find them. Then find someone who wants to buy them."

"Sounds rough. Do you like it?"

A real smile curved her mouth, making Trent's heart kick hard. She had such a nice mouth. He really wanted to know what it felt like against his. Now that she was staying here, maybe he'd . . .

Whoa. Down, boy. Not gonna happen. She needed his support and protection, not one more thing to defend herself against.

"I was born for this job," she said. "I don't care that the pay is lousy and the hours suck and I never know where I'll be going next. Most people would hate that, but not me. I get to see the world and nothing else even comes close to that." Her eyes were shining as she spoke. Her whole face lit up with a contagious kind of excitement.

"I know what you mean. I felt the same way about being a cop. Not everyone gets it, but for some people, it's in the blood."

"So, why aren't you doing it anymore? What made you stop?"

He never should have brought it up. He'd been too swept away by the smile on her face to see the trap before he landed in it. "There was an accident. I . . . shot my partner." And a kid.

He couldn't bring himself to admit that part. Intellectually, he knew he'd had no choice. The kid was armed. High. Deadly. Trent had done what he had to, but it had killed something inside him, too.

"Oh, God, Trent." She laid her hand on his. "I'm so sorry."

He shrugged, using it as an excuse to pull away from her touch. He didn't want her pity. He didn't deserve it. "It's ancient history." For everyone but John and that boy's family.

"Not if they won't let you be a cop anymore. Certainly, they know you didn't do it on purpose. How could they fire you for an accident?"

"I wasn't fired. I quit."

"Quit? I thought you said it was in your blood."

"It is."

"Then why did you quit?"

"I couldn't take the chance I'd fuck up again. I couldn't ask another partner to take that chance either."

She was quiet for a long time, watching him. Trent felt her gaze but kept his eyes firmly on his plate. No way was he going to look at her and see whatever was going through her head. "I bet you were good," she said finally.

He shrugged. "Not good enough. Ask John."

"Your partner? He's still alive?"

"Yeah, if you want to call it living. I hit his spine. Paralyzed him." Why was he telling her this? Why couldn't he keep his damn mouth shut?

"How long ago was this?"

"Two years." One month and three days.

"How's he doing now?"

Shame made his face go hot. "We don't talk much anymore."

"He's still angry at you," she guessed.

"No, that's the thing. He's not. He keeps trying to get me to call him, go see him."

"Why don't you?"

"What's there to say? 'Sorry I fucked up your life, man. Have a nice day.'"

"You should call him. If he's forgiven you, it might be time to forgive yourself."

Not in this lifetime. "I'll pass."

"Who knows, you might even be able to forgive yourself enough to take that job Bob said you could have anytime you wanted it."

Trent shoved away from the table, needing to get away from this conversation. It was too dangerous. "I'm going to put clean sheets on the bed."

He'd almost made a clean break, but he wasn't quite fast enough to get beyond earshot.

"I never took you for the kind of man to run away."

Trent came to a halt, shocked at the anger ricocheting through him at her words. His back was to her and his hands were curled into tight fists. "I'm not running," he ground out through clenched teeth.

Her tone was flippant, matter-of-fact. "Sure you are. You ran from your career, from your partner, and now you're running from me."

"Leave it alone, Elise," he warned. "I'm helping you. Don't repay me by butting in where you're not wanted."

"Someone's got to talk some sense into you."

He spun around, lashing out at her with his voice. "Why? You don't let anyone change *your* mind."

"That's different."

"How?"

"You know how. I'm willing to risk my life to save Ashley."

"And I'm willing to risk my happiness to save whatever sorry bastard would get assigned to me as a partner." He was shouting now, and he never shouted. He preferred calm, cool logic, but Elise drove him past all reason.

"You made a mistake," she said. "You can't fix it, but you can move on."

"Is that how you'll feel if Ashley ends up dead? You made a mistake, but it's time to move on?"

She jerked like he'd punched her in the gut. "Of course not."

"Then don't try to tell me how I should feel. You have no idea what you're talking about. John was like a brother to me."

"One you refuse to talk to. I can see how close you are."

Before he said something else he'd regret, he turned on his heel and left, feeling like an asshole of the highest order. He never should have brought Ashley into this. He never should have brought it up, period.

He never should have abandoned John just because he didn't want to face his own mistakes.

Hell. This night was getting worse by the second. Might as well call John and make his misery complete. Maybe then this nagging ache in his chest would ease, even if it was only a little.

Trent's hand shook when he picked up the phone. He didn't have to look up his old partner's number. He still knew it by heart. He dialed and prayed to God no one was home.

Ashley tried not to panic. She'd never taken care of so much as a goldfish, and now the life of another woman was in her hands.

At least she still had two, unlike Constance.

Gary had cut off Constance's hand. There was nothing wrong with it, but he'd gone at her like a surgeon removing a tumor—calm and silent as he worked. He'd stopped the bleeding, stitching her up like he knew what he was doing—like he cared whether or not she lived.

Constance had screamed the whole time.

Ashley sat there in shock, doing nothing to stop it from happening.

She still wasn't sure she'd really seen that happen. This had to be some kind of drug-induced nightmare. Maybe whatever he'd spiked her drink with Friday night was making her have some kind of hallucinations, and all of this was just a dream.

Constance let out a low moan of pain that broke off in a sob. The sound was real—no drug-induced delusion.

He'd put Constance in Ashley's room with her, locked them in and left.

"I'm here," said Ashley, not knowing what else to say. "He's gone now. You're safe." It was the biggest lie she'd ever told, but she was going to keep on telling it until they got out of here. And they would get out of here. Ashley refused to allow any other possibility to enter her mind.

She looked at the timer Gary had left. She couldn't give Constance any more pain medication for another twenty minutes. Gary had given her instructions on how to care for Constance and warned her that if she messed up, he'd kill them both.

Ashley believed him. She just wasn't sure that he'd use the gun, making it quick and relatively painless. After seeing the smile on his face while he used that bone saw, Ashley didn't want to know what kind of death he might be able to devise.

Constance groaned again, making Ashley's chest tighten in panic. She didn't know what to do to help her. She didn't know how to fix this.

She smoothed the blond hair away from Constance's face, hoping to sooth her. "Just lie still. I'll give you some medicine soon."

Constance's blue eyes opened a slit and tears leaked out both sides. "Give me all the pills. Please. Let me die."

"No. We're going to get out of here."

"No, we're not. There is no way out."

"You don't know that. We'll find a way. *I'll* find a way." She wasn't sure how, but she'd think of something.

"You don't understand. He'll come back. It's what he does."

Ashley looked at the clock again. Fifteen minutes left, then maybe Constance could sleep and give her some time to figure things out. "It'll be okay."

Constance let out a sound soggy sound of defeat. "That's what I told Susan."

"Who's Susan?"

"She was the one I was assigned to help. The way you're supposed to help me."

"I don't understand. Where is she now?"

"He killed her. Just like he's going to kill me. And you."

"You don't know that."

Constance sucked in a pained breath. "I do. I watched it happen to Susan. That's why he pairs us up like this, so we'll know what's coming. So we can be more afraid. Everything he's doing to me now, he'll do to you next."

Ashley's stomach gave a lurch and she had to grit her teeth against the urge to puke. "No."

"I was there when Susan died. Susan was there when Marcy died. Before Marcy, there was Joann, Corey, Stephanie . . ."

Blood rushed to Ashley's ears, cutting off the rest of the names. The list kept going. Ashley saw Constance's mouth move like in a dream.

She pushed away from the bed and stumbled across the room. She needed fresh air, but there was none to be had. She couldn't lift her face to the sun and feel warm and free. All she could do was sit here in this room with a woman she didn't know and wait to see if what Constance said was true.

Unless they got out.

Surely, someone was looking for so many women, looking for her. Elise would look for her, she was sure. But how long would it take to find them, and would it be too late?

Ashley had to get them out. She raced to the door and pulled on it, knowing the act was futile even as she tried. There was nothing in the room to pry it open with. The hinges were on the outside.

Maybe she could break a hole in the wall.

She picked up a chair and slammed it into the wall. The legs bounced off, stinging her arms and merely scratching the ugly beige paint. Beneath that paint was concrete. The walls were concrete, like a prison cell.

"Shit," she spat, furious at herself for getting into this mess, devastated that she couldn't find a way to get Constance out.

"Stop!" shouted Constance. "If he sees you doing that, you'll only make him angry."

"Maybe I want to piss him off."

Constance's voice was pinched with pain. "If you're going to do that, at least give me those pills first."

Ashley checked the clock as she went to the injured woman's side. Eight more minutes. "I'm not going to kill you."

"I'm already dead. You'd be saving me more torture. Maybe yourself, too. He might get so angry that he kills you outright."

"He's not going to kill either of us."

Constance clenched her jaw in pain. A fine layer of sweat stood out along her pale skin. "I told Susan the same thing. God, I wished I'd listened to her. She was right, about all of it."

"We're going to get out of here."

It was still a few minutes early, but Ashley gave Constance two pain pills anyway. She swallowed them and grabbed the front of Ashley's shirt. "He'll paint your fingernails first. He likes your hands to be pretty before he takes them. First the left one. Then the right. After that, he'll pick some part of you to keep as a memento. He'll cut that part out of you, then cut off your head. You'll still be alive when he picks up that bone saw. I've seen it. *I know.*"

"You're making this up to scare me." And it was working.

Constance shook her head and closed her eyes. Her voice came out as a defeated whisper. "When you're the one strapped to that chair, you're going to wish you'd listened to me. At least by then he won't be able to hurt me anymore. I'll be dead."

Elise sat at the table for a long time, clinging to that little spark of hope inside her that told her Ashley was still alive.

Maybe Trent hadn't tossed his careless remark at her to hurt her, but it had anyway.

She knew she'd hit a nerve, talking about his partner, but did she back down? Of course not. She never knew when to back down, which made her a good reporter, but not such a good friend.

After all the help Trent had given her, he didn't deserve that.

She pushed herself up from the table, stowed the

remainder of the pizza in the fridge, and went looking for him. The house was small enough he wasn't hard to find. He was in what she guessed was his bedroom, sitting on the bed. The door was cracked open, allowing her to hear what he was saying.

"Hey, John. It's Trent. Sam said you called. Call me back when you can. No rush."

He'd called his old partner.

She'd bullied him into it, which made her feel like a bitch. It wasn't her business. She should have stayed out of it. Too bad she didn't know how.

He probably didn't want to deal with her right now, so she took her laptop to the second smaller bedroom to work. She cleaned away some space on his cluttered desk and started searching the Web for other missing women.

Hours later, she had a list of area women who'd gone missing in the past five years. It was huge—too many to manage—so she cut it down to the women who were near Ashley's age. She broke that list into two: those who had been found, and those who hadn't.

She had just finished looking up contact information for the one case that didn't fit either list when Trent came in and put his hands on her shoulders.

"It's late. You should try to get some sleep. I made up my bed with clean sheets for you."

He was touching her. That was a good sign he wasn't still mad at her for butting her nose into his business.

"I'm sorry I hurt you," she told him, covering his hands with her own. His skin was so warm, and her fingers were chilled from hours of typing and the things she'd read.

So many women were missing and never found. Ashley could not be one more. Elise wouldn't let that happen.

"Forget about it. We're both a little wound up."

"Understatement of the year."

"What have you found?" he asked, looking at her scribbled notes.

"Plenty. None of it good. I'm going to start talking to some of these people tomorrow. Maybe they can shed some light on Ashley's abduction."

He pointed to the article on the screen and the picture of the smiling young blond woman next to it. "What's this?"

"She's the one who lives closest to Ashley. The police found her amputated hand, but that was all. They don't know if she's alive or dead, but prints confirmed the hand was hers."

"Did they get her prints from a criminal record?"

"No. Her mom had one of those kits done when she was a kid. That's what they used to compare the prints from the hand."

He squinted at the screen. "This case isn't that old, just a few weeks. I wonder if that hand matches the body we saw."

Elise shivered at the memory. Trent must have felt it, because his hands slid over her arms as if to warm her. "I don't know. I plan on going to see this woman's mother tomorrow. If she doesn't know about the body, I'll tell her." She wasn't sure how she was going to find the courage to talk about it, but she knew she had to find a way. If this woman's mother was anything like

Elise's, she was going to need all the emotional support she could get.

Not that Elise was all that strong herself right now.

"I'll go with you."

"No. I don't want you to miss any more work because of me. I'll be fine."

"You sure?"

No. "Yeah."

"You should get some sleep, then."

He was right. She was exhausted, and her eyes burned from staring at the screen too long without a break.

She stood, and Trent let his hands fall away. She missed his touch immediately, and without thinking about it, she stepped up and pressed herself against his lean body in a hug. Her arms slid around his waist, and her cheek lay over his heart, hearing the deep, steady beat that seemed to soothe her like magic.

Trent hugged her back, rubbing his cheek against the top of her head. His muscles contracted, hardening against her stomach and breasts. The warm strength of his body surrounded her. The scent of his skin filled her head.

For the first time in days, Elise truly believed everything was going to be okay. Maybe it was some kind of illusion he created with his presence, but whatever it was, she was thankful for it. She felt like herself again. Strong. Confident. Hopeful.

She lifted her head to tell him that, but the words froze in her throat. He was staring down at her with a look so hot and full of need, it shocked her. It wasn't compassion or sympathy, it was lust, pure and simple. The golden chips in his blue eyes glowed as his gaze moved to her mouth. His cheeks were dark with lust and he pulled in a deep breath.

He was going to kiss her. She could see his intent clear in his face, feel it in the way his arms had tightened around her.

Instantly, she felt herself soften, felt all the cold parts deep inside her start to heat.

"You should walk away," he told her in a voice ragged with arousal.

Elise was beyond words. She simply shook her head. She wanted this basic human contact. She needed it.

Trent leaned down and pressed a soft kiss against her mouth. It felt so good, so warm, but it wasn't nearly enough. She slid her fingers through his hair and kissed him back, holding him in place while his kiss expanded until it became her whole world.

A sigh escaped her lips, parting them. His tongue feathered inside to taste her, and all her pent-up fear and frustration liquefied into meaninglessness, leaving her reeling, almost giddy with relief.

He tried to pull away, but she wasn't going to let that happen. She knew what was waiting for her outside the consuming pleasure of his kiss, and she wasn't ready to face it. Not yet.

She pushed him back until he hit the wall and pinned him there. Sure, he was strong enough to get away if he wanted, but he didn't seem in a hurry to go anywhere. She had him right where she wanted him.

Elise went up on tiptoe and kissed him harder.

Wow. The word kept going through Trent's mind over and over.

Elise was a wild woman. She clung to him, kissing him like she was dying of thirst and he was the last drink of water on the planet.

A man could get used to being needed like that. Fast.

Her slender fingers curled around his neck, pulling him down so her lips could eat at his, kissing him with the kind of frenetic abandon Trent hadn't witnessed since his youth. She tasted so good, satisfying some part of him he hadn't realized was hungry. And her body . . . Lord, have mercy. Every sweet curve was rubbing against him, burning him up. He could feel the soft press of her breasts against his ribs, the hard little peaks of her nipples through their clothing.

He wanted to get her naked so he could feel her breasts without any barriers.

Her lips trailed down to his neck, and he felt the sharp sting of her teeth for an instant before she stroked the sting away with her tongue. The first playful nip had his dick standing at attention. The second nearly made him lose it right there in his shorts.

She pulled the hem of his shirt up and kissed a meandering trail across his chest and down his stomach. Trent ripped the shirt off the rest of the way, deciding it was time to do the same to her. He'd been dying to see her breasts, to feel them in his palms, against his tongue.

There were ten million buttons down the front of her dress and Trent cursed every one of them. The last few were more than his patience could stand, and as he ripped the dress open the last few inches, they went flying to the far corners of the room. A pretty pink bra offered her breasts up to him, and he didn't bother trying to resist.

He drew his fingers over the naked top curves, followed the straps up to her shoulders and slid them down. Undoing a clasp was beyond him, but with a couple of tugs, she was bare, with her bra hanging useless over her ribs.

Wow. He'd never seen anything so pretty in his life, and he was going to take his time and enjoy the view.

Elise tried to obscure his view by continuing her trail of kisses south, but Trent stopped her, pulling her face up so he could stare at her.

"So beautiful," he managed to tell her, though the words were garbled and thick.

She gave him a smile that was somehow both demure and sexy all at the same time. She stepped back, unfastened her bra, slid her panties down and left the strappy heels on.

Wow.

About a million fantasies were on the verge of coming true right here and now.

She pressed her naked body against his, making him shudder. Hot. Soft. Perfect.

Trent kissed her again. There were no other options. If he didn't get another taste of her, he simply wasn't going to survive. And as soon as he was done with her mouth, he was going to find all those other sweet spots he was dying to taste.

Elise gave as good as she got, while her slender fingers worked at the waistband of his jeans. She didn't bother pushing them down, just slid her fingers inside and wrapped them around his throbbing cock.

Trent nearly came right there and pressed his forehead to hers while he sucked in huge breaths of air in an effort to regain some control. They didn't help. It had been too long since he'd taken care of his body's needs, and he was on a hair trigger.

Before it was too late, he gathered her hands and picked her up. He wasn't going to do this on the shabby carpet. Not with Elise. He didn't have silk sheets or anything fancy, but at least the bed was clean and comfortable and wouldn't rub her back raw once he got her under him.

He laid her down on his bed. She looked like an offering, her skin glowing against the navy-blue sheets. A rosy flush had spread across her chest, and her nipples were stiff, dark peaks that made his mouth water.

Trent didn't trust himself enough to lose his shorts yet, but he toed off his shoes, shed his jeans, and lay down next to her.

She reached for him, but he captured her hands and held them at bay while he looked his fill. She was quivering, and her eyes were a deep, slumberous green. He'd never seen anything half as sexy as she was right now.

"Are you going to tease me all night?" she asked.

"No. Just for a few more minutes."

He cupped her breast and watched her eyes flutter shut. She arched her back toward him, letting out a soft, sweet sigh.

She refused to be held still, and her clever hands escaped his grip, only to pull his hand down her body to where she wanted him to touch her. Trent was gentleman enough to oblige, parting the soft curls to find her slick and hot. He slid one finger inside her, feeling the tight clench of muscles grip him like a glove.

A shiver coursed through her, and she clamped her thighs together, trapping his hand.

Trent flicked his tongue across her distended nipple, and she sucked in a hissing breath. Her hips writhed, taking his hand along for the ride. Her fingernails bit into his arm, clinging to him like a lifeline. A high, needy noise rose up in her, then was suddenly cut off as she held her breath.

A climax rolled through her body, shaking her with the force of it. Trent was right there with her, keeping her riding high with his fingers between her thighs and his mouth on her breast.

He was about ready to come himself, just watching her, when she began to relax and ease back down.

It was the single most sexiest thing he'd ever witnessed, and he was already dying to see it again.

"I'm sorry," she panted.

"Don't be." He didn't sound like himself. His voice was too rough and thick, but she seemed to understand his words.

She opened her eyes and stared up at him. "It's been a long time for me. I couldn't seem to stop it."

Boy, did he understand that. "I don't mind. Really."

Elise's smile was full of womanly intent. "Good, because I'm not done with you yet."

"Thank God. I'm about to explode here."

"Well, then," she said as she moved to all fours, with those sexy heels sticking out behind her, "why don't you put on a condom and I'll show you a really nice time."

Condom. Right. He had those somewhere.

He scrambled to look in his bedside drawer and there they were—four of them, which was probably enough to make a dent in his serious case of lust for Elise.

Some kind of warning went off in the back of his mind, but she was holding her hand out for them, smiling at him like he was something good to eat.

There was no way Trent was going to last if he let her slide one of those rubbers over his hard-on, so he shucked his shorts and tore the first pack open with his teeth, ready to do the job himself.

That's when he saw it. The expiration date. They'd expired. A year ago.

A shout of denial rose out of him until he thought the top of his head would blow off.

"What?" she asked, frowning in concern.

"Expired."

She grabbed up the wrapper. "Really expired. It's been awhile for you, huh?"

"Unfortunately, a really long while."

Trent flopped down onto the bed and covered his eyes with his arm. He couldn't look at her like this knowing he couldn't have her, and there was no way he was going to risk using a condom that was as likely to break as not. Even though he was disease-free, he didn't see how she could do the job she loved while pregnant.

He wouldn't take her beloved job away from her. He knew how much that sucked.

Her weight shifted on the bed, then he felt the warmth of her fingers slide down his abdomen and over his thighs.

"You're not helping," he groaned.

"Yes, I am. Just lie back and enjoy. We're not going to need a condom for what I'm going to do to you."

Hope forced him to lift his arm and peek at her. She'd straddled his legs, gloriously naked and flushed from her own orgasm. All she wore was a satisfied smile and those strappy heels.

"Oh yeah?" he forced himself to ask.

She wrapped her hands around his cock and stroked him slow and steady. "Oh yeah."

"You don't have to do this."

"Shut up, Trent."

Trent shut up. He didn't make another sound until he felt her lips slide over him, hot and slick, just like she'd been around his finger. The groan he let out was completely involuntary.

For a woman who hadn't been with a man in a long time, Elise had no trouble remembering what she was doing. Trent tried to hold out, tried to make the pleasure last as long as possible, but he was no match for Elise's clever fingers and hot, suckling mouth.

His body went tight, and his orgasm slammed into him with the force of a battering ram. Pleasure pounded through him, so intense it was nearly pain. The world fell away, leaving only Elise and the physical joy she wrung from his body. She stayed with him the whole time, stretching out every second of it.

When it was over, Trent was a boneless pile of man, weak and spent. He used the last bit of his strength to pull Elise against his side and pin her there with one arm.

He didn't have the strength to explain to her that he wanted her right there, next to him, nor did he want to deal with any argument she might give. If she was here, he knew she was safe, and he needed to know that.

If anything happened to her, he didn't think he'd survive.

Constance had a fever.

Ashley had no idea what to do. She didn't have any aspirin to give her, only the pain pills that barely seemed to work.

Constance was bathed in sweat, shivering uncontrollably. Long, low moans of pain vibrated out of her chest, making Ashley sick with worry.

She pressed a cool, wet cloth to Constance's head. The woman flailed around, trying to bat it away with her hands, but there was now only one, and she bumped the bandaged stump against her cheek. A cry of agony ripped from her lungs, echoing off the concrete walls.

Ashley went to the door and pounded on it, shouting for help. No one came.

For the thousandth time, Ashley wished Elise was here. She would have known what to do. She was brilliant and brave. She wasn't afraid of anything. Not even that monster Gary would have scared Elise.

But Elise wasn't here. Ashley had to deal with this on her own. Somehow.

She wet a towel, stripped the blankets off Constance's shivering body, and draped the towel over her. Constance jerked and hissed in a pained breath.

"Cold," was all she said.

"I know. I know it's cold, but we need to get your fever down."

"I need to go home." Constance tried to push herself up, but her body was too weak to cooperate.

Ashley felt helpless tears run down her face. She stroked the other woman's forehead, hoping to calm her. "It's okay, Constance. You're home. I'm going to take good care of you." The lie tasted like acid, burning her tongue, but what else could she do? She was trapped here, helpless.

"I'm so cold."

Footsteps thudded out in the hallway, growing louder. Gary was coming back.

Surely he'd see how bad Constance was and let her go to a hospital. Wouldn't he?

He unlocked the door and stepped inside. In one hand he had a tote stocked with manicure supplies. In the other, a handgun.

"It's time," he said, holding the manicure kit out to Ashley.

Fear had been with her so long, she hardly even noticed it anymore. It was simply a part of her, like her heart and lungs. She had no control over it. "Time for what?"

"Time for you to paint her nails. Make her pretty."

"No, she's too sick. Can't you see that? She needs a hospital."

"You should have done a better job of taking care of her."

"I'm not a doctor," Ashley nearly screamed. "I don't know what I'm doing. You've got to get her help."

A sickening half smile tilted Gary's mouth. "I'll give her all the help she needs soon enough. I'll even let you watch to make sure I do it right. I know how much you liked watching."

Not again. Ashley couldn't go through that horror again. Neither could Constance.

Ashley realized in that moment that everything Constance had told her was true. He wasn't going to let Constance go. He wasn't going to let either of them go. He was going to kill her, too.

Gary lifted the gun, pointing it at Constance, then he lifted the manicure kit out to Ashley. "Do it."

The tiny part of her mind that had not yet accepted her fate started praying. Ashley stepped forward and took the handle of the kit, staring at the fingernail files and bright red polish as if it were a live snake.

There was no way out of this. She had no weapons— even the fingernail files were made of cardboard, and despite what the airlines thought, clippers were not a weapon. She didn't have the strength to take him on unarmed. She didn't have the brains to find any other way out of this.

All she could do now was make this as easy on Constance as possible.

She took the shivering woman's right hand and went to work. By the time she was done, both women had bright red smudges of nail polish all over them, but it was the best Ashley could do with her hands shaking like they were.

"Good. Now help her up. We're going back to the room."

He didn't have to tell her which room.

He'll take your left hand, then your right.

Constance hadn't been lying.

"Let me take her to the bathroom first. She hasn't been all day."

"There's no time."

"She's probably going to wet all over the place. Do you really want to clean that up?"

Disgust marred his handsome face for a moment. "Fine, but be quick."

Ashley bore most of Constance's weight as she helped her into the bathroom. Gary didn't even bother to object when she shut the door. He knew there was nothing either woman could do to stop him. He was in total control.

Ashley eased Constance down onto the toilet, then took the bottle of pain pills from her pocket and counted them. Twelve.

She wasn't sure if it was going to be enough, but she had to try.

She pushed several pills into Constance's mouth and held a glass of water to her lips. "Drink, honey. It'll all be over soon."

At least for one of them.

CHAPTER TWELVE

Elise had spoken to two abduction victims this morning and knew instantly that she wasn't on the right track. Neither of the women's kidnappers had been caught, and she thought that whoever had taken them might have taken Ashley, but she was wrong.

The first woman had been abducted by a black man—clearly not the man in the photo—and the second woman by one of her old boyfriends. Elise had shown that woman the photo of the stalker in Ashley's backyard, and she was positive that was not the man who'd taken her.

She sat in her car, looking over the lists she'd made, wondering how many more dead ends she was going to hit before she found some kind of lead to go on. Her eyes kept going to the one anomaly—the missing woman whose hand had been found. Susan Maloney.

Susan's mother lived only a half hour away from where Elise was now. Maybe it was best to go speak to her just so Elise could move on. If she could rule out

Susan's kidnapper, then maybe she could also get the image of that headless, handless corpse out of her head.

Yeah, right.

Elise found Susan's childhood home without any trouble. It was in an older, well-maintained neighborhood, with towering trees and perfect lawns. She got out of her car, walked up the flower-lined sidewalk, took a deep breath and rang the doorbell.

She didn't know if this woman was aware of the handless body in the Chicago morgue, but she knew she had to tell her, just in case it was her daughter lying there.

A ragged woman opened the door. Her clothes were stained and wrinkled and her gray hair looked like it hadn't been combed in a week. "Yes?" she said in a dry voice.

"Are you Susan Maloney's mother?" asked Elise.

Her mouth tightened into a hard, angry ring, driving the blood from it. "No reporters." She started to shut the door, but Elise slapped her hand against it to stop her.

"I am a reporter, but that's not why I'm here. My sister is missing. I need to speak to you."

The woman paused, on the edge of indecision.

"Please. Just a few minutes."

Finally, the anger faded from Susan's mother, leaving her looking deflated, like a month-old balloon. "Come in."

Elise stepped inside. It smelled stale in here, a little like old garbage, a lot like despair. Dust lay on every surface. Clearly, the outside of her home was kept up by a service, or it would have looked a lot more like the inside.

She led Elise to her living room, which was filled with

newspapers and stacks of unopened mail. She motioned for Elise to sit on the couch, so she sat.

"My name is Elise McBride. My sister is Ashley."

The woman plopped down in a weary pile and nodded. "I saw you talking about her on the news. I'm sorry."

Elise swallowed back the wave of fear and grief that rose up in her throat. She needed to concentrate and make this as brief and painless for Mrs. Maloney as possible. "Can you tell me what happened to your daughter? I've read the articles online, but sometimes they leave things out—things only a mother would know."

Mrs. Maloney stared out the window. "Susan went missing last month. She went to work, left, and no one saw her again."

"Where did she work?"

"The music store here in town. She teaches piano there. She's always loved to play. I don't know what she'll do now, with only one hand."

Oh, God. Elise's stomach twisted with sympathy for this woman, and guilt that she had to make her talk about it one more time. There was nothing she could say to make this any easier, any better, so she settled for, "I'm so sorry, Mrs. Maloney."

"The police will find her."

"I'm sure they will." Elise couldn't bring herself to mention the body. It made her a coward, but she couldn't do it. She couldn't be the one to put this woman through that.

Mrs. Maloney dug in a box of tissues, found it empty. Elise pulled a travel pack out of her purse and handed it to her.

"Thanks."

Elise nodded. "I know this is hard for you, and I hate to ask, but do you think you could look at a photo for me?" She unfolded the paper and handed it across the coffee table. "This is the man I think took Ashley. Do you recognize him?"

Elise sat back as the woman stared at the picture, confident she'd hear what she'd heard all day—that Mrs. Maloney had never seen the man before.

Instead, the woman started to shake. The paper fluttered around in her hand until Elise was sure she could no longer focus on the image.

"I know him," she whispered. "I saw him outside the music shop the day Susan went missing. I'd had lunch with her that day and was late for a doctor's appointment. When I dropped her off, I was in such a hurry I almost backed into him. He was headed into the store."

A sick sense of panic welled up inside Elise. She didn't want this woman to know the man in the photo. She didn't want her sister's disappearance tied to Susan Maloney and her severed hand.

Whoever had taken Susan had hurt her. Elise couldn't stand the thought of someone doing that to Ashley.

She had to get out of here. She couldn't stay any longer and witness this woman's devastation. It was like seeing her own possible future—ragged, dirty, and full of despair.

"Thank you for your time," said Elise as she plucked the photo from Mrs. Maloney's hands. She tossed her business card on the table. "Please feel free to have whoever's working your daughter's case call me." Just not today. Please, God, not today.

Elise had to absorb this new turn of events, adjust to

it. She was standing on shaky ground, and the slightest upset would send her tumbling over the edge of grief and hopelessness.

Ashley needed her to stay strong and keep her wits about her. It was the only way she was going to find her sister before it was too late—before there was more than one piece of Ashley to be found.

On the way to her car, Elise stopped long enough to empty her stomach on the perfect flowers lining Mrs. Maloney's sidewalk.

Her hands were still shaking when she drove away and went to the nearest convenience store to get something to wash the taste of bile from her mouth. She got back on the undivided highway, blindly heading for Trent and the solace only he could give her.

She was miles away from anyone, on a deserted stretch of cow-lined road, when she realized that the car behind her had been there since she'd left Mrs. Maloney's home.

She was being followed.

Trent attached the last sprinkler head and turned on the water to test the system he'd just finished installing.

It worked perfectly.

"Looks good," shouted Sam from his truck. He'd just pulled up to the curb, so Trent turned off the water and went to see what he wanted.

"I just finished," he told his brother.

"I can see. And look at you. Where'd all that shaggy hair go?"

Trent ran a hand over his buzz cut, enjoying the

familiar feel tickling his palm. "Got it cut over lunch." He'd also picked up some condoms. Lots of condoms.

"It's been a long time since I've seen you look so respectable. Who's the woman?"

Trent felt a grin tug at his mouth. "Who says it's a woman?"

"I pull up here to find you're finished early, looking like you give a damn. And, you were whistling. Doesn't take a genius to figure out you got laid."

Sort of. He was looking forward to the real thing later tonight, praying Elise was still on board, too.

Trent deflected the intrusion into his personal life with years of practice. "Why are you here? Checking my work?"

Sam grunted in amusement. "Like I need to. No, I'm on a mission from Mom. She wants to know if you're coming this weekend."

"What's this weekend?"

"The cookout. With Busty. Remember?"

"Oh, right. Sorry. It's been a long week."

Sam grinned and rubbed his hand over Trent's trimmed hair. "I bet. Are you really not going to tell me who the girl is?"

"Elise."

"Ashley's sister?"

"Yeah."

The grin fell from Sam's face. "They still haven't found her, have they?"

"No, but we're doing everything we can."

"*We?*"

"The police."

"Ah. For a second there, I thought you might be including yourself in the investigation."

Trent shrugged. "I've been helping when I can, but there's not much I can do but try to keep Elise out of trouble."

"I can see the method you've chosen to do that. Good choice."

"It's not like that."

"No? Should I tell Mom to give you Busty's phone number?"

"No. Not interested."

Sam's blue eyes, so much like Trent's own, stared at him as if trying to unravel some mystery.

"What?" asked Trent.

"I'm just trying to figure out if this flashback to the old you is due to the woman, or to the fact that you're doing the only thing you've ever really loved."

Honestly, Trent wasn't sure either. "I'm not working for Bob."

"Maybe not on the books, but I'd bet my truck that you're getting involved in the investigation."

"I'm not doing anything illegal."

"Never said you were. But whatever you're doing, whether it's the investigation or the woman, it suits you. You should keep doing it. I like having my brother back."

"I never went anywhere," growled Trent.

"Sure you did. Your body was here, but your heart wasn't. All the lights were out. Until now." Trent opened his mouth to respond, but Sam cut him off. "I'll tell Mom not to call Busty. I'll tell her you'll bring Elise to the cookout instead."

"I don't even know if she'll still be in town."

"Then keep her here. It's Wednesday. The party is Saturday. I'm sure you can think of something fun to occupy her time for three or four days."

Yes, he could. He could think of a lot of things to do with that much time. In fact, the ideas roaming around in his head would likely take up a solid month. Or three.

Trent's phone trilled out its ring, vibrating against his hip. He fished it out of his pocket, saw it was Elise and his heart jumped in his chest, just like it had when he was a teenage boy and the girl he was crushing on had called.

"Heya, Elise," he said as he answered.

"Trent, thank God." Her voice was pitched high and thin with terror.

Fear slid through him, kicking his adrenaline pump into high gear. "What's wrong?"

"I'm being followed." She shrieked, and he heard tires squeal. "They're trying to run me off the road!"

CHAPTER THIRTEEN

Elise gripped the steering wheel tighter and took the next turn way too fast. Her car veered to the side of the road but stayed on it. Barely.

Trent's voice sounded calm and steady in her ear. "Listen to me carefully, Elise. I'm going to get you out of this."

Thank God for Bluetooth. There was no way she'd be able to hold the phone and drive right now. "I'm all ears."

"Tell me where you are."

Elise told him, giving him the name of the road she'd just crossed. "I think I'm about two miles from Highway 57."

"Okay. Keep moving, no matter what. They might have guns. Do you understand?"

If she stopped, they might shoot her. Oh, yeah. She got the message loud and clear.

"If you have to go through a light or stop sign, hit the horn to warn people as best you can, but keep moving. I'm going to guide you to the closest police station."

"It's deserted out here right now. Just me, the cows, and the two guys behind me trying to kill me."

She heard Trent talking to someone else, asked him to pull up a map on his phone.

Elise glanced in her rearview mirror. The car behind her was closing in. If they got close enough to her, they might ram into her again, and this time they might manage to knock her into a spin. Or a telephone pole.

"About a mile ahead, you're going to cross some railroad tracks. Right after that, take your first left."

"First left after the tracks. Got it."

Her hands were sweating so much it was hard to hold the wheel steady. She gunned the engine, hoping that whoever had done maintenance on this rental car had been a diligent, thorough person.

"I've contacted the state police, and the highway patrol is on their way. Hang in there, sweetheart."

"I'm hanging." Just barely. "I like the sweetheart thing, by the way."

She'd never run a stop sign in her life, but she blasted through that last one, leaning hard on her horn, even though she saw no one around.

"That's good to know. You're doing great. Can you see a license plate?"

Elise checked. "No front plate. Sorry."

"What about the men? Can you see them?"

Her rearview mirror vibrated too much to make out any details. "No. Just two heads."

The railroad tracks loomed ahead of her. The sedan behind her was only a couple of feet away from the left side of her bumper.

The gas pedal was already mashed to the floor. She couldn't make this thing go any faster.

"I'm at the tracks," she told Trent, just as she hit them. She went airborne for half a terrifying second before landing with a thud. The street he'd mentioned was maybe a quarter mile ahead.

Elise hit the brake so she could make the turn. The car behind her tapped her bumper, knocking her into a turn too early.

Her rental car whipped around. She panicked and crammed her foot down on the brake as she tried to control the spin. She heard herself screaming, heard the tires doing the same.

Trent's deep voice barked something in her ear, but she didn't have any spare attention left to understand what he was saying.

The car slid sideways toward a deep ditch running alongside the road.

Lights flashed in the distance, creating a blue arc in her field of vision.

The car tilted to one side as it left the road. The seat belt burned her shoulder, crushing the air from her lungs. She slammed to a halt inside a mushroom cloud of air bags, and the engine went dead.

Elise was too stunned to do anything for a few seconds. The side air bag had deflated enough so she could move it, and the only thing she could see out her side window was sky. That didn't make sense, and it took her a minute to realize the car had landed nearly on its side. Gravity was doing a fine job of pulling her toward the passenger's side of the car.

"Elise!" shouted a voice in her ear. Trent.

Her words came out weak from lack of air. "I'm okay." But not for long if she didn't get out of here. She wasn't going to stay here where she'd be an easy target.

Outside, she heard sirens but couldn't see the road to tell where they were coming from. Nearby, an engine roared and tires squealed. "They're getting away!"

"Let them. As long as you're safe, that's all that matters."

She tried to undo her seat belt, but it wouldn't budge. "I think I'm trapped."

"Stay put. Help is on the way. *I'm* on the way."

The sirens grew louder until it sounded like they were inside her head, then cut off suddenly. "I think the cavalry's here," she told Trent.

An officer's dark face peered into her car, past the deflated bag. "Ma'am, are you hurt?"

"No. Just stuck."

"Okay. I'll be right back. Don't try to move." The officer disappeared again.

As if she had a choice. "Trent?"

"I'm right here, sweetheart." Beneath his voice was the sound of an engine being put to a speed test.

"Slow down. I can hear you speeding. I'm fine. The bad guys ran away. The police are here."

"I need to be there, too."

"In once piece would be nice."

The sound of his engine tapered off. "You're sure you're okay?"

"I think I might have a bruise. Wanna kiss it?"

"How can you joke at a time like this?"

"Seemed like the thing to do, seeing as how I'm stuck

here, practically hanging upside down with nothing better to do."

He let out a grunt she couldn't interpret. "All that blood rushing to your head, huh?"

"Gotta do something with it. Might as well entertain myself in the bargain."

He lowered his voice until it was a soft, comforting caress. "You're scared to death, aren't you, sweetheart?"

"You have no idea," she said, stifling a sob. "I really thought they were going to kill me."

"So did I."

"It's not a coincidence, is it?"

"No. It's not."

"Guess it means I'm on the right track."

"Elise," Trent said in a warning tone, "you're not thinking what I think you are, are you?"

"Depends. I'm thinking that if I've pissed people off enough to come after me, then I'm getting really close to finding my sister. I'm thinking they figure they've scared me away. I'm also thinking they're wrong."

The officer's dark face appeared in her window again. "I bet you're ready to get out of there, huh?"

"My ride's here, Trent. Gotta go."

"Wait, Elise—" She pulled the earpiece out before he could finish pissing her off with some sort of macho demand that she back off from looking for her sister.

She had enough to deal with right now without adding him to the list of people she had to fight. After today, that list was already two men too long.

When Trent found Elise, she was sitting in the back of an ambulance. She looked like she'd been tossed around, but there was no blood. Thank God. He didn't think his shredded nerves would have been able to take the strain of seeing her bleed on top of everything else.

When she saw him striding toward her, her body sagged with relief. The walk across the hot pavement seemed to take forever, but when he got to her, she fell into his arms like she'd been made for just that spot.

"Are you okay?" His words were muffled by her blond curls as he pressed his face into her hair, but he couldn't pull away enough to make them any clearer. He wasn't letting her go anywhere for a while.

"Yeah. Just shaken up a bit."

The fist around his heart relaxed enough that he could breathe again. He pulled in the scent of her, filling himself with it.

"I'm taking you home," he declared. "As soon as they're done with you here."

He was taking her home, and keeping her there— safe, where no one could hurt her again. He wasn't exactly sure how he was going to convince her to let him do it, but he'd find a way and make it work.

This was the very last time Elise McBride was going to step into harm's way.

Gary spent the whole day angry and restless. Ashley had stolen his fun last night, drugging Constance like that. She had been so groggy she hadn't cared what happened to her. She hadn't even screamed for him.

Ashley had ruined everything, and Gary was going to see to it that she paid for this rebellion.

When he took her hands, there would be no pills. No relief. She would pay back every one of the screams she'd stolen from him tenfold. And he would make sure she knew it was coming.

He gunned the engine as he headed toward Gloria, desperate for some kind of relief from his anger. People at work were looking at him too much, noticing his fidgety restlessness.

Gary had to do something about it before people started asking questions.

He knew Gloria's schedule well enough now that finding her would be no trouble. And when he did, he'd bring her home.

It was Ashley's turn to make Wendy whole.

CHAPTER FOURTEEN

Trent had been too quiet on the drive home. Elise had tried to talk to him—joke with him—but nothing worked.

His brother, on the other hand, had no trouble keeping up his end of the conversation. Apparently, he'd come along with Trent to make sure he didn't kill himself on the drive.

Sam was hot. Not as hot as Trent, but definitely mouthwatering eye candy. The angles of his face were softer than Trent's, and he smiled more, which was nice. He was just as tan as Trent, with muscular arms and shoulders he hadn't created in a gym.

Elise sat sandwiched between the two men in the front of Trent's truck, stifling a naughty little fantasy.

Maybe those air bags had hit her harder than she'd thought.

"So," said Sam, trying to fill the awkward silence in the truck, "looks like you've found a lead on Ashley's disappearance the hard way."

"It found me, if that's what you mean."

"What are you going to do now?"

Elise shrugged, making her shoulder whine in pain. "Keep going. I'm on the right track looking into the disappearances of the other women."

"We are *not* going to talk about this right now," growled Trent.

"Why not?" asked Elise.

"Because he doesn't want me involved," said Sam.

Trent's words were harsh and clipped. "None of us should be involved. It's a police matter."

"Ah," said Sam, as if he'd figured out a great mystery.

Elise looked from one brother to the other. "From where I'm sitting, it's a family matter."

"You're going to get yourself killed," said Trent.

Elise could hear the amusement in Sam's voice. "I thought you didn't want to talk about it."

Trent pulled up next to a white Ford and stopped. "Get out."

Sam shook his head and got out. "Take the rest of the day off, man. It's going to take you that long to find a chill pill big enough to fix what's wrong with you." He unlocked the white truck and got in.

"I like him," said Elise.

"That makes one of us—at least right now."

She started to scoot across the bench seat now that Sam was gone, but Trent put a hand on her thigh, stopping her. "Stay where I can feel you."

Given in such a rough tone, the order shouldn't have made Elise's toes curl, but it did. He kept his wide hand on her thigh, like he was going to hold her in place.

He had nice hands. Big, with long, strong fingers.

They were scarred in places, rough in others, but she remembered how good they could make her feel.

Her adrenaline had been running high from the chase and all the questions afterward from the police. Her body was on high alert, vibrating with a bundle of energy she could not dissipate.

Maybe Trent would help.

"I want you to leave my brother out of this," said Trent.

"I had no plans to involve him."

"He'll try to charm you into telling him what he wants to know."

"I'm not easily charmed," she said.

"No? I didn't seem to have any trouble, and I'm a jerk."

She snorted. "Hardly. Besides, you're cuter than he is."

Trent shot her a look so full of disbelief it was comical.

"Don't worry," she assured him. "I won't get Sam into any trouble."

"I'll hold you to that."

It wasn't the only thing she wanted him to hold her to. A bed. A wall. It all worked for her.

They were near his house, and she guessed that as soon as he got her through the door, he'd start yelling at her about taking risks and how she wasn't going to keep looking for Ashley now that those men had come after her.

She wasn't interested in deflecting that kind of garbage, so she decided to turn his mind to something more constructive—like helping her vent all this fidgety restlessness.

Elise covered his hand with hers and slid it higher

along her leg. "Did you remember to buy those condoms?"

He snorted. "Like I'd forget something that important. I might forget to breathe, but I wasn't going to forget those and be empty-handed again."

"Good," was all she said. It was all she had to say. He understood what she meant.

His fingers curled into her flesh, massaging her in a sultry caress. "If you think I'm going to toss you inside and go at you like some kind of animal, you're wrong."

"What a shame. I think I'd enjoy that right now."

He let out a sharp breath, like someone had punched him in the gut. "You're trying to distract me."

"Among other things. I don't handle adrenaline well."

He pulled his truck into the garage and triggered the door to shut behind them, blocking out the bright sunshine. In the dim glow of the garage, he looked almost feral, with deep shadows cast over his face.

Elise unbuckled the seat belt and slid her body over his, straddling him. She was a bit more awkward than she would have liked, and she was afraid her ass was going to set off the horn, but Trent didn't seem to mind.

He took her hips in his palms and pressed her down against his erection.

Thanks to last night, she knew just how hard and thick he was, how he filled her hands and then some. It made her mouth water and her stomach flutter in anticipation.

She saw his jaw harden, saw a look of determination steel his features, and she knew he was about to push her away. She didn't want that. She wanted him to drive away the fear that was still shaking her body. She wanted him to take away reality for a little while, so Elise could regroup and regain her strength. But mostly, she wanted to feel safe and alive in the arms of a man who made her soul sing and her blood heat.

Before he could change his mind, Elise kissed him. She cupped his face in her hands, held on tight, and kissed him for all she was worth.

She flicked her tongue against the seam of his mouth, begging him to let her in, and he did with only a slight hesitation. His groan of pleasure tasted better than the finest chocolate. She didn't understand how she'd survived this long without it.

His hands clenched against her hips, and she could feel him warring with himself, trying to hold back and stop this from going any further.

She couldn't let him do that. Not now. Not when her body was aching and so hot, she thought her skin would melt.

"Take me inside," she said against his mouth.

He pulled away and looked at her. The golden slivers in his blue eyes seemed to catch and hold the dim light. "I shouldn't. You're hurt."

"I only hurt when you don't touch me."

His nostrils flared and a deep, primal rumble rose up from his chest. "Get inside."

Victory. She could feel it in the fine tremors his hands were giving off, see it in the way his pupils dilated as he stared at her mouth.

Elise scrambled from his lap and got out of the truck. Trent reached under the seat to grab a sack and was right on her heels.

She wasn't taking any chances he'd change his mind,

so she started shedding her clothes as she moved to the bedroom. By the time she got there, all she had on was her bra and panties. Trent stood in the doorway, watching her as she slid those off, too.

Elise had never been shy or modest, despite her mother's efforts to the contrary, but never before had she felt quite like she did right now. Trent's eyes were fixed on her, roaming over her as if he was memorizing her curves. He looked at her like her nakedness was a gift—a precious treasure she was sharing with him.

She stood there, letting him watch as he tossed the sack on the bed and stripped out of his own clothes. The ridges in his abdomen were tight with lust, and his chest moved heavily with every breath he took.

She'd never seen anything so beautiful, so mesmerizing as Trent. All he had to do was breathe and her body softened, heated.

He crossed the room, his movement slow and steady. "Lie down."

Clearly, playtime was over. The man standing in front of her meant business, and she could hardly wait to see what he had in mind.

Elise stood there, ignoring his rough order. All the remnants of adrenaline in her blood lit on fire and snaked through her system, making her body hum.

Trent's erection stood out proudly from his body, and Elise couldn't help but stare. Her mouth watered, remembering the feel of him, the taste of him on her tongue. Her knees went weak, and she nearly fell to the floor right there so she could get another taste, but Trent had other ideas. He grabbed her arms to steady her, then pressed his body fully against hers.

Elise's head spun at the contact. He was living heat, pure pleasure, hard and smooth and rough all at the same time. She couldn't untangle so much sensory input at once.

Trent didn't give her a choice. He took her mouth in a kiss, sliding his tongue past her lips, piling yet more sensation onto her already overloaded mind.

She welcomed him into her mouth as she was dying to welcome him into her body. His hands slid over her arms and shoulders, so gentle on the bruised spot, then back down, over her ribs to her waist.

Her world spun and tilted for a moment, and when it righted itself, she was lying down as he'd told her to do, and he was hovering over her with a pleased smile curving his mouth.

"You like to win, don't you?" she asked him.

"You have no idea." He bent his head to flick his tongue across one nipple.

Elise jerked and sucked in a breath. Her hands went to his head, telling him without words that she wanted him to stay right there and do that some more. His short haircut tickled her palms and added one more sensation onto an already oversized pile.

"I like your haircut," she breathed out between wicked swipes of his tongue.

"Oh, yeah?"

"Yeah."

"What do you think about this?" he asked, then moved his head so the short strands brushed over her nipples.

A wave of sparkling pleasure rushed down her body and pooled in her belly. She let out a sound she was

204 Shannon K. Butcher

sure only whores should make, but Trent didn't seem to mind.

He gave a low chuckle as his body shifted down the bed. "If you liked that, you're going to love this." Pure male confidence rang in his tone, and she was struggling to figure out what he meant when his hands pressed her thighs wide and his tongue swept over her labia.

He drove all thoughts from her head. His fingers slid along her flesh, opening her to his devastating tongue and wicked lips. She felt his warm breath wash over her, felt his probing fingers slide inside her, finding just the right spots. She was flying high, straight toward a hard, fast climax, when he stopped.

She tried to lift her head to see what he was doing, but it was too heavy. She heard the crunch of paper, something rip, a plastic crinkle that was barely audible over her labored breathing, and then he was there, hovering over her.

His face was set, his jaw bunching as he lowered his forehead to hers. His skin was damp with need, and the thick tip of his erection was pressing against her, begging entrance.

Elise slid her hands over his hips and urged him toward her. He sank in, slow and steady, filling her up until there was no room left to breathe. Not that she cared. Trent was in her arms, in her body. She didn't need anything else.

"Wow," he breathed out, holding still and deep. He twitched inside her, grazing nerve endings that hadn't been reached in years. Maybe never.

"Amen."

"You okay?"

Words escaped her, so instead, she gripped him with her inner muscles and let him be the judge.

His mouth came down onto hers, giving her a ferocious kiss. And then he started to move.

Elise had always preferred to be a participating partner in bed. She liked to take charge once in a while and keep a man on his toes, but with Trent, that wasn't going to happen—at least not today. The man didn't leave her room for any such plans. He didn't leave her room enough to think straight. Her whole body was alive, taking what he had to give, and loving it.

His muscles bunched and flexed around her as he moved, dragging her into a hard, devastating climax. Her body shimmered, fell apart into shards of pure sensation. Her mind was a pile of splintered little pieces, and still he did not relent. His pace slowed, but that was all.

He speared his fingers through her hair and angled her mouth for a deeper kiss. She could taste his determination, feel it in the steely weight of his powerful body moving against her. There was something more going on here than merely sex; she just couldn't gather enough of her wits to figure out what it was.

Trent said something, growled it into her mouth, but she didn't understand. How could she when he kept moving, kept pushing her higher?

He leaned back, shoved his forearm under her hips, angling her body so each thrust created slick friction over her clit.

Need coiled tight inside her. She clutched his shoulders and dug her fingers into hot, hard muscles.

"I won't let you," he said, staring into her eyes.

This time she understood the words, even if she couldn't make sense of them.

"Less talk. More kiss," she said, grabbing the back of his neck to pull him down. She needed his mouth on hers again, needed to taste the slick skin just inside his lower lip.

She was close—hovering on the edge of another round of weightless ecstasy—and she needed to feel that again. She needed that pleasure to drive away all the fear and grief and ugliness that had invaded her life, even if it was only for a few, brief seconds.

And like the man of her dreams, Trent gave her what she needed and then some. He shoved her over the edge of pleasure, hurled her toward the sun and let her burn. It went on forever, that flying, screaming pleasure he'd given her. And then he was there with her. She felt him tense, felt him throb inside her, heard his ragged shout of release.

As the last bit of endless sensation wore off, satisfaction filled Elise, making her glow. Trent's body was heavy and replete on top of hers, protecting her from the rest of the world. Her body was humming and content.

In that single moment, nothing else mattered. She was safe and happy, and Trent had made it happen.

Trent extracted himself from Elise's clinging limbs and flopped onto his back.

She'd killed him. It was the only explanation for the way he felt now.

All his rage and frustration were gone. He was too worn out for any of that. All that was left was a satisfied kind of warmth swelling up inside him. If he didn't know better, he would have thought it was almost like happiness.

She rolled onto her side and tossed her arm over his ribs. He needed to get rid of the condom, but it could wait a minute. Having Elise reach for him might not. For all he knew, this would be the last time she ever did.

The thought left him feeling helpless, angry.

He wanted to make her love him. Make her stay. And if that kind of mental track didn't scare the hell out of him, he didn't know what would.

She had a life, a career. He was just a pit stop along the way for her, and that was fine with him. Or at least it should have been.

He'd almost lost her today. A hundred different things could have happened, ending her life. Those thugs could have shot her. They could have run her off the road a few feet one way or another, driving her car into a tree. Another car could have been on the road, causing a head-on collision.

He could think of so many ways she might have died, it was hard to believe she'd walked away with hardly a scratch.

Trent traced the long red parallel marks on her left shoulder—the ones the seat belt had caused. She'd have a hell of a bruise there by tomorrow, but other than that, she was fine.

It was a miracle—one he wasn't going to throw away because she insisted on looking for Ashley.

The guys in the car had sent her a message: Back off.

Trent was going to see to it that she listened.

Ed Woodward flipped through the six-year-old file, scanning it for any clue that this cold case was connected to the one he was working now.

The crime scene photos showed a woman's partially decomposed headless, handless body. Only this woman was also missing one of her breasts.

It was the kind of thing that should have turned his stomach, but he was way past that now. After the photos he'd seen today going through the archives, he was confident nothing could shock him.

Only three of the deaths he'd looked into seemed to have any similarities to the Jane Doe in the morgue. That's not to say they were definitely connected, but there was a chance.

And then there was the second pile of files. The ones where only part of a body had been found. Those were the ones he was most interested in. He wasn't convinced that Jane had been mutilated to hide her identity, especially since they'd found her hand. If someone was really trying to cover up who she was, why didn't he burn her prints away with acid or fire? Why toss her hand into the river and hope for nature to do the job?

No, something in his gut was nagging him, telling him there was more to this than what appeared on the surface.

The stitch marks. That's what kept throwing him for a loop. This wasn't just some Mafia hack job. If it had been, why would there be suture marks?

If some sicko was out there, killing women, cutting them apart, and sewing them up again, why? Did he get off on it? Was it some kind of ritual? Was he sending a message to other women somehow? And why sew up the part that had been taken off?

What the hell had it been sewn to?

The whole case left a bad taste in his mouth and a sick feeling in his stomach. He wasn't sure which of the cases stacked in front of him, if any, were connected to his Jane Doe. What he was sure of was that whoever was doing this wasn't going to stop unless someone made him.

Ed was going to be that man.

Gloria had no choice but to go grocery shopping. She hadn't stocked the cupboards since she moved, and her kitchen was empty. There wasn't a single piece of fruit or slice of bread to be had. Peanut butter on a spoon had been both breakfast and lunch, but she couldn't stomach the thought of making it dinner, too.

She grabbed a bright red shopping basket and headed for the produce section. Standing in front of a display of zucchini was a man she was sure she'd seen before. She couldn't place him, but she'd been on high alert since the incident on campus, and she wasn't trusting anyone right now.

She veered right, making a clear path around him when he looked up and caught her eye. He had a puzzled look on his face and a spindly zucchini in his hand.

"Excuse me," he said to her, "but could you help me?"

Her body went tense with suspicion, and she took a half step away from him. "Um, I'm kinda in a hurry."

His tone was deep with disappointment. "That's okay. I'm sure someone else will be by in a minute."

She let out an almost inaudible sigh, feeling like a loser for not helping him when she was in the middle of a brightly lit store full of people. "What do you need?"

"Is this squash?" he asked.

"It's one kind. What kind are you looking for?"

His brows drew together in puzzlement. "I don't know. The recipe just said squash. My mother is on a strict diet since her heart surgery, and I wanted to cook her something, but I guess it's not as easy as it looks."

Now Gloria felt like a total bitch. Here he was, trying to take care of his sick mom, and she was treating him like Jack the Ripper.

She stepped closer and offered him a sympathetic smile. "That's so sweet. I'm sure she'll love whatever you make." She picked up a yellow squash and handed it to him. "Try this one. Mix it with the zucchini, and you'll be set."

"Thank you," he told her, sacking the vegetables.

"No, thank you. It's good to know there are still nice guys left in the world. Lately, I've begun to wonder."

His smile widened, deepening into a more seductive grin. He took a small step toward her, letting her know he was interested. "I don't suppose you'd like to go out with the last remaining nice guy, would you?"

She hesitated for a moment. The last thing she needed was another Ken in her life, but she missed dating—missed being with someone. Maybe not this guy, but someone.

"You don't remember me, do you?" he asked.

"You look familiar, but no, sorry. I don't."

"I work at your bank. You changed your address the other day."

"Right. I remember now."

"So, what about it? Do you think you could go out with a stuffy banker?"

"I'm really not interested in dating right now. Sorry."

He reached into his pocket and took out his business card. "Here's my number in case you change your mind."

He placed his card in her hand, and his fingers grazed hers. They were oddly cold, like he'd been holding those chilled veggies for too long.

Gloria tucked his card into her pocket. "I'm sure I'll see you around," she said and left him to finish her shopping.

It only took her fifteen minutes to grab enough food for the week, and she had just loaded it into the trunk of her car when she noticed her rear tire was flat. Totally flat.

Great. That was all she needed—being stuck changing a tire when she was sure some wacko was stalking her.

"Need some help?" came a man's voice.

Gloria whirled around, her heart pounding in her throat, but it was just the guy from the bank.

She pressed her hand over her heart in an effort to slow it and gave him an embarrassed smile. "You scared me."

"I'm sorry. I didn't mean to." He nodded toward the tire. "Do you have a spare?"

She went to the trunk and moved her groceries aside to access the spare tire. "I think so," she said. "I've never had to use it before."

The banker stepped up behind her, and that feeling of eyes on the back of her neck slammed into her full force.

She whirled around to see who was watching, when a white cloth covered her nose and mouth, filling it with a vile stench.

She tried to scream, but all she managed to do was suck more of the awful vapor into her lungs.

Her legs went weak. The world around her shimmered, then wavered toward blackness. The last thing she saw was the banker open the back door of his car so he could shove her in—the same luxury car that had been following her on campus.

Gloria's body hit the backseat, driving the breath from her lungs. Her cheek grazed the supple leather interior, and then she felt nothing.

Elise was up well before dawn, revising her list of people to interview today, when Trent shambled out of the bedroom and found her at his dining room table.

"Can't sleep?" he asked.

His eyes were puffy from sleep, and he wore only a pair of low-riding pajama bottoms that left the rest of his body on glorious display.

She'd had him inside her only a few hours ago, but her body was heating and softening, aching for him again. The man was clearly addictive, and if she didn't watch herself, she'd end up doing something stupid and fall for him.

The two of them would never work long-term. He had roots here, a family that needed him. She couldn't see him giving all that up to travel around the world with her. Besides, what would he do with himself? How would he earn a living? She barely earned enough to support herself, much less two people.

And the idea of giving up her life to settle down felt more like a prison sentence than a future.

It was best if she kept things in proportion and remembered that while it was okay to enjoy him while she was here, that's all she could do. As soon as she found Ashley, she'd move on, and so would he.

Yesterday, that idea wasn't nearly as daunting as it was today. It had been difficult resisting him before, but now that she knew how good all those muscles felt under her fingertips and tongue, how perfectly they fit together, resisting him was nearly impossible.

She cleared her throat and pulled her eyes back to her laptop screen. "I slept for hours, thanks to your vigorous efforts to wear me down."

He gave her a knowing grin. "You needed the rest."

"I know. Thank you. It helped clear my head enough to figure out what I need to do next."

"And what's that?"

"First, I have to rent another car. Then, I'm going to talk to the detective who was assigned to Susan Maloney's case and see if he has any possible leads. Maybe if he has some suspects in mind, the photo might give him some direction as to who to go after. I also need to talk to the press again today. Ashley's story is losing weight, and I don't want people to forget she's still missing."

"You're not serious." His tone was sharp with anger, making her look up at him again. His mouth was tight and his brows were drawn together in a scowl.

"Of course I'm serious. Why wouldn't I be?"

"You were nearly killed yesterday."

She'd been trying hard to forget. Thinking about those terrifying moments nearly froze her with panic, which wasn't going to do Ashley any good. "That means I'm getting close. Susan Maloney is the key. If I can find out what happened to her, I'll find Ashley."

"What makes you so sure she's the key?"

"Her mother recognized the man in the photo. She saw him the day Susan went missing."

Trent let out a harsh, scoffing sound. "How could she be sure that was the same guy? The photo is horrible at best. It shows a white guy with at least one eye and one ear. A lot of people match that description. It doesn't even give a clear idea of what color hair or eyes he has."

"She was sure." Elise was, too. She'd seen the woman's reaction and knew it was real.

"The woman's daughter is missing, right?"

"Yeah."

"And they found her kid's hand, but nothing else."

"Right."

"Was she acting lucid? Was she thinking clearly? Or was she crazy out of her mind with worry, grasping at any straws she could find? You went to her with your story of a missing sister, showed her a guy you think did it. Of course she's going to think that's the kidnapper. What did you think she was going to do?"

"She wasn't making this up."

"Maybe not intentionally, but people like her don't make reliable witnesses. Surely you know that."

"No. I don't. She saw this guy, Trent. She saw him the day her child was abducted. That's why she remembered him—he was etched into her mind."

"You believe her because you want to, because you want to find a lead. I get that you feel out of control, and that you need to do something, but you can't be sure that woman's daughter has any connection to Ashley."

"If I'm on the wrong track, then why did those guys come after me? They followed me from Mrs. Maloney's house."

"My guess is that they'd been following you since we left Sally's. Someone there destroyed the video footage of Ashley coming in and leaving Friday, which means someone is covering this up. Whoever is doing that was one of the guys who went after you, or he was the one who ordered the hit. They would have followed you whether you went to that woman's house or the freaking grocery store."

"You weren't there, Trent. You didn't see the look of horror on this woman's face when she saw the photo. I'm sure she recognized him."

Trent rubbed a hand over his short hair. "You could put fifty guys in a room and every one of them would look similar to the man in that photo. You're fooling yourself if you think otherwise. I've seen lineups in action. I've seen witnesses pick cops that were planted in the lineup, claiming they were the ones who raped them. Emotional people make horrible witnesses."

Mrs. Maloney had definitely been emotional. Maybe Trent knew what he was talking about, but Elise couldn't take that chance. "What if you're wrong?"

He pulled out a chair and sat down next to her. His eyes caught and held her gaze, and the sympathy she saw there made her chest ache. He took her hands in his and his thumbs trailed over her skin in a caress as gentle as his voice. "What if I *am* wrong? What if visiting this girl's mother is the thing that caused those men to try to kill you? Would it be so bad to let it drop?"

"If it means not finding Ashley, then yes."

"You're willing to risk your life on a guess?"

It was more than a guess. It was a feeling. An instinct. "Absolutely."

"I won't let you."

Shocked outrage rocketed through Elise. She jerked her hands from his and forced herself not to scream the words. "You don't have any say in this."

"Last night gave me the right to have an opinion."

"It gave you the right to an opinion about what sexual positions you like, what brand of condoms to use, about whether you sleep on the right or left side of the bed. It didn't give you any right to tell me what to do."

"Someone needs to stop you from getting yourself killed."

She shut her laptop and stood from the chair. "I'm sick of people telling me how dangerous this is. I understand that investigating my sister's abduction is not the safest thing I can do, but it's the *only* thing I can do. I can't leave her out there alone, waiting to see what will happen. If you want to act like my mother and keep me under your thumb, then I'll find another place to stay."

Elise turned to leave, but Trent stopped her, wrapping a hand around her arm. "If you leave, those guys will find you again, and this time, they'll succeed in killing you. Who will help Ashley then?"

"I'm not backing down, Trent. If you have a better idea of how to go about finding Ashley, I'll listen, but I won't give up on her."

"I'm not asking you to. I'm asking you to be careful—

let the police handle the dangerous stuff. Maybe those guys only meant to warn you to back off, but it could have been more than that. They could have been sent to kill you."

"Why? Wouldn't that only create more buzz, attract more attention? Not only is my sister missing, but I end up dead. That's going to turn a lot of heads and make people ask a lot of questions."

"Not if you die in a car accident. It would be easy enough to say you were overwrought with emotion or fatigue and lost control of your vehicle."

She hadn't thought about that angle. She hadn't let herself think about the car chase at all, but it made sense. "They'd make it look like an accident so no one would ask questions."

He nodded. "The fact that you got away to tell the tale will either back them off, or make them more desperate to finish the job before you tell too many people what happened. Either way, there's more going on here than one missing girl. Maybe Ashley found herself a boyfriend who's in the Mob. It would explain why thugs were chasing you."

"They didn't come after me here, so either they don't know where I am, or they've already backed off, right?"

"Who knows? What we do know is that you're not safe. You can't pretend you are just because you don't like the idea of being more careful."

"I'm fine with the idea of being more careful. I'm just not willing to sacrifice results."

"It's your only safe option. I'm sorry."

Elise knew he was trying to help. She also knew she

was in danger, but not as much as Ashley was. She had to focus on what was important and let everything else fall away, no matter how appealing it was to sit back and let other people take care of her problems, put themselves in danger.

She looked up at Trent, hating what she knew she had to say. "We had a great time together last night. I like you, and you're sexy as hell, but I think that the sex has given you the impression that things between us have changed. They haven't. I'm here to find my sister, and you're the Hot Lawn Guy who lives across the street. I don't have the energy to fight you, too, so I think it's best if I check into a hotel."

Anger darkened his cheeks. "You think running away is going to fix things? You think that's going to make you safe?"

"No, I think it's going to save me valuable time by not having to argue with you over every move I'm going to make."

"You're safer here, with me."

"Maybe, but Ashley *isn't* safer. Neither are you with me here. If those guys come after me again, I don't want you to get hurt."

Outrage made his features tighten and his voice clipped. "I know how to protect myself. I can keep us both safe."

Elise took his hand in hers. "I'm tired, Trent. I'm scared out of my mind. I can't stretch myself much thinner without breaking, and trying to convince you what I know I need to do is taking up too much of my attention."

"I will not let you do this. I don't want to be the one to ID your body when those thugs find you."

"Then don't. This isn't your business anymore. Forget I was ever here."

It didn't take her long to pack her stuff. By the time she was done, the rental car company had already sent someone with her new car—a sporty model with plenty of horsepower. Just in case.

CHAPTER FIFTEEN

W"hen we hit oil, we usually quit digging," said Sam.

Trent looked at the deep hole he'd carved into the earth. It was way too big for the bush he was planting, but not nearly big enough to contain his frustration and worry for Elise.

"Sorry," he said as he started to fill it back in.

Sam bent and tapped the bush out of the plastic pot. "Yesterday, you were like the brother I remembered. Even with Elise in trouble, you still handled yourself the way you used to. Today, you're back to being a surly bastard. What the hell happened?"

"Forget about it. I'm here, doing the job. I even came in early to make up for the last few days."

Sam slit the tangled roots with his knife and dropped the bush into the hole Trent had refilled partway. "I don't give a shit about the lost time and you know it. What I do care about is you." He stood, brushing the dirt from his hands. "I thought you were coming back to us."

"What the hell is that supposed to mean?" asked Trent. "I never went anywhere."

"Sure you did. Maybe you showed up for work, and family get-togethers when we twisted your arm, but it wasn't really you. Your heart wasn't in it—not since you moved back from Chicago."

Not since he'd shot his partner and killed a sixteen-year-old boy.

Trent's gut flooded with acid and guilt, mixing with the coffee he suddenly wished he hadn't had.

"Yesterday, when we were driving out to find Elise, you were back. I saw the man you used to be—confident, rock-solid, there to do whatever it takes."

"I always do whatever it takes."

"Then why aren't you out there looking for Ashley?"

"Because I'm not a cop."

"Neither is Elise. It hasn't stopped her."

Much to his dismay. "That's because she's not smart enough to know when she's in over her head. I tried to warn her, but she didn't want to listen. She packed up and left so I'd quit wasting her time."

"Are you that bad in bed?"

"No, dickhead. She was tired of me harping about how dangerous looking for Ashley is."

Sam shook his head, staring at Trent like he was the idiot here. "Ashley is her sister. She's not going to back off because she almost had a car accident."

"Obviously."

"If you really want her to be safe, you'd be with her right now, backing her up, giving her your insight."

"I'm not a fucking cop, Sam!"

"Yes, you are! You don't wear the badge anymore, but

you were born for the work. You never stopped being a cop; you just stopped going to work every day, and it's killing you. It's eating you alive from the inside out. We were all sure you'd see that by now, but apparently, you're either too blind or too stupid to see the truth. You never should have quit."

Trent thrust the shovel into the ground and gripped the handle hard to keep from reaching for his brother. Anger burned hot and bright inside him, fueled by each careless word Sam flung his way. "You don't know what you're talking about. Back the hell off."

Sam took a belligerent step forward, just like he used to do when they were teens. "No. There's too much at stake here. You've had plenty of time to sulk and pout over what happened two years ago, but it's over now. Move on."

"Move on? You've been saying that for years, like I can flip some kind of switch and make all the shit I did disappear."

"You made a mistake. According to John, it wasn't even that—just a case of bad timing."

Bad timing. Trent would have laughed out loud at Sam's ludicrous statement if there had been one shred of humor to be found. "I shot my partner in the back. I killed a kid."

"Shit happens."

"Just like that. You dismiss the destruction of so many lives with a fucking bumper-sticker slogan?"

Trent had to walk away. If he didn't, he was going to punch Sam in the head to knock some sense into it.

Sam grabbed his arm. Trent tried to jerk away, but Sam was strong, and he refused to let him go. "It would be great if you could give up this guilt you're carrying around, but at this point, I'm not going to ask for miracles. What I am asking you to do is get out there. Help Elise find Ashley before it's too late."

What he wouldn't give to be able to do that—to do something meaningful again, something real. "The cops don't need me."

"But Elise does. She's not going to back down."

Not even when thugs were out to hurt her.

Sam sidestepped in front of Trent, barring his path. "Please, Trent. If you won't do it for Elise, do it for me. Ashley's a sweet girl. She's delicate, fragile. She needs you right now, and apparently, the police do, too. Help them."

What if he couldn't? What if he tried and failed?

A small, hopeful voice inside him whispered to him, taunting him. What if he *didn't* fail?

What if he found Ashley? Saved her? What if he stood by Elise and somehow made a difference?

A sense of purpose trickled into him, filling him up. He had to try. He had to help. He couldn't stand by and plant bushes while Elise threw herself in harm's way, all alone.

"I'll need some time off," he told Sam as he headed for his truck.

"It's yours. Take as much as you need."

Trent didn't even take the time to gather his tools. He left them on-site. He didn't give a shit if he ever saw them again, so long as he found Elise before it was too late.

*   *   *

Gary paused the TV, stopping on the image of Elise McBride's tearstained face as she pleaded with the public to help her find her sister.

She was beautiful in her grief. Perfect.

He'd thought Gloria had been a gift, but now he realized he'd taken the wrong woman.

Of all the women he'd found, Elise looked most like his beloved wife. Maybe it was the tears, the sweet pain straining her features, but Elise was almost the spitting image of Wendy.

Gary closed his eyes, remembering the moment he lost her. She'd stared at him from the passenger's seat of their wrecked car. He'd gone too far and hurt her that night. She liked the pain he gave her, begged for it, but that night, he'd given her too much, and she'd stopped breathing.

Gary had panicked, packed her into the car and driven like hell itself was nipping at his heels. He hadn't seen the patch of ice until it was too late.

He could still smell the cold, mixed with the scent of blood and gasoline. He could still feel the slight weight of Wendy's severed hand in his lap, so beautiful and perfect in its stillness.

It was the last gift she'd ever given him.

Wendy had woken during the accident. She'd stared at her hand, too, shocked and confused, as the last of her life drained from her crushed body onto the floorboards. Gary saw the realization that she was dying set in, saw the fear and panic as it changed her face from merely pretty to breathtakingly perfect.

In her last moments, as death swept over her, as she

realized she was helpless to prevent it, Wendy had been the perfect woman.

As hard as Gary had tried, no matter how many women he'd been with during their last moments, he'd never again been able to find that perfection. Until now.

Elise McBride.

He needed her. He needed to bring her home, where she belonged. If Ashley's disappearance had made Elise's face glow with tears, Gary could only imagine how lovely she'd be when he allowed her to be with her sister again and witness Ashley's final moments.

It was Ashley's turn to die, but Elise would be there to take care of her. She'd be there to hold her sister's hand.

Elise felt like she was being watched. She could feel her skin crawling under the contact of a stranger's eyes.

She scanned the street in front of the Haven police station but saw nothing out of place.

Maybe it was just her imagination running wild. All of Trent's worry had gotten to her, and now she was seeing things that weren't there. She hoped.

At least she was at the police station for her appointment with Bob Tindle. If she was safe anywhere, it was here, surrounded by cops.

As she headed inside, she realized that even though there were armed officers everywhere, she still didn't feel as safe as she had with Trent. She was pretty sure it was some kind of sick joke the universe was playing on her, but she wasn't laughing.

Lawrence saw the proof of the hired help's failure walk inside the police station. Not only had the men he'd hired failed to kill Elise McBride, they'd also failed to kill her desire to find her sister.

He wasn't a picky man. He didn't ask that they shed her blood simply because they could. All he asked was that they scare her away, make her crawl back into whatever hole she'd crawled out of. If she'd done that, he would have left her alone.

But no. She had to keep digging into her sister's disappearance.

Pretty soon, she, or someone like her, was going to uncover the truth. Gary wasn't going to stop. Lawrence accepted that fact. His brother was a sick man, and he would continue to dismember and kill women for as long as he could hold a bone saw.

It was Wendy's fault. If she'd lived, Gary would have continued on as he'd been doing, entertaining himself with their games.

But Wendy was gone now, and Lawrence had to step up and take care of his brother. His only options were to stop his brother by killing him or to take care of the nosy woman.

As tedious as it was to find good hired help, Lawrence had no choice. He couldn't bring himself to hurt his own brother, nor did he want to dirty his own hands with Elise McBride. That's why he hired professionals.

He dialed one of his contacts in Chicago—a man who owed him a favor for the drugs he'd transported inside the lining of a casket. If anyone would know where to find dependable help to deal with Elise, this man would. He probably had a little black book full of reliable hit men.

*   *   *

Trent wasn't going to go to Elise empty-handed. If she thought he was trying to butt in, she'd never let him help, and although what she was doing was dangerous, it was a lot more dangerous without him there to cover her back.

The more he did to help her, the faster this would all be over, and she'd be safe again.

A lot of people at the Chicago PD owed Trent favors after his years on the force. He called in every one of them before noon, and what he got in return was a phone call from Detective Ed Woodward.

Trent told him everything he knew, everything Elise had found, and what she suspected about the connection to Susan Maloney.

"Ashley lives farther away than all the other girls, but she fits the profile," said the detective.

"What profile?"

"She's young, single, attractive, and artistically gifted. I hadn't seen that part of the pattern until last night when I was looking through the old case files. That seems to be the unique thing that links the women together."

"How far back did you go?"

"Likely not far enough, now that I'm sure it's a serial killer we've got on our hands. He's probably been doing this for years, but it's taken until now to see the pattern."

"Making the bodies hard to ID helped cover his tracks," said Trent. "I'm impressed you saw something that obscure."

Detective Woodward gave a rough grunt, as if he was uncomfortable with Trent's praise. "I'm still going through files, but I'm sure I haven't found all the victims yet. I've put in some calls to other jurisdictions farther out from Chicago to see if there are any other unsolved cases that match these. The FBI may have some victims to add to the pile."

"How many so far?" Trent didn't need to be more specific. The detective would know he was asking about corpses.

"Twelve bodies in three years in Chicago. Six more possible cases with only body parts, all heads and hands."

Body parts. The thought of what those women must have gone through made Trent's lungs tighten. "What are the odds that Ashley isn't one of this guy's victims?"

"I wish I knew. All I can say is the fact that she's an artist makes her a prime target."

"What can you tell me about Susan Maloney?"

"She's a musician. We found her left hand a few days ago. Honestly, I think we'll find the rest of her any day now, washed up on a riverbank. That's another thing these cases have in common—the victims were all dumped into water instead of being buried."

"Do you have leads to go on? Any suspects?"

"Not yet, but like I said, things are just now coming together enough that we can see the connection between these women. Maybe in a few days, I'll know more."

"Ashley may not have a few days."

There was a brief silence, followed by a weary sigh. "I know. I'm sorry."

"I want to help."

"I wish you could. I've heard about you for years. John Laree says you've got some of the best instincts he's ever seen."

Trent's hand locked around the phone, making his knuckles ache. "You talked to John?"

"Sure. All the time. He misses you."

Blood rushed through Trent's body, but he started to shake with cold all the same. How could John miss him? How could John even stand to think about him?

Trent couldn't speak. The silence stretched on for long, uncomfortable seconds.

Finally, Detective Woodward spoke, but Trent didn't hear much of what he said. He only caught the end. "So, what do you think?"

"What?" Trent's voice was barely loud enough to be heard.

"I said, why don't you make the drive up here, take a look at the evidence, and see if those instincts of yours have gotten rusty."

It was an offer too good to refuse. Not only could he be a part of something bigger than himself again, he could also ask Elise to go with him. Surely she wouldn't turn down a chance like this. And when she agreed, she'd be right at his side where he could make sure she was safe.

"Sure," he heard himself tell the detective. "I'd love to."

"Good. Get here as soon as you can. Tonight would be good."

"It will be late."

"That's okay. I'll be here."

The knock on Ashley's front door made Elise nearly jump out of her skin. She froze in place, like a bunny hiding in plain sight. Only her pounding heart and shaking hands moved.

"Elise," said Trent from the other side of the door. "It's me."

A wave of relief swept through her, unlocking her muscles.

"I know you're in there," he said.

Her car was parked in the driveway. Ashley's garage was too full of junk for her to hide the car inside. She knew it displayed her presence, but it was a risk she had to take.

Elise got up and unlocked the door. He stood there with an overnight bag on his shoulder, bathed in sunshine, glowing with health and strength. She'd never seen anyone look better than he did right now. It took her several stuttering heartbeats to remember that he was the enemy. He stood in her way.

"I'm busy."

"I know. I came to help."

"I don't have time for your kind of help. You've already told me how dangerous this is. No need to waste your breath any longer."

"No. I mean really help. I'm not going to try to stop you anymore. In fact, I've been on the phone with the Chicago PD for the past several hours."

A giddy sense of relief swelled up inside her, making her sway.

Trent caught her by the arms and held her steady. "Whoa. When's the last time you ate?"

She ignored his nosey question. "Really? You really talked to them?"

"Yeah. Why?"

"I haven't been able to get them to return my calls. I think I've contacted the wrong person, but they haven't called me back yet so I could find out who I should talk to."

"Ed Woodward is our contact. He seems sharp."

Our contact. That sounded really good. Not being alone in this—having someone who knew his way around the system—was more than she could ask for. The fact that it was Trent was an added bonus.

Elise stepped up close enough to hug him. She buried her face against his shoulder, pulling in the scent of his skin. It filled her up and loosened knots of fear that made every one of her muscles ache.

His arms closed around her, holding her tight.

He was warm and solid and so steady she wanted to cry. Until this moment, she hadn't realized how much she'd come to depend on him these last few days. Sure, she was getting along without him today, but she was more afraid. More tense. Too much of her attention was spent on her surroundings, and whether or not those two men who'd chased her were going to jump out at her when she least expected it.

When Trent was with her, she could shed some of her fear and worry, and relax enough to think straight.

She pulled away a mere inch, so he could understand her words. She wasn't willing to let him go yet. "What did you find out?"

"Plenty. I'll tell you on the drive up. If you're willing to go with me, that is."

At this point, she was desperate for some direction. Bob Tindle had no new news for her, and no one from the Chicago PD had returned her calls. She'd been going through Ashley's e-mail, hoping that someone might have responded to her plea for help, but all she'd found were letters of condolence.

Everyone acted like her sister was already dead. After the tenth one, she'd stopped reading them. She didn't need any reminders of how much the odds were stacked against them.

"Of course I'll go. When do we leave?"

"Now, if you can."

"My bag is still in my car. I hadn't checked into a hotel yet." She hadn't wanted to give anyone time to break into her room while she was out today. If she picked a hotel right before she was forced to sleep, she figured it would be safer that way.

"Good. Do you want to take your car or my truck?"

"Did you learn how to drive when you trained to be a cop? I mean, like evasive maneuvers, and what to do in a chase, and stuff."

"Sure did."

Elise reached into her pocket and pulled out the keys. "We'll take my car, but you drive. Just in case those guys show up again."

Trent's expression darkened at the reminder of the danger she'd been in, but he said nothing. He simply took the keys and nodded.

Trent kept a careful eye on the road behind them and had seen no signs of anyone following them. Either no one was there, or they were so good he had no hope of spotting them.

"You're getting more tense with every mile," said Elise as they neared the station where Detective Woodward was going to meet them. "Are you worried about this meeting?"

"No."

"Then what are you worried about?"

That his old partner might ambush him. That he might be lurking around the station and force Trent to face demons he wasn't anywhere near ready to face. "Nothing."

"Liar."

She was right, and it was time to change the subject before she started poking around in uncomfortable places. "Are you sure you're ready for this?" he asked her.

"Of course I am. Why wouldn't I be?"

"There will likely be photos of victims. You should avoid looking at them."

"I'll be strong, Trent. You don't have to baby me."

He parked the car and they stepped out onto the hot pavement. "I'm not babying you. I just don't think that looking at that stuff is going to do you or Ashley any good. We don't even know if her disappearance is related to any of these others."

"You said this guy goes after creative women—dancers, musicians, artists. That's a connection."

"Or, it could be a coincidence. Your best bet is to go through the mug shots and see if any of them match the photo from Ashley's backyard."

"I thought you said that picture was no good—that anyone could be the guy if he had at least one eye and one ear."

"You might get lucky." He opened the front door of the station for her. Cool air washed over them, and it was scented with old coffee and dogged determination. Trent remembered that smell. This wasn't his precinct, but it still smelled the same, still felt the same.

His abdomen tightened as if he expected a punch in the gut, but his pulse sped up with excitement. Part of him was scared shitless being here again, but the rest of him was howling in joy, champing at the bit to get back to work. This was where he belonged, and he hated himself for fucking it up. He'd hate himself even more if he let himself take the chance and fucked up again.

Elise's voice swept over him, helping to quiet his jangling nerves. "You're trying to protect me, which is sweet, but stop it. I'm here to make progress, no matter what it takes."

He respected the hell out of her for that, even though he knew it was bound to get her into more trouble.

Trent signed them in, and within minutes, Detective Woodward came to meet them. He looked to be in his mid-thirties, with premature gray hair and skin darkened by too much coffee and not enough sleep. He thrust his hand out toward Elise. "Ms. McBride. Good to meet you."

"You, too, Detective."

He turned his attention on Trent and gave his hand a firm shake. "Officer, uh, I mean, Mr. Brady."

The slip had been intentional. Trent could see it shining in the detective's eyes—a look he'd seen John wear too many times not to recognize it.

"I see you've been talking to my old partner again," said Trent, letting the other man know he'd been caught.

"We spoke."

Trent had to ask. "Is he here?"

"No. But I could call him," offered Detective Woodward.

"No, thanks. I got it covered."

Woodward smiled. "He said you always did."

Elise stared from one man to the other as if trying to figure out what was going on. "Ticktock, gentlemen."

"Of course," said Woodward. "If you'll both follow me, I have a room cleared out for us to use."

He led them back to a dingy interrogation room. The table was already stacked with file folders. A half-empty cup of coffee sat on one corner and a ragged notebook lay open, topped with a chewed-on pencil.

Woodward waved toward the pair of chairs set out for them. "Have a seat, and let's see what we can do for each other, shall we?"

Elise wasted no time getting to the point. She explained everything in brief, factual statements, covering everything from her last conversation with Ashley up to the e-mail she'd read this morning from Ashley's friends. "My sister has been missing for nearly a week now. Here's the photo of the guy I think abducted her—the one she took the day she disappeared." She pulled it out of a notebook and handed it to him.

Woodward glanced at the photo and nodded. "I've seen this. Haven police sent the electronic file over yesterday. I've asked one of our computer guys to put the file through a filter, or whatever it is they do, and see if they can clean it up."

"Can you use face recognition software?" asked Elise.

Woodward shrugged. "If we get a clearer shot, maybe,

but we only have part of his face. That's going to make it hard to match. Plus, there's no guarantee he's in any of our databases. We'll go through the motions, but don't hold your breath."

"So what do we do?"

"First, I'm going to ask you a bunch of questions about your sister to help determine her habits and see if the man in this photo is really the same guy who took Susan Maloney. I've been working on his MO, picking up bits from all the cases I think are connected. And I'm not alone. There are five other cops lending a hand, too. Plus, I have a friend at the Bureau who does profiles, and she's already agreed to help."

"What good will a profile do?"

"It will give us a general idea of who we're looking for, how far away from his home he'll tend to go to find his victims, things like that. Then we can use that to figure out where to start looking for your sister."

Elise swallowed and clasped her hands tightly in her lap. "Ashley may not have that much time."

"I know, but we're going to work as hard and fast and long as it takes to find this guy."

Trent covered her hands with his in an effort to comfort her. "It's a good start. I suggest we let him take the lead and do whatever we can to help, okay?"

Elise nodded. "Okay. I hate sitting here. I feel like I should be out looking for her or something, but if this is what will work, then I'll sit here."

"Great," said Woodward as he picked up his chewed pencil. "Let's get started."

Four hours later, Elise was still answering questions about her sister, even though she was melting with fatigue. An hour after that, Trent called a halt. "That's enough for tonight. It's late."

Woodward looked at his watch, and his brows twitched in surprise as if he hadn't realized the time. "He's right. We'll call it a night, and tomorrow we'll pick up where we left off. In the meantime, I'll send all this over to my buddy at the Bureau and see what she can make of it."

"I can keep going," said Elise.

"But I can't," lied the detective. Trent guessed the man could keep going for hours yet, but he appreciated his trying to protect Elise.

"We'll go check in at the hotel down the street." Trent scribbled his cell phone number on the top sheet of the battered notebook. "Call if you need us."

"Will do."

Trent put his arm around Elise as they walked back out to the car. He wasn't sure if she let him do it because she liked it, or if it was because she needed the support. He could feel her fatigue trembling through her limbs. Or maybe it was fear.

Either way, he didn't like it much.

He tucked her into the car and went around to his side. As the engine came on, the clock glowed bright green.

"It's after midnight," she said in a somber voice. "Ashley went missing a week ago today."

"Don't think about that. It won't do her any good. You have to focus on the here and now."

"I'm not going to fall apart on you and get all emotional. Don't worry."

"I don't care about an emotional outburst, sweetheart. I care about you." He more than just cared, but he didn't let himself go there. There was no point. Their lives were too different. Even if he walked away from everything to be with her—his family, his job, his friends—it would never work between them. He'd be a weight around her neck, keeping her from reaching her goals.

He loved her too much to do that to her.

Trent's hand fumbled with the keys. He wasn't sure when he'd fallen in love with her, but he had. It should have been a comforting, freeing feeling, but it wasn't. Without a future, what good would his love do either of them?

She reached for him and slid her fingers around his arm. "You're a good man. I'm lucky you caught me breaking into Ashley's place."

"I thought you weren't breaking in. At least that's what you told Bob."

"I'll tell you everything one day when we're not sitting outside a police station."

One day. That sounded suspiciously like she was talking about the future—that she'd be around long enough for them to have one.

Trent was enough of a fool to let that bubble of hope swell up inside him. "I'll hold you to that."

CHAPTER SIXTEEN

While Trent waited with the car in the loading zone of the hotel, Elise checked them in.

She felt fragile and stretched thin. Trent had been right beside her all day, rock-solid, and she knew that without him, she'd likely be a basket case by now. Even being away from him long enough to get them a room left her feeling edgy and vulnerable.

She asked for a room with only one bed. The idea of sleeping in his arms again was a lure that was too potent for her to resist. She needed every advantage she could find to hold herself together long enough to find Ashley, and right now, Trent was her advantage.

The clerk handed her two key cards and pointed toward the elevators. Elise took the keys, trying to pay attention to what the woman said, but all she could think about was getting back to Trent. As she hurried off, a man in waiting behind her stepped up to the counter. Apparently, they weren't the only ones getting in late.

Elise walked out of the hotel. Trent was right in front

of the doors, in the rental car, keeping watch around him as if he expected trouble. He was probably right to do so.

She climbed back in the passenger's seat and handed him a plastic key card. "We're in room 412. The clerk said we could use the side door coming in from the garage with our keys."

"Do you want to grab some food, or just go to sleep?"

He was probably starving, and it had been a long time since she'd eaten, too. "Food, if you can find something open."

"There's a store down the street that's open all night. We can grab some granola bars or something."

"Sure."

They made quick work of finding food, parked in the hotel's garage, and went up to their room.

Elise carried the sack of sandwiches and fruit they'd found, along with their drinks, while Trent carried the luggage. He slid his key in the door and opened it for her to go in.

As she set the drinks down, she saw a movement out of the corner of her eye. She jerked her head up just in time to see a masked man lift a silenced pistol.

There wasn't even time to draw in a breath to scream before Trent was moving. He shoved her out of the way and went flying at the man. As he closed the distance, he swung one of the overnight bags at the gunman. It batted the man's arm aside as the weapon fired, barking in the silence of the hotel.

Trent rammed his body into the masked man's, taking control of his weapon arm.

Elise steadied herself against the wall, stood there, shocked. Unmoving. She wasn't even sure if this was real.

"Get out!" shouted Trent.

She couldn't move. She was rooted to the spot, staring in horror as Trent took a hard blow to his jaw.

Trent rammed the man's hand into a desk, trying to dislodge the gun.

Another bullet screamed across the room and plowed through the ceiling.

What if there was someone in the room above them?

Finally, that thought shook her locked-up body loose and she was able to move. She picked up the icy drink next to her and hurled it at the masked man's back.

He jerked in shock, then kept fighting, but that fraction of a second's distraction was enough to give Trent an opening. He did something with his leg that swept the man's feet out from under him. The man went down against the desk, but Trent didn't let go of his arm.

The gun barked again. Trent snarled, lifted the man's hand, weapon and all, then slammed his elbow against the edge of the sturdy desk.

Elise heard the bone break, followed by the man's stifled scream of pain.

The weapon fell from his limp fingers, clattering onto the desk.

Trent forced the man the rest of the way to the floor using his broken arm for leverage. He pinned him there with a knee to his back.

Elise saw a dark wet spot forming on the man's sleeve.

"Give me the phone cord from the wall," said Trent. His voice was harsh, guttural.

Elise ripped the cord out of the wall and tied the man's hands together behind his back where Trent held them. He made short, pained grunts every time his broken arm shifted.

Her stomach rolled with every sound he made, every accidental brush of her skin over his.

As soon as she was done, Trent checked the knot, pulled the man's mask off and tossed it aside. "Who sent you?" he demanded.

The man said nothing.

Trent leaned his weight on the knee he had against the man's spine. "Who the fuck sent you?"

This was not going to end well. Before it could get out of control any further, she got her cell phone out, dialed 911, and told the dispatcher what had happened. They were only blocks from a police station. It wasn't going to take long for the cops to get here.

She just had to keep Trent from killing this man until then.

Half a second longer and Elise would have been dead.

That was the thought that kept spinning around in Trent's head as he stared down at the piece of shit bleeding on the carpet.

If he'd hesitated upon seeing that weapon, she'd be the one bleeding right now, and Trent would likely be right there with her.

He patted the man down, looking for a wallet or anything to ID him. The guy didn't even have spare change. The only thing on him was a hotel key card and a spare clip of ammo.

Trent's blood went cold, soaking up all the heat of battle.

This man was a professional. A hired killer.

What the hell had they gotten mixed up in? Whatever it was, it was a lot more than just a serial killer. A killer wouldn't want to hire someone to do the work for him. He'd take care of the job himself.

Trent rolled the man over, making him cry out as his weight shifted onto his broken arm. He grabbed the front of his shirt and snarled, "Tell me who hired you."

The man stared up at him. Those dark eyes were empty. Soulless. This was the kind of man who could shoot two unsuspecting people in their hotel room while deciding what to have for breakfast.

"Don't hurt him, Trent. He might know where Ashley is." Elise came forward, but he didn't dare look at her. Not yet. He wasn't going to risk taking his eyes off this killer even for a second, which was why he saw there wasn't even a flicker of recognition on the man's face when she'd mentioned Ashley's name.

If he knew anything about her, he had one hell of a poker face.

"Do you know where my sister is?" asked Elise.

The man's eyes moved toward Elise, and Trent slapped him to get his attention. "Don't even look at her."

A slight smile lifted one side of the hired killer's mouth. Trent had shown him a weak spot and the fucker was enjoying it. If he got the chance, he'd exploit it.

Trent wasn't going to give him the chance.

"Hand me the gun, Elise."

"I don't think that's a good idea."

Sirens filtered through the hotel room windows. The police were here.

Trent was tempted to get it himself, but he knew that if he took his weight off this man for even an instant, Elise would be the one to pay. He might be bound, but that didn't mean he couldn't find a way to hurt her, or at least get away to do so later.

Trent wasn't going to let that happen. "Give. Me. The. Gun."

"No." Her voice was firm and unyielding.

"I can make him tell me what he knows," lied Trent.

"Fine, then you can do it once the police are here to witness his confession."

There would be no confession. A man in his field didn't talk and keep breathing.

Heavy footsteps pounded in the hall and Elise went to the open door to wave the police inside.

As the officers took control of the scene, Trent let go of his prey, knowing he'd lost his chance to rid the world of one more threat.

Gary wanted Elise, but she was nowhere to be found. He was normally a patient man, but he detested having his schedule interrupted.

Ashley was becoming burdensome. He was tired of her. Angry at her for what she'd done to Constance.

It was time for her to be of use. She owed him for what she'd taken away, and Gary was going to see to it that she paid her debt.

Constance was gone now, but she wasn't done serving a purpose. She was going to bring Elise right to him.

Gary needed Elise. He needed to see that perfect,

beautiful fear and grief shining in her eyes again. He'd watched it over and over on the news, but it wasn't the same. He wanted to see it in person. In the flesh.

He knew she loved Ashley, and that when she watched him turn Ashley from a whiney, brainless twit into a beautiful, perfect woman, Elise's eyes would shine, and her skin would glow. Her pain would be exquisite, acute, making her beautiful beyond words. Perfect, just like Wendy had been.

Eventually, Elise would fail him, becoming imperfect. All the women did. She'd no doubt have to take her own turn under his scalpel and saw, but he'd planned something special for her—a kind of thank-you present for the pleasure she was destined to give him.

Both Elise and her sister would live together forever, side by side, the two halves of their hearts stitched into one whole. Just like sisters should be.

It was dawn by the time Trent and Elise had finished answering all the police's questions.

Trent's body was still humming with adrenaline, tight and tense. Elise, on the other hand, sat limp and exhausted beside him.

He needed to find a place for her to sleep, and he wasn't about to check them back into that hotel.

They'd been gone for no more than twenty minutes to get food, and that hit man had found them. Trent wasn't taking that kind of risk again.

Detective Woodward opened the door of the interrogation room. "You're free to go now."

Trent stood and offered his hand to Elise. He was more than ready to be out of here. Experiencing crime from the victim's side made him feel caged in and restless. He wanted to be out there, doing something.

He wanted to be in Woodward's shoes.

"Did you get anything out of the guy who attacked us?" asked Elise.

Woodward held the door open for them to leave. "No, but we know this guy. He's a hired gun—works for anyone with enough cash. He's wanted for questioning in connection with several unsolved homicides. We've got guys in with him now, talking to him."

"He's not going to say anything," predicted Trent.

"Maybe not, but we caught him in the act this time. He's not going to be slipping away anytime soon."

"How did he get the key to our room?" asked Trent.

"He killed the night clerk, so maybe he made his own, or found a housekeeping key lying around."

Another death. Trent felt his chest tighten.

"The clerk died?" asked Elise.

"I'm afraid so."

She squeezed Trent's hand hard as they made their way down the hall. "What is going on? What does this have to do with Ashley?"

Woodward shrugged. "I wish we knew. I'm beginning to wonder if she didn't get herself mixed up in some kind of organized crime. We know that hit man worked for the Outfit, even if we can't prove it."

Elise leaned against Trent's side. She was shaking with fear or cold or both, so he wrapped his arm around her. "So, what do we do now?" she asked.

They walked past several desks. Even this early, the place was starting to bustle with activity. The smell of fresh coffee wafted through the station. A low drone of voices filled the air with purpose.

"Get some rest. Come back in a few hours. Maybe we'll have more to go on."

Maybe. No promises. Trent could hear the frustration in Woodward's tone. Having the silent hit man in custody had gotten them no closer to Ashley.

"Any suggestions where to stay? Someplace safe?" asked Trent.

"I've got one," said a man behind Trent.

Every muscle in his body clenched, locking down hard. Air flew out of his lungs and he stood frozen for a long, excruciating second. Slowly, he turned around and faced John Laree, his old partner.

"How about you come stay at my place?" asked John.

Trent looked down at the man in a wheelchair, the man who'd taught him so much.

The last time he'd seen John he'd been pale and weak. His face had been haggard with pain and hard with determination. He'd been in a motorized wheelchair then, but now, John's arms bulged under the sleeves of his CPD T-shirt—clear evidence that he'd gotten well past needing the motor.

John was tan and smiling. His graying hair was trimmed to the scalp, and his bright blue eyes were as clear and sharp as a cold mountain stream. The signs of pain were gone, and it was almost like he was happy to see Trent again.

Trent knew better. No way was John happy to see the man who'd stolen his life.

John thrust his hand out. Trent had no choice but to take it, or be even more of an ass than he already was.

John's hand was strong and warm, rough with calluses. "It's good to see you, man. You're a hard guy to get ahold of."

Trent couldn't speak. His tongue was glued to the roof of his mouth.

Elise stepped forward and shook John's hand. "I'm Elise McBride. Trent's friend."

"John Laree," was all Trent managed to choke out.

"So, I hear you two have some trouble on your hands. Why don't you come back to the house and get a little sleep. You both look like you could use it."

"Thanks," said Elise. "We'd love to."

"But we can't," added Trent, his words fast and clipped with panic. "I've already brought enough trouble down on you. I won't bring any more to your doorstep."

"Hell, Trent. No one knows where you're going but me and Ed. And he sure as hell won't spill."

"Not a word," agreed Woodward.

"Besides, Carol would love to see you again."

"Carol? I thought you two split up," said Trent.

John shrugged wide, powerful shoulders. A broad grin spread over his face. "A lot's changed. If you'd given me your phone number, you'd know about all of it. Instead, you hightailed it out of here as soon as the doctors sent me home."

He'd wanted to stay, but that would have been selfish. Once he'd seen John was going to make it, he thought he owed the man the decency of never having to look at him again. "I thought it was best."

"Well, you were wrong," said John, in that same casual lecturing tone he'd used to teach Trent too many things to count. "You always were a bonehead."

John spun his chair around easily, like it was a part of him. "Come on," he said as he rolled away. "I already told Carol you're coming, and if you make me disappoint her, I'm going to have to beat the hell out of you."

Trent stood there, unsure what to do for a moment, but Elise had no similar problems. She took her overnight bag from Trent's shoulder and headed after John.

"You'd better go," said Woodward. "I'm pretty sure John could take you."

Lawrence hated incompetence. He expected precision and effectiveness from those he employed.

Hired hit men were no different.

The man had come highly recommended, and yet Elise and her ex-cop boyfriend were still nosing around in Chicago, with the police, no less. His contact on the CPD had seen them only moments ago—right after the hit man he'd hired had been arrested and hauled in for questioning.

Clearly, Lawrence was going to have to take matters into his own hands. He wasn't about to do anything drastic—no sense in dirtying himself. But this time, the man he hired was going to be supervised. He'd go himself and make sure the job was done right.

And then after that, he was going to have to do something about Gary—get him to leave town, maybe go out to the West Coast. He'd dirtied the waters here. It was time to move on.

And if he didn't want to go, then Lawrence would

simply have to supervise the job of having his brother killed, too.

John Laree's house was the last place on the planet Trent wanted to be.

They followed him home and pulled in front of a quaint little house crammed up against its neighbors. There wasn't much yard to be had, but what was there was lush and green. A long ramp wound its way from the drive up to the front porch, and each side of it was lined with bright pink petunias.

"You shouldn't be so tense," said Elise. "Clearly, the man doesn't hate you."

"He should." Trent got out of the car before she could say anything else. This was bad enough without her added commentary.

He pulled their overnight bags out of the trunk and headed up to the door. John had already got there ahead of him and was unlocking it.

"You really don't need to put us up," said Trent.

"Sure I do. It's the safest place in town, and your lady friend looks like she's about to fall over."

Elise did look tired, but Trent could think of better places for her to catch some sleep than here.

Like anywhere.

John rolled inside and called out, "Carol, I'm home."

The house was small but homey. Lace doilies and matching curtains gave the place a distinctly feminine look, but Trent figured John probably didn't care what Carol did with the place as long as she didn't get rid of the TV. Family pictures covered the walls, along with macaroni art and crooked crayon drawings.

The air smelled like cinnamon and bacon, with a hint of pine cleaner lurking beneath the stronger scents. A radio was on in another room, giving off the bouncy beat of an old Beach Boys song.

Carol came bustling out of the kitchen. She was younger than John, maybe fifty-five, and wore a floral apron around her pudgy middle. As soon as she saw Trent, her face broke into a smile and she rushed past John to reach up and hug him around the neck.

Her smooth cheek was cool against his, and she smelled like fresh cooked bacon. She said something, but Trent was too stunned to get his ears to function. He couldn't believe that she was hugging him like he was her long-lost son, when she should have balled up her fist and slugged him in the gut.

He'd nearly killed her husband, and she was hugging him.

"I think you've embarrassed him enough, Carol," said John. "Why don't you come meet his friend, Elise."

Carol pulled back enough to kiss Trent's cheek, then wiped off the lipstick mark she'd left behind. "It's so good to see you again."

While John made introductions, Trent tried to figure out what the hell had just happened, and why he was wearing a smear of lipstick on his cheek instead of a bruise.

Carol's voice drifted across the living room, hitting Trent but not really sinking in. "I've got some coffee on, and the cinnamon rolls are almost done. They're just the kind out of the can, but they're pretty good. I'll scramble some eggs and we'll have a nice breakfast. I bet you two are starved after your ordeal."

Ordeal. That was one way of putting almost being killed by a hired hit man.

"You ladies go ahead," said John. "Trent and I need a few minutes."

Carol brushed her hands over her apron, her smile faltering for the first time. "Don't be long. Business and breakfast don't mix, and cold eggs are only good for dogs."

"Just a minute, honey. I promise."

Carol nodded and took Elise by the arm, leading her away.

"Have a seat," said John. He was using his training-the-rookie voice, and Trent responded before he'd even realized what had happened.

"You've been avoiding me for more than a year. Care to tell me why?" asked John. "I thought we were friends."

"Of course we were." *Were*, not *are*. Trent winced at the slip.

If John noticed, he said nothing. "Then why?"

Trent wasn't sure how to explain, so he just spat it out. "At first I didn't want to interfere with your physical therapy. I knew you'd be mad as hell at me, so I stayed away."

"Mad? Is that what you thought?"

"I shot you in the back. Of course you had a right to be mad."

John let out a scorching, humorless laugh. "That kid was high as a kite, heavily armed, and scared out of his mind. He raised his weapon and aimed at you, and you did the only thing you could—the thing I taught you to do. You shot back."

"And hit you."

"Yeah, well, serves me right for jumping in the way."

How could he be so flippant? How could he act like it was his fault?

Trent clutched the arm of the couch in frustration. "That's not what happened. You jumped on him to keep him from shooting me."

"And your bullet hit me instead of him. It was an accident. I always knew that, even before the investigation cleared you of any wrongdoing."

"Knowing it was an accident didn't make it any easier on you. I ruined your life!"

John spread his hands and motioned around the comfortable living room. "Does my life look ruined to you? I have a nice place, a wife who loves me, and time to play with my grandkids. What's ruined about that?"

"You'll never walk again. You'll never be a cop again."

John scoffed. "There's more to life than being a cop, son. Apparently, two years hasn't been long enough to teach you that."

"You loved being a cop."

"Sure I did. But I love my life more. I love my wife, my kids, and my grandkids a hell of a lot more. If it hadn't been for leaving the CPD, Carol would have never come back to me. She left me because of the job—she couldn't stand wondering if I'd come home after my shift every night. After the accident, after being separated for a year, she came back to me. We're better than ever. Stronger."

"You should have been able to leave on your own two feet."

John shrugged. "Four wheels work just as well. Besides, if it hadn't been for the accident, I never would have left. I'd never have had the guts to leave—it's all I knew. I have you to thank for making me realize it was time for a change."

"Thank? You're psychotic."

"The world has a way of changing shape when something like this happens. I choose to see it as an improvement. Besides, I still do good work. I go to schools and talk about gun safety, drugs, gangs, you name it. I'm still out there, fighting the good fight." He moved his chair toward Trent. "What about you? Are you fighting the good fight, Trent?"

No. He was passing time, letting life slide by, wondering if it was worth the trouble. "I work for my brother now."

"The family landscaping business? You always said you'd rather die than do that job."

And he'd meant it. Doing the one thing he despised most seemed like a good punishment at the time. Still was.

Trent looked away, staring at the wall of photos behind John. Half a dozen different kids smiled out at him, hamming it up for the camera.

John put his hand on Trent's knee. It was as far as he could reach from the wheelchair. "You're the one whose life was ruined that day, not mine. If you want to keep beating yourself up over it, there's not much I can do, especially when you won't even give me your phone number."

"You have it now," said Trent.

"And I'm going to use it and keep using it until you

stop being a bonehead. Eventually, you'll give up and come back to work just to get me to shut the hell up."

Not likely, but Trent said nothing. He didn't want to dash John's hopes on top of everything else he'd done to him. No matter how well his life was going now, it couldn't excuse what Trent had done to his friend.

"Breakfast is ready," called Carol.

"We'd better get in there. She doesn't like to be kept waiting."

Trent remembered all the nights they'd worked late. John had never once worried about making Carol wait, even before they separated.

"I imagine your girlfriend doesn't like being kept waiting either. They never do."

"She's not really my girlfriend."

"No?" John shook his head. "Then you really are a bonehead. It's sad that even though I'm pushing sixty and stuck in a wheelchair, I've got a better life than you."

Ashley knew she was next, she just didn't know how long it would be until Gary came in and brought that manicure kit with him.

Over the past few days—or what she thought were days—she'd changed. Seeing Constance suffer and die—killing her—had freed Ashley in some small way.

She was no longer afraid. She knew she was going to die in here; it was just a question of how much damage she did on her way out.

The one summer she'd spent at camp had bored her out of her mind. All she cared about was the hour every day they'd worked on art projects. They made stained glass out of colored marbles, and used a hammer and nails to texture copper sheets into raised images of flowers. She still had those projects in her garage somewhere.

But in all that boredom, listening to what kinds of plants she could eat and how to survive a rattlesnake bite, some of the information must have leaked in, because she realized that she had everything she needed to start a fire.

Burning this place down was a giant step up from having her hands chopped off with that bone saw.

She could still hear the grating noise beneath Constance's screams of pain. For as long as she lived, she'd never forget that sound.

Luckily, that memory wasn't going to be with her a long time.

The trick was going to be timing the fire so that Gary would go up right along with his prisoners.

That thought gave Ashley pause. She was going to have to kill another woman—the one she heard crying after Constance was dead. Her blood was going to be on Ashley's hands when she met whatever judgment awaited her after this life. She'd already killed Constance. Now she was going to kill again.

She wondered if there was just one woman down here with her, or if there were more. How many lives would she end with this plan?

But what choice did she have? She could kill the women who were here now, or risk letting Gary hunt down more after he'd killed them himself. The women trapped here were dead one way or another, just like her. If she acted now, she might save countless others from the horror Constance had to face.

If she could take Gary out, it was worth a shot—worth the stain on her soul.

Ashley rounded up the things she'd need—a couple of pencils, some pencil shavings from the sharpener Gary'd given her, a narrow strip of fabric ripped from her sheet, a plastic hanger, and several pieces of sketch paper crumpled into balls.

Now all she had to do was wait until she knew he was home—until he walked down the hallway outside the door, bringing them food.

As soon as he was here, she'd start the fire and pray it spread fast enough to kill the devil himself.

CHAPTER SEVENTEEN

Carol showed them to the guest room, which was clearly a place where the grandkids stayed, judging by the stuffed animals piled on top of the race-car bedspread.

"I hope the bed's not too small," said Carol as she gathered up the stuffed animals and stowed them in the closet.

Trent had been silent through breakfast and still seemed to be less than talkative. Elise gave Carol a reassuring smile. "It's fine, really. Thank you."

Carol covered her mouth and her eyes were round with shock. "Oh, my. I forgot to ask if you even wanted to share a bed. I just assumed you were . . ." She waved her hands nervously.

"Sharing isn't a problem," said Elise.

"Okay, then. I'll leave you in peace. The bathroom is down the hall, and I'll set out towels for you to use. I'm headed to the market for a while, but John will be here if you need anything." She slipped out the door, shutting it behind her.

Trent sat on the edge of the bed and pulled off his shoes. His back was rigid and tight, and his usual fluid movements were jerky and sharp.

"You're awfully quiet," said Elise.

"Sorry."

"Something happened between you and John, didn't it? Ever since you talked to him you've been silent."

"It's nothing."

"Nothing has you tied in knots, then."

"I'm fine." He pulled his shirt off over his head, baring the broad expanse of his back. Muscles she remembered feeling under her palms stood out in tense ridges. The urge to run her palms over him made her hands sweat.

She tried pretending she didn't notice the way his body made her feel, but it was harder than it should have been. "No, you're not. You're strung so tight you're about to snap."

"It would be a really good idea for you to leave this alone."

"How can I when you only have to deal with this because I dragged you up here?"

His words were clipped and angry. "I chose to come."

"Because you wanted to help me. It hardly seems fair that you're suffering because you were trying to be a nice guy."

He skinned out of his jeans and sat back down on the bed, making it rock with his sudden weight. "I'm not suffering because I tried to be nice. I've made mistakes, and facing up to them sucks, but I'm a grown man, so that's what I'll do. I suggest you leave it alone and get some sleep."

Elise left her T-shirt and panties on, but got rid of the bra. Even as tired as she was, she didn't think she could sleep in it. "How can I sleep when you're upset?"

"Be creative. I'm sure you'll think of something."

She ignored his snippy statement and slid under the sheets. Trent hadn't even so much as tried to see her undress, which was a bit disappointing. She'd certainly enjoyed watching him.

Finally, he lay down beside her on the double bed. His long body took up most of the room, but she didn't mind the brief brushes of his rougher skin over hers. His leg grazed her shin, and his hair gave her a tickling caress. Everywhere their bodies met, his was hard and masculine, reminding her just how effective he'd been in that fight. Knowing he was there with her was nice. Comforting.

She'd almost drifted off to sleep when his voice rose up, vibrating with guilt. "The night I shot John, I killed a sixteen-year-old boy."

Shock jolted through her. "What?"

"He'd stolen a car. He was high as a kite, didn't know what he was doing. And he was armed. He shot at us." He pulled in a deep, sucking breath. "I didn't know how old he was until . . . after. His mother showed up and screamed at me, asking me how I could kill a child."

"She should have been asking herself why her sixteen-year-old was running around doing drugs and carrying a weapon."

"She was a single mom. Had four kids, worked three jobs." He said it like it excused the outcome.

Maybe it did. Maybe this woman didn't have the kind of support system Elise's mother did. Maybe she didn't have an apartment building full of neighbors ready, willing, and eager to report anytime they left the apartment for something other than school, or anytime they stepped out of line. If it hadn't been for their mother's protective streak, maybe she and Ashley would have gotten into a lot more trouble than they had. Maybe they would have been on the streets like that young man.

That was a lot of maybes, and Elise bet her bank account that the grieving mother had already punished herself by going over every one in detail.

"You did what you had to do," said Elise.

Trent let out a humorless laugh. "Good thing I don't have to make those kinds of decisions anymore. The world is a safer place now."

"Hardly. Who knows what the kid would have done if you hadn't stopped him."

"That's what everyone said. The kid had a record. He was headed for prison. A walking lost cause." He didn't sound convinced.

"And what do you say?"

"I say we'll never know for sure now, will we?"

Elise found his hand and laced her fingers through his. "You'll also never know how many people you might have saved from that teen's violence. I can't imagine what it must be like to live with something like that, but how long are you going to punish yourself?"

"This isn't about me."

"Sure it is. You gave up the job you love. Did you do it because you're afraid you'll accidentally shoot the wrong person again, or afraid you'll shoot the right one?"

"Everyone will be fine so long as I never pick up a weapon again. You instinctively knew that when I had that hit man on the ground. You made the right call not handing me the gun."

"Maybe. Maybe not. He could escape custody, or get out of jail and kill someone. Killing him might have saved lives. I guess we'll never know for sure." Throwing his words back at him made her feel petty now that they were out of her mouth.

His fingers tightened. "This conversation ends right here, Elise. It's none of your business."

His harsh comment didn't faze her. She was used to dealing with difficult people, trying to get an interview. Trent wasn't going to thwart her that easily. "Ashley's disappearance was none of your business, but that hasn't stopped you from getting involved. Why should it stop me?"

"That's different. You need my help."

"Maybe you need mine. Maybe you need someone to knock some sense into you."

She felt his hand fist in the sheet, drawing it tight. "What I need is for everyone to leave me alone."

"So you can wallow in misery?"

His voice rang with warning. "Leave it alone, Elise."

Not likely. She never knew when to stop. It was one of the things that made her a good reporter. "Leave it alone, so you can drag your whole family down with you while you're wallowing? Is that really fair?"

"Fair would have been that kid behind a desk at school instead of being stoned and behind the wheel of a stolen car. Fair would have been John walking again. Life isn't fair."

"Seems to me that would grate against a man like

yourself—one who devoted his life to upholding the law."

"My life is over."

And that was the root of the problem. He'd given up. He'd stopped living. "It doesn't have to be. You can choose to keep on doing good. In fact, helping me out means you already are."

"It's not the same."

"Why not? Because I'm not paying you? Because you're not wearing a badge?"

"You don't understand. I don't deserve another chance. Even ignoring the fact that I killed a child, I also nearly killed my partner. An error in judgment that big is not something I can overlook."

"Then don't. Decide you're going to learn from it. Move on."

"Is that what you'll do if we don't find Ashley? Move on?"

Elise couldn't go there. Not if she was going to be of any use to Trent. She pushed away the fear and panic his words evoked and refused to give up. "What will it take for you to forgive yourself? Do you need to save a life to balance things out?"

"It doesn't work like that."

"Then how does it work? If you were the one sitting in John's wheelchair, and he'd been the one who accidentally shot you, would you want his life to be over? Would you want him to be miserable?"

"Of course not. This is not about revenge, or evening the score. I just can't take that kind of risk anymore. If that means I plant bushes for the rest of my life, then so be it. It's honest work."

"But not the work of your heart."

A bleak laugh fell from his lips. "Good thing I'm not some starry-eyed teen who thinks that's the end of the world, then."

"You're giving up on yourself."

"Why do you care? It's not like we have a future together."

She let go of his hand, rolled over on her side and leaned on her elbow. "First, that doesn't mean I don't want to make you see reason. Second, who says we don't have a future?"

"Anyone with half a brain. You have a job you love, traveling around the world, doing important work. I don't."

"You could."

"Could what?"

"Have a job you love. Even if you're unwilling to wear a badge, you could do something else. You could go into private security, or become a PI."

"I'm not going to carry a gun."

"So, don't. Find another way. If this thing between us turns out to be more than just sex, then we'll make it work for as long as we can."

He shook his head in grim amusement. "I could just see it now. You come back to Haven three weeks out of the year, spread out here and there, and I sit at home, waiting for you to show."

"Yeah, okay. Maybe the long-distance relationship thing isn't for us, but we won't know until we try, right?"

"You deserve a husband who isn't fucked up."

"Whoa. Who said anything about marriage?"

"That is the logical progression of a lasting relationship."

"Not with me, it's not. As far as I'm concerned, marriage is an invitation to misery."

"So, you don't believe in commitment?"

"I never said that. I just don't believe in standing up in front of the world and declaring something will last forever when everyone knows that's a huge, steaming pile of shit."

"Wow. And you thought I was cynical."

"I'm realistic. Marriage doesn't work. Why bother?"

"It can work, at least when people love each other." Something desperate and hopeful shone in his eyes. Maybe he was simply looking for something to distract him from all the guilt he suffered.

"People always love each other at first. But it goes away. It fades."

He shook his head. "Not the real thing. It's rare, so maybe you've never seen it, but I have. I see it every time I visit my parents."

Elise wanted to believe, but she knew better. Like the tooth fairy and the Easter bunny, true love was just a pretty story told to young children—one they learned was a lie as soon as their parents split up.

Still, she couldn't stand the thought of destroying the lie for Trent. She remembered how good that lie felt. "That must be nice."

He studied her face for a moment, frowning. "You don't believe me."

"I believe you believe it."

"Here I was, feeling sorry for myself when you're the one who's really got issues."

"No, I don't."

"You may not realize it, but somewhere along the way, you got your brain scrambled. When all this is over, I'm going to take you home to my folks and show you how wrong you are."

He could show her whatever he liked. It wouldn't change anything. At most, he'd show her two people who tolerated each other out of convenience or habit. At worst, he'd see through the childish illusion and become even harder and more cynical. "No, thanks. I'll pass."

"Are you afraid you're wrong?"

"No. I'm afraid you'll figure out *you* are. I don't want to do that to you."

He had the gall to smile at her like she was some kind of foolish kid. "It's going to be fun to watch you eat those words."

"If you say so."

"It's going to be even more fun to show you how good a marriage can be between two people who love each other."

"You are the most marriage-minded man I've ever known. We haven't even been on a date yet."

"My talk of marriage makes you nervous because a woman like you could never love a man like me."

He was wrong. She realized it then. It jumped out at her, scaring the hell out of her. She *could* love him, despite his bout of unreasonable self-doubt and his foolish beliefs about marriage. He'd been kind to her, kind to Ashley. He took care of the people around him and when he messed up, it hurt him deeply. He wasn't the kind of man who gave up on other people. Just on himself.

Elise didn't want that for him. Even if what they had was a product of stress and adrenaline, she didn't want him to suffer once this thing between them was over, and she was gone. He deserved better than that.

Maybe, if she tried hard, she'd find a way to show him that—to prove it to him. Until then, all she could do was prove to him how much he meant to her, how much she cared for him.

She climbed on top of him, straddling him, and forced him to look into her eyes. The golden chips swimming in his eyes glowed with self-doubt, but Elise was going to find a way to change that. "You're wrong," she told him, letting him see the truth in her words. "A woman like me would be lucky to love a man like you. But even that won't matter if you don't love yourself."

"That sounds a hell of a lot like bullshit. But I like it anyway."

"Good." She kissed the tip of his nose.

"Sweetheart, when you look at me like that, it makes me forget all the mistakes I've made."

"And what happens when I do this?" She kissed his mouth, nibbling at his firm lips. His body went tight beneath hers, his penis thickened and hardened against the gusset of her panties, but she tried valiantly to ignore it.

"I forget what day of the week it is, or why I should care."

"And this?" she asked, deepening the kiss, tasting the warmth of his mouth, feeling the sharpness of his teeth against her tongue.

"I forget my own name."

"But do you know mine?"

"Elise," he said, as he cradled her head in his hands and kissed her back. "Elise McBride."

She smiled down at him. "I'm glad you remembered."

He stared at her mouth. "If you don't get off me, I'm afraid I'm going to forget we're sleeping in someone's guest room."

She wiggled her hips against his groin, feeling his erection twitch. Only the thin cotton of their underwear separated them. "Maybe that's what I want."

"To scandalize Carol?"

She ran her hands over his chest, feeling the hard contours of his muscles gliding under her fingers. "She went shopping. John's gentleman enough not to listen, or at least to pretend he didn't."

"We're not going to do this here."

That sounded too much like a challenge for Elise to resist. She whipped her shirt off over her head, making her blond curls fly around her face.

Trent's gaze honed in on her breasts and his hips bucked beneath her.

Her blood went thick and hot in her veins, making her feel languid and breathless. The only time she truly stopped thinking about all the danger and worry was when Trent made her come. All she could think about then was surviving the rush of pleasure long enough for him to do it again.

He gripped her hips, but his arms froze, as if he wasn't sure whether to pull her closer or lift her away. "We're not going to do this," he whispered.

Elise merely smiled and cupped her breasts in her palms, offering them to him in open invitation.

Trent groaned and closed his eyes.

As if she'd let him escape that easily. The man needed to have a little fun, to let go. And she was just the woman to make it happen.

She leaned down so that her nipples grazed his chest and pressed her open mouth against the side of his throat.

Trent sucked in a breath and let it out in a harsh curse. "You play dirty."

Elise grinned against his neck and flicked her tongue out to taste his skin. His taste went to her head. He made her feel sexy. He made her feel unstoppable, like a force of nature. With him at her side, there was nothing she couldn't do.

In that moment, Elise realized that she was going to do whatever it took to keep him. They'd deal with whatever problems they had to, but in the end, he was going to be hers for as long as they could make it last.

"I'm not playing at all," she said.

He rolled her over and covered her nipple with his mouth. He drew her deep, making rocketing streaks of sensation rip through her until they pooled in her womb. Trent's fingers slid over her ribs and belly, and snaked down to her labia. He didn't need any help finding the spot that made her squirm. His aim was perfect. She was moments away from making John blush with her screams, and all it took was the tip of one finger.

He stopped at the last second and said, "Oh, no, you don't. I'm not letting you get away that easily—not after the way you teased me."

"Teasing is when you're not willing to follow through. I'm willing." Ready and eager.

Trent's fingers moved, leaving her hanging. Sexual need gripped her by the throat and didn't let go.

He slid his hands beneath her panties and pulled them off, then he settled down between her splayed thighs. The first flick of his tongue had her lifting up off the bed. The second had her jerking the other pillow over her face to keep from embarrassing them. After that, she lost count.

Trent teased her, tortured her, and nearly made her beg to let her come. Every time she got close, he backed off until she was ready to scream.

Elise wasn't the type of woman who begged, but she was seriously considering it when he moved away, leaving her panting and covered in a sheen of sweat.

Her arms were almost too weak to move, but she managed to get the pillow off her face long enough to see him get a condom out of his bag. He rolled it on and came back to her, giving her no time to change her mind.

Not that she would.

She thought he'd cover her body with his and take her, but instead, he lifted her up until she was straddling his hips again.

"Like this," he told her. "I want it like this."

Elise was more than happy to oblige.

Trent's head was about to explode. Elise was the most beautiful, sexiest woman he'd ever seen.

She sank down on him, taking him slow and deep. Each rocking motion she made as she worked to join them fully made her breasts jiggle enticingly. He liked breasts as much as any straight man, but Elise's drew his attention like no other woman's ever had. They made his mouth water and his palms ache to touch.

Her eyes were closed and her head was thrown back as she rode him. Each graceful curve and soft hollow of her body called to him to touch and taste. Her skin was softer than any he'd ever touched, and the scent of it drove him wild.

His body hummed with need, demanding release, but he held it back and enjoyed the view. He could watch her like this—all pink and blissed out—forever. It was the kind of sight a man could drown in and be happy he'd had the chance.

Her pace sped, and the soft sighs escaping her lips became needful cries. She was close. He could feel the fine tremors inside her, vibrating along the length of his cock, and he knew he wasn't going to last much longer either.

Her fingers curled against his chest, clutching and releasing in time with her strokes. Her thighs clamped his. She held her breath, pressed down fully, driving him as deep as he could go, and then she flew. Her cry of release was sweet and clear, filling his head and making him feel complete somehow.

There wasn't time to figure it out, though. His dick had other plans as his climax slammed into him and shoved him over the edge of pleasure. His muscles locked down as he throbbed in time with Elise's body. Each milking squeeze made him gasp and jerk as he came inside her.

Finally, when his lungs were burning and his throat was raw, the climax slowed and gave up its stranglehold.

Elise collapsed against him, panting. Trent stroked her back with clumsy hands. He wanted nothing more than to give into the pull of sleep, but he couldn't risk the condom leaking.

He lifted her away and eased her down onto the bed. She didn't bother to open her eyes.

Trent pulled the sheet up over her naked body, took care of the condom, and went right back to her side.

He belonged here with her. Maybe it was the sex talking, but he felt right here, stroking her cooling skin, feeling her slowing heartbeat.

He wasn't much of a believer in perfection, but as far as he was concerned, Elise was the perfect woman.

Gary was back. Ashley heard his steady, even gait outside her door.

She pressed her ear against the cold metal, listening. She heard his voice, then the sound of another heavy metal door shutting. Another door opened, he spoke, closed the door.

There was at least one other woman down here—one woman who was going to die tonight by her hand.

Ashley stifled a shiver and glanced at the table where her tools lay. She'd made sure not to leave any obvious signs of what she intended to do, for fear he'd stop her. Gathering everything from her hiding place under the blankets would take precious seconds, but she had no choice. She had to risk those seconds and hope that Gary wasn't able to escape this building before it was too late.

A key slid into the lock and she jumped back away

from the door. A second later, Gary appeared, holding a tray of food.

He shut the door behind him and set the tray down on the table. The whole time, he watched her, his oil-slick eyes narrow with suspicion.

"What has my pet been up to today?" he asked her.

"Nothing," she said, a little too quickly.

His brows lifted. "Really? Why don't I believe you? And why are your cheeks pink?"

Ashley's hands flew to cover her cheeks, cursing herself for allowing a guilty blush to give her away. "Maybe I caught Constance's fever."

A slow, sinister smile twisted his mouth. "Not yet, you haven't."

He stepped toward her and Ashley backed away, unable to stop her instinctive reaction. She bumped into the wall and pressed herself against it.

Gary closed the gap between them, almost touching her. "But you will. Soon."

He cupped her cheek in his hand. She caught the scent of something harsh and floral, like rubbing alcohol and perfume. Or fingernail polish remover.

Ashley's stomach heaved, and she ground her teeth to keep from throwing up. She couldn't stand the thought of being any weaker than she was.

She tried to jerk her head away from his touch, but his fingers slid through her hair, holding her in place with a tight grip.

"You never told me you had a sister," said Gary.

It took a moment for the meaning of his words to sink in. "You stay away from her," warned Ashley.

Gary let out a laugh that sounded cultured and

elegant, like he was at some kind of cocktail party. "She's looking for you. I think I'm going to let her find you."

"Don't you dare."

"She'll take good care of you, I'm sure. Right to the very end."

Dear God, no. Not that. Ashley couldn't let that happen. She couldn't let Elise go through what she had gone through with Constance.

Gary leaned forward until his nose was against her neck, and he breathed in deeply. "I love that smell," he said. "Terror and helplessness. I just can't get enough."

He pulled back to look down at her. "I'm not going to be able to wait much longer. Good thing your sister is clever and resourceful. It won't take her long to figure out the clue I left her."

"What clue?" asked Ashley, dreading the knowledge even as she asked for it.

"The one I carved into Constance's stomach."

Elise woke up to find Trent watching her. Judging from the fading light outside, she'd slept the whole day away.

"Did you get any rest?" she asked him. He was fully dressed, unlike herself. It had been hot in the bedroom. The southern windows had allowed the sun to heat the room all day, and now it was nearly stifling. She'd kicked the sheet off at some point, leaving her completely nude.

"Enough." The golden flecks in his eyes were glowing bright as he stared down at her naked body.

"What time is it?"

"Almost seven."

She'd been asleep for hours, despite the heat. Apparently, she'd reached the end of her strength and needed to recharge. She only hoped it made a difference in the search for Ashley. "Has Detective Woodward called?"

"Not yet. He probably didn't have anything new to report."

Disappointment rose in the back of her throat, bitter and searing. "I was hoping he would. I'm not sure where we go from here without any leads."

"I'll call him for you." Trent fished his phone out of his pocket and dialed. "Hi, Ed."

He listened briefly and from the way his face hardened, Elise knew it wasn't good news.

She pressed a hand to her mouth to hold back the cry of denial. She was tired of jumping to the conclusion that Ashley was dead every time the phone rang, but she couldn't seem to make herself stop. Her mind just went there of its own volition, and there was nothing she could do to stop it.

"It's not Ashley," Trent said to her. Into the phone, he said, "We'll be there as soon as we can." He hung up.

"What?" asked Elise.

"You need to get dressed. They found another body— Susan Maloney. Or what's left of her."

Ashley's hands shook as she used the strip of fabric stretched across a plastic hanger to spin the pencil, trying to create enough friction to light the little pile of wood shavings and paper strips on fire.

Her dinner sat untouched next to her. The condensation forming on the plastic cup of ice water slid down the side, marking off the seconds as they passed. Every slow drip made it less likely that Gary was still here to die along with them in the fire.

If she could get the blasted thing started.

Frustration rose up in her, hot enough to make her throat burn, but it did no good in helping spark a blaze. Her arm was tired, but she refused to give up so soon. A rest break might allow that devil to get away to kill again.

He wanted Elise. Ashley wasn't going to let him find her.

She forced her arm to move faster, ignoring the burn deep in her muscles.

A wisp of smoke more delicate than her last shred of hope wafted up from the pencil.

Ashley held her breath, fearing she'd blow out the spark before it had time to take root.

A bigger tendril of smoke rose up, and inside the nest of pencil shavings, she could hear a faint crackle of burning wood.

She kept the pencil spinning, and in seconds, the infant fire was born. With as much care as her trembling hands allowed, she moved a crumpled ball of paper near the tiny glowing spot. It blackened, then glowed as it caught fire.

Everything she needed was close at hand. She grabbed the roll of toilet paper and fed it to the small fire, making it grow. Next, she lit the edge of her sketchbook and took it over to the bed.

The blanket went up in a whoosh of heat and light, giving off acrid smoke.

Ashley coughed and stepped away, instinctively covering her face with her hands. Not that it was going to help her much. In a few more minutes, the smoke would overpower her and she wouldn't live long enough to know whether or not her plan to kill Gary had worked.

She backed against the wall and slid down to the ground, watching as the flames crept higher.

CHAPTER EIGHTEEN

There was no way Trent was going to let Elise see Susan Maloney's body. She didn't need that kind of image in her head at all, much less tied to her sister.

If they never found her, this was the picture that would fill Elise's mind every time she wondered what had happened to Ashley.

Both her hands were missing, as was her left leg from the knee down. Her head was also gone. A perfect two-inch square of skin had been removed from her stomach, leaving a gaping wound. There was no blood, but streaks of mud were smeared across her pale flesh. Bits of vegetation were tangled in her pubic hair, along with a film of green slime from the water.

Trent looked back up the weed-infested hill to where Elise stood behind the yellow plastic tape. She was wringing her hands, standing on tiptoe in an effort to see what they'd found. Trent was confident she couldn't see the body from there. It was in a shallow depression near the water's edge, hidden by grass and debris.

Detective Woodward had been right to make her stay

back. He'd given her the story that she didn't know how to not contaminate a crime scene. Trent could go because he did, which was why he was well back from the area, but that's not why he was standing here over the mutilated body of this poor woman.

He was there because Woodward knew Elise shouldn't be, and unless Trent was here, she wasn't going to take no for an answer.

"How did you know it was Susan?" Trent asked Woodward.

"Birthmark. Her mother told us about it when she went missing. We'll have Mrs. Maloney ID her, just to be sure, but it's a safe bet that the head we found downstream belongs to this body."

Susan's head.

"Is he getting sloppy?"

"A few hours ago, I would have said yes."

"But not now?"

Woodward shook his head. He hadn't stopped looking at Susan's corpse, like he was trying to memorize it or something.

Maybe he was forcing himself to face the consequences of not finding this psycho yet.

Woodward sighed. "I didn't want Elise to know yet, not until I talked to you, but we found another body three miles from here."

A sick sense of doom cascaded through Trent's limbs. "Ashley?"

"No. This time he left all the pieces together in a trash bag so we could ID her."

"Then why don't you want Elise to know?"

"Because her name was carved into this woman's body."

"Elise's name?"

"Yeah. Along with a bunch of numbers. We've got guys working on what it might mean, but it's clear the message was for Elise."

"He wants her," said Trent, feeling the truth of it sitting cold in his belly.

"That was my guess."

"He's not going to get her." No way was Trent going to allow that asshole to lay a finger on Elise. Not while he still drew breath.

"I figured you'd say something like that, which is why I was hoping you could help me convince her to go into protective custody."

"She's not a witness."

"No, but the Bureau is stepping in to help with the case, and they're willing to foot the bill."

"What are they getting out of it?"

Woodward finally took his eyes off Susan and gave Trent a guilty stare. "Bait."

"Fuck that," snarled Trent. "There's no way I'm letting her put herself out there like that."

"It's not your decision. I know she'll want to do this."

"So do I, which is why we need to convince her not to, rather than trying to talk her into dangling herself in front of this psycho like a worm on a hook."

"I know these guys," said Woodward. "They'd be careful with her. She'd be safer than she is now."

"I don't see how."

"For one thing, she won't have armed assassins breaking into her hotel room anymore. She'd be under guard 24/7."

"It's not worth the risk."

"Maybe to you it's not, but what about to her?"

"Don't you dare tell her about the other body, or the message."

"I don't want to tell her unless she's willing to go with the feds. Otherwise, she might try something stupid and try to take the killer down herself. That's why I need your help here."

"If she doesn't know, she can't act."

"It's not like she won't find out. It's not exactly easy to hide news about a dead body from the press."

"Fine, then hide the message. Cover it up. Don't publicize it."

"So, you think we should pretend we never saw it, let Elise go along her merry way and hope this guy doesn't catch up to her before we can find him? I've found unsolved cases dating back ten years that might be connected to this guy. Do you really think a guy who can kill for that long and get away with it—without us even knowing he exists—is going to be easy to find?"

"I know he's not, but you've got to be closer now. There's got to be evidence somewhere on these bodies, surveillance footage, people who saw him. Something."

"Believe me, we're working all the angles. There just isn't anything solid to go on right now. The bodies are clean. No fibers, no prints, no skin under the fingernails, no semen. If we found the bone saw he used, we could probably connect it to the bodies, but we have no idea where to start looking. We've got young, blond, female undercover officers working to bring him out of hiding, but so far, he hasn't taken any of our bait. That's why we need Elise."

"No. You can't ask her to do this."

"I'm sorry, Trent. I thought you'd see how important this is, but since you don't, I have no choice but to tell her everything and let her make up her own mind."

"If you do, she'll get herself killed." Mutilated and sliced up into pieces like the woman lying in the muddy weeds.

"If I don't, a lot more women are going to die. I can't take that chance."

"It's not your chance to take. It's hers." And Trent was going to see to it that Elise left the country before she could.

Elise saw Trent march up the riverbank, his face grim. An officer lifted the yellow police tape to let him pass, and he headed right for her.

Trent took her arm and swept her up in his wake. "Time to go," he said.

"Where?"

"To the airport. I'm getting you on the next flight out of here. Decide where you want to go."

"Go?" She had no idea what was going on, or what he'd seen that had spooked him, but she wasn't about to let him manhandle her like this.

Elise straightened her legs, trying to stop him, but he simply lifted her up with one strong arm and kept on walking toward the car. She swatted him, but he didn't slow.

"Put me down right now and tell me what the hell happened down there."

"I will. On the way to the airport."

They reached the car, and he set her down long enough to unlock the doors with the remote. Elise took the opportunity to swipe it away from him and tucked the keys deep into her pocket.

She backed up so he couldn't reach her. "Now, Trent. You're going to tell me now."

His face had hardened into a murderous expression, making the muscles in his jaw bulge. "Give me the keys."

"Not until you stop acting like a Neanderthal, tossing me around as you please, ordering me to do things. I don't take kindly to being bossed around."

He pulled in a deep breath that stretched his shirt over his pecs, then let it out slowly. "I'm sorry if I offended you. I'll explain everything if you just get in the car. Please."

Detective Woodward walked toward them, his stride hurried. He had a worried look on his face, but when he saw Elise standing there, it changed to relief.

"Good. You haven't left yet," he said. "My friend from the FBI is at the station asking for you."

"Me?" said Elise.

"Yeah. She wants some time with you, if you don't mind."

"Why?"

"She thinks it will help complete her profile of the killer."

Elise had no idea how it could help, but she was willing to play along. "Sure. Anything I can do to help."

"I was just taking her to the airport," said Trent in

a tone that indicated the detective should have already known that.

Woodward glared at him. "I know all about what you were doing."

"That makes one of us," said Elise. "Care to fill me in? Trent won't."

Trent shot him a look so thick with warning, the air between them wavered.

Detective Woodward hesitated. "He's worried about you. We all are."

"Worry less about me and more about Ashley, and I'll be fine."

"Bodies are piling up, Elise. You should leave town and let the police and FBI handle it from here."

"Is that why you were taking me to the airport? To shove me on a plane and get me out of the way?"

Trent didn't even have the decency to look guilty. "They don't need your help anymore. You're only going to get in the way."

"Then why is there someone waiting at the station to talk to me?"

Trent glared at the detective. "Because Woodward is an ass."

Elise didn't know what was going on between these two, but she had other things to worry about. "Are you going to let me down there to see Susan?"

"No," said both men at the same time. At least they agreed on something.

"Why don't you go back and meet with the profiler, and Trent and I will go over some things here."

"I'm going with her," said Trent.

"She'll be fine at the station, surrounded by cops."

"I'll drive her and come back."

Woodward gritted his teeth. "I was hoping you'd stick around a bit longer. There's something I wanted to show you. I'll get a patrolman to escort her back."

Trent looked at Elise for a long time, as if trying to decide.

Screw that. She'd been making her own decisions for a long time now, and she wasn't about to hand the reins over to someone else.

She dug the keys out of her pocket and walked around the car to the driver's side. "Call me if you need me." She got in the car and shut the door.

"Elise, wait," said Trent.

She started the engine, rolled down the window, and cast him an impatient stare.

"I . . . Be careful." He'd been about to say something else, but Elise didn't have the time to figure out what.

"I will." Then he leaned through the window and kissed her, and she no longer cared about what he was going to say, or why he was acting so odd. All she knew was that his mouth was on hers, his breath was filling her lungs, and the scent of him surrounded her.

It was a sweet, gentle kiss, tinged with helpless desperation. He pulled away slowly, caressing her cheek with his thumb. He looked into her eyes, and the splinters of gold shone bright, surrounded by blue. "Stay safe. I'll come get you as soon as I can, and then we'll talk."

"There's nothing to talk about. I'm not leaving until we find Ashley."

"You could get hurt."

Part of her wondered if it wasn't already too late. Walking away from Trent wasn't going to be easy. She'd fallen for him somewhere along the way, and even though she knew their two lives could never blend together into one, leaving him was going to hurt.

"We all get hurt sometimes," she said. "I'll survive."

Ashley woke up with the stench of smoke stinging her nostrils. She opened her eyes, expecting to see the flames, feel the heat of them searing her skin, but instead, all she saw was textured white ceiling.

She blinked a few times, trying to clear her head. Had she dreamed about setting the fire? If so, why did she smell it?

Her head was pounding and her throat was raw. She needed some water to ease her throat and wash away the grit drying her eyes, but when she tried to get up to go to the bathroom, she couldn't move.

Her arms and legs were strapped down.

Panic exploded behind her eyes, and a high cry of fear bubbled up out of her.

"Good," said Gary from somewhere on her left. "You're awake."

He sounded cheerful.

Ashley turned her head, more because of reflex than because she wanted to see him. His clothes were charred, and he had a nasty burn on his forearm. His usually flawless hair was mussed, and a fine chalky powder coated the glossy strands. His face was pinched with rage, but it was his eyes that scared the hell out of her. Those oil-slick eyes were bulging with fury, glowing with malice.

Instinctively, she tried to run away from whatever he had planned, but there was nowhere she could go. She thrashed around uselessly, making the table she was strapped to vibrate against the concrete floor.

"That was a naughty trick you tried to pull," he said as he reached beneath the table and did something to make a metallic clicking sound. "Now I have to punish you."

The table started to move, folding her into a sitting position.

Panic throbbed through her system with every beat of her heart. Tears streamed from her eyes, burning hot against her cheeks. She fought against the bonds holding her down, but it was no use. The restraints held firm, thrusting her into his mercy.

The man had none. If she hadn't realized it before, as soon as he stepped aside enough to clear her view, she was sure.

A young woman who couldn't have been more than twenty sat trapped into the chair Constance had died in. She was held in place with wide leather bands, and a blue cloth had been shoved into her mouth. The pitiful whimpers she made were barely audible over the sound of Ashley's racing pulse.

"You tried to kill us all tonight," said Gary. "It almost worked, too. I never would have thought you were that resourceful, but now I know better. Thankfully, I had a fire extinguisher on hand."

He moved across the room to the frightened, gagged girl.

"Of course, your room was destroyed. I'll have to rebuild it before I can have another guest stay there."

"Good," she spat out with bravado she could only pretend to feel. "Serves you right, you sick fucker."

"Sick?" he said, his tone filled with a creepy kind of blandness, as if he were discussing his dry-cleaning bill. "Hardly. I simply like things a certain way."

"You *like* cutting off women's hands?"

"Among other things."

Ashley was going to puke. She was going to lose her stomach right here and vomit all over herself, making matters worse.

"But today, we're going to try something new. You wanted to set us all on fire, so I'm going to give you your wish. Sort of."

He lifted an acetylene torch, twisted the knob to start the flow of gas, and lit it. A blue flame shot out like a spear.

The gagged woman let out a muffled cry of panic.

Ashley was beyond making noise. Her throat had clamped down hard, shutting off her air supply. She knew what he was going to do. She could see the excited gleam glowing in the oily depths of his gaze as he smiled at her.

Gary moved the torch toward the young woman's bare toes. "We'll start at the bottom and work our way up, shall we?"

CHAPTER NINETEEN

Elise thought the FBI profiler looked too young to know what she was doing. Her dark hair was pulled back into a tight bun, and the glasses perched on her dainty nose had lenses too small to be of any use other than making her seem more intelligent. She wore a black pantsuit, but the cut was too trendy to be reassuring.

Agent Robin Laurens looked like she was playing a role in a TV show, and had been cast for her good looks rather than what was inside her head.

"Can you tell me a bit about what kind of men your sister dated?" asked Agent Laurens.

"I don't see how this is going to help." Elise also didn't understand why she'd thought this was a good idea when she could be back at the crime scene with Detective Woodward, helping look for clues. Sure, she wasn't trained, but that didn't mean she couldn't help. Maybe she'd see something they didn't—something only she would know about Ashley that would help find her. What if something that belonged to Ashley was there and they didn't recognize it?

Agent Laurens swept the glasses from her face in a dramatic move. "I realize this is difficult for you, but it's important. Having an accurate profile of the killer can help track him down. It can help us understand his patterns and define an area in which to look for him. It can even tell us what kind of profession he may have."

Elise gripped the paper cup of coffee and sighed in frustration. She was here, she might as well play along. "Ashley likes calm guys."

"Calm?"

"Steady, levelheaded. She doesn't go for the flighty artistic types—she butts heads with them too much."

"What else? Any physical characteristic she might find more appealing?"

"She appreciates men who stay in shape. She goes for men who are older than her by a few years—late twenties, early thirties."

"How old is she?"

"Twenty-two."

Agent Laurens scribbled something down. "What about hair color, eye color?"

"She wasn't fond of blonds when we were younger, but she hasn't mentioned any similar aversion since she was out of high school. Her tastes may have changed."

"Does she tend to date a lot of men?"

"Yeah. She said she was too young to settle for just one. She likes the attention she gets from a new guy— one who isn't bored with her. She likes the thrill and excitement of a new relationship."

"Do you know of any men she's rejected who might want to exact some kind of revenge on her?"

Elise shook her head. "If there was one, she wasn't aware of it, or at least she never mentioned it to me."

"Do you think she would have hidden something like that from you?"

"No, I don't. And if I'd thought there was some scorned lover in the mix, I would have mentioned it a long time ago. I'm not an idiot."

Agent Lauren's lips tightened in irritation. "I'm sorry if I came across as accusing you of that. It wasn't my intent."

"I should be doing something more than sitting here with you. This isn't getting us anywhere."

"It will, Ms. McBride. I know what I'm doing."

"I hope so, because my sister has been missing for a week now. If we don't find her soon . . ."

Agent Laurens laid her hand on Elise's arm. "There are a lot of people working on this case. We'll find this man and put him away forever."

"That's great, but I'm much more interested in finding Ashley."

Ed Woodward walked into the small office with Trent right on his heels. Whatever was going on had Trent mad enough that his face was dark red and his mouth was drawn into a thin, flat line.

"Hey, Robin," said the detective. "Glad you could come."

"No problem, Ed. I owe you after that thing last fall."

"Mind if I interrupt for a minute?"

"Go ahead." Agent Laurens stood and offered Detective Woodward her seat.

"This is a mistake, Woodward," said Trent.

Elise looked from one man to the other, trying to figure out what was going on. "What's a mistake?"

Detective Woodward placed a notebook in front of her. Across the page was scrawled a bunch of numbers. "Any idea what this means?"

Elise had no clue. "Sorry. What is it?"

"Don't." Trent uttered the harsh command.

"Don't what, Trent? Why are you acting so odd?"

"I don't want you involved in this any more than you already are."

"The message was left for her," said Woodward to Trent.

Elise frowned at the men in confusion. "What message?"

Woodward pointed to the paper. "These numbers. They were left on a victim."

"On Susan?"

"No. On the other victim we found tonight."

Another victim? Elise started shaking and her mind jumped once again to that single conclusion that scared her the most.

She pushed her chair back from the table and looked at Trent. She trusted him to tell her the truth. "Was it Ashley?"

"No."

"Her name was Constance Gregory," said Woodward. "And the man who killed her left this message for you."

"How do you know it was for me?"

"It had your name on it," said Trent, stepping over whatever Woodward had been about to say.

Elise looked at the paper again. There were six numbers on the top line, eight numbers on the middle line, a dash and eight more numbers on the last line. "Can I see the note?"

Trent spoke first. "No."

Woodward gave Trent a hard stare, then said, "It's evidence we don't want you to contaminate, but this is exactly how the message was written."

Elise stared, read the numbers aloud. "One-two-one-four-eight-eight. One-twenty-one, four-eighty-eight." Eighty-eight. That was the year Ashley was born. "Twelve, fourteen, eighty-eight. That's Ashley's birth date." A rush of victory flooded through her, until she realized what that meant. "He's giving me a message about my sister."

"What about the rest of it?" asked Woodward. "Does it mean anything to you?"

She ran through all the dates she could remember in her head: her parents' birthdays, anniversary, the dates they died. Nothing fit.

Agent Laurens leaned over her shoulder. "Do you have a copy of the note? A photograph?"

Woodward pulled her aside, opened a folder for Agent Laurens to see, and shut it again.

Her face had gone pale and she swallowed convulsively.

"Let me see," said Elise.

Trent stepped in front of Woodward, blocking him from sight. "You don't want to see this."

"She doesn't need to see it," said Agent Laurens. "I think I know what the numbers mean."

"What?"

"They're coordinates. He used freckles for the decimal places."

"Freckles? The note had freckles?" And then it hit Elise. He hadn't written the message on paper. He'd written it on a victim. That's why they didn't want her to see. "I can handle looking at crime scene photos."

"Not these," said Trent.

Agent Laurens had regained her composure, though her voice was not as steady as before. "You don't need to handle it. Latitude forty-one, longitude negative eighty-eight. That's near here, right?"

"Yeah," said Trent. "It's just south of here."

Elise froze in her seat. "He could be telling us where she is." Or where her body was.

Trent left the room and headed for the closest PC. Everyone followed.

He brought up an Internet connection and located the coordinates on an aerial map. "It's Sally's."

"The bar where Ashley was last seen?" said Woodward.

"Yeah."

"Does that mean Ashley is there?" asked Elise.

Woodward picked up a phone and dialed. "We'll know in a few minutes. I'll get some men over there to search the place."

Elise went back into the office and got her purse. "I'm going, too."

Trent shot up from the PC and caught her arm before she could get away. "It will take you at least a couple of hours to get there, even if you speed. Stay here, and you'll know what's going on sooner than if you drive there."

"But what if she needs me?"

"We don't even know if she's there. It's more likely

this is some kind of trap to lure you out where the killer can find you. If she needs anything, the authorities on the scene can handle it."

Elise hated waiting, sitting and doing nothing, but Trent was right. She was better off here, where the communication between police was best. Anything she heard over the phone would be secondhand knowledge.

The minutes ticked by. It was nearing the height of the rush at Sally's. The place would be packed. It was going to take the police a while to search the place.

Trent laid a comforting hand on her shoulder. Elise sat on the edge of her chair and watched the clock.

Gary needed new prey. It had been days since he'd last hunted, and already his mind was itching for the right target.

Gloria hadn't done anything to appease him—she hadn't done anything to settle the restlessness crawling inside him. He'd had to sacrifice her to teach Ashley a lesson: She was not in control. He was.

But in teaching that lesson, his beautiful dancer was no longer beautiful. She was a blackened corpse lying in a shallow grave—not even worthy of becoming part of his Wendy.

Gary didn't think he'd ever again be able to smell the scent of burning flesh without remembering the sound of her screams. His ears were still ringing.

At least he'd managed to wash her charred scent out of his hair.

He swept through the pulsing crowd at Sally's, looking for his next target. The brunettes and redheads faded into the background, leaving the blondes burning bright in his vision. There were so many to choose from, but he knew what to look for. He could see the signs of an artist from a mile away. They carried themselves differently— looked at the world differently. There was something ethereal about them that he couldn't quite describe but knew instantly on sight.

A dancing woman bounced into him, jarring him as he passed. Gary righted her back onto her feet.

She flashed him a wide smile. "Sorry," she shouted over the music.

He continued on without responding. She wasn't worthy of his notice.

She wasn't Elise.

That's what his problem was. He couldn't find Elise.

He realized in that moment that none of these women were going to suit him, not even as a temporary distraction. He'd already chosen the woman he wanted.

Gary's phone buzzed against his hip. He pulled it out and answered his brother's call, though he doubted he'd be able to hear anything over the music. "Hello?"

". . . Sally's . . . out."

Gary pressed the phone tighter against his ear. "What?"

"Police raid . . . get out."

Ah. So they'd found Constance.

A slow, simmering excitement bubbled up inside him. If the police had his message, it would only be a matter of time before Elise did, too. She'd come here soon.

"Hold on," he said to Lawrence.

Gary made his way toward the exit. He wasn't worried about the police showing up. Even if they checked his ID, it wouldn't matter. His record was clean. He paid his bills, paid his taxes, voted. He'd never had so much as a speeding ticket. He even served jury duty when called. Anyone looking at him would see exactly what he wanted them to: a law-abiding citizen who did his civic duty.

As soon as he was outside and in his car, he asked, "What did you hear?"

"An informant of mine at the CPD heard they're going to raid Sally's. It's going down right now. You're there, aren't you?"

"I'm leaving." But he'd watch from a distance, searching for a glimpse of Elise. Once the fanfare died down, she'd come here. She'd want to see for herself that Ashley wasn't here.

Of course, Gary couldn't pounce on Elise here. Doubtless, the police would be watching her, using her as bait in a trap that wouldn't spring. No, he'd wait until later, when no one was watching, to make his move. All he needed was for her to come back where he could find her. Then she'd be his.

"What did you do? How did they find you?" Lawrence's demands stabbed Gary's ears, ruining his anticipation.

"They haven't found anything I didn't want them to."

"Then why are they raiding Sally's?"

"Because I asked them to."

"Are you mad?" shouted Lawrence.

"I want Elise McBride. The only way to find her is to draw her out of hiding."

"She's not hiding, you idiot, she's in Chicago with the police."

"How do you know?"

"I know a lot of things. I keep my ear to the ground. I use my contacts."

The Mob. Lawrence used to transport drugs and firearms for them in coffins. Knowing him, he'd probably even burned a few bodies for them like he used to do for Gary. "I thought you quit doing favors for them years ago."

"I do what I'm told. You should follow my example and go home. Stay put until all of this dies down."

"I want Elise."

Lawrence let out a long, gusty sigh. "Fine. I'll bring her to you."

"I want to do my own hunting."

"I don't care what you want. If you get caught, you're going to mess up everything I've worked so hard to create."

"Everything *you've* worked to create? What about my work?"

"You kill women. You chop them up into pieces. There's no profit in that."

"And it's all about profit to you, isn't it?"

"That, and prestige."

"It's more than that," said Gary. "You get excited being around all those dead people. You get a rise out of playing the somber, sophisticated comforter to the families, while behind the scenes, you're toying with their loved ones."

"I do not!"

"Have you ever screwed one of them?"

Gary could hear his brother sputtering with rage on the other end of the line. "I've never been anything but professional."

"Except when you ran drugs for the Mob."

"Enough! This isn't a game. You're going to get caught. You're going to ruin everything."

Of course it wasn't a game. Gary was deadly serious. "You don't have to tell me that. Just stay the hell out of my business."

"Go home, Gary. Stay away from Sally's. I mean it."

Blue lights glowed in the distance. It was time to move on. "Is Elise still in Chicago?"

"Yes, why?"

"I'm going to go find her." It was Friday night. He had the whole weekend before he had to be back at the bank. He could think of a lot of things he could do with Elise, Ashley, and an entire weekend.

Just the thought was enough to make his body heat. His pulse sped up, making him feel warm and complete again for the first time since he'd killed Constance.

"If I help you find her, you have to promise me you'll move away. I know better than to think you'd ever stop, but you've got to go. I'll help you buy a new identity. You can start over fresh somewhere else."

Gary liked living here, but he knew better than to defy Lawrence openly. He'd take the help he needed to find Elise, and then they would talk. He'd explain that this was his home, and he had as much right to live here as Lawrence did. If he didn't like it, *he* could leave.

Besides, now that Ashley had burned down part of his guest quarters, he had plans to renovate. This time, he'd build in a sprinkler system, just in case another one of his guests got creative. He couldn't tolerate that kind of mistake again.

Maybe he'd add some more rooms while he was at it.

He had a suspicion that once he'd gotten a taste of how sweet those two sisters were together, he was going to want more.

"Whatever you want," said Gary. "Just tell me where she is."

CHAPTER TWENTY

Woodward was still on the phone with Bob Tindle, who was in charge of the raid on Sally's Bar, so Trent went back to the office to break the bad news to Elise.

Her head jerked up as he came through the door. The look of hopeful expectation widening her gray-green eyes nearly broke his heart. He wanted so much to be able to tell her that Ashley was safe and sound.

"I'm sorry. Other than some illegal drugs, they didn't find anything at Sally's."

Her body seemed to bow under the disappointment. Her voice was small, defeated. "I really thought she'd be there. I thought this might be over."

Agent Laurens, who was sitting on the other side of the desk, stood up and quietly left the office. She shut the door behind her, leaving Elise and Trent alone.

Trent didn't hesitate to take advantage of the privacy. He pulled her into his lap, wrapped his arms around her, and held her close. The feel of her cheek against his chest gave him a sense of comfort, of rightness. He hoped she felt the same, though he doubted anything as mundane as a hug was going to make her content right now.

"I'm sorry, sweetheart. We were all rooting for a happy ending." Just not expecting one.

Trent's greatest fear had been that they'd find Ashley's body—that she'd have some message carved into her skin in that spidery, scrawled writing. If that had happened, Ashley's nightmare would be over, but Elise's would just be starting. She'd have to live with that memory, with the knowledge that she'd failed to find Ashley before it was too late.

It wouldn't have been Elise's fault. There wouldn't have been anything she could have done to change the outcome, but she would spend the rest of her life wondering. She'd spend the rest of her life playing the what-if game.

What if she'd come back to the U.S. sooner? What if she'd found that photo as soon as she arrived? What if she'd talked to the right person and gotten the one lead that could have located Ashley before she died?

Trent knew how draining the what-if game was. He knew how it could eat at a person's soul until they questioned every decision they made, every action they took until their life became stagnant and useless.

He didn't want that for Elise. She was a good sister. A good woman. She deserved better.

"So, what now?" she asked. He could hear the weariness winding through her words, but still she pushed on.

Time to man-up. As much as he hated the idea of letting her go, he knew it was time. If she stayed around longer, she might get hurt. "I think you should leave town. Go back to work."

"While Ashley is still missing? Are you crazy?"

"There's nothing more you can do. We've got a ton of police working on her case, and now the FBI's Violent Crimes Task Force is on the job, too. They'll find her."

"I can't move on with my life like nothing's happened."

"When they find her, you can come back." As long as they'd also found the sicko who'd taken her. The fact that he'd addressed his macabre message to Elise meant he'd fixated on her. Until he was behind bars—or dead—the safest place for her was well outside his reach.

She shook her head, and he could feel the soft slide of her blond curls over his shirt. "I can't. I have to stay and help, even if I'm not really helping."

"It's not safe. If you stay, the FBI will ask you to play bait."

Her head popped up. "Really? Agent Laurens didn't say anything about it."

"Maybe not yet, but the longer this drags out, the more likely it becomes that she or someone else will approach you about it."

"You make it sound like a bad thing. Why wouldn't I want to help them?"

"Because it's dangerous?"

"Yeah. So?"

"So, you could get hurt. Killed."

"I could also help them find Ashley. I could help them stop this killer."

"It's too risky."

"It's my risk to take. I get to decide if it's too risky or not."

Even though it pissed him off, he forced himself to say, "Of course you do, but you have to realize that the chances of something like that working are slim. If this guy is smart enough to have been killing women for years without anyone seeing the pattern, then he's smart enough to see through a trap."

"I have to take the chance, Trent. She's my sister."

And if Trent wanted to be there to make sure she was properly protected, he had to go along with her decision. If he didn't, she'd dump him on his ass like before and go do as she pleased without him. He had no illusions to the contrary. Ashley was a lot more important to Elise than he was, as much as it chafed him to admit it.

"Okay. If you're sure you want to do this, then let's go talk to them. We can at least see what kind of plan they have—how they're going to handle security details to ensure your safety."

"You're not going to fight me on this?" she asked.

"Would it do any good?"

"No. Sorry."

Trent pushed out a sigh and helped Elise to her feet. "That's what I figured you'd say. Let's go find Detective Woodward and see who we should talk to."

He started to walk away, but Elise wrapped her hand around his arm to stop him. She looked up at him, her eyes shining with gratitude. "Thank you, Trent. It means a lot to me to have you on my side."

She was so pretty, it nearly broke his heart to look at her. She had no idea how fragile she was—how vulnerable she was going to be if she went through with this.

He wished like hell there was some way to stop her, and he wondered if telling her he loved her would make a difference.

Trent's world ground to a halt as he realized the monumental shift his life had just taken. He loved Elise, and not just a little. It wasn't a crush or infatuation or lust, not this soul-deep feeling of completeness he had when she was near—of total and utter rightness. He loved her the way his dad loved his mom—enough to give her whatever she wanted, even though he hated every second of it. He hadn't meant to love her, but he did, and now he had to sit by and watch her put herself in danger to save a sister who might already be dead.

If he didn't do something to stop the words, they were going to spill out and make a bad situation worse. She didn't believe in love that lasted forever. She didn't believe in marriage, even though he couldn't imagine his life taking any other course than one that ended up with his ring on her finger.

He was a sap for feeling that way. Foolish. Things were stacked way too high against them for him to be considering something so huge and permanent.

He couldn't let her know how he felt. He didn't want to put that kind of pressure on her right now when she was already dealing with so much emotional overload.

Rather than say the words, he bent his head and kissed her mouth. She responded immediately, giving him what he wanted, letting him taste and feel her heated response.

"If you're trying to distract me with sex, you're going to have to at least find a room without spectators."

"Don't tempt me," he said. "I'd much rather have you

spread out naked, wet, and panting on the floor in front of everyone, than have you dangle yourself on a hook."

She laid her hand over his heart. "I'll be fine. Everyone will take good care of me, and I'm sure they won't let me take any unnecessary risks."

"You've got a lot more faith than I do."

"Of course I do. I have you on my side, right?"

"Every step of the way, sweetheart."

She beamed at the endearment. "Good. Now, let's go get this over with so I can get my sister back."

Trent said nothing; he merely nodded his head and led the way out the door.

Gary made the drive to Chicago in record time. At this time of night, the roads were nearly empty.

He cruised through the parking lot outside the police station, searching for Elise's rental car. His brother had been keeping track of her for a while, and he even knew the license plate number for the Mazda she'd been driving.

One of these days, Gary was going to have to talk to him about keeping secrets. Lawrence let slip that he'd hired people to kill her, and if that had happened, Gary would have had to punish him for taking away his sweet, lovely Elise.

Killing her was going to be his joy, and no one was going to take that away from him. All her screams, all her tears, belonged to him.

Gary spotted the sporty red car and parked in the slot next to it. He hated waiting, but it was better than walking into the police station and trying to sneak her out. This was much better. Besides, the anticipation wouldn't hurt him. Good things came to those who waited, and Gary was willing to be patient for just a while longer.

He adjusted his mirrors so he'd see her coming, then opened the file folder he'd brought with him.

It was full of articles Elise had written, each one succinct and eloquent. He didn't much care for the emotional pieces about sick children in countries crawling with famine and poverty. As far as he was concerned, those countries could fall off the face of the planet and it would be an improvement. She was wasting her time writing about that kind of drivel.

But the rest of the articles were good. Artistic, even. His sweet Elise had a level head and a keen insight.

Maybe he should keep her brain instead of her heart. Wendy had never been very bright, so replacing her brain with Elise's wasn't a bad thought.

No. There was no need to go to that trouble. It would only mess up Wendy's hair if he sawed her skull open. It had taken him months to get her blond hair to look just like it had the night of the accident—disheveled from their sex games, shining in the glow of moonlit snow, spattered with blood from her gushing wrist.

Gary liked Wendy's hair the way it was. He didn't want to ruin perfection.

With that decision made, Gary put the hat from the police costume he wore on his head and went back to reading the articles while he waited for Elise to come to him.

It was still dark when Trent and Elise left the police station to drive over to the Chicago division of the FBI. Even though it was so late it was nearly early morning, a special agent had been assigned to meet with her and discuss their options.

Apparently, they wanted to catch the guy who was abducting and killing women as badly as Elise did.

"I still think this is a bad idea," said Trent as he walked beside her.

"I know, but at this point, we've run out of options."

"That doesn't make me feel any better."

"The sooner we do this, the sooner it's all over, and the sooner we can go back to our lives."

At least he could. There was no way Elise was going to be able to leave Ashley alone again. Not after this. Her sister was going to need her to be there for her and help her get over this trauma. And just like now, Elise wasn't going to take no for an answer.

Her plans to travel the world and find those compelling stories were just going to have to wait until . . . whenever. She'd already had three years of her dream. That was more than most people ever got. Ashley had to come first, even if it meant putting Elise's life on hold indefinitely.

The security lights overhead cast deep shadows over the parking lot. Even as late as it was, the lot was still half full, giving proof to exactly how many men and women were at work keeping their city safe.

Beside her rental car, a uniformed officer sat in his car, talking on his cell phone. His window was down, and she could hear him saying something about a missing woman. Whether he was talking about something related to her sister's case or not, Elise wasn't clear.

On the ground beneath his car door was a shiny CD

that caught her attention. He must have dropped it when he got in his car and hadn't realized it.

"Want me to drive?" asked Trent. "I know the way."

"Sure." Elise handed him the keys.

He used the remote to unlock the doors. Elise went around to the passenger's side, trying to hear more of what the officer was saying without looking obvious about her eavesdropping.

The car rocked as Trent got in.

Elise picked up the lost CD, and tapped the man on the shoulder to get his attention. "Excuse me. I think you dropped this."

The man in the officer's uniform snapped his phone shut and said, "Thank you. That was kind."

He turned his head toward her. Shadows fell across the right side of his face, allowing her to see only a portion.

He was the man from the photo. The one who'd taken Ashley.

Elise pulled in a breath to scream and warn Trent, but it was too late. The man grabbed her wrist, capturing her. A matte-black gun appeared in his free hand and seemed to suck away the light all around him.

From the corner of her eye, she saw Trent start to move.

"Don't," said the man. "I will shoot her before you can stop me."

Trent froze in the driver's seat.

The man let go of Elise long enough to get out of his car, but he kept his eyes and his gun on her the whole time. She didn't dare move.

"Hand me your cell phones," he said.

"Do what he says, Elise."

She couldn't. Her body was stuck in place except for the slight tremors that shook her every few seconds.

Trent held his phone out, but not so far that the man didn't have to reach for it. She wasn't sure if he was trying to piss the killer off, or if he was trying to create an opportunity to grab the gun.

Humor laced the man's voice. "Nice try, but I'm not a stupid man. Elise, take the phone from him and toss it on the ground."

Elise managed to move enough to obey.

"And yours, too," said the killer.

"It's in my purse."

"Then dump the whole purse. You're not going to need it anymore."

Oh, God. That didn't sound good at all.

A hot wave of fear swept through her, making her break out into a sweat.

"Now," he ordered.

Elise took her purse from her shoulder and tossed it onto the asphalt at the killer's feet.

"Good. Now, I'm going to take you to see your sister. You'd like that, wouldn't you?"

Elise nodded.

"Say it. Say you want to go with me."

"I want to go with you."

A pleased smile pulled his mouth wide. "Let's go, then. I don't want to keep you waiting." He opened the car door for Elise. "I'm going to get in back, and your boyfriend is going to drive away, nice and slow. Understand?"

Trent gave a jerky nod. She could feel the anger and frustration radiating from him.

"Don't try anything heroic. Not only will it get the woman killed, we both know heroics are not your strong suit. The best thing you can do is follow orders like a good boy."

The killer kept the gun pointed at Elise while he opened the back door and got inside. Behind her, she felt the seat shift like he'd pressed something hard against it.

She had no doubts about what that hard thing was, nor did she doubt he'd use it.

"Close the car door," ordered the killer.

Elise's sweaty hand slipped on the handle, but she managed to get it shut.

"Where to?" asked Trent. His voice was tight and seething with barely controlled rage.

"South."

Trent started the engine and drove south.

CHAPTER TWENTY-ONE

Trent kept looking for an opening to take this guy down, but he saw none—at least none that wouldn't end with a bullet in Elise's back.

The fucker in the backseat never let down his guard. Hell, Trent hadn't even seen the man blink.

He'd ditched the hat a few miles back, giving Trent a clear view of his face. He was average-looking. He'd never stand out in a crowd, which was probably why he'd gotten away with killing for so long. He didn't look crazy or deranged. He didn't look like a killer. He looked . . . plain. Except for his eyes. They were dark, set deep in his face, and never missed a thing. His gaze darted between Trent, Elise, and the road, keeping watch over everything.

Trent had been hoping for a moment of distraction so he could try to get that gun away from Elise's back, but so far, there'd been none.

They'd been on the highway for a few minutes when Trent decided it was time to find a way to get inside this guy's head. If he could talk to him, maybe he'd be able to find a weakness—something he could exploit and use to save them. If nothing else, it might distract him enough that Trent could make a move.

"You're the one who took Ashley?" he asked, already knowing the answer.

"You know I am."

"Is she alive?" asked Elise. Her voice was breathless with fear.

"Yes. I've taken good care of her."

Not good. The confidence this guy oozed was not a good sign.

"How long have you been doing this?" asked Trent.

"Doing what?"

"Abducting women. Killing them."

"Not nearly long enough."

Trent glanced in the rearview mirror. "How many?"

A slow, creepy smile slid along the man's mouth. "That would be telling."

Traffic was light. Trent was speeding as fast as he dared while splitting his attention between the road and the killer. With any luck, they'd get pulled over, or the sirens might distract the man with the gun long enough that Trent could grab it and get it off Elise.

The fact that the muzzle of that weapon was only inches from her spine made every hair on Trent's body stand on end.

He gripped the steering wheel tighter and moved around a slow van. "How far are we going?"

"You'll know when we get there."

"We need to stop for gas."

The man laughed. "Nice try, but no."

Elise twisted her hands in her lap. They were shaking

so hard Trent had no trouble seeing it from the corner of his eye.

"Is Ashley . . . okay?" she asked.

"She's still in one piece. For now." The killer's satisfied smile filled the rearview mirror. "Has anyone told you what lovely hands you have?"

Elise made a sound like she was going to be sick.

"Leave her alone," growled Trent.

"Or what?"

"Or I'll plow this car into the median."

"The gun would go off and your pretty friend would end up like your former partner."

He'd considered that, which was why he hadn't done that very thing already. There was still a chance he'd find another way out of this mess. He wasn't sure what that was yet, but his eyes were wide open, looking for anything that might present itself.

"Slow down," said the killer. "We wouldn't want anyone pulling you over for speeding, would we?"

"No one is out at this time of night."

The man moved the gun up to the back of Elise's head. "Slow. Down."

Trent eased off the accelerator.

City turned to suburbs, and suburbs turned to rural countryside as they moved out of Chicago. He weaved over the road, praying someone would report him for drunk driving, but all he got for his trouble was a horn blast that made Elise jump in her seat.

Trent had lost track of how far they'd gone when the man said, "Exit here."

This didn't look good. The area was remote. Isolated.

Perfect for doing whatever one wanted without any witnesses.

The only good news was that they must be getting close to wherever it was they were going. Maybe close to Ashley. Once they stopped, Trent would have the opportunity to take the man out.

He hoped.

"Go left at the end of that fence."

"Where are we going?" asked Elise.

"Home."

"Is Ashley there?"

"Yes. She's going to be so happy to see you."

Trent turned where the man indicated. The road was a single-lane gravel path that led into blackness. There were no streetlights out here, only one distant yellow glow that indicated someone lived nearby.

The car slewed around on the loose gravel, so Trent slowed down. He flipped on his brights to get the lay of the land, but all he saw was rolling farmland, broken here and there by fences, trees, and rocks. Off to the right, his headlight gleamed off a small private lake surrounded by trees.

Small, but large enough to hide all sorts of crimes. And bodies.

"Pull over here," said the man. "Next to the water."

Warning bells gonged around inside Trent's head. If he didn't do something soon, neither one of them were going to make it out of this alive. This man was no amateur. He was armed, and he knew his way around out here. Trent didn't.

"Get out. Both of you."

Elise opened her door and got out. Immediately, the

killer grabbed her and shoved the gun against her back hard enough to make her wince.

Trent got out but left the car running, the lights on and the door open in case they needed to get away fast.

The killer jerked Elise's hair hard enough to make her gasp in pain, and gave Trent a knowing smile. "Move away from the car."

Trent moved.

"Come around to the front where I can see you better."

Trent went and stood in the beams of the headlights. He kept his body loose, his eyes on the killer. In the light, he could now see that the uniform the man wore wasn't an official one. It carried the wrong emblem, but it was probably close enough to fool most people. The hat was the real thing, though. So was the gun.

Anger burned hot and acidic in Trent's throat. If he ever managed to get his hands on that asshole, he was going to see to it that he suffered before he died for hurting Elise.

The killer pulled something off his belt and handed it to Elise. "Tie him up nice and tight."

He pushed her forward, making her stumble. She caught her balance and hurried to Trent's side. Fear made her face pale, but she was holding it together. Her whole body shook, but she hadn't shed a single tear or broken down the way most people would have.

It only made him love her more.

"Hold your hands out for her," said the killer.

Trent saw what she carried. It was plastic zip-tie handcuffs.

Once those went on, he was going to have a hell of a

time stopping the man from doing whatever it was he had planned.

"Nice and tight. No wiggle room."

"I'm sorry," whispered Elise.

Trent kept his voice low, barely a whisper. "It's okay. Just do what he says so you don't get hurt."

"Hold your hands up and let me see," ordered the killer.

Trent held them up in the headlights' glare, showing the killer she'd done as he'd asked.

"Elise, open the trunk. You, walk over here."

The man waited for him at the back of the car. The trunk popped open.

The killer was going to stuff him in the trunk and send the car into that lake. Trent was sure of it. Why else would he have stopped here next to the water? Why else was a dock on a lake so small, wide and sturdy enough to support a car's weight?

If Trent was going to do something, now was his last chance.

Trent moved like he was going to comply like a good little docile prisoner. He shuffled his feet over the dirt and kept his eyes down.

"Get in."

"No!" shouted Elise.

The killer grabbed her arm hard enough to make her squeak in pain. The barrel of the gun went to her head. "Get in the trunk."

Trent lifted his head and looked into Elise's eyes. "I love you," he told her. He might never again get the chance, and he didn't want to let the opportunity go by.

Her eyes widened with shock, and something gloriously beautiful took hold of her features. The fear was wiped away, and what was left in its place was the fierce determination of a woman who was going to get what she wanted.

She lifted her foot and pulled her elbow forward at the same time. Trent had been in enough fights with his brother to know what she planned even before she finished moving.

He charged just as her foot slammed down on the killer's, and her elbow flew into his gut.

The gun slipped away from her head, and that was all the opening Trent needed.

He barreled into the killer, giving him the full brunt of his momentum. His hands were still confined, and as they fell, he lost his balance.

Elise yelped and backed away.

Trent couldn't free his hands, so he slammed both of them into the killer's face. Blood spewed out from his nose, but it didn't seem to faze him. He let out a roar of fury and punched Trent in the neck.

With his hands bound, Trent was off-balance. He couldn't seem to steady himself.

The killer lifted the gun.

Trent realized too late that he hadn't unarmed the man.

He rolled away, trying to make himself a moving target.

He heard the boom as his body jerked from the blow. A searing pain swept out from his side, consuming him.

Elise screamed.

The gun went off again, only this time, Trent felt nothing.

CHAPTER TWENTY-TWO

Ed Woodward hung up the phone and stuck his head into the room where Agent Laurens was going over all the crime scene photos. "Hey, Robin, Ms. McBride never showed up to her meeting with Special Agent Sinclair. I can't get her or Trent on their cell phones."

Robin glanced at her stylish watch and frowned. "They've been gone almost two hours."

"Either Trent convinced her not to cooperate, or something happened. Come on."

"Where are we going?" Robin stood and followed him out the door.

"To check security footage of the parking lot and see who was driving. I wouldn't put it past Trent to simply take off with Elise to keep her out of this."

They turned the corner and walked past the back entrance of the station. Robin came to an abrupt stop.

Ed turned to see what she was looking at. "What?"

"Do your officers usually carry purses?"

Ed looked to where she pointed. Dave Fowls had just

come in from the parking lot. He clutched a brown purse in his hands.

"No."

"It's Elise's," said Robin as she headed for the man, her stride long and confident.

Ed hurried after her. "How do you know?"

"I was trying to avoid looking at the cheap, mud-brown thing all day. Believe me. It's hers."

Ed wouldn't have known a cheap purse from an expensive one if his life depended on it, but Robin was always impeccably dressed. He trusted that she knew her way around a handbag.

He lifted his voice so Dave could hear him over the station's noise. "Hey, Dave. Is there ID in that purse?"

Dave reached inside and pulled out a passport as Robin and Ed reached his side. "Elise R. McBride. Isn't that the lady whose sister is missing?"

"Yes," said Ed, "and now she is, too."

Elise watched in horror as the killer shot Trent again.

Blood bloomed out over his shirt and darkened one thigh. Trent stopped moving and lay still and quiet in the dirt.

The killer stood up, keeping Trent in his sights the whole time. His shoulders rose and fell with his labored breathing, and he wiped a hand across his face.

In the glow of the headlights, Elise saw blood wet on his fingers.

He didn't even bother to turn around when he said, "He's still alive. Try to run and I'll shoot him in the head."

Elise stood right there, not daring to move a muscle.

I love you.

He'd said those magic words to her, and they'd changed her entire world. He hadn't just been saying them as a distraction either. She'd been looking into his eyes when he spoke. He'd meant every word.

He loved her, and now he lay on the ground, bleeding because of her.

She never should have taken the risk of fighting back. If she hadn't, Trent wouldn't have attacked. He wouldn't have been shot.

She was shivering with shock by the time the killer walked toward her. He wasn't pointing his weapon at her, but he didn't have to. She knew he'd use it if she so much as twitched.

She wasn't afraid of dying as much as she was of not being able to save Trent. "Let me stop his bleeding," she begged.

"No, I'll do it," said the killer. "But first, let's make sure you don't run off."

He grabbed her wrist and dragged her across the broken ground to a tree. He looped one end of the plastic handcuff around her wrist and the other around a thick branch of a young tree. He pulled the plastic tight until it cut into her skin, securing her in place.

"Stay put."

"Please hurry," she said. "He's losing a lot of blood."

The killer smiled at her, then went back to where Trent lay. He pulled his booted foot back and kicked Trent in the ribs with a force that would have incapacitated a grown man.

Trent didn't even flinch. His body flopped over the ground, and he lay still and silent.

It was then that Elise realized the man had lied. He had no intention of helping Trent. He was going to kill him. She'd been a fool to think otherwise.

Maybe he'd lied about Ashley being alive, too.

Elise felt hot tears fall down her cheeks.

The man dragged Trent over the ground, heedless of the blood seeping from his side. He holstered his gun, then heaved Trent up toward the open trunk of the car.

Elise could see what came next. He wasn't going to kill Trent quickly. He was going to drown him.

Fury swelled inside her, making her vision blur with the force of it. She was not going to stand here and let this happen. Chances were she wasn't going to survive the night. She sure as hell wasn't going to spend her last moments being a victim.

She pulled at the cuff on her wrist. The tree branch swayed but bounced back. She pulled harder, trying to work the plastic loop toward the narrow end of the branch.

The thin bark scraped away as she tugged, leaving behind green scars in the wood. Her wrist started to bleed, but that was the least of her worries. The killer had managed to lift Trent's bulk into the trunk.

Trent was too big to fit easily, but the man shoved hard several times until the trunk lid latched.

Elise pulled harder, moving the cuff a couple of inches until it ran into a smaller branch. With her free hand, she bent that branch, trying to break it, but it was too green to snap.

Leaves dropped from the tree, shaken loose by her efforts.

The killer got into the car and drove it onto a wide wooden dock. He got back out and went around to the rear of the car. He fetched a jack from a large plastic tub at the end of the dock and shoved it under the back of the car.

As he started to jack the car up off its back wheels, Elise knew she was nearly out of time.

Frantically, she jerked on the cuff and the tree limb, trying to make one give way. She managed to break the smaller branch off, but it left behind a stubby bit of soggy splinters behind. She was going to have to get the cuff over that bump.

Blood leaked out from under the plastic, making it slip along her skin. She twisted to get a better angle and pulled with all her strength. The hard edge burned as it cut into her flesh, but she didn't ease off the pressure.

She glanced over her shoulder and saw that the car had been jacked up all the way. The killer found a heavy stone and was hauling it back to the open driver's door.

Elise let out a cry of denial. She was not going to let this man kill Trent.

She gathered up some of her blood and smeared it on the knobby bit of wood, hoping to lubricate it. Another tug told her the idea worked. The cuff slid over the bump. The sudden release of pressure made her stumble, but she regained her footing and pulled the cuff the rest of the way off the skinny branch.

Leaves flew everywhere, sticking to the blood on her wrist, but she didn't stop to clear them away. She sprinted over the ground as quickly and silently as she could.

The killer was leaning inside the car. Suddenly, the engine roared and the back tires spun as if someone had floored the accelerator.

The noise hid her approach.

He straightened, closed the car door and went around to the back of the car.

Elise's feet hit the dock, making a hollow thud as she ran.

The killer saw her coming. He gave her a sickening, pleased smile and kicked the jack out from under the bumper.

The spinning wheels hit the dock, and the car shot off like a rocket.

The man drew his gun and aimed it at her. Elise didn't care. She didn't slow. She was going to dive into the water after Trent and get him out of that trunk.

The car hit the water with a huge splash and a crunch of breaking plastic.

The killer must have realized her intent, because he dropped the weapon and launched himself at her.

Elise leaped to avoid him, but she wasn't fast enough to clear the end of the dock and go into the water. The killer snagged her around the waist and slammed her down onto the weathered wooden boards.

He'd knocked the air from her lungs, but she didn't stop fighting him. There was still time to save Trent.

She scrambled, trying to claw her way out from under him, but he bore down on her, pinning her in place. His arms were wrapped around hers, and his weight kept her legs immobile. The only thing she could move was her head.

Elise looked toward the water, praying Trent would

come swimming out at any moment. The car sank fast, releasing huge bubbles of air as it went. The headlights cut through the murky water, making it glow a dull brown-green.

Finally, the last bit of bumper disappeared below the surface of the water. One more giant air bubble gurgled to the top, and then nothing. No movement. No Trent.

"No!" screamed Elise. "Trent!"

"He's gone," said the killer. "He's breathing in that dirty water right now. It's filling his lungs, choking the life from his body."

Agonizing fury consumed her, making her stronger, faster. She exploded into movement, knocking the killer's arms away from hers. She managed to crawl two feet away before he grabbed her ankle and pulled her back away from the water.

Splinters dug into her skin, but she didn't stop kicking and punching.

Her blows landed, but did little good. He let out a grunt of pain, then balled up his fist and slammed it into her temple.

Lights blinded her for a moment and then disappeared, along with everything else.

Gary dragged Elise down the dock, enjoying the sound of her head bouncing along the wooden planks.

The bitch didn't know her place, but she would soon enough. Once he got her home, she'd realize just what happened to women who refused to obey.

Once he got back onto the rocky ground, she got too hard to drag, so he hefted her over his shoulder and headed toward his house. It was only a half mile away, and the exercise would do him good.

He checked over his shoulder, just to make sure that the ex-cop boyfriend hadn't surfaced, then headed for home. Once he had Elise safely locked away, he could clean himself up and see to his bleeding nose.

And then, finally, it was going to be time for the McBride sisters to have a little family reunion.

He could hardly wait.

CHAPTER TWENTY-THREE

The shock of cold water rushing into Trent's mouth woke him up.

He sputtered, spitting the water out, instinctively moving toward the dwindling source of air he felt on his face.

Within a few speeding heartbeats, everything came back to him. The drive from Chicago that ended at the isolated expanse of farmland. The lake. The fight with the cop-impersonating killer that left him with two bullet holes, at least. Maybe more. His entire body was a mass of writhing pain, and he was twisted to fit into a small, confined space, unable to move and see what worked and what didn't.

The trunk. He was in the trunk of the Mazda.

And the car was sinking into the lake.

Panic seized him and he fought it back, knowing that it would kill him. There was still a little bit of air left, and until that was gone, until the water filled the trunk, equalizing the pressure, there was no chance of getting out.

He didn't have much time, and he didn't want to waste a second of it. He tried to move his hands to feel for a way out, realized they were still bound, and started searching the trunk for something sharp enough to cut through the plastic cuffs while he waited for the trunk to fill with water.

Survival instincts roared at him to flee, to fight his way out, and he had to grit his teeth to hold them back.

The water level in the trunk was still going up, taking away the pocket of air he had left. He sucked it into his lungs, trying to oxygenate his blood as much as possible so he could hold his breath longer when the time came.

Another gush of water filled his mouth. Panic rioted through his limbs, making them shake. If he didn't find a way out soon, he was going to drown down here, alone in the dark, while that killer did whatever he wanted with his sweet Elise.

He had to get out and save her. He'd seen what that man had done to all those poor women. He couldn't let that happen to Elise.

He wasn't sure if he'd be able to swim with his wet clothes dragging him down and the gunshot wounds weakening him, but he guessed that trying to swim while also handcuffed was going to be impossible. He'd sink like a stone.

Trent's fingers searched over the bumps of the sheet metal around him. Something sharp stung his fingertip as it sliced it open. He had no idea what it was—the edge of a piece of metal of some kind—but if it could cut his skin, it could probably cut the plastic ties.

It took him a precious few seconds to maneuver his bound hands to get the right angle, but he managed to make it work. He sawed back and forth, raking the plastic against that bit of metal.

Water rushed into his nose, and he had to push with his legs to shove his face up high enough to take another breath.

The plastic broke. His wrists flew apart, scraping his knuckles as they dragged across the metal trunk lid.

He ripped his hands free and felt around for the trunk release. This car was new enough to have one inside, probably similar to a light switch—designed so kids would flip it to turn on the lights if they got stuck.

His fingers were a bit numb, but he found the lever and triggered the release. The trunk lid didn't move. He was going to have to shove it open.

The position was awkward, and a searing pain shot out from his thigh, but he managed to brace himself and push the lid up with his legs. The thing felt like it weighed a ton, but it moved sluggishly through the water, letting out the last few tiny air bubbles that had been trapped.

Trent's air supply was gone, but at least he knew which way was up as he followed those bubbles.

The headlights were still on, gleaming through the murky water. The beams landed on a bright green Volvo with smashed windows—Ashley's car.

He hoped that meant she was nearby, and that Elise was, too.

His head broke through to the air, and he sucked in huge gulps of oxygen. He treaded water, but every kick burned his thigh, every stroke made his ribs throb in protest.

He wasn't going to be able to keep his head above

water for long with his wet clothes and shoes bogging him down. He had to get to shore and hope that the killer with the gun hadn't noticed he was still alive.

Trent headed for the dock. It was closest and would provide cover from any stray bullets headed his way.

He had no idea how long he'd been unconscious—how long Elise had been on her own with the killer. Had he had time to hurt her? Was Trent already too late? The idea that he'd find Elise hacked into pieces the way those other women had been made him want to scream in rage and denial. He couldn't let that happen. He had to hurry, but his limbs were sluggish with cold and blood loss. The gaping holes in his body weren't doing him a hell of a lot of good either. He was going to have to stop the bleeding soon, or he'd end up being no good to anyone.

As he swam, no bullets flew past him, nor did he see anyone at the edge of the lake. The moon overhead was bright enough to see by, now that his eyes had adjusted.

He made it to the dock and clung to one of the wooden supports while he gasped for breath. Getting up onto land was going to be a bitch, but he didn't have any options. And every second he rested was one more second Elise was in jeopardy.

Trent reached up, gripped the end plank, and used what was left of his strength to haul himself up and over the edge.

Pain roared through his abdomen at the motion. Something was definitely not good somewhere inside his gut. He lay on the deck, bleeding and panting as the wave of pain passed over him, leaving him weak and shaking.

After what seemed way too long, the pain faded

enough for him to move. He lifted his soggy shirt, looked down at the bullet hole and saw a slow stream of blood seeping out. A quick swipe over his back told him there was no exit wound, so the bullet was still in there somewhere.

Lovely.

The hole in his thigh was more ragged and bled a lot more, but it had gone through part of the muscle and out the other side. Ugly and painful as hell, but not that serious. He hoped.

Heedless of whatever muck he'd picked up in the lake, Trent ripped his shirt in half, tied part of it around his thigh to slow the bleeding, and the other half he tied around his waist in the hopes it would keep the bullet from moving around in his abdomen and doing any more damage.

By the time he was done, he was weak and nauseated from the pain, but at least he'd done what little damage control he could.

Now, it was time to find Elise before it was too late.

He pushed himself to his feet and scanned the area. There were no signs of life, no movement nearby. The only thing he could see was the wavering light of a yellow bulb obscured by the trees.

He wasn't sure if Elise had gone toward that light, but he didn't have a whole lot to go on here. If she wasn't there, maybe there'd at least be a phone he could use to call for help.

Right now, in the shape he was in, it was his best bet.

With slow, shambling steps, he moved over the dusty

ground, leaving a visible trail of water and blood behind him.

Elise didn't want to open her eyes. She knew monsters waited out there beyond the calming blackness of sleep.

Her head pounded, and her ribs ached like she'd taken a beating. Her wrist felt like it was on fire, consumed by a searing, stinging pain.

It was all the pain that told her she was still alive, she wasn't dreaming, and that everything she remembered was real.

Trent was dead.

I love you.

He was gone forever. He loved her, and now he was gone.

How could he have loved her? How could he love someone who failed so utterly?

She'd failed to find a way to save him. She'd failed to keep Ashley safe. She'd failed to find her when she went missing, and now she was going to fail again.

The man who'd killed Trent was going to kill her, too.

Elise wondered if she'd see Trent again after she died. And if she did, would he forgive her for not finding a way to save him?

She had no answers, only a bleak sense of helplessness and the sure knowledge that all her chances to redeem herself were now gone.

"Please, wake up," came Ashley's frightened voice.

Elise's eyes snapped open and light drilled into her

brain, making her hiss in pain. She raised her hand to shield her eyes. "Ashley?"

"I'm here," said her sister. She was close.

Maybe Elise was already dead. But if so, why did she hurt so much?

Elise forced herself to open her eyes and accept the pain the light caused. At first, everything was a brilliant, searing halo, but slowly, things started to come into focus.

She was in a hotel room—a dank, oppressive hotel room. Everything was bland, lifeless beige. She was on a bed, leaving smears of drying blood on the beige bedspread. There were no windows, only the noxious fluorescent lighting overhead.

Ashley was beside her, sitting on the edge of the bed. She looked pale, gaunt. Haunted.

Dark smudges of fatigue made her green eyes glow fever bright. Her long hair fell lank and dull around her too-thin face. Worry had edged deep lines around her mouth and between her brows.

The last week had aged Ashley at least ten years.

Even though her ribs protested the movement, Elise pushed herself up and hugged her sister. Her thin body felt good in Elise's arms—something real and solid to latch onto.

Ashley began to shake. Her weak arms tightened, and a nearly silent sob burst violently from her body, like she'd been holding it in for years.

"I'm sorry," cried Ashley. "I'm so sorry he found you. I didn't want to be alone. I kept wishing you were here, and now you are, and I'm so sorry."

"Shh." Elise stroked her hand over Ashley's hair, trying

to soothe her. Either she wasn't making much sense, or Elise's brain wasn't firing on all cylinders yet. Either way, she needed to take stock in their situation and figure out how the heck they were going to get out of it. "It's okay. Now that I'm here, we're going to get out of this place together."

"You don't understand. I tried. We all tried. It won't work. There is no way out."

Elise pulled back and cupped her sister's face in her hands. Tears flowed over her fingers, leaving streaks in the dried blood on Elise's hands. "Yes, there is. But you need to get ahold of yourself and answer my questions, okay? We may not have much time."

"He said he was coming back for me as soon as you woke up." She swallowed hard. Her eyes closed, wringing tears of defeat from them, and she whispered, "He painted my fingernails."

Elise wasn't sure why that upset Ashley so much, but clearly it meant something more. "Did he hurt you?"

"Not yet. He will, though. When he comes back, he's going to take me to that room and strap me down. And then he's going to cut off my hand." A sob shook her body before she controlled it. "He's going to make you watch, Elise."

Elise's stomach heaved at the thought. She didn't know what kind of torture her sister had endured this past week, but whatever it was, the effects of it were glowing in her eyes, haunting her features with pain.

"No. That's not going to happen. I won't let it."

"You can't stop him. He's too strong. I tried, and he killed her. He burned her while I watched . . . Oh, God." Ashley pushed away and curled into a ball. She rocked on her side, gritting her teeth and making a horrible, high-pitched noise of torment.

Elise watched her sister, too shocked to think. She'd seen Ashley upset, seen her mad enough to break dishes and sling paint across the room. She'd seen her cry like her heart was broken when some high school kid broke up with her. But she'd never seen anything like this— never seen this soul-deep anguish, never heard that wounded animal noise being wrenched from her chest.

The man who'd taken them had broken Ashley, killed Trent, and Elise was going to make him pay.

She moved from the bed to search the room for a means of escape. The door was locked and made of metal. There was no window to break, and the hinges were on the outside. The only weakness she could see was the knob. Maybe she could break it off and unlock the door that way.

Her body was sluggish and every movement hurt her ribs. Maybe he'd kicked her after she'd gone unconscious like he had Trent; maybe he'd broken one.

Trent.

I love you.

She couldn't go there. She couldn't think about that right now and still function. If she stopped long enough to let those thoughts invade her head, she'd be curled into a ball and rocking the way her sister was.

She had to stay strong, so she shoved him out of her mind and focused on the task at hand.

She needed something hard, something she could use as leverage or something heavy enough to smash metal and break it.

There was a chair, but it was mostly plastic and not

heavy enough to do any damage. The small round table, though, that might be solid enough to do some good.

Elise tipped it over and picked it up by the base. Her ribs felt like they were on fire, but she ignored them. She lifted the table as high as she could and slammed it down hard on the doorknob.

The noise was deafening in the insulated quiet of the room. Vibrations from the impact numbed her arms.

The doorknob remained solid and undamaged.

"I told you," said Ashley. "There's no way out."

"There's always a way out. We just have to find it." Before the killer came back.

"Gary will be here soon. He probably heard the noise and knows you're awake."

Gary? The killer's name was Gary? "What's his last name?"

"I don't know. I just met him at the bar. He was . . . nice. He bought me drinks." She sucked in a breath that shook with self-loathing. "How long have I been here?"

"A week."

"Only a week? It seemed so much longer."

"It's almost over now, Ashley. I promise." Maybe it was an empty promise, but one she was willing to make all the same. "I need you to be sharp, okay? We might find an opening when he comes back, and if you get one, run. Don't wait for me."

"I can't leave you here with him."

"You run and get help. I mean it."

"I don't even know where I am."

"Just find a road and flag down whoever you can."

Ashley covered her ears and started rocking again.

"Stop talking like this. It won't work. We're going to die in here."

Elise wished she had the time to be gentle, but that wasn't a luxury either of them could afford. She knelt on the bed, grabbed Ashley's shoulders, sat her up, and gave her a hard shake. "Pull yourself together," she ordered. "We *are* going to get out of here."

"That's what I told Constance. She knew the truth, but I didn't believe her. I told her we'd find a way out. I told her everything would be okay, but it wasn't. He hurt her. He cut off her hands. He made me watch. He made both of us watch."

"That's all over now." It was a lie, but one Elise had to tell. If they got out of this, the nightmare wasn't going to be over for Ashley for a long time. Maybe never.

"This is what I get for not listening to Constance. My punishment. I should have listened. I should have killed her sooner."

Ashley killed her? That didn't seem possible. It had to have been a trick Gary played on her to torture her more. "You didn't kill anyone."

"I did." She reached out and grabbed Elise's arm. Her fingers grazed the deep gashes the cuffs had left on Elise's wrist, making pain streak up her arms.

The fear in Ashley's eyes was desperate, pleading. "Listen to me. Don't make me wait, don't make me suffer like I made Constance suffer. Kill me. Give me the whole bottle of pills so I don't have to watch him take my other hand. Promise me."

Elise had an idea of what Ashley meant, but she refused to even consider killing her sister. "Stop talking like that. As soon as he comes back, I'm going to fight him. I'm going to bash his head in with that table and it will all be over. We're going to get out of here."

"I should have listened to Constance. I should have believed her. I'm so sorry."

"Constance is dead. We're not. I need you, Ashley. Don't give up on me. I can get us out."

Ashley shook her head as tears slid down her gaunt cheeks. "I'm so sorry."

CHAPTER TWENTY-FOUR

Gary was going to have two black eyes come tomorrow morning. By Monday, he was going to have to figure out a colorful story to tell his coworkers so they wouldn't get suspicious.

His nose had finally stopped bleeding, and he'd put on a clean set of scrubs.

Finally, after all the waiting, he had both sisters in residence, and he wanted to do this right. Take his time. Savor it.

The look of horror on Ashley's face when he'd dumped Elise in her room had been one he wouldn't soon forget.

Maybe he should start carrying a camera. He enjoyed watching his recordings over and over, but there wasn't always time to set up a video camera to capture a moment. A camera made much more sense.

He slipped on a pair of canvas shoes that he'd washed since he'd dumped Constance's body. The bloodstains hadn't all come out, but he didn't mind. He was just going to have to bleach them again tonight anyway, after he was done with Ashley.

Gary headed back to the kitchen to sterilize the instruments he was going to need tonight. The routine was soothing, reassuring in its monotony.

He left the tools to boil and headed downstairs to check on the girls. Neither of them were as docile as he liked, but he didn't mind a bit of a challenge. They were going to be worth it.

He made sure his pistol was ready to fire and unlocked the door. He didn't trust them not to fight back, but he knew how to use one of them against the other. He was in control here, and it wouldn't take them long to figure that out.

Gary pushed the door open. A chair flew through the opening, nearly smashing into his head.

"Nice try," he said, "but you're wasting our time."

He peered into the room. The lights were off. He couldn't see much beyond the doorway.

Two could play that game.

He flipped off the hall lights, casting them all into darkness. He waited for a few seconds while his eyes adjusted. It didn't do much good—there was no natural source of light down here.

Slowly, he moved forward. "I'm armed. I suggest you be careful what you throw, or one of you might end up with a hole in her pretty head."

Neither woman spoke. He could hear their frightened breathing sawing in and out of their lungs, but it was hard to tell exactly where it was coming from.

He stepped forward, feeling his way through the

doorway. His foot kicked something light that made a dry sound, like wadded-up paper.

Too late, Gary realized he'd just stepped into a trap. The sound had told them where he was.

Something hard and heavy slammed into his stomach. It crushed the air out of his lungs.

Rage at his own incompetence burst behind his eyes, making his head throb. These women were going to pay for that.

He ignored the pain and shot forward, groping blindly for one of the women. His hand brushed something soft, and a startled cry of fear spilled out, telling him where to aim.

He reached out, caught a fistful of hair and jerked it back toward his body. The woman stumbled into him, knocking him off balance. It took him a second to regain his footing and wrap his arm around a slender throat, cutting off a sobbing scream of terror.

"I've got a gun to her head," he called out into the darkness.

The scrambling sound of movement he'd heard a moment ago went still. A soft click sounded from across the room, followed by a blinding light cascading from the bathroom.

Elise stood there, bathed in a halo of light, her face twisted in a snarl, looking like an avenging angel. Beautiful.

Gary adjusted his weapon so it was aligned with Ashley's temple. "I will kill her just to teach you a lesson," he said to Elise. "If you don't believe me, ask Ashley about Gloria."

A beautiful, wounded sound rose up out of Ashley at the reminder.

Gary's cock stirred to life.

Elise lifted her hands in surrender.

"Good. Now, walk out that door and down the hall."

"No," sobbed Ashley. "No, no, no."

"Do it."

Elise looked at her sister, then back at Gary. "You're going to kill us both. A bullet to the head is a much nicer way to die than what you've got in mind."

Gary lowered the gun until it was aligned with Ashley's intestines. "A gut shot isn't. Care to test me and see if I'll do it? It will take her days to die. She'll be in horrible pain, and I'll make you watch every minute of it."

Elise swallowed visibly. Her fists were clenched at her sides, and she was shaking with anger. "Take me. Let her go and take me instead."

"What possible reason could I have to do that?"

"If you do, I promise to cooperate. Do whatever you like. I'll be docile, I'll scream and fight—whatever gets you off. Just let her go."

Gary found himself actually considering it. Wendy had always been willing to play his games. She'd always been selfless, just like Elise was being right now.

Maybe that's what he'd been missing all these years. He'd been searching for the perfect woman—one who could make him feel the way Wendy did—but he'd been going about it all wrong.

He couldn't force a woman to be what he needed. She had to do it of her own free will.

Of course, he couldn't let Ashley go. She'd report him to the authorities and his fun would be over. He wouldn't allow himself to be confined as a prisoner. But he had to make Elise think he'd let Ashley go.

It was a win-win situation. He'd get to experiment with a willing victim, and if Elise lied, he could bring Ashley back and continue on as he'd originally planned.

"Okay," he said. "I'll let her go. You stay here, and I'll be right back."

"I want to see you let her go. I want to see her walk away."

"You're in no position to make demands. We'll do this my way, or not at all. You said you'd do whatever I want."

She was quiet for a long moment, looking at Ashley with so much compassion and love, he could almost feel what it was like to be willing to sacrifice oneself for someone else.

He never would have even considered doing such a thing for Lawrence, and he wondered briefly if that made him a bad brother. Not that he cared. Lawrence had never done anything to warrant such a sacrifice.

"Can I have a minute alone with her? Please?" asked Elise.

It was the "please" that gave Gary pause. This was what he'd wanted all along—that play of emotional agony between two sisters. How much more agonizing could it be than to say good-bye for the very last time? How much more beautiful?

"Come with me," he ordered without turning around to see if Elise followed behind her sister's dragging body.

He opened the door to his operating room and tossed

Ashley inside. Elise rushed forward to help her sister from the floor.

Gary pressed the power button to start his recording equipment and left them alone. Whatever they had to say, he'd capture it and watch it later when he was in bed tonight.

Besides, it was time to fetch his instruments. He wanted to see how long Elise could lie still while he cut her. Wendy's record was twelve minutes. Maybe Elise would break it.

Trent's vision was going in and out of focus, which didn't exactly fill him with confidence.

The ground beneath his feet seemed to reach up and trip him every few steps. He stumbled yet again and fell to the dusty ground. His nose was only inches from the dirt, so the dark, wet spot was easy to see in the bright moonlight. Blood. Not his own, but the killer's. He'd come this way, and this spot was proof of it.

He was right on the killer's trail.

A surge of adrenaline spiked through him, dulling the pain and giving him the added burst of strength he needed. He wasn't going to give up and let the killer have Elise.

He loved her. She was strong and brave and loyal. Completely selfless. Sexy as hell. She made him feel needed, useful. How could he not love her? How could anyone not love her?

She needed him, and he wasn't going to let her down. He was in rough shape, but he was the only shot she had for a rescue. All he needed was a phone so he could call for help. He just needed to hang on long enough to get to the house.

Trent pushed himself to his feet. He felt the warm trickle of more blood slide down his leg as the makeshift bandage moved.

At the rate he was bleeding, he was going to have to hurry or he wouldn't even have the strength to make a call.

The yellow light he'd seen was closer now—only a few yards away. He could see that it was a porch light, a bare yellow bulb beside a simple wooden door. A plain white curtain hung over the glass, shielding his view of the inside, but a faint light leaked through the fabric.

He saw no movement, no sign that anyone was inside, but there was nothing else out here—nowhere for anyone to go.

Trent prayed Elise was inside, that he hadn't driven her somewhere else. There was an old Cadillac sitting beside the house, but that was no guarantee the killer hadn't driven her away in another vehicle.

There was only one way to find out, and time was sliding away with each drop of blood that leaked out of him.

As quietly as he could manage, Trent moved up to that door and turned the handle.

It was locked.

The door was old and loose in the frame. The knob was even older. Trent pulled a credit card out of his dripping wallet and eased the latch open.

The door swung in with a wickedly loud squeak.

Trent froze, bracing himself for another bullet, but no bullet came. He listened hard, but only heard the beating of his heart and the sound of blood struggling to pump through his veins.

Bugs flew past his head, flocking to the light over the kitchen sink. Trent stepped inside, not bothering to close the door and make another racket.

The kitchen he stood in was old, run-down. The butcher-block countertops were scarred with use and split with age and neglect. A pot of water boiled away on the gas stove, and sticking out from the top, Trent could see a metal handle of some kind gleaming under the stark light.

On the wall, there was an old rotary-dial phone. He wasn't sure if the thing still worked, but he was willing to give it a shot.

Keeping his eyes and ears open for sounds of any company, Trent went to the boiling pot, grabbed a blue towel sitting on the counter, and lifted out one of the instruments. It was some kind of saw with fine, serrated teeth.

A bone saw.

A shiver of revulsion moved through him as he realized what he held in his hand. How many women had been tortured with this instrument?

As weapons went, it wasn't a great one, but it was better than the dainty scalpels and clamps he had to choose from in the bottom of the pot. For the first time in two years, he wished for the dense weight of a gun in his hand. Beggars couldn't be choosers, and he sure as hell wasn't going to walk around bleeding *and* weaponless.

He put his back to the wall and lifted the phone out

of the cradle. A dial tone buzzed in his ear, sounding like a chorus of angels. Hallelujah.

He dialed 911, praying the old phone would work with the relatively new system.

The operator came on the line asking what his emergency was, and her calm, professional voice seemed to scream through the phone into the silent kitchen.

Trent rattled off his old badge number, hoping it would light a fire under the local authorities if they realized he knew the difference between a problem and a real emergency. "I've tracked the serial killer the CPD is looking for to this location. I need immediate backup."

He didn't wait to see what she said. He couldn't give her an address, but since this was a landline, he hoped they could trace it. Rather than waiting around to see what she had to say, he simply let the phone dangle at the end of its curly cord and went looking for Elise.

It took every ounce of strength Elise had not to cry. Chances were good this was the last time she'd ever see Ashley again, and she didn't want to waste whatever few moments they had left with tears.

"I'm not going," said Ashley. "I'm not going to leave you alone here with him. He's a demon, not a man."

Elise took her sister's hands in hers. They were cold from fear, trembling. Ashley's fingers were long and slender—the hands of an artist. Elise knew that losing them would end Ashley's life, even if they made it out of this alive.

She had to convince Ashley to go and not look back. If that killer got the chance, Elise was sure he'd go after Ashley as soon as he was done with whatever he'd planned for her. Before that happened, Ashley needed to be far, far away.

"This is the best chance we have. You have to run for help."

"Then you should be the one to go. You're stronger than I am. Faster, too."

"I can't run. I think I have a broken rib."

Ashley's face crumpled in misery. Tears slid unchecked down her cheeks. "I won't leave you."

Elise hugged her sister tight. She didn't know how much time they'd have before he came back. "Please, do this for me. Be strong for me."

"He's going to hurt you. He's going to kill you."

Elise couldn't think about that now. She had to pretend it wasn't going to happen, that everything was going to be fine. If she didn't, the hopelessness of her situation would crash down on her and bury her alive. She had to stay strong for just a few more minutes.

She swallowed down the urge to scream out her helpless rage, to rant at the unfairness of all this. How could she find the one man on earth who could love her despite all her flaws, only to lose him? How could she finally find her sister, only to become a victim of a madman?

Elise pulled away from Ashley's embrace, making sure her face was a calm mask. "If you don't go, he'll kill both of us."

"I should be the one to stay. I was the one who was stupid enough to fall into his trap."

She gave Ashley a shake to stop that train of thought before it got started. There'd be plenty of time for her to think about that later, if she was lucky enough to survive. "No, Ashley. I can't run. You have to go."

Tears wet Ashley's cheeks. Her eyes were huge and luminous with fear. "I wish you'd never come for me."

"Of course I was going to come for you. I love you." It was so easy to say to Ashley. Why couldn't she have said the same thing to Trent? Why couldn't she have admitted the truth to herself earlier? She loved him, and she was never going to get the chance to tell him.

"I love you, too," said Ashley.

"Then be strong for me. Get away from this monster, and get help so that no one else has to go through what we have. Promise me."

Ashley's voice wavered, but she whispered, "I promise."

Gary went to fetch his toys from the stove. When he reached the top of the stairs leading into the kitchen, he came to a dead stop.

Small puddles of muddy, bloody water were all over his kitchen floor. The back door was open. The phone was off the hook, dangling by its cord. The bone saw was no longer boiling away on the stove.

The ex-cop boyfriend. Somehow he'd survived.

Gary had no idea how he'd gotten out of that trunk, but he'd found a way. He should have put a bullet in his head when he had the chance. Now, he was going to have to subdue the man all over again.

Only this time, the boyfriend was armed. With *his* saw.

The man had already shown he was willing to throw himself into danger—right at a loaded weapon—if that's what it took to do the job. Gary wasn't willing to take that kind of risk again. He needed to be smarter this time.

He needed leverage.

Luckily, he had what he needed downstairs. Once Gary had Elise in front of him, playing human shield, her boyfriend would think twice about charging at them with the bone saw he'd stolen.

CHAPTER TWENTY-FIVE

Trent had searched the entire first floor of the house, and so far he hadn't found a serial-killing psycho, only empty rooms.

Well, not exactly empty. One of them had been turned into a home theater with a huge video library. A stack of DVDs were sitting out, ready to be viewed. The top one was labeled "Constance, Volume 3."

Constance Gregory. The woman who had been chopped up into chunks so she fit in a garbage sack. The woman with Elise's name carved into her skin.

What would he carve into Elise's soft skin if Trent didn't find her first?

Trent suffered through the wave of revulsion that hit him. He didn't have to see that video to know that whatever was on it wasn't good, and it was probably a lot worse than what was on the first two volumes.

He didn't stay and poke through the rest of the videos. Not only did he not want to tamper with evidence, he also didn't want to waste the energy. With every second that ticked by, he lost another few drops of blood. The way his vision wavered, and his legs felt like lead weights, he figured he didn't have a whole lot of seconds left.

But until he found Elise and knew she was safe, he had to keep moving. He shuffled his feet over the worn hardwood, trying to keep his weight off his injured leg as much as possible.

A bedroom was next. It, too, was void of serial-killing psychos, but it did have a nice 9mm semiautomatic handgun sitting on the bedside table.

Trent took that as proof that God was on his side, and he limped over to the weapon. He dropped the saw, picked up the gun, released the magazine, found it full, and slipped it back into place, working the slide.

He hadn't touched a gun since that night two years ago, but he hadn't forgotten how to use one. The deadly weight of it in his palm was reassuring. Comfortable.

Now, all he needed was that psycho, and his job here was done. If he could keep his eyes and trigger finger working that long.

A wave of dizziness made him sway. He gritted his teeth and let his fear for Elise seep in. He'd been trying to shut it out, ignoring what could be happening to her right now, for fear that he'd break down or give up. But he needed that fear and the adrenaline it poured into his system to keep going just a little longer.

He let himself imagine what could happen—saw her perfect body lying in pieces, smeared with dirt and algae. The image enraged him, made his blood pound through his veins. He was *not* going to allow that to happen. If it took every last bit of life he had in him, he was going to find that man and kill him.

Only a few more steps. He'd find the killer in the next room and it would all be over.

But the killer wasn't in the next room. Or the living room. Trent had searched the whole first floor and hadn't found him yet. He'd wasted precious time searching in vain.

The creak of old wood trickled in from the kitchen, almost too faint to hear. Trent thought he'd imagined it, but it happened again.

The psycho was in there.

A surge of deadly satisfaction ripped through Trent. His body responded when he ordered it to move and find the bastard. He kept to the shadows as best he could, but his wobbly gait made it hard to stay balanced. His leg had been a throbbing mass of pain, but right now, all that fell away. He couldn't feel anything but the reassuring weight of the handgun in his grip.

"I've got your woman," called out the psycho. "I know you're here. Show yourself."

"He's got a gun, Trent!" That was Elise's voice, high and strained with fear.

Elation trickled over his skin like cool rain. She was still alive. There was still a chance to save her.

Trent peered around the doorframe, into the glaring brightness of the kitchen, and saw the situation. He pulled his head back before the psycho could blow it off.

He wasn't lying. He had Elise in there with him, plastered against his front like a living shield. Even on his best day, with rock-steady hands, Trent wouldn't have been able to make a shot like that without hitting her. Today was not his best day. His hands were shaking like the rest of him, getting worse by the second as his blood pooled on the floor at his feet.

Damn it!

How the hell was he going to get them out of this?

"I'll shoot her if I have to," said the psycho. "We both know what happened the last time you held a gun. If you try to shoot me, you'll only hurt her the same way you hurt your partner."

"He's going to kill me anyway, Trent. He's going to kill both of us. Don't listen to him."

The killer roared, "Shut the fuck up, you bitch!"

Elise yelped in pain, but Trent had no idea what he'd done to her. The only thing he knew was that he couldn't let the man do it again. Not to his Elise.

He stepped around the corner, aiming the gun at the psycho's head. He had to use two hands to keep it steady, and he still wasn't doing a great job. The shredded remains of the plastic handcuffs dangled from his left wrist, vibrating in time with his unsteady grip, blatantly displaying exactly how unsteady it was.

The killer shoved the gun against Elise's cheek. "Drop it or I'll shoot her."

"You shoot her, and you won't have time to blink before I kill you."

"Tough words for a man who can barely stand. Look at you. You're leaking like a sieve."

"Worried about your floor? You won't have to worry about anything for long."

"Shoot him, Trent."

"Yes, Trent," said the killer. "Shoot me. Go ahead. I dare you."

Trent had maybe two inches of clearance on the left

side of the man's head. The rest of him was covered by Elise. Unfortunately, her head was right next to those two inches.

The night he'd shot John came back to him, pounding him with a barrage of memories. He remembered pulling the trigger. He remembered John's pained scream. He remembered the blood—heaping gouts of blood pouring out of his friend's back.

If he missed, it would be Elise's head bleeding.

"You can do it, Trent," she said. "I trust you."

She shouldn't. She knew what he'd done—the mistakes he'd made. How could she trust him?

"He's going to kill all of us if you don't."

That much was certain.

Trent's vision grayed out at the edges. It was creeping inward, blinding him by slow degrees. He felt cold, numb.

Elise stared at him, her eyes bright with trust, her expression pleading.

A little more of his vision faded. He couldn't see the man's feet anymore. Suddenly, it got hard to breathe.

"Please, Trent. Don't let him kill us. I love you."

Had he imagined those words? Surely, he was hallucinating. But what if he wasn't?

He had to find out, and the only way he had a shot at that was to take it.

Trent leveled the weapon, lined up the sights on the killer's left temple, and fired.

The gun bucked in his hands. Blood bloomed out from the killer's head. Elise slammed her arm up, knocking his weapon away from her face, and ducked away.

Trent fired again, this time aiming at center mass,

now clear of the woman he loved. He hit something, but he couldn't tell what. All he saw was the killer stumble backward before that gray tunnel closed down to a pinpoint and winked out entirely.

He felt his body hit the ground, and this time, he couldn't get back up.

CHAPTER TWENTY-SIX

Elise kicked the weapon away from Gary, well out of his reach.

He was thrashing around on the ground, holding his chest.

Trent had collapsed and didn't look good. His skin was pale and there was a lot of blood on his clothes.

She couldn't deal with both of them, and she couldn't go to Trent until she was sure Gary wasn't getting back up. She needed something to tie him up with.

Elise looked around for something she could use, and saw Ashley standing at the top of the stairs, staring at the man who had held her hostage and tortured her for the past seven days.

"He didn't lock the door," she said in an eerily calm voice. "When he grabbed you, he didn't lock the door."

"Help me find something to tie him up with, Ashley. Trent's bleeding"

Ashley bent down and picked up the gun Gary had been using. The thing looked huge and alien in her hands. She leveled it at Gary. Her hands didn't shake. "Go ahead and take care of Trent. I won't let Gary up."

Ashley stared at the bleeding man lying on the cracked vinyl floor. The demon lay broken but not destroyed.

Blood frothed from Gary's mouth. He stared at Ashley, his oil slick eyes wide with rage and hatred. He tried to say something but he choked on his own blood, and the words were too garbled to understand.

Not that Ashley cared what he had to say. There were no words to make up for what he'd done. No possible redemption.

The gun was heavy in her hands and surprisingly warm. The red polish on her thumbnail shone like wet blood against the dull black surface of the gun.

Gary gripped his chest as if trying to hold in the blood that leaked between his fingers.

He was dying.

He hadn't suffered nearly enough for her to let him die so easily. He deserved to suffer first, to be afraid, to be in pain.

He deserved to lose his hands.

Ashley leaned down so he could see her face. She looked into his tainted eyes, at his hands, then back again. Her gaze was deliberate—slow—so he'd see what she was going to do before he did it.

Gary's eyes rounded in fear, and it was the most satisfying thing Ashley had ever witnessed.

That satisfaction wouldn't make up for the terror and pain he'd caused so many women, but it felt good all the same. She supposed that made her a smaller person, but so be it.

Ashley leveled the gun, aimed for his hand—an easy thing as close as she was to the demon—and fired.

The weapon shuddered in her grip, and Gary's hand exploded into a ragged mess of flesh and bone. He screamed, a gurgling wail of agony.

A grim sense of justice filled her as she aimed the gun at his other hand.

A gun went off behind Elise. Gary screamed. Elise jumped, turned around in time to see Ashley shoot Gary again. His hand exploded in a spray of blood and pulpy bits. The other hand was already a bloody mess.

He'd been holding his chest, and both of Ashley's shots had gone through his hands and into his body. He jerked, trying to suck in a breath. A panicked look stretched his features into a grimace.

Ashley didn't seem to notice. She walked across the kitchen, as if in a trance, set the gun beside the stove, picked up a steaming pot of something and walked calmly back to Gary's side.

She tipped the pot, spilling its contents onto Gary's groin and abdomen. Boiling water splashed down onto him, along with shiny bits of metal that stuck into him like silver quills. Gary screamed out in agony. His body arched up off the ground, then went suddenly limp.

Ashley dropped the metal pot on top of him and stood there staring, unmoving.

Not once did her expression change. It was as calm and tranquil as if she'd been sleeping, only now, a steady flow of tears fell down her face and wet her shirt.

The sirens grew louder. Trent's eyes fluttered open for a brief moment.

"You safe?" he asked.

"Yes. We're all safe. You hold on. Help's here."

Elise split her time between Trent's hospital room and Ashley's house. She hated leaving either one of them, but at least Trent had a constant stream of family coming in to sit with him. Elise was the only family Ashley had.

Trent had woken up only once since they'd done surgery to remove a bullet and repair the damage Gary's gun had wrought, but he hadn't stayed awake long, and it was clear he wasn't lucid. The doctor assured her he'd recover; he just needed time for his body to heal and fight off infection.

Elise stroked his hand, silently willing him to hurry up. She needed to see for herself that he was okay. Until then, she wasn't going to be able to take a full breath.

The door to Trent's room swung open and his parents walked in.

Elise had met them once before, but she hadn't been able to talk with them. As soon as she knew Trent had someone at his side, she'd raced out to go check on Ashley.

Leann Brady looked young enough to be Trent's sister, but there was no mistaking the maternal concern tightening her features. She had shoulder-length hair that had only begun to show a few silver strands at her temples. Her blue eyes glowed with tears, and a crumpled tissue was clutched tight in her fist.

Trent had gotten his mother's coloring—dark hair and blue eyes—but his build had come straight from his father.

Alan Brady was a tall, lean man, tan from years spent working under the sun. He had one leathery arm around Leann's waist, holding her close. His eyes were the color of autumn sunshine, glowing with the kind of determination that would make grown men step out of his way.

He glanced at Elise, then to where she touched Trent's arm. He nodded, as if pleased by what he saw, then led Leann over to the far side of the bed.

"How is he today?" asked Alan.

"Better," she said, because she wanted to believe it was true.

"Has the doctor been in yet this morning?"

Elise nodded. "Around seven."

Alan's brows lifted. "You were here that early?"

"That late. But now that you're here, I should go back to my sister."

"How is she doing?" asked Leann. She clutched her husband's arm with one hand, and with the other, she stroked a loving caress over Trent's head.

Elise almost lied but stopped herself at the last minute. "She has a long way to go."

"You'll help her get through this. We all will. Our family is yours now."

The offer of help rang inside Elise like a church bell—full of beauty and hope. She had to swallow twice before she could speak. "Thank you."

"You go on and see to your sister," said Alan. "We'll stay with Trent."

Alan put his arm around Leann and hugged her close. She looked up at him, and the love shining between them, glowing in that simple gaze, was almost palpable.

Elise stood there in shock, staring, intruding upon

their private moment. But she couldn't stop looking. She'd never seen anything like it before.

After all the years they'd been together, they still loved each other. They weren't bound by convenience or habit, stuck in a marriage that neither one wanted. They truly loved each other.

If she hadn't seen it with her own eyes, Elise never would have believed it.

She stumbled away from the hospital bed, feeling like her world was shifting beneath her feet. With each step, her internal landscape changed, leaving her reeling from the shock.

She had to get out of there before everything she'd thought true was ripped from her and she had nothing left to cling to.

Trent had been right. The tooth fairy and the Easter bunny were real.

CHAPTER TWENTY-SEVEN

Trent woke up to find his old partner, John, next to his hospital bed.

"Hey, ugly," said John, giving him a weary grin. "Took you long enough to wake up. Guess you really needed your beauty rest."

Trent's head was a bit fuzzy, and it took a minute for everything that had happened to come back to him. The last thing he remembered was passing out after shooting the killer.

A quick glance around the stark room told him Elise was nowhere to be found.

"Where's Elise? Is she okay?" A spurt of panic lanced through him, and he tried to sit up.

Bad move.

Pain radiated out from his side, stealing his breath with its intensity.

John wheeled his chair forward and pushed Trent back down, not that it was a hard thing to manage, as weak as he was. "Whoa there, hero. Take it easy. Elise is fine. She's been here the last two days. She just left to go check on Ashley."

"Ashley?" Had she been there, too? Trent couldn't remember.

"Yeah. She's okay, too. A little fucked in the head, but she'll pull through. That woman of yours won't have it any other way."

Trent let out a long sigh and waited until the pain dwindled down to something less ferocious.

"Want me to get a nurse?" asked John.

"Not yet. Tell me what happened first."

"Well, Ed knows more than I do, but he's a bit busy weeding through all the evidence they found at Maitland's house."

"Maitland?"

"Gary Maitland was the asshole's name. That house in the boonies you found was his late wife's family home. Maitland had been bringing women there for years, torturing them and killing them. And he would have kept right on doing it if you hadn't stopped him."

"Is he alive?"

"I don't know if he was when you got done with him, but he sure as hell wasn't once Ashley finished bringing down justice."

Trent wished he'd stayed conscious long enough to see that. "Good. That's good. He deserved whatever he got."

"You don't know the half of it. They found videos of dozens of women he'd killed. He had parts of them in this big walk-in freezer in the basement. Apparently, he took pieces from each and sewed them together. I saw photos, and let me tell you, Bride of Frankenstein doesn't even begin to cover it."

Trent really didn't want to imagine. He was sure he'd see the crime scene photos eventually, but he was in no hurry to add that image to the ones he already had in his mind.

The memory of Elise in that killer's arms, with a gun pressed against her soft flesh, was more than enough terror for one lifetime. He broke out in a cold, shaking sweat just thinking about it.

"Maitland had a brother that has Mob connections. He runs a funeral home, and evidence is stacking up against him, too."

"What did he do?"

"Ed's pretty sure he helped cover up the murders by cremating some of the bodies, maybe burying them with other corpses."

"That would explain why it took years to find the killer."

John nodded. "I figure we'll be finding cases connected to this guy for a while. With all those pieces of women in his freezer, we'll be able to get some DNA, maybe close some cold cases and give some families peace."

Trent wasn't sure how much peace any family would get from knowing that their daughter or sister or wife had been in this man's hands. At least they'd know what had happened to their missing loved ones. "I hope you're right."

"You did good, son. I know it had to have been hell, but you came through."

Barely. It had been too close. He didn't think he'd be

able to relax again until he could see Elise with his own eyes and know for a fact she was okay.

"I'd really like to see Elise," said Trent. "Think you can manage that?"

"Sure. You get some rest and I'll rustle her up. Maybe get you some nice drugs while you wait."

"Thanks. And thanks for being here."

John shrugged. "I owed you, after all those hours you spent by my hospital bed."

"You knew I was there?" Trent had always been careful to leave as soon as John had started to wake up. He didn't think the man deserved having to face his shooter on top of trying to recover.

"Of course I did. You kept trying to sneak away, but I knew. You've always been my friend. It's just taken you a couple of years to remember it. That's all."

"You don't have to be nice to me. You don't have to stick around. I understand if you never want to see me again."

"Listen up, Trent. This whole thing where you avoid me is over as of right now. I think I've given you more than enough time to pout, so get over it already. Once you're up off this bed, you and I are going to have a nice, long talk about why you should go back to work at the CPD."

The idea made Trent's pulse race, but that sickening sense of doom he used to get whenever he thought about becoming a cop again was gone. Instead, there was a heady kind of excitement. Hope.

Maybe John was right, and it was time to rethink things. "Sounds good."

John gave him a slow, satisfied nod. "I'm so glad

you're not going to make me beat some sense into you. I've been working hard on pretending to be civilized lately. Carol likes it when I do."

"I'm glad you see things her way."

"She didn't give me much of a choice. God, I love that woman, even if I don't deserve her."

Trent didn't deserve Elise either. Maybe that meant there was hope for them, too. He wanted there to be.

"Sit tight," said John. "I'm going to go find someone who can drug you up, then I'm going to record whatever you say so I can hold it against you later."

Trent smiled as he closed his eyes, and like magic, when he opened them again, Elise was standing beside him, holding his hand.

She smiled down at him, blinking relieved tears from her eyes. "Hi."

"Hi, yourself."

She looked tired. Her eyes were shadowed with fatigue and red from crying.

He wished like hell he had been awake to hold her while she did.

"How are you feeling?" she asked.

He lifted the arm they'd hooked up to the IV. "Pretty good, thanks to whatever happy juice they pumped into me. What about you?"

She looked fragile, like she might fall over. Trent patted the space on the bed next to him in invitation.

Elise eased down to perch on the edge of the mattress. It wasn't good enough. He wanted her stretched out beside him, close enough he could feel her heart beating. Preferably naked. But he'd take what he could get.

"I have a cracked rib, a few bruises. I'll live. Thanks to you."

Thanks to him? "All I did was pull the trigger. You were the one who was going to pay the price if I missed."

"I knew you wouldn't."

The way she said it, so calmly, so matter-of-factly, eased something deep inside Trent that had been clenched and tense for years.

Trust. She'd given him her trust without hesitation, and somehow, that gift had taken root inside him and sprouted into a tiny, quivering blade of trust in himself. He wasn't sure how it had happened, but he accepted the gift, and whatever magic lay behind it, gratefully.

Trent tugged her arm so she'd lie down beside him. He wasn't sure the hospital staff would appreciate him sharing his bed, but they could all go screw themselves for all he cared. He needed this.

She was careful not to bump his wounds, but she snuggled into his side like she'd been dying to get close as much as he had.

"How's Ashley?"

He felt her body go tense. "Physically, she's fine. Mentally . . . she has a long way to go. But she's out of bed and painting again."

"That's good. It might help her heal."

Elise shook her head. "I don't know, Trent. She's different now. That carefree, weightless quality she had before is gone. Her paintings are dark now."

"Dark? How so?"

"She used to paint birds and dogs. Now, sometimes it's hard to tell what she's painting. They're abstract, with lots of angry slashes of red and black. The one she was working on when I left looked like a pool of shadowed blood more than anything else."

"It's only been a couple of days, right?"

"Three."

He'd slept longer than he thought. "Let her work things out. Give her time to realize she's safe."

"Of course she's safe now. Gary is dead."

"Her mind might know that, but you know Ashley. She's emotional. It may take time for her heart to catch up."

"I hope it doesn't take long. I'm so worried about her."

"Don't worry. We'll help her through this. Whatever she needs."

Elise nodded and her body began to relax again. Trent knew it would be a while before things were back to anything resembling normal, but he wasn't sure how much more time he had before Elise left. There were some things they had to get out in the open.

"So, where to now?" asked Trent.

"What do you mean?"

"I mean, your overnight bag is sitting by the door. I assume that means you're headed back to Hong Kong."

She stiffened, then leaned up and stared at him like she was ready to slap him. "Oh, no you don't. You're not getting off that easy. That bag is full of your clothes, not mine."

Relief made him smile. "Easy? You call this easy?"

"You don't get to tell me you love me, then take it back just because you're not dying anymore."

He looked right into her eyes. "I'm not taking anything back. I still love you."

Her glare turned to a weepy look of relief. His poor Elise had been through the wringer, and clearly, her emotions had been sent for a loop. "You do?"

"Yeah."

"You're not taking it back?"

"Hell, no. And just so we're clear, once I get out of this place and back on my feet, I'm going to find you in whatever country you're in. I figure I can watch your back. Keep you safe while you go out and get all those exciting stories."

"You'd do that? You'd go with me? Travel the world?"

"If that's what it takes to be with you, then yes. So, where will you be? Hong Kong?"

She sniffed and shook her head. "I'm done with excitement for a while. I thought I'd try something a little closer to home."

Hope drove away all the pain lingering in his bones. "Chicago?"

"I was thinking more along the lines of Haven. I want to be near Ashley."

"Move in with me," he said without even thinking. But now that the words were out of his mouth, he felt like a genius. "I'll fix the place up so it's not such a hole. Get rid of the flowered wallpaper, get new carpet."

"I don't care about any of that. I could live in a tent with you and be happy."

"Really?"

"Yeah, but I can't move in with you."

His hopes deflated, and the deep throb of his wounds came back full force. "I see."

Sam walked into the room, and Trent was glad for the interruption. It gave him something to think about besides the gaping hole she'd dug in him with her rejection.

Elise held up her hand to Sam, telling him to stay back, then took Trent's chin and turned his face, forcing him to look at her. "No, you don't see. I want to move in with you, but I can't. Not yet. Ashley needs me now. But when she's better . . ."

Trent felt a victorious grin stretch his dry lips.

"I'm going to be taking care of Ashley," Sam announced.

Elise sat up, staring at Sam in indignation. "What gives you the right to make that call?"

"Ashley did. She doesn't want to burden you. She asked me if I'd stay with her for a while so you wouldn't."

"She doesn't want me?"

"She doesn't want you to give up your life for her. Besides, I wasn't there that night." His mouth twisted around the words as if they left a bitter taste in his mouth.

"So you don't understand what she went through," said Elise.

"I won't remind her of what happened either. And if she wants me to understand, she's going to have to talk to me about it." He put his hands on his hips, and Trent knew from a lifetime of experience that meant his brother was not going to back down. "You'd coddle her. I won't."

"So, you're going to ease her fears and help her readjust to life by being an asshole?"

"No, but I'm also not going to let her skip her therapy sessions, and I won't let her lie in bed all day anymore."

A guilty blush spread up Elise's neck. "She's tired. She needs her rest."

"She needs professional help, and I'm going to see to it that she gets it."

Trent hated seeing Elise wound up like this, but Sam was right. Ashley likely needed more than Elise was able to give.

He stroked her arm, hoping to soothe her. "Let him try. If it doesn't work out, you'll be right across the street to set him straight."

She turned and looked at him. "I haven't agreed to move in with you yet."

"No, but you will."

"I will, huh?"

"I'm a confident man. I'm sure I'll find some way to convince you. Whatever it takes. However long it takes."

"You can't even get out of bed yet."

"I'm most persuasive in bed," said Trent.

Sam made a choking sound. "Clearly, I've come at a bad time. I'll come back later, after all the mushy crap is over. I suggest you make it quick. Mom and Dad are on their way." He left, closing the door behind him.

"So, what do you say, Elise? Are you going to have mercy on a man who nearly died and give in?"

She let out a gusty sigh, but a secret smile played at the corners of her mouth. "I suppose I can move in with you for a while. Once you're back on your feet again, I can think of a few good uses for a man like you."

"Oh, yeah?"

She nodded. "At least three."

"Opening jars, killing spiders, lifting heavy things?"

"Okay, maybe four."

She settled back down beside him, fitting at his side

just right. "You know, if I move in with you, you may never get rid of me."

He was counting on it, but he decided to play it cool. No pressure. "Why's that?"

"Because the more I'm with you, the more I love you."

The words rolled around inside him, lighting up all the dark, weary spots he'd developed over the years. A wide grin stretched his mouth. "Maybe I should hand-cuff you to me."

"How about we save the kinky stuff for after the bullet holes close up."

"Good point."

"I'm trying to be serious here."

"Sorry. Must be the drugs. Go on with your serious-ness. I'll behave."

Her fingers laced between his and she held on tight. Trent didn't think she even realized she did it. "What if this doesn't work out between us?"

"What if it does?" he asked. "I'm willing to take the risk. Are you?"

"It scares me."

"That means you're sane. Marriage is a big deal."

"Whoa. Who said anything about marriage?"

"That is where we're headed, Elise. There's a lot going on right now, and we need time to adjust to it, but I love you, and I want you in my life forever."

"Marriages fall apart."

"Wrong. People *let* marriages fall apart. A good mar-riage isn't something that happens to you; it's something you make happen. You work at it, like my folks did."

"I never had a good example of a functional relationship. I don't even know what one looks like. At least I didn't until I met your parents. You were right. They still love each other after all those years."

"So will we."

Her voice was small and unsure. "You think?"

"I know. I won't let it happen any other way. I love you too much to let go. We'll live here if you want, we'll travel the world if you want; but whatever it is we do, we'll do it together."

She shook her head, but her smile was as bright as the happy tears shimmering in her eyes. "You're an amazing man, Trent. You actually make me believe in miracles."

"Who needs miracles when I've got the perfect woman?"

Elise grinned. "Perfect, huh? I'm going to remind you of that every time we fight."

"Fine, but I'm going to remind *you* of it every time we make up."

"Deal."

EPILOGUE

The sound of Ashley's blinds rolling up jolted her awake. The bright light streaming in through her windows made her groan.

"Rise and shine," came Sam's cheerful voice. "Time to get up."

"I'm tired."

"Too bad. You've got things to do today."

He'd been saying that for weeks now, waking her up in the morning, whether or not she liked it. "I really hate you, Sam."

She could hear the smile in his voice. "I know. I brought coffee."

Ashley's brain perked up at the thought. She pushed herself up, blinking so her eyes would adjust to the sunshine. "So, what's on my schedule today that's so damn important I need to be up before noon? I don't have any therapy sessions."

"No, but my birthday's tomorrow and I thought you might want to paint me something."

Ashley sipped her coffee, which was loaded with

cream and sugar, just the way she liked it. "Yeah, right. Like I'm going to reward my torturer with a birthday present."

Sam sat on the edge of the bed, his blue eyes shining in the sunlight. How could anyone be so handsome first thing in the morning?

"I'm partial to yellow," he said.

Yellow.

Ashley's hands started to shake, making rings vibrate along the surface of her coffee.

She'd been through a gallon of red and black paint in the last few weeks, but not one drop of any other color. She just couldn't bring herself to put color back into her world. Her memories were all still covered in shades of blood and darkness.

Gary was dead. He couldn't hurt her anymore. She knew that, but he still haunted her at night. If it hadn't been for Sam sleeping on the couch, only feet away, she wasn't sure she'd still be able to face the dark.

He laid one strong hand on her knee. "I have to go to work now, but I'll be back for lunch. I'll make you some of that fruit salad you like."

Ashley nodded and watched him walk away, heard him get in his truck and drive off.

Time to get moving. Staying busy helped her pass the time and kept her mind off the horrors she'd witnessed.

She shambled out to her easel, coffee in hand. A blank canvas stood waiting for her. She had no idea what had happened to the painting she'd done yesterday—Sam always took them and put a fresh canvas up for her— but she was glad that whatever dark, bloody mess she'd painted yesterday wasn't staring at her.

Today was a new day. A fresh start.

Tomorrow was Sam's birthday. He liked yellow.

Ashley's hands shook as she picked up the tube of yellow paint.

The first few strokes of color burned her eyes, but something inside her shifted, loosened. Relaxed.

Her brush flew over the canvas, and before she knew it, sparks of green and swaths of blue appeared, revealing a field of daisies.

It wasn't her best work, and she wasn't sure how a macho guy like Sam would feel about daisies, but for the first time since the night Gary had abducted her, Ashley smiled.

Dear Reader,

I've always said that reading a romance novel allows us to fall in love all over again without cheating on our spouse. So, when I say I'm in love with dozens of men, my husband just rolls his eyes and grins. He knows he's at the top of my list.

As the heroes of my first published novels, the men of the Delta Force trilogy hold a special place in my heart. David is the grieving widower from NO REGRETS, Caleb is the guilt-ridden soldier from NO CONTROL, and Grant is the lonely playboy from NO ESCAPE. I love them all, and I hope you will, too. Those boys need all the love they can get.

Of course, each one of them has eyes only for his special lady, but that's okay with me. If they didn't, I don't think I'd love them nearly so much.

So, if you're looking to fall in love with some handsome, sexy, noble men, there are three special ones I'd like you to meet . . .

Enjoy!

Shannon K Butcher

THE DISH

Where authors give you the inside scoop!

♥ ♥ ♥ ♥ ♥ ♥ ♥ ♥ ♥ ♥ ♥ ♥ ♥ ♥ ♥

From the desk of Shannon K. Butcher

Dear Reader,

For thirty days, I lurked inside the mind of a deranged serial killer. And let me tell you, it may be an interesting place to visit, but I'm glad I don't have to live there. Thirty days was long enough, and I spent every one of them looking over my shoulder, in the backseat of my car, and under my bed. Just in case.

Luckily, I had some professional help with the profile for the killer in LOVE YOU TO DEATH, but little did I know how much more it would creep me out when I realized I was creating this character from bits and pieces of real people and real crimes. In fact, it creeped me out so much that the security system and our dog were no longer enough. I went out, bought a gun, and learned how to use it, just in case someone like Gary decided to come calling.

Ridiculous? Probably. But my SIG SAUER, its magazines holding eighty bullets, and I all feel much better.

This book opened my eyes to a world that I'd never

really thought about before. Sure, we see reports on the news about murder and abduction, but there's always a kind of distance to those stories. This project forced me to put myself inside the heads of both the victims and the killer, and after doing so, every story I've seen on the news has suddenly become real—a waking-up-with-nightmares, buying-a-gun kind of real.

Being able to write about two people who fall in love during such a difficult time was something I wasn't sure I could do, but I hope I pulled it off. Elise and Trent and their love for each other brighten up the darker parts of this book, and their relationship highlights just how important it is to have someone to lean on when things become impossible.

I won't spoil the end of LOVE YOU TO DEATH, but I can confidently say that I've never felt more satisfied with the justice I've inflicted on my deserving characters than I did with Gary. I hope you agree. And if you do decide to crawl inside the mind of a serial killer by reading this book, I recommend doing so with the lights on and the doors locked.

Enjoy!

Shannon K Butcher

www.shannonkbutcher.com

♥ ♥ ♥ ♥ ♥ ♥ ♥ ♥ ♥ ♥ ♥ ♥ ♥ ♥

From the desk of Kate Perry

Dear Readers,

Hot naked men!

An unorthodox beginning, I know, but you have to admit it caught your attention. Also, it's vastly more interesting to talk about hot naked men than it is to discuss, say, tutus. Not to mention that hot naked men and my Guardians of Destiny series go hand in hand. Tutus? Not so much.

For instance, in the first book, MARKED BY PASSION, we have Rhys, the British bad boy who's got it all—except the woman who sets him on fire. Rhys is hot on so many levels, and when he strips down . . . I'd suggest keeping an extinguisher on hand.

And then there's Max, the hero of CHOSEN BY DESIRE, the second Guardians of Destiny novel. A past betrayal has Max closed off—until he meets the right woman, who makes him want to bare it all. Naked, he's a sight to behold. Plus, he's got a big sword, and he knows how to use it.

Unclothed, finely chiseled men. Sassy heroines who tame them. Kick-ass kung fu scenes. Much more exciting than tutus, don't you think?

Happy Reading!

Kate Perry

www.kateperry.com

♥ ♥ ♥ ♥ ♥ ♥ ♥ ♥ ♥ ♥ ♥ ♥ ♥ ♥ ♥

From the desk of Sue-Ellen Welfonder

Dear Reader,

Sometimes people ask me why I set my books in Scotland. My reaction is always bafflement. I'm amazed that anyone would wonder. Aside from my own ancestral ties—I was born loving Scotland—I can't imagine a place better suited to inspire romance.

Rich in legend and lore, steeped in history, and blessed with incredible natural beauty, Scotland offers everything a romantic heart could desire. Mist-hung hills, castle ruins, and dark glens abound, recalling the great days of the clans and a time when heroism, loyalty, and honor meant everything. In A HIGH-LANDER'S TEMPTATION, Darroc MacConacher and Arabella MacKenzie live by these values—until they are swept into a tempestuous passion that is not only irresistible but forbidden, and acknowledging their love could destroy everything they hold dear.

In writing their tale, I knew I needed something very special—and powerful—to help them push past the long-simmering feud that could so easily rip them apart. With such fierce clan history between them, I wanted something imbued with Highland magic that would lend a dash of Celtic whimsy and lightness to the story.

Fortunately, I didn't have to look far.

One of my favorite haunts in Scotland had just the special something I needed.

It was the Thunder Stone, an innocuous-looking stone displayed on the soot-stained wall of a very atmospheric drovers' inn on the northwestern shore of Loch Lomond. Said to possess magical powers I won't describe, the stone is often borrowed by local clansmen. I've eyed the stone each time I've stopped at the inn and always thought to someday include it in a book. A HIGHLANDER'S TEMPTATION gave me that opportunity.

Changed into a prized clan heirloom and called the Thunder Rod in A HIGHLANDER'S TEMPTATION, the relic provided just the bit of intrigue and lore I love weaving into my stories. I hope you'll enjoy discovering if its magic worked. *Hint:* Darroc and Arabella do have a happy ending!

With all good wishes,

www.welfonder.com

Want to know more about romances at Grand Central Publishing and Forever? Get the scoop online!

GRAND CENTRAL PUBLISHING'S ROMANCE HOME PAGE

Visit us at www.hachettebookgroup.com/romance for all the latest news, reviews, and chapter excerpts!

NEW AND UPCOMING TITLES

Each month we feature our new titles and reader favorites.

CONTESTS AND GIVEAWAYS

We give away galleys, autographed copies, and all kinds of fun stuff.

AUTHOR INFO

You'll find bios, articles, and links to personal Web sites for all your favorite authors—and so much more!

THE BUZZ

Sign up for our monthly romance newsletter, and be the first to read all about it!